From the Pages of
the *Paradiso*

The glory of Him who moveth everything
Doth penetrate the universe, and shine
In one part more and in another less.
(Canto I, lines 1–3, page 3)

A little spark is followed by great flame.
(Canto I, line 34, page 4)

"The greatest gift that in his largess God
Creating made, and unto his own goodness
Nearest conformed, and that which he doth prize
Most highly, is the freedom of the will,
Wherewith the creatures of intelligence
Both all and only were and are endowed."
(Canto V, lines 19–24, page 23)

And all my love was so absorbed in Him,
That in oblivion Beatrice was eclipsed.
(Canto X, lines 59–60, page 51)

"That which can die, and that which dieth not,
Are nothing but the splendor of the idea
Which by his love our Lord brings into being."
(Canto XIII, 52–54, page 67)

"Thou shalt have proof how savoreth of salt
The bread of others, and how hard a road
The going down and up another's stairs."
(Canto XVII, lines 58–60, page 89)

While the eternal pleasure, which direct
Rayed upon Beatrice, from her fair face
Contented me with its reflected aspect,
Conquering me with the radiance of a smile,
She said to me, "Turn thee about and listen;
Not in mine eyes alone is Paradise."
(Canto XVIII, lines 16–21, page 93)

"Now knoweth he how dearly it doth cost
Not following Christ, by the experience
Of this sweet life and of its opposite."
(Canto XX, lines 46–48, page 105)

Like as a lark that in the air expatiates,
First singing and then silent with content
Of the last sweetness that doth satisfy her,
Such seemed to me the image of the imprint
Of the eternal pleasure, by whose will
Doth everything become the thing it is.
(Canto XX, lines 73–78, page 106)

Not only does the beauty I beheld
Transcend ourselves, but truly I believe
Its Maker only may enjoy it all.
(Canto XXX, lines 19–21, page 157)

But my own wings were not enough for this,
Had it not been that then there smote my mind
A flash of lightning, wherein came its wish.
Here vigor failed the lofty fantasy:
But now was turning my desire and will,
Even as a wheel that equally is moved,
The Love which moves the sun and the other stars.
(Canto XXXIII, lines 139–145, pages 176–177)

THE PARADISO
DANTE ALIGHIERI

TRANSLATED BY

HENRY WADSWORTH LONGFELLOW

With an Introduction and Notes
by Peter Bondanella
and Julia Conaway Bondanella

Illustrations by
Gustave Doré

George Stade
Consulting Editorial Director

BARNES & NOBLE CLASSICS
NEW YORK

ℬ
BARNES & NOBLE CLASSICS
NEW YORK

Published by Barnes & Noble Books
122 Fifth Avenue
New York, NY 10011

www.barnesandnoble.com/classics

Dante is believed to have composed *The Divine Comedy* between 1308 and 1321, just before his death. Longfellow's translation of *The Paradiso* first appeared in 1867; the present text derives from the Bigelow, Smith & Co. edition published in 1909.

Published in 2006 by Barnes & Noble Classics with new Introduction, Notes, Biography, Chronology, Map of Paradise, Inspired By, Comments & Questions, and For Further Reading.

Introduction, Notes, and For Further Reading
Copyright © 2006 by Julia Conaway Bondanella and Peter Bondanella.

Note on Dante Alighieri, The World of Dante Alighieri and the *Paradiso*, Map of Paradise, Inspired by Dante and the *Paradiso*, and Comments & Questions
Copyright © 2005 by Barnes & Noble, Inc.

Diagrams on pages 190, 192, 219, 233, 276, 277, 284, 337 are reprinted from *Dante's Paradise*, translated with Notes and Commentary by Mark Musa (Bloomington: Indiana Univ. Press, 1984). Used by permission of the publisher. Diagram on page 182 is reprinted from Dante Alighieri, *The Divine Comedy*, translated by John Ciardi (New York: W. W. Norton & Company, Inc., 1977). Used by permission of the publisher.

The Paradiso
ISBN-13: 978-1-59308-317-5
ISBN-10 1-59308-317-3
LC Control Number 2005935856

Produced and published in conjunction with:
Fine Creative Media, Inc.
322 Eighth Avenue
New York, NY 10001
Michael J. Fine, President and Publisher

Printed in the United States of America
QM
3 5 7 9 10 8 6 4 2

Dante Alighieri

Dante Alighieri was born in Florence in 1265 to Alighiero Alighieri, who appears to have been a moneylender and property holder, and his wife, Bella. Alighieri's was a family of good standing. Much of what we know of Dante's earliest years comes to us from *La Vita Nuova* (*The New Life*, completed around 1293), in which he tells the story of his idealized love for Beatrice Portinari, whom he encountered just before his ninth birthday. Beatrice died in 1290 but remained Dante's idealized love and muse throughout his life. Sometime around 1285 Dante married Gemma Donati, with whom he had three sons and a daughter.

Dante's public life is better documented than his private life. It is known that he counted among his closest friends the poet Guido Cavalcanti and the philosopher and writer Brunetto Latini, who is generally credited with bringing classical literature to thirteenth-century Florence. Dante began an intense study of theology at the churches of Santa Maria Novella and Santa Croce in 1292, and was well-versed in classical literature and philosophy as well as religious thought. Membership in a guild was a requirement to participate in the government of Florence, and Dante partook of this privilege after enrolling in the Arte dei Medici e Speziali (Guild of Physicians and Apothecaries), in 1295. He was elected to serve as a prior, the city's highest office, in 1300.

By early 1302, however, Dante had fallen out of favor in Florence. The Guelphs, the ruling body with whom Dante's family had long been associated, had split into two factions, the White and the Black Guelphs. Dante aligned himself with the Whites, who were opposed to the intervention of Pope Boniface VIII and his representative, Charles of Valois, in Florentine politics. While Dante was in Rome with a delegation protesting papal policy, Charles of Valois entered the city and a proclamation was issued banishing Dante and others, ordering them to be burned alive should they fall into the hands of the Florentine government.

Dante never returned to Florence, even after the exiles were granted a pardon. He probably began *La Divina Commedia* (*The Divine Comedy*) around 1308, during his extensive travels throughout Italy. The work brought him fame as soon as it began to circulate (in hand-copied form, at a time when the printing press had not yet been invented). Dante's travels took him to Verona, where he resided on and off for some six years, and finally to Ravenna, where he died on September 14, 1321, after falling ill in Venice.

Dante Alighieri is considered to be one of the world's greatest poets. In the words of the twentieth-century poet T. S. Eliot, "Dante and Shakespeare divide the modern world between them. There is no third."

Table of Contents

The World of Dante and the *Paradiso* ⋆ IX

The Story of the *Paradiso* in Brief ⋆ XIII

Introduction by Peter Bondanella
and Julia Conaway Bondanella ⋆ XIX

Map of Paradise ⋆ LXXVI

the *Paradiso* ⋆ I

Endnotes ⋆ 179

Six Sonnets by Longfellow ⋆ 347

Inspired by Dante and the *Paradiso* ⋆ 351

Comments & Questions ⋆ 355

For Further Reading ⋆ 359

The World of Dante and the *Paradiso*

1265   In May or June (exact date unknown), Dante Alighieri is born to Alighiero Alighieri, a Florentine moneylender and renter of properties, and his wife, Bella, daughter of a family of good standing. (Dante discusses his ancestry in *Paradiso* [*Paradise*], cantos XV and XVI.)

1272   Bella dies.

1274   According to his later collection of poetry and prose *La Vita Nuova* (*The New Life*), Dante lays eyes on Beatrice Portinari for the first time during festivities on May 1. Throughout his life and career Dante cites Beatrice as his muse and as the benevolent force in his life, maintaining that she inspired the best part of his work.

1281   Dante, some scholars contend, studies at the universities of Bologna and Padua.

1282   Dante's father dies, leaving a modest inheritance of property.

1283   Dante passes Beatrice in the street and she greets him. The encounter inspires a visionlike dream, which Dante recounts in a sonnet that he circulates around Florence. One of the readers, the poet Guido Cavalcanti, becomes Dante's friend and mentor. About the same time Dante finds a role model and teacher in Brunetto Latini, a writer and influential Florentine politician and man of letters.

c.1285 Dante is married to Gemma Donati, to whom he was bethrothed when he was twelve and Gemma was ten.

1287   Beatrice marries Simone de' Bardi, member of a wealthy clan.

1288   Dante's son, Giovanni, is born. Dante and Gemma will have three more children, Pietro, Iacopo, and Antonia.

1289   It is believed that Dante, having been trained in knightly warfare, fights in the battle of Campaldino on June 11, when the

Guelphs, with whom Dante sympathizes, defeat the Ghibellines. On August 16 Dante goes into battle again, this time against the Pisans to restore the fortress at the village of Caprona to the Guelphs, from whom the Ghibellines have captured it.

1290 Beatrice dies in June.

1292 Dante begins to study theology, first at the Dominican church of Santa Maria Novella, then at the Franciscan church of Santa Croce. His theological readings will have a profound influence on his works.

c.1293 Dante completes *La Vita Nuova*, which he had begun around 1283 to celebrate his beloved Beatrice.

1295 Dante enrolls in the Arte dei Medici e Speziali (Guild of Doctors and Apothecaries), which includes philosophers as well. Membership in a guild gives him a say in the Florentine government. Dante's friend and mentor Brunetto Latini dies.

1300 Dante, a persuasive and eloquent speaker, is appointed to Florence's highest office as one of the city priors. He holds this office from June 15 to August 15. Florence is once again divided into warring factions, the White and the Black Guelphs. Dante's sympathies lie with the Whites, who favor independence from papal authority; in what he considers to be the best interests of Florence, he must concur with the priors when they send Guido Cavalcanti, a Black and his longtime friend, into exile on the Tuscan coast, where he dies of malaria. Dante travels as part of a mission to the city of San Gimignano to rally Tuscan cities against the territorial ambitions of Pope Boniface VIII.

1301 Dante goes to Rome to ask Pope Boniface VIII to help prevent the French Charles of Valois, a papist sympathizer, from entering Florence. Charles takes the city in November, and the Blacks harshly regain power.

1302 On January 27 Dante is accused of corruption and bribery, fined, and sentenced to two years in exile. When he does not reply to the charges, his home and possessions are confiscated, and on March 10 his sentence is increased; he is now banished for life and condemned to be burned alive if he ever returns to the city.

1303– 1304	Dante travels throughout central and northern Italy and affiliates himself with other Florentine exiles. He appears to have been much dissatisfied with his colleagues. Dante arrives for a stay in Verona, as a guest of Bartolomeo della Scala, son of a local ruling family.
1306– 1308	Dante works on *Il Convivio* (*The Banquet*), a philosophical treatise on poetry influenced, in part, by the writings of Aristotle. Throughout these years he travels to Lucca (where some think he encounters his eldest son, Giovanni), Arezzo, Padua, Venice, and other cities. It is believed that Dante probably begins work on *La Divina Commedia* (*The Divine Comedy*), turning first to the *Inferno* (*Hell*), in 1308; he will complete the larger work shortly before his death in 1321.
1309– 1311	In January Dante attends the coronation, in Milan, of Henry VII of Luxemburg as king of Lombardy. Dante views Henry as the rightful ruler of Italy and writes two impassioned letters to the Florentines, imploring them to open their gates to Henry.
1312	Dante begins a six-year stay in Verona, interrupted by frequent travels, as a guest of Cangrande della Scala, a powerful political leader. While in Verona, Dante revises the *Inferno*, writes and revises *Purgatorio* (*Purgatory*), and begins *Paradiso*. His second son, Pietro, joins him in Verona.
1313	Henry VII dies, putting an end to Dante's hopes of returning to Florence.
1315	Dante refuses an offer from Florence allowing him to return if he pays a reduced portion of a fine imposed upon him at the time of his exile; he calls the pardon "ridiculous and ill-advised." Another decree is issued against Dante, as well as his sons, condemning them to beheading if they are captured. The *Inferno* gains recognition throughout Italy.
1319– 1321	Dante stays in Ravenna as a guest of Guido Novello da Polenta. Two of Dante's sons, Pietro and Iacopo, his daughter, Antonia, and his wife, Gemma, join him. Antonia enters the convent of Santo Stefano degli Olivi in Ravenna, taking the name Sister Beatrice.
1321	Dante travels to Venice to help negotiate a peaceful resolution to a disagreement that has arisen between Ravenna and Venice.

During his return to Ravenna across marshy lands, he contracts malarial fever; he dies on the night of September 13–14. He is buried "with all the honors deemed worthy of such an illustrious deceased man," writes Giovanni Boccaccio, the author of another great fourteenth-century Italian masterpiece, the *Decameron*. Dante's remains are in Ravenna's church of San Francesco, though Florence has tried repeatedly to have them moved to the poet's place of birth.

1337   Florence establishes the Chair of Dante, an academic position for the preservation and study of Dante's works. This position was first held by Giovanni Boccaccio, who was not only a friend of Dante's, but whose own literary perspective was influenced by the poet's writings and who was one of Dante's first biographers.

The Story of the *Paradiso* in Brief

BY HENRY FRANCES CAREY

CANTO I. The Poet ascends with Beatrice toward the first heaven; and is, by her, resolved of certain doubts which arise in his mind.

CANTO II. Dante and his celestial guide enter the moon. The cause of the spots or shadows, which appear in that body, is explained to him.

CANTO III. In the moon Dante meets with Piccarda, the sister of Forese, who tells him that this planet is allotted to those, who, after having made profession of chastity and a religious life, had been compelled to violate their vows; and she then points out to him the spirit of the Empress Costanza.

CANTO IV. While they still continue in the moon, Beatrice removes certain doubts which Dante had conceived respecting the place assigned to the blessed, and respecting the will absolute or conditional. He inquires whether it is possible to make satisfaction for a vow broken.

CANTO V. The question proposed in the last Canto is answered. Dante ascends with Beatrice to the planet Mercury, which is the second heaven; and here he finds a multitude of spirits, one of whom offers to satisfy him anything he may desire to know from them.

CANTO VI. The spirit, who had offered to satisfy the inquiries of Dante, declares himself to be the Emperor Justinian; and after speaking of his own actions, recounts the victories, before him, obtained under the Roman Eagle. He then informs our Poet that the soul of Romeo the pilgrim is in the same star.

CANTO VII. In consequence of what had been said by Justinian, who together with the other spirits have now disappeared, some doubts arise in the mind of Dante respecting the human redemption. These difficulties are fully explained by Beatrice.

CANTO VIII. The Poet ascends with Beatrice to the third heaven, which is the planet Venus; and here finds the soul of Charles Martel, king of Hungary, who had been Dante's friend on earth, and who now, after speaking of the realms to which he was heir, unfolds the cause why children differ in disposition from their parents.

CANTO IX. The next spirit, who converses with our Poet in the planet Venus, is the amorous Cunizza. To her succeeds Folco, or Folques, the Provençal bard, who declares that the soul of Rahab the harlot is there also; and then, blaming the Pope for his neglect of the holy land, prognosticates some reverse to the papal power.

CANTO X. Their next ascent carries them into the sun, which is the fourth heaven. Here they are encompassed with a wreath of blessed spirits, twelve in number. Thomas Aquinas, who is one of these, declares the names and endowments of the rest.

CANTO XI. Thomas Aquinas enters at large into the life and character of St. Francis; and then solves one of two difficulties, which he perceived to have risen in Dante's mind from what he had heard in the last Canto.

CANTO XII. A second circle of glorified souls encompasses the first. Buonaventura, who is one of them, celebrates the praises of Saint Dominic, and informs Dante who the other eleven are, that are in this second circle or garland.

CANTO XIII. Thomas Aquinas resumes his speech. He solves the other of those doubts which he discerned in the mind of Dante, and warns him earnestly against assenting to any proposition without having duly examined it.

CANTO XIV. Solomon, who is one of the spirits in the inner circle, declares what the appearance of the blest will be after the resurrection of the body. Beatrice and Dante are translated into the fifth heaven, which is that of Mars; and here behold the souls of those who have died fighting for the true faith ranged in the sign of a cross, athwart which the spirits moved to the sound of a melodious hymn.

CANTO XV. The spirit of Cacciaguida, our Poet's ancestor, glides rapidly to the foot of the cross; tells who he is; and speaks of the simplicity of the Florentines in his days, since then much corrupted.

CANTO XVI. Cacciaguida relates the time of his birth; and, describing the extent of Florence when he lived there, recounts the names of the chief families who then inhabited it. Its degeneracy, and subsequent disgrace, he attributes to the introduction of families from the neighboring country and villages, and to their mixture with the primitive citizens.

CANTO XVII. Cacciaguida predicts to our Poet his exile and the calamities he had to infer; and, lastly, exhorts him to write the present poem.

CANTO XVIII. Dante sees the souls of many renowned warriors and crusaders in the planet Mars; and then ascends with Beatrice to Jupiter, the sixth heaven, in which he finds the souls of those who had administered justice rightly in the world so disposed as to form the figure of an eagle. The Canto concludes with an invective against the avarice of the clergy, and especially of the pope.

CANTO XIX. The eagle speaks as with one voice proceeding from a multitude of spirits that compose it; and declares the cause for which it is exalted to that state of glory. It then solves a doubt, which our poet had entertained, respecting the possibility of salvation without belief in Christ; exposes the inefficacy of a mere profession of such belief; and prophesies the evil appearance that many Christian potentates will make at the day of judgment.

CANTO XX. The eagle celebrates the praise of certain kings, whose glorified spirits form the eye of the bird. In the pupil is David; and, in the circle round it, Trajan, Hezekiah, Constantine, William II, of Sicily, and Ripheus. It explains to our Poet how the souls of those whom he supposed to have had no means of believing in Christ, came to be in heaven; and concludes with an admonition against presuming to fathom the counsels of God.

CANTO XXI. Dante ascends with Beatrice to the seventh heaven, which is the planet Saturn; wherein is placed a ladder, so lofty that the top is out of his sight. Here are the souls of those who had passed their life in holy retirement and contemplation. Piero Damiano comes near them, and answers questions put to him by Dante; then declares who he was on earth; and ends by declaiming against the luxury of pastors and prelates in those times.

CANTO XXII. He beholds many other spirits of the devout and contemplative; and among these is addressed by Saint Benedict, who, after disclosing his own name and the names of certain of his companions in bliss, replies to the request made by our Poet that he might look on the form of the saint, without that covering of splendor, which then invested it; and then proceeds, lastly, to inveigh against the corruption of the monks. Next Dante mounts with his heavenly conductress to the eighth heaven, or that of the fixed stars, which he enters at the constellation of the Twins; and thence looking back reviews all the space he has passed between his present station and the earth.

CANTO XXIII.   He sees Christ triumphing with his church. The Saviour ascends, followed by his virgin Mother. The others remain with Saint Peter.

CANTO XXIV.   Saint Peter examines Dante touching Faith, and is contented with his answers.

CANTO XXV.   Saint James questions our Poet concerning Hope. Next Saint John appears; and, on perceiving that Dante looks intently on him, informs him that he, Saint John, had left his body resolved into earth and that Christ and the Virgin alone had come with their bodies into heaven.

CANTO XXVI.   Saint John examines our Poet touching Charity. Afterward Adam tells when he was created, and placed in the terrestrial Paradise; how long he remained in that state; what was the occasion of his fall; when he was admitted into heaven; and what language he spake.

CANTO XXVII.   Saint Peter bitterly rebukes the covetousness of his successors in the apostolic see, while all the heavenly host sympathize in his indignation: they then vanish upward. Beatrice bids Dante again cast his view below. Afterward they are borne into the ninth heaven, of which she shows him the nature and properties; blaming the perverseness of man, who places his will on low and perishable things.

CANTO XXVIII.   Still in the ninth heaven, our Poet is permitted to behold the divine essence; and then sees, in three hierarchies, the nine choirs of angels. Beatrice clears some difficulties which occur to him on this occasion.

CANTO XXIX.   Beatrice beholds, in the mirror of divine truth, some doubts which had entered the mind of Dante. These she resolves; and then digresses into a vehement reprehension of certain theologians and preachers in those days, whose ignorance or avarice induced them to substitute their own inventions for the pure word of the Gospel.

CANTO XXX. Dante is taken up with Beatrice into the empyrean; and there having his sight strengthened by her aid, and by the virtue derived from looking on the river of light, he sees the triumph of the angels and of the souls of the blessed.

CANTO XXXI. The Poet expatiates further on the glorious vision described in the last Canto. On looking round for Beatrice, he finds that she has left him, and that an old man is at his side. This proves to be Saint Bernard, who shows him that Beatrice has returned to her throne, and then points out to him the blessedness of the Virgin Mother.

CANTO XXXII. Saint Bernard shows him, on their several thrones, the other blessed souls, both of the old and new Testament; explains to him that their places are assigned them by grace, and not according to merit; and lastly, tells him that if he would obtain power to descry what remained of the heavenly vision he must unite with him in supplication to Mary.

CANTO XXXIII. Saint Bernard supplicates the Virgin Mary that Dante may have grace given him to contemplate the brightness of the Divine Majesty, which is accordingly granted; and Dante then himself prays to God for ability to show forth some part of the celestial glory in his writings. Lastly, he is admitted to a glimpse of the great mystery; the Trinity, and the Union of Man with God.

Introduction

Dante's Life and Times

We know little about the private lives of Homer and Shakespeare, the only two poets who may be said to rival Dante's influence in the Western tradition or, indeed, his genius. Some critics have raised doubts about the authorship of the *Iliad* and the *Odyssey*, and about the rich poetry and drama of Shakespeare. But Dante Alighieri, the man whom the nineteenth-century British writer and critic John Ruskin called "the central man of all the world," is unquestionably the author of the great epic poem we call *The Divine Comedy*, of which *Paradiso* is just one of three parts. Dante the man remains inextricably tied to the content and action of *The Divine Comedy*, both as its narrator and as its central protagonist. Many of the important events in his life figure prominently in the work, and the reader, to whom a good many of these biographical details are not immediately transparent, must seek out information in annotations that centuries of scholars and commentators have compiled.

The problematic quality of autobiographical details in Dante's works is that they may allude to real, historical events that actually occurred or to fictional events from Dante's fertile imagination. It is not always easy to separate fact from fiction. Dante the Poet is also the epic's protagonist, Dante the Pilgrim. It required a breathtaking act of poetic license for Dante to make himself the hero of an epic, a genre usually populated by warriors and heroes. The results, however, have silenced any critical objections to such presumption. Scholarly debate over Dante's poem has continued since its first appearance in manuscript in the early fourteenth century. The unbroken tradition of writing about Dante from that time to the present remains unparalleled in its complexity and breadth by that on any other major Western author, including Shakespeare. Yet despite all we know about Dante (much of this gained from the poem itself), problems arise because there is not a single extant autograph manuscript of his many works, including his poetic masterpiece. Every one of his many works has come down to us in such a complicated manuscript tradition that his contemporary editors can still carry on heated debates about which text should be accepted as the best one or whether, indeed, some of his minor works are actually to be attributed to his own hand.

A child born on a day between May 14 and June 13, 1265, in the Tuscan city of Florence, Italy, was christened in the Baptistery of San Giovanni on March 26, 1266, with the name Durante Alighieri, later contracted to Dante Alighieri. Dante's family—the father Alighiero and the mother Bella—was not particularly wealthy or distinguished but was sufficiently well off that Dante could later participate in the republican government of Florence, eligibility for which rested primarily upon economic status. According to Dante's testimony in *La Vita Nuova* (*The New Life*), he first encountered a girl named Beatrice Portinari when they were both eight years of age; he saw her again nine years later, in 1283. A decisive encounter in his poetic and intellectual development, this meeting inspired Dante's unrequited love for Beatrice (who died in 1290) and led him to begin writing poetry. Dante married a woman named Gemma Donati (the marriage contract is dated 1277), and he apparently had four children.

Dante must have enjoyed a very good education, probably from the schools that had grown up around the ecclesiastical centers in Florence—the Dominican church of Santa Maria Novella; the Augustinian church of Santo Spirito; and the Franciscan church of Santa Croce. He certainly received stellar training in Latin grammar (he would later compose a number of works in Latin) and must have read extensively in the Latin classics and rhetoric books typically employed in medieval education. The poet also came under the influence of Brunetto Latini (1220–1295), under whose tutelage he probably encountered not only the works of Aristotle and Cicero but also important works written in Old French, such as *The Romance of the Rose*, and the troubadour lyrics written in Old Provençal. One work attributed to Dante but still contested by some scholars, and probably written between 1285 and 1295, is *Il Fiore* (*The Flower*), a series of 232 sonnets summarizing *The Romance of the Rose.*

The lyric poetry Dante produced between the early 1280s and the mid-1290s holds much greater importance in his poetic development. These ninety or so poems of undoubted attribution represent a kind of artistic workshop for the young aspiring lyric poet. The poems display a variety of metrical forms: sonnets, sestinas, *ballate* (dance songs with repeating refrains), and *canzoni*, ode-like "songs," as the name implies, consisting of a number of stanzas of varying lengths and a shorter envoy. Dante considered the *canzone* to be the noblest form of poetry. This kind of poetry was popular among the major groups of lyric poets Dante admired, imitated, and sometimes criticized: the Provençal troubadours, such as Arnaut Daniel and Bertran de Born; the Sicilian School of poetry that flourished from around 1230 to 1250, the members of which included Pier della Vigna and Giacomo da Lentini, the probable inventor of the sonnet; the Tuscan school led by Guittone d'Arezzo; the Bolognese group of poets led by Guido Guinizzelli; and what came to be known as poets of the *dolce stil novo* ("sweet new style"), a group of Tuscans including not only Bonagiunta da Lucca, Cino da Pistoia, and Guido Cavalcanti, but also Dante himself. Dante places a number of these individuals in *The Divine Comedy* as testimony to his own literary development and to his argument that poetry represents one of humanity's most noble callings.

Had Dante stopped writing poetry with his lyric production and never composed *The Divine Comedy*, he would be remembered only by medievalists as the author of two works. These are a moderately interesting Latin treatise on political theory, *De Monarchia* (*Monarchy*), completed during the last decade of his life, and an unfinished Latin treatise on vernacular language and its use in poetry, *De Vulgari Eloquentia* (*On Eloquence in the Vernacular Tongue*), probably written between 1302 and 1305. Without *The Divine Comedy*, there would have been little reason for Dante to have composed the unfinished Italian work *Il Convivio* (*The Banquet*), a philosophical consideration of poetry that is also inspired by religion. In fact, rather than being admired for the often abstract and ethereal love lyrics typical of the "sweet new style" (the term itself comes from a line in *The Divine Comedy*), Dante would be recognized primarily for *La Vita Nuova* and four explicitly sensual lyrics called the *rime petrose* (literally, "rocky rhymes"). These reveal his interest in metrical experimentation and a highly sophisticated understanding that the courtly love celebrated by the Provençal poets—often Dante's models—was firmly based on requited lust rather than unrequited love. Such a poetic reputation would not have attracted much critical attention during the past six centuries from anyone but highly specialized scholars.

Dante's love poetry, however, led to the stroke of genius that ultimately saved him from so unremarkable a future. Dante had the immensely clever idea of taking thirty-one of the lyric poems he had composed concerning an unrequited love for the girl named Beatrice and setting them within a prose frame. Although not widely read and immediately eclipsed by the appearance of his great epic, *La Vita Nuova* (probably completed around 1293) represents a fundamental step forward in Dante's poetic and intellectual development. The Italian prose framework of the work allowed Dante to comment on his own work. This idea of a poet who presents a series of poems on love and then includes his own readings of the works was a unique invention that flirts with a postmodern conception of literature as an ironic revisitation of what has been written in the past. *La Vita Nuova* represents a precocious first step toward Dante's decision to become the protagonist hero of an epic poem filled with self-critical images of its author. This little work already contains the key distinction in *The Divine Comedy* between protagonist and narrator, who are the same person but are viewed from different perspectives. But even more important was the revolutionary role of Beatrice in *La Vita Nuova*. By the addition of the prose commentary, Dante projects Beatrice as one whose name, life, and effects upon the narrator are associated with blessing and salvation and especially with the number nine (the square of three, the number of the Trinity). Her death nearly destroys the narrator of *La Vita Nuova*, but in the process of mourning, Dante envisions a Beatrice who has become a figuration of Christ and a guide to his salvation, even before her dramatic appearance in *The Divine Comedy*.

Did Beatrice really exist? We know that there was a real person named Beatrice Portinari who died around the time Dante says his Beatrice did. Did she really have such an influence upon the young

Dante, or does Dante simply invent this conceit in order to embark on a revolutionary treatment of a woman's role in a poet's life? It is impossible to prove or disprove this influence, for we only have Dante's word. Whether or not the young Dante was so struck by Beatrice at the age of eight that she led him to poetic glory, Dante does state that this early *innamoramento* transformed his life and mind. In the process, Dante raised the poetry of praise, the most traditional role of medieval love poetry, to the highest possible level, surpassing the traditional claims of courtly poetry that a woman's love (sexual or chaste) refined a man. Dante affirmed that a woman's love could lead a man or a poet to God with its Platonic overtones, and this bordered on blasphemy. At the same time, Dante stepped back from the avowed sensuality of troubadour lyrics and created a literary relationship between the lover and his beloved that would later come to be labeled "platonic."

For approximately a decade between the time *La Vita Nuova* was completed and his exile from Florence in 1302, Dante divided his activities between writing and active participation in the communal government. In 1289 Dante took part as a cavalryman in the battle of Campaldino, in which the Florentine Guelphs were victorious against the Ghibellines of the nearby Tuscan city of Arezzo. Guelph and Ghibelline traditionally refer to Italian political factions allied, respectively, to the papacy and to the Holy Roman Empire. But the intense and bitter rivalries within the city-state governments of Italy made things more complicated than that. If your enemy was a Guelph, you became a Ghibelline, and vice versa. Conflicts between families and clans were often more important than the more weighty issues of empire versus papacy. Florence was traditionally Guelph, as were most of the city-state republics intent upon removing themselves from the restrictions of either church or state, but even the Guelphs divided into warring factions. The Black Guelphs were most extreme and had the closest ties to the papacy. The White Guelphs (Dante's party) were generally more moderate in their politics.

In 1300 Florence boasted a population of around 100,000; it may have risen to 120,000 before the Black Plague of 1348 devastated the city, as it did most of Western Europe. This Italian city-state was a crucial player in the politics of the period because of its central location, its vibrant republican government, and particularly its enormous wealth. Its flourishing textile industry (specializing in luxury goods of wool and silk but also more humble fabrics made from cotton and linen) and its international banking business dominated world trade and commerce—even rivaling that of Venice, a commercial city and seafaring republic. Florentine politics reflected not only the struggle between Ghibellines and the two factions of Guelphs but also the class conflict between the impoverished mass of humble workers, on the one hand, and the two groups of economically well-off people who governed and who were themselves often in conflict. These were the elite, upper-class patricians who represented a small number of powerful families and were not really noble in the medieval or feudal sense, and the more numerous but less prestigious middle-class merchants, artisans, notaries, lawyers, manufacturers, and shop-keepers who were members of the various guilds and corporations in the city-state. The politics of the city remained turbulent because of friction between various groups. Although members of the groups were often connected to each other by ties of family, religion, and friendship, conflicts often turned into violence, riot, and warfare, with financial ruin and exile being the favorite punishment for those who lost the struggle. Constant internal conflict led quite naturally to a search for outside allies, further complicating the situation within Florence.

In the fourteenth century, the Florentine florin served as the standard currency for the entire European economy. Its value was carefully maintained: 24 karats of purely refined gold, accepted almost everywhere in the known world as legal tender. Rapid commercial communications operated by the Florentine banks, the invention of double-entry bookkeeping, and shrewd dealings abroad made Florence the capital of the major service industry of the Middle Ages. When Tuscan banks began to collect papal revenues all over Europe, the profits were enormous. Based upon high banking charges and incredible profits from the luxury goods produced by the textile industry, the Florentine economy supported a huge building program between 1250 and 1320. The popular monuments now visited by busloads of foreign tourists each year—the Bargello, the churches of Santa Croce and Santa Maria Novella, the Duomo of Santa Maria del Fiore, the

Palazzo Vecchio, numerous family palaces—were all begun during Dante's lifetime. Florentines were so omnipresent in the economic life of Western Europe that they were called the "fifth element" by a pope—the other four elements, of course, were earth, fire, air, and water. Florentine bankers collected taxes for various foreign monarchs and loaned money to both sides in European wars, gaining a reputation as usurers for their trouble. Florentines ran at least one European navy, and like their counterparts in Venice, they journeyed as far as China and India in search of profit. In the process, they began to patronize architects, painters, and sculptors in such an enthusiastic and sophisticated manner that the city soon became the artistic capital of the known world. By the time Dante, Petrarch, and Boccaccio died, they had virtually created Italian literature and fixed the Italian language in the form that we know it today. Unlike Old French or Old English, Old Italian is just Italian, thanks to the example of Dante and his two brilliant successors, together known as the "three crowns of Florence."

Religious life in Florence was vibrant, and the cloister and pulpit concerned Florentine citizens as much as the bank and the factory did. In fact, a significant part of the city's remarkable artistic production was directly linked to religious patronage. Religious organizations also contributed a great deal to the daily life of the city. The life of a medieval Florentine was marked from the cradle to the grave by religious ritual; time was told by canonical hours, and the passing of the seasons was marked by religious holidays, saint's days, and church processions. Moreover, the city's clerics provided much of the education and religious confraternities supplied much of the social assistance before the advent of a welfare state. One of Tuscany's wealthiest citizens in the next century, Francesco Datini, began his ledger book with the telling phrase "In the name of God and profit." The relationship between economic wealth and moral corruption, the latter caused by a society that avidly pursued profit and tried to retain its religious devotion, would provide Dante with one of the key themes in *Inferno* and *Purgatorio*—the moral and ethical corruption of both Church and society brought about by the wealth produced by the "new people" that Dante's essentially conservative social views could not abide. Florence also boasted some of the greatest reformist, fire-and-brimstone preachers of the time, figures who reflected the great popular piety of both the masses and members of the ruling classes and the intelligentsia. Echoing the concerns of these preachers, Dante sometimes seems like an outraged Jeremiah, but his moral indignation over corruption and evildoing was shared by many of his fellow citizens. In spite of Dante's reservations about the "new people" who were busily making Florence into the most exciting place in the Western world, Florence, between the thirteenth and the sixteenth centuries, became a cultural and commercial center that would rival Athens and Rome in its brilliance.

Once the merchant class determined that internal conflict was bad for business, the city government found a novel way to limit the strife. In 1293 a fundamental constitutional change, the *Ordinamenti di Giustizia* (Orders of Justice), took effect in Florence, supported by the Guelph faction. Essentially, it limited political participation in the republican government of the city to members of the major guilds or corporations—basically merchants, bankers, magistrates, notaries, and the moneyed classes. It is important to remember that medieval guilds were not modern labor unions: Membership usually excluded common workers and included only people with property or money. In 1295 Dante joined the Arte dei Medici e Speziali (Guild of Physicians and Apothecaries)—the same guild to which most artists in Renaissance Florence subsequently belonged, because apothecaries provided the materials for paintings. He was elected to serve a two-month term as one of the seven city priors, but fulfilling his civic duty proved to be disastrous for Dante. The elevation to this office identified him as an important White Guelph and made him a target when the more radical Black Guelphs seized power from the White Guelphs. While serving as one of three Florentine ambassadors to Pope Boniface VIII in Rome in 1302, Dante was sentenced first to exile and then to death if he should ever again set foot in his beloved native city of Florence.

Dante's exile lasted until his death, in 1321, from malaria at Ravenna, where he enjoyed the protection and patronage of Guido Novello of Polenta, after receiving the same type of hospitality from Cangrande della Scala in Verona. He wrote *The Divine Comedy* during his long years in exile, and his body was laid to rest not in Florence but in Ravenna, where it remains to this day. In spite of Dante's life in exile and the composition of the poem outside his native city, *The Divine Comedy* has a distinctive Florentine and Tuscan character. The poem often reflects the partisan struggles that swept over Italy during Dante's day, and in so doing it allowed the poet ample opportunity to pay back his political foes. Many of the most memorable figures in the poem are essentially minor historical characters who played a role in the internecine factional struggles of fourteenth-century Florence and who had a personal effect on Dante's life. The depictions inspired by Dante's rancor and righteous indignation—or, occasionally, by his admiration—have transformed many of these minor figures, condemned to a Hell or saved in a Purgatory or Paradise of Dante's invention, into major literary characters.

An Overview of The Divine Comedy

Several times in the poem, Dante refers simply to his creation as the *Comedy*. A subsequent sixteenth-century edition of a manuscript published in Venice during the Renaissance added the adjective "divine" to the title, where it has remained ever since. The poem is an epic, owing a good deal of its structure and content to the epic tradition that began in Western literature with Homer's *Iliad* and *Odyssey*—works Dante could not have read, since he knew no Greek. Few readers of Virgil's *Aeneid*, however, would ever know the Latin epic better than Dante, who absorbed many of the lessons he might have learned from a direct reading of Homer through an indirect encounter with Homer in Virgil's poem. In celebrating the birth of the city of Rome, destined to rule the classical world by Virgil's lifetime, the Latin poet could not have predicted that his imperial capital would eventually become the capital of Christianity, or that the Latin race would be fully Christianized. The link of medieval Rome to both the Roman Republic and Empire, on the one hand, and to the rise of Christianity, on the other, was never far from Dante's mind when he considered what Rome meant to his own times. Virgil's Latin epic became the single most important work in the formation of the ideas that would eventually produce *The Divine Comedy*. Dante also read carefully other Latin epics that are less popular today. One such book was Lucan's *Pharsalia*, a work that described the Roman civil wars and was also full of horrible monsters and marvelous sights. He admired two Latin epics by Statius: the unfinished *Achilleid*, a treatment of Achilles in the Trojan War, and the more important *Thebeid*, a poem treating the fratricidal struggles of the sons of Oedipus in the city of Thebes. Ovid's *Metamorphoses* provided Dante with the most influential repository of poetry about classical mythology.

Nonetheless, no classical precedent really exists for the overall structure of *The Divine Comedy*, in which the author is also the epic protagonist, an Everyman who is not a warrior or a city founder. Homer or Virgil would never have dreamed of making themselves the heroes of their epic works. Dante the Pilgrim in Dante the Poet's epic takes a journey that the Poet believes must be taken by every human being. No matter how many trappings of the classical epic *The Divine Comedy* may contain—invocations to the muses, masterful epic similes, divine messengers sent from the deities, lofty verse, and monsters and other figures cited from the literature or mythology of ancient Greece and Rome—the underpinning of the entire poem is fundamentally religious. It is a Christian epic and, more specifically, a Catholic epic. For the first time in Western literature, the values and ideals of an epic poem derive from the fundamental tenets of Christianity as they were understood during the Middle Ages. This means Catholicism as mediated by the dominant theology of the time—the scholasticism of Saint Thomas Aquinas—as well as the writings, teachings, and examples of such figures as Saint Augustine, Saint Francis, Saint Benedict, Saint Dominic, Saint Bernard, and Saint Bonaventure. Ancient philosophy, in particular the works of Cicero, Boethius, and Aristotle, came to Dante filtered through these Christian lenses, as did the traditional Ptolemaic picture of the universe as earth-centered and the classical rhetoric and erudition often based on either Scholastic commentaries in Latin or Latin translations of Arabic commentaries on Greek texts. It is important to remember, however, that all of Dante's sources are filtered through his own unique poetic intelligence to serve his own personal, historical, religious, and literary purposes.

The most important philosopher of the Middle Ages in Italy as in Europe was Aristotle, the sage Dante calls the master of "those who know" (*Inferno* IV: 131). By the time Dante was born, more than fifty of Aristotle's works had been translated into Latin, although these works were often read alongside Scholastic or Arabic commentaries. Plato was virtually unknown during Dante's time, except for an incomplete

Latin translation of the *Timaeus*. Certainly Dante would also have gained some insight into Platonic thought through some of the neo-Platonists to whom Augustine refers in his *Confessions*. The emergence of Plato as a rival for Aristotle would not occur until the Medici family of fifteenth-century Florence sponsored the publication of Latin translations of the entire body of Plato's works.

In addition to his profound knowledge of Christian philosophy and theology, Dante had a familiarity with the Bible that was extensive for his time, an era when most Catholics may have heard scripture cited only in sermons, or read to them out loud during the celebration of the mass, or even depicted in narrative fresco painting and tempera altar pieces in the churches. In the centuries before the Reformation declared that every man could be his own priest, few laymen actually read the Bible. Dante was certainly an exception to this general practice, and the Bible he would have read would have been some version of Saint Jerome's Latin Vulgate. In *The Divine Comedy*, Dante draws almost 600 references or citations from the Bible, compared to almost 400 from Aristotle and almost 200 from Virgil. Interestingly enough, the number of classical and biblical citations is almost identical, an eloquent testimony to Dante's conscious desire to synthesize the classical and Christian traditions in his poem. Dante's familiarity with Catholic ritual and music also shines forth in the poetry, mainly in *Purgatorio* and *Paradiso*, where it is associated with harmony and order.

The theme of Dante's epic work is the state of souls after death. Consequently, the entire work is subdivided into three parts, each corresponding to one of the three possibilities in the Christian afterlife. In *Inferno* XX: 1–3, Dante refers to the part of the poem devoted to Hell as "the first song" ("la prima canzon"). *Canzone* means "song" in a generic sense but may also refer to a specific poetic genre, a relatively long composition, the rough equivalent of the ode, with a number of stanzas and an envoy. Dante valued the Italian *canzone* form for its rich poetic possibilities. At the end of *Purgatorio*, in canto XXXIII: 140, he employs another, even more suggestive term for the three major parts of the work—referring to *Purgatorio* as "this second canticle" (*questa cantica seconda*). If labeling his complete epic poem a *canzone* recalls Dante's origins in his secular lyrics, both the amorous and the moralizing variety, calling each of the poem's three parts (*Inferno, Purgatorio,*

Paradiso) a *cantica*, or canticle, reminds us of the religious nature of their content, since the term retains the biblical suggestion of Song of Songs (*Cantica canticorum* in the Vulgate Bible). The two terms Dante employs when referring to his poem also reflect Dante's intention to synthesize very different literary and philosophical traditions in his epic, blending the secular love lyrics of *La Vita Nuova* and the tradition of courtly love with the greatest lyric poetry of the Bible.

Besides the terms Dante uses to refer to the three parts of his epic poem (the number of parts suggesting the holy trinity), Dante employs the term *canto* (first mentioned in *Inferno* XX: 2) for the name he gives to the 100 subdivisions of the three canticles of his poem. The word suggests both poetry and song and singing in Italian, appropriate to the epic tradition, which emphasized the act of singing. The cantos in the poem are divided as follows: thirty-four in *Inferno* and thirty-three in both *Purgatorio* and *Paradiso*. Dante obviously considers canto I of *Inferno* to be a kind of general prologue to the work. Thus the poem may be said to reflect the following numerical structure: 1 + 33 (*Inferno*) + 33 (*Purgatorio*) + 33 (*Paradiso*) = 100. Given Dante's fascination with symbolic numbers, the suggestive quality of this arrangement is certainly intentional.

Dante's poem contains 14,233 lines of hendecasyllabic verse in *terza rima*. The length of each canto may vary from between 115 and 160 lines. Hendecasyllabic verse, following Dante's noble example, became the elevated poetic line of choice in Italian literature, just as the peerless example of Shakespeare's blank verse of iambic pentameter has privileged that poetic form in English. In general, the most successful English translations of Dante, such as Longfellow's, have always been in blank verse, not in rhymed verse. Italian poetry is not scanned by feet but by counting the number of syllables in a line. Since most Italian words are accented on the penultimate syllable, hendecasyllabic verse generally contains eleven syllables with the tenth accented. Lines of ten syllables or even twelve syllables occur in the poem infrequently but still follow the general rule governing accents: In the first case, the tenth or last syllable is accented, while in the second case, the tenth syllable of a twelve-syllable line retains the accent.

Dante's great metric invention was *terza rima*. This incomparable narrative form has stanzas of three lines (tercets) in which the first and third lines rhyme with each other, and the second lines rhyme with the first and third lines of the next tercet. The formula for *terza rima* may be written as follows: *aba bcb cdc d . . . wxw xyx yzy z*. Note that each canto begins with a pair of alternating rhymes but ends on a single line. The rhyme scheme also makes run-on lines (*enjambement*) infrequent in the poem, since the focus is upon rhymes at the end of lines. English, compared to Italian, is relatively impoverished in rhymes, and this explains in large measure why most attempts to repeat Dante's *terza rima* have met with dismal failure in English translations. The trinitarian association with a rhyme scheme that relentlessly repeats itself in series of threes seems obvious. What is less obvious but probably also intended by Dante is that *terza rima* helped to protect his manuscripts from changes by scribes (either accidental or intentional) and eventually by proofreaders after the advent of printing. We may not have an autograph manuscript of *The Divine Comedy*, but even after the passage of nearly seven centuries, the text of Dante's poem that has been established for us today represents an amazingly accurate version of what Dante must have written, thanks in part to the meter the poet invented that has helped to insure the integrity of the text.

Dante's Paradiso: *Conception, Geography, and Its System of Merits and Rewards*

Readers of *The Divine Comedy* often fail to ascend to Paradise, even though *Paradiso* is the narrative and poetic end of the Pilgrim's journey toward freedom. It is, we suppose, not surprising that Dante's readers find the blood and gore of Hell's arena to be so appealing, or even the ascent of a high, punishing peak of Purgatory to be enticing. And both Hell and Purgatory fall within the earth's sphere, one descending to the center of the earth and the other reaching toward the heavens, making them somehow more tangible. Yet noted novelist Umberto Eco, among other contemporary readers, believes that the *Paradiso* is the most extraordinary of the three canticles of *The Divine Comedy*. Its spectacular lights, textures, colors, and sounds, its glorious poetry, its concrete physics, its high-minded philosophy and theology, its refined expression of the deepest religious feelings are all qualities that contradict the notion of a "dark" Middle Ages. The Poet never stumbles in creating a spectacle for the eye, ear, mind, and heart. In short,

Dante's *Paradiso* is as imaginatively and intellectually engaging as *Inferno* and *Purgatorio*.

Dante's originality lies not only in his choosing to write a comedy in Italian rather than an epic tragedy in Latin, but in his creation of an unusual epic hero—a contemporary Christian seeking salvation, who is also himself. His fiction is that Dante the Poet, now older and wiser, looks back on his own pilgrimage to the other world, a journey made by his protagonist, Dante the Pilgrim. The Pilgrim has suffered a midlife crisis of faith described in the first canto of *Inferno*, which provides the introduction to the whole *Divine Comedy*. Weighed down by sin, he cannot ascend the mountain toward the light beyond the trees. Light, which is the light of God, becomes the central image in *Paradiso*. The Pilgrim requires God's grace, which is conveyed through the assistance of three heavenly ladies (*Inferno* II: 49–142), one of whom is Beatrice, and the revered Latin poet Virgil. Dante the Pilgrim learns much about the human struggle to stay on the straight path to God during his sometimes horrifying descent into the pit of Hell and his challenging climb through Purgatory. His experience in Paradise proves that virtue has substantial spiritual rewards. Dante's strategy draws readers, who may have suffered some type of spiritual crisis themselves, into a story that focuses upon a single individual's struggle to gain a clear vision of his goals in life and in death. His story of salvation is one that can inspire, even in our own age. The twentieth-century Christian writer C. S. Lewis read Dante's *Paradiso* a year before his own conversion to Roman Catholicism.

At every step in his journey, the lessons the Pilgrim learns show him that although sin has internal and personal causes as well as external and social causes, the individual ultimately remains responsible for his own fate. *Inferno* brings him face to face with the consequences of choosing evil—an eternity of pain. In *Purgatorio*, he learns that love is the motivating force of all human action. Even souls that remain stained by sin at death can be saved. Purgatory is where the Pilgrim discovers the reassuring truth that love of God and repentance, even at the moment of death, ensures salvation. Once the Pilgrim has understood the lessons of Hell and Purgatory, he is prepared for Paradise. He has learned how to free himself from the dark wood of sin and to open his heart to God's love.

In Paradise the Pilgrim learns that the supreme goal of all human endeavor is to find and to love God. Dante sees salvation, however, as a complex process of learning and loving: educating the mind and heart, through study of philosophy and theology, through the practice of good, and through emulating good examples, both religious and secular. Daily choices create the individual human personality, the Aristotelian *habitus*, and God dispenses punishments and rewards that fit them. The Christian afterlife is one in which true justice is assured, and Dante demonstrates how to achieve salvation through the education of the Pilgrim, who represents all humankind. His rhetoric in the opening cantos of *Inferno*, declaring that he is not Aeneas or Paul, serves to emphasize that he becomes both Aeneas and Paul. He goes to Paradise, where he is admonished to share his visionary experiences upon his return to earth for the benefit of his fellow Christians.

All three canticles of *The Divine Comedy* teach the spiritually deficient Pilgrim, who represents Dante himself and Everyman, what it really means to love truly, how difficult it is to remain on the straight path to God, and the rewards of salvation. Just as Dante's *Inferno* vividly depicts the horrifying conditions, both physical and mental, of the damned, *Purgatorio* and, most of all, *Paradiso*, reveal the nature of the community of the blessed. He draws on medieval tradition for two of the ideas central to *Paradiso*: the paradox of equality and hierarchy among the blessed, and the idea that the search for religious knowledge accompanies the discovery of the centrality of love. The idea of a rank among the souls in Paradise is coupled with the idea of the relative equality of the blessed. But this hierarchy is quite different from the earthly ones. The highest ranks are open to all, and nobility by birth is replaced by the ideal of spiritual nobility. Rather like Saint Augustine, Dante the Poet emphasizes the love of God over every other type of loving.

Paradiso, with its brilliant images and the perfection of its heavenly geometry, seems somehow less solid and substantial than the two terrestrial realms, the abyss of Hell and the mountain of Purgatory, with their gritty realism. Although he has experienced the horror of Hell, the pain of purgation, and the exquisite beauties of the Earthly Paradise, Dante the Pilgrim remains unprepared for the startling and unique beauties of Paradise, where he realizes that his journey through heaven is a journey toward the ultimate freedom. Sometimes blinded by the lights, overwhelmed by the music, and confused about the souls he sees, he has much to learn about the nature of blessedness. It is in Paradise that he finds the answers to his questions about salvation. The true reality is, of course, to be found in Paradise with God.

Dante's *Comedy* is filled with the author's creative synthesis of physics, philosophy, theology, history, politics, literary, and artistic tradition; it is full of his own idiosyncratic judgments, views, and opinions, expressing his political and poetic aspirations. In *Paradiso*, Dante's poetic creativity, historical analysis, theological and philosophical discourses, and political diatribes—especially against the Holy Roman Empire and the city of Florence, from which Dante writes his poem in exile—and his denunciations of corruption in the Church, reach their culmination. *Paradiso* reshapes many of the ideas, issues, themes, and poetic images that link the three canticles. As the Pilgrim moves beyond the human, he is, he tells us, "transhumanized"—one of the neologisms (new words) he creates in the third canticle to suggest that his experience of heaven is beyond the power of normal language. Indeed, one of the major themes of *Paradiso* is ineffability—the Poet often interrupts his narrative to exclaim that he scarcely knows how to describe his experience to the reader. Another common connection between the canticles is the image of the stars that ends each of the three canticles. This image lifts the Pilgrim's eyes—and those of the reader—toward the heavens, which the Poet depicts as perfect and free of anomalies or blemishes, a reminder of the perfection of creation and the perfection of God's every judgment.

The question of divine justice is not unique to Christianity or to Dante, who takes inspiration from the Old Testament as well as from pagan philosophers and such writers as Plato, Cicero, and Virgil, who conceived of an afterlife in which punishments are proportionate to the crimes and rewards proportionate to good deeds. Divine justice in Dante's epic is never simply about gruesome punishments of those who sin; it is also about the rewards given to those who love God and the communion of the just. Throughout the *Comedy*, the ideal of love stands as a measure of goodness—souls in Hell are willfully and obstinately lacking in love for God, for others, or for themselves, whereas those in Purgatory have repented of their misdirected, deficient, or excessive love of things. The level of a soul's love for God determines his or her rank in the hierarchy of heaven, and it is God's love, we learn at the end of *Paradiso*, that "moves the sun and the other stars" (XXXIII: 145).

Dante's Christian vision of the afterlife draws upon widespread beliefs in ancient civilizations, especially upon those from the classical and Judeo-Christian traditions. The Greeks believed in the immortality of the soul, and in Greco-Roman tradition, souls go to an underworld after death. Eventually this underworld was divided into regions for the good and the wicked. In Plato, Cicero, and Virgil, those who have lived good lives are generally rewarded with a pleasant afterlife, while the wicked are destined to punishments that often fit their crimes and are, in some cases, eternal.

The concept of life after death existed in Judaism but was not greatly elaborated. Old Testament texts refer mainly to an undefined dark place called "Sheol," sometimes described as a pit. Writers began to make spatial distinctions between lower places or infernal regions, and heaven, the home of the blessed. Judaism developed the notion of separate areas of the underworld for the wicked and the good (as told in the Bible, 1 Enoch 22: 1–14), and the New Testament offers the story of Lazarus, which describes different places reserved for the good and the sinful (see Luke 16: 26). Future bliss came to have a role in Jewish thinking by the Roman period, but mainly among the Pharisees. The idea of heaven as the final abode of those who love God is chiefly a Christian development; the idea of heaven in the New Testament normally refers to where God lives rather than an actual place. Details about heaven arise mainly in the Book of Revelation, with its vivid depictions of the throne of God and the Lamb with elders, angelic hosts, and the blessed who pay joyful homage. These ideas and images contribute to Dante's future elaboration of the Christian afterlife, in which Paradise is the ultimate goal.

Dante links the regions of Hell, Purgatory, and Paradise spatially and cosmologically through the Aristotelian-Ptolemaic model of the cosmos. This geocentric model, the product of observation, deduction, and calculation, is sometimes described as the first mathematical paradigm that attempted to explain the motions of the heavens. Dante's use of this model, accepted by the Church, lends great concreteness to his vision of the other world as well as to theological correctness. In this paradigm, a motionless earth lies at the center of a universe composed of nine concentric crystalline spheres made up of ether, containing the seven known heavenly bodies. Revolving around the motionless earth at the center are the moon, Mercury, Venus, the sun, Mars, Jupiter, Saturn, the fixed stars, and the Primum Mobile, which moves the whole. In the Christian scheme, the Empyrean Heaven, the abode of God, the angels, and the blessed, lies beyond the Primum Mobile. The substance of the sublunary region is composed of four mutable elements: earth, water, air, and fire. Since earth is the heaviest element, the natural place for this planet is the center of the cosmos. The heavens, it was theorized, are made up of an immutable substance, the ether or quintessence (fifth element). The substance of the moon, contaminated by its proximity to the earthly, goes through phases and is marked by spots. Given this notion of an imperfect world in a perfect and orderly universe, Saint Thomas Aquinas, the thirteenth-century religious and philosopher, could transform the Aristotelian-Ptolemaic universe into a Christian universe governed not by a Prime Mover but by God.

In constructing his Paradise, Dante adapts and refines medieval cosmology to serve the purpose of his narrative of redemption. The structure of the other world through which the Pilgrim travels reflects the Ptolemaic model. The design of every part of Dante's universe is based upon the perfect geometric image of the circle and the sacred number three. With the Ptolemaic template, Dante divides all three realms of the afterlife into nine circular spaces. Hell has a circular and funnel shape that descends to the center of the earth, where Satan is located—the place reserved for the most vile sinners. Purgatory's mountain, a reverse image of Hell's funnel, is likewise divided into nine sections that narrow gradually as the mountain ascends. Dante's Paradise embodies the Aristotelian-Ptolemaic assumption of the perfection of the heavens, and it includes the seven heavenly bodies, the Sphere of the Fixed Stars, and the Primum Mobile, beyond which is the Empyrean. By adapting this harmonious model of the cosmos with all its interconnections to his construct of the afterlife, Dante emphasizes the perfect order of God's cosmos, another of the central themes of the *Comedy*. In *Paradiso*, Dante completes his depiction of

God's cosmos as a result of rational design, even though at the end he admits it may not be entirely comprehensible to the human mind.

Another classical idea that influenced Dante's discussions of the cosmic order and the stellar influences on the fate of individuals is the idea of the "chain of being" (a term used by eighteenth-century English poet Alexander Pope) or the ladder of being (*scala naturae*). Plato and Aristotle suggest a classification of all entities in the universe based on the degree of their innate perfection—that is, the degree to which they resemble God. In God's universe, described by Saint Thomas Aquinas and others, being is hierarchical and interconnected, in descending order from God, to the angels, human beings, plant life, and basic matter. Dante's concept of divine justice also contains hierarchy: Individual merit or virtue is the criterion of judgment. Virgil explains in *Purgatorio* XXV: 42–79 that the human soul itself goes through the lower stages of being to the highest: The fetus first has the vegetative soul, then the animal, and last, by direct action of God, the intellective soul. Within his *Comedy*, Dante depicts great variation in human merit, which ranges from the worst sinner, Judas, to the best of all human beings, the Virgin Mary. Yet the chain of being is different from the order of the physical cosmos, because one's place on it is determined by one's actions and choices; it is possible for humans to learn and earn their salvation, if they also have God's grace.

Many other connections between the three realms of the afterlife exist. Besides the common themes of love, individual responsibility, justice, diversity, and perfect order in God's cosmos, Dante succeeds in creating an afterlife that is appealing to the mind and imagination. *Paradiso* is as full of history as *Inferno* and *Purgatorio*. The colorful people typical of the two lower realms are present in Paradise, but the residents of Dante's heaven are exemplary human beings who can contribute to the Pilgrim's spiritual progress in a positive fashion. A great many are saints, theologians, martyrs, and other religious figures, but, as always, Dante surprises us with a heaven that is home to breakers of vows, lovers, glory-seekers, and just rulers who are perhaps a bit more concerned with power and fame than with the state of their souls. Throughout his *Comedy*, Dante states and restates his belief that a good society, and one in which people can cultivate the good, can exist only if the institutions of both church and state have just leaders. Some of the central figures in his critique of church and state appear in more than one canticle. Among others, Dante's nemesis, Pope Boniface VIII, and Ulysses, the most famous hero of antiquity, are mentioned in all three canticles as leaders who have failed their followers.

Dante develops his own "house rules" for Paradise, often following current thinking on the topic. The reader of the *Comedy* does not so much confront Church doctrine as Dante's poetic elaboration of doctrine. Dante enriches tradition with his own poetic devices to make his other world come alive. In this way, *Paradiso* is no different from *Inferno* or *Purgatorio*. Even if the doctrinal discussions in Paradise seem relatively orthodox, Dante the Poet still creates the "house rules." He discovers at the beginning (canto I) that the law of gravity no longer applies in the celestial regions, where he is almost instantaneously raised upward, because all things instinctively seek their proper place in the hierarchy of God's heaven. In the *Comedy*, light and love are most intense near God and least so as one descends toward the pit of Hell, the lowest and darkest part of the universe. The Pilgrim eventually learns that love—not the kind he once felt for Beatrice, but love of God—is the motive force within the universe. As the Pilgrim ascends, Beatrice's eyes and the light become more and more brilliant, reflecting their proximity to God.

The issue of the location of souls in Paradise is complicated. Although the souls the Pilgrim encounters actually reside with God in the Empyrean, they come to him in the eight "planetary" spheres in a spectacle suited to human comprehension and to Dante's narrative. All the souls dance and sing to express their joy and satisfaction, and they can read Dante's questions in the mind of God. Like the souls in Purgatory and some of the less sinful souls in Hell, the saved take great delight in meeting the Pilgrim. But their goal is not to be remembered like the souls in *Inferno*, nor are they eager, like the souls paying penance in Purgatory, to send the Pilgrim on his way. Their joy in responding to the Pilgrim's questions only increases their radiance. Dante's heaven is thus a place of eternal celebration.

No longer does Dante see the "aery bodies" or well-defined shades typical of Hell and Purgatory. Sometimes the Pilgrim can see no more than dim reflections of the human form, and even these are sometimes drowned in flashes of light or in the various symbolic shapes created by groups of soul-lights. Their spiritual quality is emphasized by the fact that the Pilgrim can scarcely make out their human forms. In the Empyrean, where individuals appear to be recognizable, Dante's vision appears to show him what the souls will be like after the Last Judgment, when body and soul will be reunited, an idea common to all three canticles. Just as the damned have different degrees of sin, so, too, the saved have different degrees of merit.

Dante most likely completed *Paradiso* by 1318 (although some have dated it to Dante's last years). Divided into 33 cantos, it recounts how Dante the Pilgrim ascends through the nine spheres of the cosmos to the Empyrean, where he finds the Celestial Rose, the site of eternal bliss. In *Paradiso*, Dante goes far beyond the lessons he has learned in Hell and Purgatory to complete this Christian *paideia*—this process of educating the Pilgrim into a good Christian who can be saved. The Pilgrim has mastered the teaching that human beings are free by virtue of their rationality to choose good or evil. Although the consequences of unrepented sin are damnation and punishment, he has also learned that repentance and God's sacrifice of Himself makes redemption possible to the very moment of death. Dante clearly advocates, however, that a proper education, good habits, and grace from on high are necessary for salvation. Love, the motivating force in the cosmos (*Purgatorio* XV–XVIII) must be properly directed toward God. In Purgatory, the Pilgrim discovered that misdirected or deficient or excessive love is the root of sin, and in Paradise he comes to understand that love directed toward God is a prerequisite for heavenly and eternal bliss.

In Dante's afterlife, all souls must conform to the divine will. In Hell, the souls of the damned are strangely eager to cross the Acheron to be judged. Souls in Purgatory are impatient to earn their way to heaven by enduring their punishments, no matter how painful. They show Dante that salvation is predicated upon turning to God and repenting of sins. Right at the beginning of *Paradiso*, it is clear that the third realm is quite different from the first two, and that natural law no longer applies. In this canticle, the Poet more frequently demands the attention of the reader, especially as he articulates the challenge of putting his vision into words. Paradise is, he tells us almost regretfully, his "last emprise" (I: 13).

The poetry of *Paradiso* is more than doctrine; it is a personal recreation and analysis of the Poet's spiritual struggles. Through the experiences of Dante the Pilgrim, the reader begins to understand that even an Earthly Paradise is no more than a dim reflection of the gloriously real thing. Unsure that all his readers will be able to follow him (II: 1–6), the Poet warns those who are unprepared for the divine vision to turn back, because he is setting his course for uncharted waters. Unlike the safer waters he finds upon leaving Hell behind him in Purgatory (*Purgatorio* I: 1–6), when the Poet begins *Paradiso*, he announces: "The sea I sail has never yet been passed" (II: 7).

Dante's journey through Paradise takes place in several stages, during each of which he learns something vital to his search for God. Almost every canto focuses upon some philosophical or doctrinal issue with the goal of disclosing truth. Earlier attempts to understand the Pilgrim's emotional and spiritual crises, the meaning of life, and the nature of the universe, among other philosophical, historical, and religious issues, find fuller expression and more certain explanations in *Paradiso*. From cosmological truths of order and beauty to spiritual truths about love, justice, and the nature of God, the discussions in each sphere of the heavens prepare the Pilgrim—and the reader—for the final beatific vision of the Trinity, the central Christian truth.

After the introductory cantos and Beatrice's first two discourses, Dante travels to the planetary spheres situated within the earth's shadow, the moon, Mercury, and Venus (cantos I–IX). The second stage moves to the highest planetary spheres, the sun, Mars, Jupiter, and Saturn (X–XXII). The third stage finds the Pilgrim in the Sphere of the Fixed Stars (XXIII–XXVII), and the fourth in the sphere of the Primum Mobile (the end of XXVII–XXIX). Passing beyond space and time to the Empyrean, the heaven that has "no other Where / Than in the mind Divine" (XXVII: 109–110), constitutes the fifth and final stage (XXX–XXXIII).

Finding Paradise in the Earth's Shadow: Cantos I–IX

The end of the narrative action in *Purgatorio* merges into the beginning of *Paradiso*. The Pilgrim has been reprimanded for his earthly ties; he has seen the great pageant in the Earthly Paradise, with its scriptural lessons of the Word, revealed. He has crossed both the Lethe, which erases the memories of sin, and the Eunoë, which restores the memories of good deeds. At noon he and Beatrice, his guide to understanding the faith, remain standing in the Earthly Paradise, from which Matelda and Statius have disappeared.

• Canto I: Ascension of Dante and Beatrice into the heavens. Dante the Pilgrim "transhumanized." Physics in Paradise. God's truth, cosmic order, and degree.

The first canto of *Paradiso* alludes to themes and images already present in the first two movements of the narrative; it also announces the principal themes, images, structures, and symbols that lie at the heart of the third canticle—order, light, motion, harmony, intellect, memory, imagination, love, joy, the sun, the eagle, the topos of ineffability or inexpressibility, geometric figures (especially the sphere, the circle, the cross, and the point), Beatrice's eyes, and the Empyrean. The canto also introduces the fundamental contrast between the two worldly realms of the afterlife and Paradise, between the sublunary world and the celestial regions, and between the human and the divine. As always, the Pilgrim remains the eager student, ready to learn from his teacher, who serves as his intellectual and spiritual guide as well as a fond, loving, and sometimes motherly friend.

In the first two canticles, the first words refer respectively to Dante's age at midlife and to his task as a poet, but the first words in *Paradiso* describe God's glory: "The glory of Him who moveth everything / Doth penetrate the universe" (I: 1–2). In the end, it is God's glory that ensures the beatific vision. It defines an essential attribute of God and the light that illuminates the universe, although unevenly in different parts. Although Dante the Poet writes of beholding this divine light at its brightest in the Empyrean (I: 1–9), he claims that no one who has ever returned has found the words to describe the experience. Indeed, the greatest challenge, the Poet tells us, is to find a way to recapture this experience that goes beyond reason, memory, or words. And on some occasions, he can escape this snare only through neologism—creating a special new vocabulary. To explain the effects of his purification in the Earthly Paradise, which he compares to the miraculous transformation of Glaucus from fisherman to sea-god, he creates the word "transhumanize" (I: 67–72). That is, like Glaucus, the Pilgrim has become more than human, and is now equipped to grow in his understanding and acceptance of God's glory and love. Moving beyond epic tradition and finding the Muses insufficient to the task of inspiring him to describe the indescribable, Dante the Poet now invokes a higher deity, the god of poetry himself—the "good Apollo" (I: 13–15). The damned are described as having lost "the good of intellect" (*Inferno* III: 18); this precise quality is of the utmost importance in Dante's heaven. Human beings can learn the good; they can learn to be good; and with God's grace, they may find the path to eternal bliss.

Throughout his journey, the confrontation with physical and moral reality shocks, astounds, and even confuses Dante the Pilgrim, whose experiences in heaven contradict his earthly expectations. In *Paradiso* Beatrice often takes on the role of the theologian/philosopher, who explains what he sees and experiences and answers his questions. In the first canto, Beatrice offers the first of a number of discourses on philosophical and theological topics. In this discourse, it becomes clear that Dante is greatly influenced by Saint Thomas Aquinas's synthesis of Platonic, Aristotelian, and Christian materials in the shaping of Church doctrine.

At one point, startled, the Pilgrim feels himself moving and wonders how a heavy corporeal body can move upward through the aery entities of the heavens. He has already experienced the paradox of the ever-greater ease of climbing as he moves upward in Purgatory, where Virgil has explained the laws of love to him. Beatrice completes the lessons of Virgil, explaining the hierarchical order of the universe in which the most perfect things move closest to God (II: 103–142). Every creature has the drive—the love—to seek God, who in His love illuminates the universe. Since the Pilgrim has been purged of the weight of sin in Purgatory (I: 130–141), his good instinct along with intellect and love (I: 120) naturally propel him upward toward God. It would be profoundly unnatural—as if flames did not fly upward—if he did not ascend in Paradise (I: 139–141). His movement and participation in the eternal order are perfectly natural, and Paradise is Nature as God intended it to be: " 'All things whate'er they be / Have order among themselves, and this is form, / That makes the universe resemble God' " (I: 103–105). What is normal on earth is not necessarily so in Paradise.

- Canto II: Solid bodies in the same space. Lunar spots. Limits of reason. Revised theory of lunar spots. Thought experiment with mirrors. "True" principles of motion and variations in matter.

The technical discussion of lunar spots in canto II raises the issue of diversity in a universe created by the one God (II: 70–72), one of the thematic cores of *Paradiso*. When the Pilgrim asks Beatrice about the "dusky spots" (II: 49) on the moon as it is seen from earth, she uses the occasion to demonstrate the limits of human reason in addressing both problems of physics and matters of the spirit. In *Paradiso*, intellect is important, but incapable of penetrating the profoundest mysteries of faith. The moon alone of the heavenly entities exhibits any imperfections. The Pilgrim tries to explain moon spots with an argument Dante presents in his *Il Convivio* 2: 13: 9, drawn from Averroës and Albertus Magnus, which attributes varying densities to lunar matter (II: 59–60). Refuting this claim, Beatrice explains that the fixed stars in the eighth heaven (the Sphere of the Fixed Stars) have different "powers" or "active principles" that influence the world below in different ways. She argues that if the marks were caused by different densities in the moon's substance, the moon could not block out the sunlight in an eclipse (II: 73–78).

To prove that lunar spots result from different qualities, or "virtues," in the lunar material rather than the density of matter, she constructs a curious experiment using three mirrors to reflect a beam of light. She concludes that the light reflected in two more distant mirrors would be of equal intensity to light reflected in a less distant mirror, even if the image is not as large (II: 82–105). Any apparent irregularities in the heavens would result, therefore, from the fact that the primary essence of creation, which originates in the Primum Mobile and God, is differentiated as it passes through the Fixed Stars, which possess "virtues," or powers, that are different from the spheres and planets below. These powers of the stars, along with the different angelic intelligences, produce the spots on the moon and the diversity in earthly things, including human souls. This argument looks back to the opening tercet of *Paradiso* and prepares Dante the Pilgrim—and the reader—for the fact that God's creation naturally exhibits different degrees of perfection.

- Canto III: Piccarda Donati's moral deficiency. Paradox of the equal hierarchy among blessed. Canto IV: Explanation of souls' appearance in planetary spheres. Justice and free will. Canto V: How to compensate for a broken vow.

In cantos III–IX, souls appear in the first three heavenly spheres that contain the moon, Mercury, and Venus, which lie under earth's cone-shaped shadow, which has not only a physical but also a moral dimension. The souls the Pilgrim meets in the first three heavenly planets are tainted by earthly considerations (IX: 118–119) and are less blessed than souls who appear in the higher heavens, and whose seat is closer to God in the Empyrean, where all souls actually reside.

As a traditional symbol of inconstancy, the moon is an appropriate meeting place for Dante the Pilgrim and the souls of women—nuns—who have failed to keep their sacred vows. Piccarda Donati's failures make her assurances that she fully experiences God's love and finds complete satisfaction in heaven puzzling. Like all of Dante's interlocutors in Purgatory and Paradise, she eagerly tells him her personal history. She explains that she and the Empress Constance have lower stations in heaven, because they failed to keep their vows when their families forced them to marry for political reasons, even though it was against their will. When Dante asks if they yearn for more, she explains that heavenly love enables them to desire only what they have, in accord with God's will. All souls are as happy as their potential allows.

In cantos IV and V, Beatrice addresses other questions that arise in the Pilgrim's mind. He wonders if the Platonic notion that a soul returns to its star at death is true, but Beatrice explains that all souls actually reside in the Empyrean and appear now in the spheres only as part of Dante's education. Although Dante admits in other parts of *The Divine Comedy* that the stars have some influence on human personality (*Purgatorio* XVI: 67–84; *Paradiso* II), he insists that their impact never interferes with the exercise of free will. Hence, when the Pilgrim asks why a person's worth would be diminished because of another's act, he learns that those forced to break their vows (as Piccarda was) failed to oppose the act with an absolute will, allowing the contingent will to submit out of fear of greater harm. In canto V Beatrice explains further that even though some vows may be changed with the approval of the Church, particularly sacred vows may not be substituted. In this declaration, Dante goes beyond the Church teachings (especially those of Saint Thomas Aquinas) that the Church has full authority to grant dispensation. Again, Dante emphasizes individual responsibility, urging all Christians to find guidance in Scripture and the Church.

Ascending to Mercury, Dante meets souls who actively pursued fame and glory in the world. The classical virtue of pursuing fame becomes a personal failing in Christianity, even though, like breaking vows and amorous desires, it has certain admirable features and does not preclude salvation.

- Canto VI: Justinian's history of the Roman Empire and the coming of Christ (first reference to Christ in the *Paradiso*). Canto VII: Beatrice discusses justice and the Crucifixion.

Cantos VI and VII take place in the Sphere of Mercury and address basic principles of religious doctrine, enunciating the role of Roman institutions in providing an environment in which Christianity could arise. Dante clearly believes that empire is—or should be—a reflection of the heavenly order and a source of peace for the world, allowing human beings to develop their talents and to learn the path to heaven. Responding to the Pilgrim, the Emperor Justinian, famous for the Justinian Code, the sixth-century revision and compilation of Roman law, raises the central theme of divine justice and the decisive role of Rome in Christian history, tying together the historical material from earlier in the *Comedy*. His long exposition of Roman history concludes with an invective against the Guelphs and Ghibellines of Dante's day, whom he accuses of betraying the sacred eagle, symbol of the Roman Empire, which had paved the way for the birth of Christ and for the spread of Christianity.

Dante consistently blames the politics of his day—both in secular and ecclesiastical institutions—for much of the evil in the world. Nonetheless, he insists that the Holy Roman Empire of his time, however imperfect a reflection of the earlier Roman Empire, is part of God's plan for the world; following some of the ideas set out in his treatise *De Monarchia*. Dante learns that despite their virtuous efforts, the souls here in the Sphere of Mercury allowed their desire for lasting fame to diminish their love of God. For this reason, Justinian and Romeo appear in this sphere, but Justinian assures the Pilgrim that they rejoice in the system of merits and rewards essential to divine justice.

The seventh canto of *Paradiso* follows a pattern common to the seventh cantos of *Inferno* and *Purgatorio*, which open the debate that rages throughout the *Comedy* on the role of political and religious institutions in human society. *Inferno* VII focuses on Fortune, the classical goddess transformed into a minister of God, and on the distribution of worldly success and wealth. The failure of princes to take their responsibilities seriously, a related issue raised frequently in the *Comedy*, lies at the heart of *Purgatorio* VII. In *Paradiso* VII, Beatrice, responding to the Pilgrim's troubling questions, analyzes the role of the Empire in Christ's Passion, the Redemption, and the punishment of Jerusalem and the Jews. If the Crucifixion was a just penalty for human sin, how could it justly be avenged by the fall of Jerusalem? She explains the effects of the Crucifixion in terms of Christ's Incarnation, when human nature was joined to that of God. Both aspects of His person were punished through the Crucifixion. Although the Jews were blameless in the just punishment of sinful human nature in the man, Dante holds that they were still guilty of sacrilege against God. Hence, the destruction of Jerusalem avenged the injustice perpetrated upon the divinity in Christ. Since sinful human beings could not have made just amends on their own, the Crucifixion alone could redeem human nature and pay the debt for the sin in the garden of Genesis.

At the end, Beatrice discusses the resurrection of the body, a subject first brought up in *Inferno*. Reflecting back on the earlier discussion of diversity in the cosmos, she notes that the elements and compounds in the material world, subject to decay, are given form and function by other created bodies (stars, planetary spheres, angelic intelligences). Primary matter, such as the angels, the heavenly spheres, and human life, was, however, created by God and therefore made eternal. Hence, the human body and soul are God's direct creations and will have a second life, but because human beings lost their privileged status by sin (VII: 76–78), they had to be redeemed by atonement commensurate with the sin of disobedience against the Creator.

- Canto VIII: Charles Martel of Anjou. Diversity in human talents. Role of stellar influences. Canto IX: Cunizza da Romano, Folquet of Marseilles, Rahab. Pursuit of false glory. Analysis of historical and political issues, with denunciations of Boniface VIII and the city of Florence.

Dante sets cantos VIII and IX in the Sphere of Venus, named after the Roman goddess of sensual love, and addresses lust once again as a diversion from the love of God. (This common human failing also plays a distinctive role in *Inferno* V and *Purgatorio* XXV–XXVII.) Love is definitely not the worst defect, but it still merits condemnation, because of its power to shape human behavior. Although Dante the Poet makes this sin the least offensive, he still views it as a distraction from loving God and focusing upon salvation. Dante's political agenda is never far from the surface in the Sphere of Venus, and the theme of diversity, put forth in the discussion of lunar spots and in the discussion of degrees of beatitude, reappears in a discussion of the laws of heredity and the division of labor.

The Pilgrim meets the soul of Charles Martel, a member of the French family of Anjou, one of the ruling families in southern Italy in the thirteenth and fourteenth centuries. Charles, whom Dante knew and admired, explores differences that exist naturally among people, even members of the same family. He observes that some of his relatives were unsuited to govern a kingdom. These include his brother Robert, whom he depicts as stingy and quite unlike himself or their father, Charles II. He concludes that the laws of heredity give rise to a necessary individuality and differentiation of talents. Besides what a child inherits from his or her parents, the stars also play a role. Since the social order depends upon the division of labor and the cooperation of people with various different talents, God has assigned powers to the spheres and stars to generate diversity. Each individual is created for a particular purpose, but has the free will to choose whether or not to fulfill his or her real talents. In Dante's view, education should help individuals develop their special attributes in accord with God's will.

In canto IX are conversion stories that seem to be appropriately exemplary for the Pilgrim, because they focus on lovers, the first of whom is Cunizza da Romano. Famous for being often married and for taking many lovers, one of whom was the troubadour poet Sordello of *Purgatorio* VI–VIII, Cunizza pardons herself for her amorous disposition. She feels no grief for her failings, since all the saved enjoy perfect bliss. It was presumably that same love, finally directed properly toward God and her neighbor, that saved her. Unlike Charles Martel, who forbids the Pilgrim from disclosing his predictions of misfortune for his successors, Cunizza openly prophesies death and punishment for treacherous political leaders in the Veneto and the March of Treviso, including members of her own family. Cunizza's words re-evoke the sinful disposition of the souls in the Sphere of Mercury, the glory seekers. She warns against striving for fame through treachery and betrayal, because she can see the punishments she predicts through the angelic order of Thrones, the third highest, whom she describes as mirrors through which the blessed may read the judgments in the mind of God (IX: 61–63).

As an antidote, Cunizza introduces the troubadour who became a bishop, Folquet de Marseilles, who provides a positive example of striving for fame through good works. Folquet wrote several crusade songs, and he later became a central figure in preaching for the Albigensian Crusade against heretics in Occitania, or southern France, a theme that looks forward to the cantos of the crusaders and martyrs (XIV–XVII) at the heart of *Paradiso*. He reiterates Cunizza's claim that for the saved in heaven, no feelings of guilt for their weaknesses remain (IX: 103–105). These souls, purged of their sins in Purgatory, have been purified by bathing in the Lethe and the Eunoë, so that, forgetting the shame of their sins, they remember the good things in their lives (*Purgatorio* XXXIII: 118–129).

The Pilgrim receives several other lessons in the Sphere of Venus. He learns that the first soul—a pre-Christian soul—"assigned" to Venus after the Crucifixion was the harlot Rahab, who, like Folquet, contributed to a matter of state by helping save the spies Joshua sent to Jericho. He also learns the significance of the fact that the earth casts a shadow on the first three heavens. Folquet then delivers a scathing speech about the corruption and greed of Pope Boniface VIII, whose damnation Dante has already predicted in *Inferno* XIX and who lacked a proper interest in the liberation of the Holy Land (see also *Inferno* XXVII: 85–93), and about the city of Florence.

Reflecting back on the regular attacks on the Church throughout the *Comedy*, Folquet shows that the worldly order, especially the social order, is left in disarray by those who should be implementing God's plan. Humans, who are free to choose between good and evil, have the responsibility of using their talents to improve life on earth and to improve their own souls. Even though the souls in the first three spheres exhibited weakness in their lives, they ultimately picked the path of the good. God, the author of order, has also, through His mercy, made reconciliation possible through Christ's death, an act of both martyrdom and of justice.

A Pilgrim's Progress and the Cardinal Virtues: Cantos X–XXII

The Pilgrim sees the cardinal and theological virtues in the guise of stars early in *Purgatorio*. Coming out into the light from the darkness of Hell, he and Virgil find in the sky four stars, which symbolize the cardinal virtues (*Purgatorio* I: 28) and help to guide them on their way. Their light illuminates the face of Cato, Purgatory's guardian and an important symbol of freedom. At the threshold of Purgatory proper, the Pilgrim sees the three stars of the theological virtues (*Purgatorio* VIII: 89). Together these virtues can help free fallen human beings from domination by the Seven Deadly Sins, from which the Pilgrim, on his journey of freedom, must find release. In the Earthly Paradise (*Purgatorio* XXIX: 120–132), the Pilgrim sees the seven virtues personified in the form of seven dancing maidens that guide him to Beatrice, who provides him with the instruction he requires to enter Paradise and attain the beatific vision.

In *Paradiso*, the cardinal and theological virtues provide an ethical framework for the spheres of the higher heavens—the spheres that lie beyond earth's shadow and beyond all possible corruption. Once the Pilgrim moves beyond the earth's shadow, he encounters exemplars possessing the qualities of character that may be associated with the four cardinal virtues: prudence, courage or fortitude, justice, and temperance. These values, derived from the classical tradition, have a personal and social dimension. They regulate one's inner and spiritual life and one's outer and social life through self-restraint in the face of fear and temptation. Interestingly, the souls in the last four planetary spheres appear in communities of the blessed that organize themselves into various symbolic configurations.

The Pilgrim now moves into the four higher planetary spheres: the sun, Mars, Jupiter, and Saturn (cantos X–XXII). As he moves into the Sphere of the Sun, he distinguishes lights more brilliant than the sun itself, a scene of indescribable beauty (X: 40–51).

- Cantos X–XIV: Saint Thomas Aquinas, Saint Francis, Saint Bonaventure, Saint Dominic.

Beginning with the Sphere of the Sun, the human form is essentially obliterated by the light, and individuals are depicted as part of a community of souls who appear together in various geometric and symbolic configurations. In this sphere, two groups of the souls of wise and learned religious figures, engaged in dance and song, form two sparkling rings around Dante and Beatrice. The beginning and end of the Pilgrim's sojourn in the Sphere of the Sun is tied together by the figure of the circle; the episode is also united by three references to the Trinity (X: 1–3; XIII: 25–27; and XIV: 28–33). As the central tenet of Christianity, the image and doctrine of the Trinity becomes central to *Paradiso*. In the Sphere of the Sun, the sphere of divine illumination, it is the truth that brings all the souls together in their joyful harmony. The residents of this sphere include the wise and learned, philosophers and theologians, whose writings, sometimes at odds in the world, guided the Church in developing its creed and canon law.

A central event in the Sphere of the Sun is the reconciliation of the Franciscan and Dominican orders. This theme recalls the Valley of the Princes in *Purgatorio*, where the saved—including former political enemies—leave aside worldly wrangling to form a harmonious Christian community (*Purgatorio* VII: 91–136). Worldly quarrels have no place in the two realms of the saved—even those of a theological nature. The Franciscan and Dominican orders originally took different theological approaches, especially with respect to the role of rational reflection in faith. The Franciscans tended to view reason as a tool for explicating faith, whereas the Dominicans, with the rise of Aristotelian philosophy, expanded and elevated the role of reason in establishing the theological foundations of the faith.

In canto XI, the Dominican Saint Thomas Aquinas tells the story of Saint Francis, paying tribute to the virtue of poverty and calling attention to the unity of Dominicans and Franciscans. His account of Saint Francis's rejection of earthly goods gives sharp focus to Dante's repeated denunciations of ecclesiastical corruption, regularly linked to the greed for secular power or wealth and the sin of avarice. Saint Thomas introduces himself and various Judeo-Christian writers and thinkers, including Albertus Magnus, Gratian, Peter Lombard, Solomon, Dionysius the Areopagite, Paulius Orosius, Boethius, Isidore of Seville, Bede, Richard of Saint Victor, and even Siger de Brabant. After more music and dance, Saint Bonaventure, who represents the Franciscan order, speaks to Dante the Pilgrim (canto XII). Just as Saint Thomas praised the Franciscans, so Bonaventure praises the Dominicans in a speech extolling Saint Dominic, their founder. He calls the Pilgrim's attention to the souls in the outer circle, among them Illuminato, Augustine, Hugh of Saint Victor, Peter Mangiador, Peter of Spain, Nathan, Saint Chrysostom, Saint Anselm, Donatus, Rabanus, and Joachim of Fiore. Both Saints Thomas and Bonaventure also condemn their own orders for growing corrupt and moving away from their founders' teachings.

It is worth noting that besides various Franciscans and Dominicans, the two circles of light include other Jewish and Christian thinkers, including Joachim of Fiore, a mystic and founder of the Cistercian order (with whom Bonaventure had serious disagreements), and Siger de Brabant (with whom Saint Thomas had sharp differences). Dante includes the names of some of the greatest medieval religious thinkers—Augustine, Peter Lombard, Albertus Magnus, Hugh of Saint Victor, Saint Anselm, and even the supposed author of the famous treatises on angels, Dionysius the Areopagite, or Pseudo Dionysius. The circles of souls also contain two biblical figures, Nathan and Solomon, who signify the two types of wisdom central to Christian thinking associated with the active and contemplative lives, introduced in *Purgatorio* XXVII, but different from the wisdom gained through an intellectual or philosophical approach. As a poet, Dante may have found the prophetic voices of Joachim and Nathan congenial.

The atmosphere of perfect concord in the Sphere of the Sun suggests Dante's own breadth of knowledge and his eclectic approach to theology. It also reveals medieval theology to be complex and many-sided. Just as there is diversity in the cosmic order and in humankind, so, too, diversity exists in the spiritual and intellectual orders. The themes of community and reconciliation also find expression in the paired circles of souls and the parallel discourses of Saints Thomas and Bonaventure. A traditional symbol of enlightenment, the sun is an appropriate symbol of the Pilgrim's educational experience in this sphere.

Cantos XIII and XIV are devoted to a single figure—King Solomon. Thomas has appeared to claim that Solomon was the wisest of men (X: 112–114), but Dante argues that since God created only Adam and Christ directly, they were the wisest of men. Saint Thomas explains that his words make no such comparison, but rather distinguish between different kinds of wisdom. He meant that Solomon's wisdom *as a king* was unsurpassed. He then picks up Beatrice's earlier theme about the limits of human intelligence (XIII: 118–120).

In canto XIV, the soul of Solomon answers the Pilgrim's questions about the radiance of the souls and the resurrection of the flesh. Solomon explains that the intensity of a soul's love for God determines its brilliance (XIV: 36–63), adding that when body and soul are rejoined after the Last Judgment, the light will be even brighter. This argument is a Scholastic doctrine based on Aristotle holding that the perfection of body and soul lies in their union and continues the discussion of the resurrection of the flesh at the Last Judgment begun in *Inferno* VI.

- Cantos XIV–XVIII (Angelic Order: Virtues): Crusaders and martyrs (Courage or Fortitude). Cacciaguida. Moral courage in martyrdom and civic life.

Whereas reason can serve as a tool of truth, courage fighting for the faith is another aspect of establishing God's order in a chaotic human world. Cantos XIV–XVIII depict Dante's encounter with his ancestor Cacciaguida in the Sphere of Mars, where the souls of warriors and martyrs configure themselves in a new geometric form, the rectilinear image of the Greek cross with its two equal axes. Dante the Poet connects this cross to the earlier figure of the circle, "the venerable sign / That quadrants joining in a circle make" (XIV: 101–102).

Although the music sung by the souls of these crusaders and martyrs is beyond human appreciation, the Pilgrim is somehow able to discern its fitting theme, Christ's resurrection and victory over death (XIV: 124–126). Warriors who defended the faith were exemplary Christian heroes in the Middle Ages, and Dante structures these cantos around his tribute to them. In canto XV, his great-great grandfather, Cacciaguida, describes his death on a crusade (XV: 139–144), and at the end of the episode in XVIII, he names a variety of famous warriors, whose souls form the cross. The papal indulgence granted to crusaders declared them to be martyrs, who would go straight to Paradise after death if they confessed their sins and repented before dying. Heroes from the Old Testament, past crusades and the French *chansons de geste*, who fought the Saracens in Spain, were often presented as examples to inspire later crusaders. The heroes forming the cross that Dante sees are defenders of the faith from Old Testament and Christian times. Cacciaguida eventually names Joshua, Judas Maccabaeus, Roland, Charlemagne, William of Orange, Renouard, Godfrey of Bouillon, and Robert Guiscard (XVIII: 34–48). The individual souls flash from their place in the cross as their names are called.

One might ask why Dante places the souls of warriors and martyrs at the heart of *Paradiso*. Dante the Poet signals the personal importance of these encounters in the Sphere of Mars when the Pilgrim encounters the crusader Cacciaguida, who, rather than reading the Pilgrim's questions in the mind of God, insists that he ask them in his own voice. This meeting between Dante the Pilgrim and his great-great grandfather Cacciaguida imitates Aeneas' meeting with his father in the Underworld (*Aeneid* VI). Anchises shows Aeneas his future in the context of Roman history, and in like manner Cacciaguida places Dante's life and future within the context of Florentine politics. The Pilgrim's encounter with Cacciaguida also echoes similar meetings with influential characters throughout the *Comedy*. In *Inferno* XV, the Pilgrim comes upon Brunetto Latini, the teacher who showed Dante how a poet may earn fame. In *Purgatorio* XV–XVIII, he hears a lecture on the core issue of love from Virgil, his first guide, who led him through Hell and Purgatory.

Responding to the Pilgrim's questions, Cacciaguida begins by giving the Pilgrim a short history of the family, explaining that the name

Alighieri belonged to his wife and that he had died during the Second Crusade (XV: 88–147). He emphasizes the family's noble origins and character, in part as a product of the mores of eleventh-century Florentine society. The culmination of the theme of Florentine corruption, begun with Ciacco and Farinata in *Inferno*, becomes personal in *Paradiso*. This corruption results in Dante's own exile that will take place after 1300, the fictional date of the Pilgrim's journey in the poem.

Although Virgil told Dante that Beatrice would reveal his future (*Inferno* X: 127–132), it is his own ancestor who tells the story. Cacciaguida's account emphasizes an idyllic early period of moral and political integrity in Florence, a city founded by Romans. The sober, simple customs of earlier times came to be tainted by the behavior of immigrants from the countryside, by the mercantile pursuit of profit, and by the factional strife among Guelphs and Ghibellines—later the Black and White Guelphs. All this will lead to Dante's betrayal and exile.

Cacciguida makes the virtue of poverty, associated with Saint Francis (XI) in the Sphere of the Sun, an element in the heroic ethos of the Sphere of Mars. Dante's typical celebration of idyllic times in early Florence stands in contrast with his condemnation of city, church, and state in his own day. The many earlier ambiguous references to Florentine degeneracy come together in Cacciaguida's clear and comprehensible prophecy of Dante's future exile (XVII). He compares Dante, who will face charges of political corruption, to Hippolytus, falsely accused and forced to flee Athens (XVII: 46–48). Nonetheless, this mistreatment will, according to Cacciaguida, ensure a much greater destiny (XVII: 97–99). Dante the Pilgrim affirms his determination to fulfill his destiny through his poetry and through revealing the truth (XVII: 118). Finally, Cacciaguida bestows special authority upon Dante's poem, calling Dante's words "a vital nutriment" (XVII: 132). From here on, Dante's references to his poem change from the term "comedy" used in *Inferno* to "sacred poem" in *Paradiso* (XXIII, XXV), recalling the divine permission for the Pilgrim's journey.

• Cantos XVIII–XX: Human and divine justice. Virtue, justice.

In cantos XVIII–XX, the Pilgrim enters the Sphere of Jupiter and meets earthly rulers, who exemplify the third cardinal virtue, justice.

The *Comedy* displays its author's deep interest in politics, especially as they relate to salvation. The process of salvation can be worked out only if earthly conditions permit, and Dante's concerns about good leaders reach a climax in this sphere.

In a spectacular show for which the Poet re-invokes the Muses, the souls arrange themselves into thirty-five letters that spell out the phrase *Diligite justitiam qui judicatis terram* ("Love righteousness, ye that be judges of the earth"—XVIII: 91, 93). This line, taken from the opening verse of the apocryphal book of the Wisdom of Solomon, connects the Sphere of Jupiter to the Sphere of the Sun, in which Solomon is described by Saint Thomas as the wisest ruler who ever lived. Additional souls congregate to enlarge the letter M (for monarchy, XVIII: 97–98), next adding to it the figure of the lily, emblem of France (XVIII: 113). Finally, the souls continue the emphasis on monarchy by refashioning themselves into the form of an eagle, symbol of imperial Rome (XIX: 101–102), the holy image of Justinian's earlier discourse on justice and empire in the Sphere of Mercury (VI: 5, 111).

In another exercise in heavenly reconciliation and community, all the souls speak with one voice through the eagle (XIX: 10–12). Departing from his usual exchanges with individual souls, the Pilgrim communicates with the eagle throughout this episode. The last political speech in the *Comedy* emphasizes the notion, earlier expressed in Dante's treatise *De Monarchia*, that the emperor receives dominion from God and spiritual guidance from the Pope. The Poet again interrupts the narrative to ask the souls of Jupiter and God Himself to punish those who, with the "bad example" of their illegitimate ambitions (XVIII: 126), have led the Church from its spiritual and evangelical mission. He castigates Pope John XXII directly for his readiness to write or to withdraw orders, especially of excommunication, for a price.

The souls in the eagle know the Pilgrim's nagging concern about divine justice: How can God condemn those born before Christ or who have never heard the gospel? The eagle expands the question beyond the virtuous pagans to all non-Christians, including those who could never have heard the gospel, with the pervasive argument on the limits of human reason (XIX: 40–99). God is infinite, and his qualities cannot be shared or known by finite creatures. Hence, God's justice is beyond human understanding, and a belief in God's goodness and judgment is simply a matter of faith. Only the illumination of God's grace can overcome the human inability to comprehend divine mysteries. The first part of the eagle's speech ends with a reprimand that has a biblical ring: "Now who art thou, that on the bench wouldst sit / In judgment . . ." (XIX: 79–80).

The eagle assures Dante that some of those who seem to know Christ will be farther from Him at the Last Judgment than some others who do not yet know Christ (XIX: 106–108). Then, opening God's book with its list of the damned, the eagle identifies some of the names in it (XIX: 115–148). This catalogue of wicked rulers opens with the deplorable example of Albert of Austria (elected emperor in 1298) and ends with the abuses of a petty tyrant in Cyprus, Henry II of Lusignan. All are infamous for their injustices, including various types of treachery, usurpation, dishonesty, cruelty, and incompetence.

In canto XX shining souls sparkle like stars or jewels and sing another ineffable song. Reading Dante's desire for more information, the eagle continues its discourse with a catalogue of good rulers, the best exemplars of the active life, who form the eagle's eye. David is the pupil of the eye, and Trajan, Hezekiah, Constantine, William II, and Ripheus form the brow. Reflecting Saint Thomas's discussion of the possible salvation of certain pagans, Dante, too, creates unexpected salvations, opening one of the most impassioned arguments for God's justice, a quality not even the blessed can fully comprehend. Constantine's donation of temporal power to the Church, regularly condemned in the *Comedy*, resulted in the perversion of the Church's mission and damage to human society. Yet his intentions have been judged good, and he is, therefore, saved (XX: 55–60). The salvation of Trajan and Ripheus, two pagans, reveal the mystery of God's judgments and the Poet's freedom to create stories that serve his purpose. God listens to prayers of love and hope (XX: 95–98). Returned to life by the prayers of Saint Gregory, Trajan found the faith that, with God's grace, led to his salvation. God bestowed special grace upon Ripheus, whose love of justice and belief in human redemption were unqualified (XX: 123–125). In this way, the Pilgrim grasps the truth that humans, who cannot know God's will, should refrain from judgment (XX: 129, 130–138). This lesson is a fitting completion of the theme of justice that has occupied the Poet throughout the *Comedy*.

- Cantos XXI–XXII: The contemplative life. Virtue, temperance. Peter Damian, Saint Benedict.

The Pilgrim now ascends to the Sphere of Saturn (XXI–XXII), which turns away from the active life in the world to the contemplative life, with its clearer focus on God. This episode marks a transition between the six lower spheres and the highest heavens. The seventh sphere displays a renewed emphasis on the individual and individual responsibility for salvation.

In Dante's time, Saturn was believed to exert an influence on individuals inclined toward the solitary life of contemplation, and Dante makes Saturn the temporary residence of souls with this predisposition (XXII: 46–47), particularly those with a monastic vocation. Monastic communities provided a supportive environment for the spiritual exercises of their members, and their way of life is sometimes associated with the fourth cardinal virtue of temperance.

The atmosphere on Saturn proves quite different from the lower heavens: The Pilgrim cannot see Beatrice's smile or hear the heavenly music. It is clear that he has a difficult lesson to learn, for which, at the moment of his arrival, he is insufficiently prepared. The souls on Saturn appear to the Pilgrim descending the golden rungs of a ladder in the sky (XXI: 28–33) that reaches up into the heavens beyond what the eye can see. Based on Jacob's ladder, this golden staircase suggests the great worth of the contemplative life.

Peter Damian descends to speak with the Pilgrim. As in his meeting with Cacciaguida, in a second deviation from the usual practice, the Pilgrim asks his questions aloud. He wonders about the absence of music and about how Peter's soul had been elected to speak to him (XXI: 55–60). The conversation here turns to the question of predestination. After explaining that the Pilgrim's powers of sight and hearing are still too weak to bear the lights and sounds of Saturn, the soul of Peter Damian explains that his soul shines brighter to the degree that God's grace allows it to reflect His own light (XXI: 79–90). Reinforcing the lessons about the mystery of God's judgments that the Pilgrim learned on Jupiter, Peter characterizes predestination as another mystery so profound that it is even beyond the Seraphim, who see God most clearly. In sharing the story of his own life with the Pilgrim,

Peter, too, inveighs against the greed and corruption of modern prelates (XXI: 106–135), and his remarks elicit a howl of indignation from the other souls in the Sphere of Saturn.

At the beginning of canto XXII, the Pilgrim is left in shock and confusion by the loud and angry response, an indication that he still lacks true insight into the nature of the contemplative life. In fact, he is at a loss, and Beatrice scolds him for failing to understand "good zeal" (XXII: 9). To remediate, the largest and brightest light comes forward to address the question the uncomprehending Pilgrim has not even been able to formulate. Saint Benedict (480–543), the founder of the first religious order in the West, the Benedictines, and the monastery of Montecassino, explains the warmth of charity and the love of God and one's neighbor—qualities that produce goodness. When the Pilgrim asks if he has sufficient grace to see his face, Benedict explains that his wish will be realized in the "remotest sphere" where high desires are fulfilled (XXII: 58–63). He then launches into an invective condemning the corruption of his order, yet another chapter in the story of ecclesiastical wrongdoing, foreshadowing Saint Peter's attack on the corruption of the modern church in the Sphere of the Fixed Stars.

At the end of canto XXII, the Pilgrim finds himself in the sign of Gemini, to which he attributes his talents, a re-evocation of the idea that stellar influences govern the mutable sublunary world (XXII: 106–123).

The Pilgrim's Final Examination and the Theological Virtues (Cantos XXIII–XXIX)

As always, Beatrice's power, the power of divine love, conquers gravity, and the Pilgrim ascends at lightning speed to the Sphere of the Fixed Stars. All that has gone before has prepared the Pilgrim for the beatific vision (XXII: 100–102), but one crucial challenge to the Pilgrim remains before he can see God: He must demonstrate that he understands and possesses the theological virtues. The cardinal virtues, attainable through human endeavor, utilize humankind's natural powers—the senses and intellect.

By themselves, the four cardinal virtues are inadequate for salvation. As the Pilgrim has observed in Limbo (*Inferno* IV)—and as the Latin poet Virgil knows (*Purgatorio* VII: 34–36)—even the individual who has achieved great merit by observing the cardinal virtues cannot attain salvation without the theological virtues of faith, hope, and charity, revealed in the Scriptures. Faith, hope, and charity have their origin in God's grace and are known through revelation; they are gifts of God acquired through baptism and knowledge of Christ that resides in the Scriptures. Dante carefully distinguishes the difference between human knowledge and revealed knowledge, between reason and revelation. Virgil, the symbol of human reason, can take him only so far on his journey, and even Beatrice, often said to symbolize revelation, has her limits. Ultimately, salvation rests upon the quality of one's faith, hope, and charity, and these virtues are positioned in the Sphere of the Fixed Stars to signal their crucial importance.

- Cantos XXIII–XXVII: Theological Virtues: Faith, Hope, and Charity. Saint Peter, Saint James, Saint John.

This third phase of the Pilgrim's journey takes him beyond the planetary spheres into a more purely spiritual realm. Enclosed between two visions of the planetary universe that involve looking down upon the earth, a "threshing-floor" (XXII: 151 and XXVII: 85), his sojourn in the Sphere of the Fixed Stars signifies his definitive movement away from the physical toward the spiritual universe. Again the focus is upon individual behavior, which, in Dante's view, figures importantly in achieving salvation. Dante the protagonist becomes the real focus of the narrative as he is examined on his knowledge of the theological virtues required for salvation. Although Saint Paul was the first to group the three virtues together (see the Bible, 1 Corinthians 13: 13) and to experience a journey to the afterlife, Dante's exam is conducted by Peter, James, and John, the three apostles who witnessed Christ's transfiguration (Matthew 17: 1–6; Mark 9: 1–8; and Luke 9: 28–36) and who perhaps best embody these virtues in the gospels. Dante's stay in the Sphere of the Fixed Stars ends with Saint Peter, the first pope, dramatically denouncing the corruption of the papacy and assigning to Dante the task of revealing what he has learned with his fellow men (XXVII: 22–66) and giving his poem its sacred purpose.

Although he is blinded by the light, when Dante opens his eyes at

Beatrice's command (XXIII: 46), he discovers that his transformation enables him to endure her smile. He is now ready to behold the triumph of Christ and the coronation of Mary, with its courtly garden imagery and light (XXIII) that serve as the necessary prelude to his examination and his experience in the Empyrean. Just as his sight has been restored, so has his hearing, and he hears the hymn "Regina Coeli." In another surprising departure from the norm, the music in the eighth sphere is recognizable, an actual church hymn, sung in praise of the Virgin at Easter. When the souls in this sphere express their joy at the idea of sharing their knowledge with the Pilgrim in the usual ways—spinning and sparkling—the Poet admits that it is impossible to find the words to describe the extraordinary sights and sounds.

Dante's examinations resemble a medieval university exam (*disputatio*) on philosophy or theology, in which the candidate would study questions announced by the master. After a brief time to prepare, the candidate set forth arguments, usually both pro and con on certain questions, without drawing definite conclusions, which was the prerogative of the master or doctor who proposed the questions. When Saint Peter, the brightest light in this sphere, descends and circles Beatrice, she asks him to test Dante on "the Faith / By means of which thou on the sea didst walk" (XXIV: 38–39). Dante's response to the question "What is the Faith?" (XXIV: 53) is, not surprisingly, a standard response based on an expression taken directly from Saint Paul in the Bible (Hebrews 11: 1): "Faith is the substance of the things we hope for, / And evidence of those that are not seen" (XXIV: 64–65). The Pilgrim explains that he has learned faith through the miracles of the Bible, and when he is asked to offer better corroboration, he asserts that the world's acceptance of Christ without verification of the biblical miracles is sufficient proof. Again, in religious matters, arguments are not based on evidence but on belief or faith. The Pilgrim then makes a profession of faith, using the language of the creeds to define the trinitarian nature of God as three beings in one.

In canto XXV, Saint James administers the examination on hope, asking the Pilgrim to define hope, to explain the degree of his own hope, and to specify its source. The Pilgrim defines hope by following standard Scholastic formulations, in particular that of Peter Lombard.

Hope, he has learned from the Scriptures, especially the Psalms and James's own epistle, is the expectation of future bliss, a life to come in which some will know God and experience the resurrection of body and soul. Beatrice answers the question about Dante's hope, since it would not be appropriate for him to do so.

As Saint John joins the souls of Peter and James in a circular dance and in song, Dante the Pilgrim feels embarrassed at finding himself blind (XXV: 137–139). He is, of course, going through yet another stage in his spiritual transformation—that process of being "transhumanized" (I: 70)—that prepares him for John's questions about love, the virtue identified by Saint Paul as the greatest of the three. Dante's explanation of charity (XXVI: 16–18) refers to the passage in the Bible, 1 John 4: 8, that defines God's existence as *caritas*, or love, which creates the good, "that gives contentment to this Court" (XXVI: 16). Charity is learned through reason and revelation. Since all goodness is in God, the Pilgrim concludes that He must be the primary object of love. He asserts that the natural world, God, the Redemption, his hope, and his faith show this to be true (XXVI: 7–66). Music fills heaven in response to the Pilgrim's successful answers, and his sight becomes even sharper than before (XXVI: 79).

Following Dante's examination by the founders of Christianity, he encounters Adam, the first human being and progenitor of the human race (XXVI: 80–142). The Pilgrim's questions would have been of interest to medieval Christians, and Adam, reading them in God's mind, poses and answers them. They include the length of time he spent in Eden (seven hours), the number of years he lived on earth (930), and his residence in Limbo before Christ harrowed Hell (4,302 years), for a total of 5,232 years elapsing between Adam's creation and the Crucifixion. Adam also discusses the origin of language and the nature of Edenic language in a way that contradicts Dante's earlier theories (*De Vulgari Eloquentia* I: 4–6). He tells the Pilgrim that he himself created his speech, which became extinct long before the Tower of Babel, since it was mutable, like all earthly things. In this way, Adam shows that the use of the vernacular, as in Dante's *Comedy*, is perfectly acceptable, because no divine model of speech has ever existed. Adam also defines sin as placing oneself in opposition to God by disobeying His rules or limits (XXVI: 117). The Pilgrim's examination is complete, and the liturgical hymn of praise to the Trinity—the "Gloria Patri"—resounds throughout the heavens to celebrate his success.

The Visions of God from the Primum Mobile to the Empyrean (Cantos XXVII–XXXIII)

After looking one more time at the earth below, the Pilgrim, his "mind enamored, which is dallying / At all times with my lady" (XXVII: 88–89) sees Beatrice as more gloriously beautiful than ever, marking their ascent to the ninth and swiftest sphere, the Primum Mobile. Beatrice instructs him further on the role of love: Indeed the motions of the heavens and time itself have their roots in the Primum Mobile, where God's love is the motive force. With a tone of righteous indignation, Beatrice deplores the perversity of human beings who pursue worldly rather than divine good, despite the beauty and order of God's universe. Both Saint Peter and Beatrice view avarice, or greed, as the cause of human depravity and the corruption of human institutions. Yet both leave the door open for hope, suggesting that God will send some form of help.

- Cantos XXVII–XXIX: The Primum Mobile. Vision of Angels. Metaphor of the Point.

A crystalline heaven in which the Pilgrim encounters no souls, the Primum Mobile encloses the eight spheres below. It imparts to them the motion that carries them along in their daily revolutions around the earth (XXVII: 109–114). Both the largest and swiftest sphere, it is closest to God and the Empyrean. Beatrice explains the importance of its proximity to God, claiming that all motion originates in the love that burns in the Mind of God. In an effort to explain his experience, the Poet creates a word to describe his condition, calling his mind "imparadise[d]" (XXVIII: 3). In his first vision of the divine, the Pilgrim sees God in the form of another perfect geometrical image, that of a brilliant point of light, around which are spinning the nine circles of the angelic hierarchy (XXVIII: 12–40). The hierarchy among the angelic orders is created by their vision of God or their distance from him and by the measure of their love. In the Primum Mobile, the principles of motion in God's cosmos become clear: The origins of physical motion lie in the spiritual motion of love, the love of God Himself.

The angels' circling is a spiritual movement arising from their love for God; this love actually moves the heavenly spheres through the medium of the Primum Mobile. Each angelic order moves one of the nine heavenly spheres, beginning with the smallest circle of angels, the Seraphim, which governs the largest heavenly sphere, the Primum Mobile (see diagram 1). The system of merit among the angelic orders is another sign of diversity in God's cosmos.

The Pilgrim struggles with an apparent contradiction between the structure of the angelic hierarchy and that of the physical universe. The smallest, swiftest circle of angels and the largest, fastest sphere are closest to God. Beatrice explains this apparent incongruity as an inverse correlation between the spiritual order (the angels) and the physical order (the spheres). She tells the Pilgrim that he must judge not by physical size and speed but by the "virtue" (XXVIII: 73), or power, of the angelic orders, which govern the spheres. Because they are nearest to God physically and spiritually, the outermost sphere (the Primum Mobile, which is physically closest to God) connects with the innermost circle of angels (the Seraphim, which is spiritually nearest to God). Just as the love of God, or the "virtues," of the other angelic ranks decreases the farther they are from God, so, too, the spheres these ranks govern decrease in size the farther they are from God. The two universes, the angelic model and the physical copy, function in a perfectly designed relationship (XXVIII: 41–42), and they both reflect the perfection of their Creator. The principle of diversity applies not simply to sublunary things, but to the most important parts of the cosmos.

Beatrice describes the hierarchy of angels according to the trinitarian principle of *Paradiso* in groups of three, from highest or nearest to God to lowest or farthest from God: Seraphim, Cherubim, Thrones; Dominions, Virtues, Powers; Principalities, Archangels; Angels. In describing the second triad of angels, she introduces the image of the flower in eternal spring (XVIII: 115–117), a pivotal image in the Empyrean, and associates the focal ideas of perfection, circularity, trinity, and eternity (XXVIII: 118–120). Beatrice ends her discourse on angels with a bit of humor about Pope Gregory the Great, who discussed the angelic hierarchy using an order different from the one followed by Saint Thomas Aquinas, which originated in the work of

Pseudo Dionysius on angels. She claims that when Pope Gregory ar-rived in heaven, he saw the truth and laughed at his mistake. Dante de-parts here from the usual tendency of medieval theologians to avoid drawing attention to this disagreement, while adding an unexpected bit of humor to *Paradiso*. He may also be amused by his own early er-ror in *Il Convivio* 2. 5. 6, where he switches the ranking of Thrones and Principalities.

Beatrice reads the Pilgrim's questions in the mind of God concern-ing the purpose of creation, the nature of the good angels, and their number. Emphasizing the theme of divine love, she describes the cre-ation as an expression of God's overflowing and limitless love, His de-sire to create other beings and things to enjoy this love. God created three substances simultaneously in a hierarchical chain of being, which involves different degrees of perfection, defined by the relative propor-tion of spirit and matter in a substance. At the top is pure essence, form, or pure act, the angels; the heavens are in the middle, a combi-nation of pure form and pure matter or of act and potential; at the bottom of this chain of being is pure matter or pure potential.

With respect to the angels, Beatrice then explains that a group led by Lucifer rebelled at the moment of their creation. When they were cast down, they created Hell within the earth. Rewarded with the power to move the heavens, the good angels, who exist in perfect har-mony with their Creator, have faculties quite different from those of human beings. Beatrice's discussion of angelology leads to her tirade against corrupt preachers and priests who lead believers astray with false teachings because they value their own wit and worldly fame rather than the truth. She also argues that it is impossible to calculate the number of angels, a question of interest to medieval people, be-cause they are not only infinite but also separate and distinct in the way in which God's light shines through them. This argument again picks up the theme of diversity among all of creation.

The Empyrean: The Metaphor of the Book and the Vision of the Trinity (Cantos XXX–XXXIII)

Paradiso is particularly full of high poetic art—complex imagery, metaphor, and simile, through which Dante the Poet shares his vision. At the beginning of *Paradiso*, Dante refers to the Empyrean as the heaven that receives most of God's light and as the "quiet" heaven of God's peace (I: 4–5, 122; II: 112). Later he depicts it as the brightest heaven and supreme sphere (XXIII: 102, 108). The Empyrean is immaterial, spiritual, and full of light, love, and joy; it is the abode of God, the angels, and the blessed.

- Cantos *XXX–XXXIII*: The Empyrean. Saint Bernard. Beatrice joins the Blessed in the Celestial Rose.

As the tenth and highest heaven, the Empyrean encompasses all of creation, but lies beyond space and time. Finally Dante has ascended to the heaven that has "no other Where / Than in the Mind Divine, wherein is kindled / The love that turns it, and the power it rains." (XXVII: 109–111). The entire journey down into Hell, up the Mountain of Purgatory, and through the heavenly spheres of Paradise gradually has educated the Pilgrim emotionally, intellectually, and spiritually to enjoy God's grace and to experience the divine vision. After the souls of the blessed have descended to greet and to teach the Pilgrim at every step of his journey, they return to the highest heaven, where they contemplate God. In the last part of *Paradiso*, the theme of ineffability intensifies, as the poem moves away from emphasis on the unhappy history of earthly corruption, with its violence and despair. Although blinded by the light, the Pilgrim feels his senses enhanced, and a new kind of sight lights up his eyes with a new kind of power, enabling him to gaze upon even the most holy sights. The Pilgrim no longer looks at God's light reflected in Beatrice's eyes (*Purgatorio* XXXI, 109–123). Now, his own eyes become mirrors capable of receiving and reflecting divine light.

Making the invisible tangible, Dante uses a series of metaphors to convey the nature of his experience in the Empyrean, which happens in stages. First, he casts the court of heaven in courtly and highly refined garden imagery. The Pilgrim sees a river of flowing light, with two banks, that becomes a sea of light in which move sparks and flowers that Dante compares to rubies set in rings of gold (XXX: 66). Beatrice reveals that this landscape of spring is symbolic of the true nature of the Empyrean Heaven, representing the angels and the elect (XXX: 61–108). As the Pilgrim's eyes are unveiled, they become more capable of seeing, and the river with its sparks and flowers are revealed as the souls of the blessed and the angels who minister to them. The court of heaven looks like a vast amphitheater in the form of a white rose with various gradations of individual souls seated in the light of God's eternal sun (XXX: 109–123). Here God rules directly and the laws of nature no longer apply.

Beatrice reveals that this vast heavenly city is nearly filled, although one place is reserved for Henry VII, the Holy Roman emperor in whom Dante had placed his hopes for world peace (XXX: 109–148). Beatrice's last words in the *Comedy* carry on her harsh condemnation of the leadership of the Church, confirming the prophecy in *Inferno* XIX: 73–75 concerning the fate of Clement and Boniface. Dante the Poet damns both Clement V and Boniface VIII one more time, without naming them (XXX: 148). The Pilgrim now sees the general plan of Paradise in its particulars, despite the size and distance. Angels spread the peace and love of God from soul to soul throughout the white Celestial Rose. The Pilgrim sees that the divine light penetrates a diverse universe in proportion to the merits of each part. Describing himself as an awestruck pilgrim, similar to the barbarian amazed by the first sight of the city of ancient Rome, he appears refreshed, but wonders how he will be able to describe his experience. When he sees the blessed in their "white robes"—in their glorified bodies as they will be at the Last Judgment—he also makes one last biting remark about the corruption of the city of Florence (XXXI: 39), sharply contrasting it with the heavenly city he now sees.

When the Pilgrim turns to Beatrice, she has disappeared. Saint Bernard has taken her place and shows him Beatrice, now returned to her seat in the rose (XXXI: 68–69). Dante's loving farewell and tribute to Beatrice describes the journey he has taken at the behest of the three heavenly ladies as a journey of freedom. Beatrice, depicted as a Christ-like figure at her appearance in Purgatory, has served as Dante's lure, guide, and instructor. Her beauty and goodness generate passion— the love that comes from God—and in her are linked love, knowledge, and revelation. At this point, Beatrice is no longer his guide, but she is, once again, the Poet's beloved, a real person, with whom he now uses the familiar form of address. Her final smile reassures him as he remains alone, without her, to meet his final challenge.

Just as Virgil, representative of human reason or natural philosophy, leads the Pilgrim to the Earthly Paradise and to Beatrice, so too, Beatrice, representative of divine wisdom, leads the Pilgrim to God. She is the real woman whom he loved on earth and who inspired his *Vita Nuova*. She is also his teacher in Paradise. In the Earthly Paradise at the end of *Purgatorio*, she has no pity for the Pilgrim. Her harsh and exacting words force him to feel the kind of true repentance that will allow him to advance on his spiritual journey. She represents the highest human understanding, the wisdom that can lead a human being toward his Creator. Although the Pilgrim learns much from the souls he encounters, it is always Beatrice who mediates every truth. She becomes more and more beautiful as they ascend through the heavens, and the Pilgrim's love increases with every argument she uses to reveal the truth, but in the end, he has learned now to love her in the proper manner. In her final appearance, it is the real woman who takes her seat in the heavenly rose. Her role is complete, for it requires a different kind of insight to experience the final vision.

The beatific vision is beyond rational comprehension and even revelation, and the Poet chooses Saint Bernard to guide the Pilgrim for the last stage of his journey. This choice neatly reflects Bernard's historical and theological reputation as a visionary mystic who had a special devotion to Mary and a penchant for writing about religious ideas in the language of love found in Dante's earlier poetry, rather than the language of scholasticism that pervades *Paradiso*. Dante would have found Bernard's idea that souls achieve perfection when reunited with their bodies at the Last Judgment congenial to his own. Bernard instructs the Pilgrim to examine the Celestial Rose from its highest point, the seat of the Virgin, who, nearest to God, remains the most fitting object of his spiritual devotion (XXXII: 138–142). The Poet, who describes himself again as a pilgrim, this time looking upon the Veronica in Rome (the first reference was in *Paradiso* I: 51), declares that trying to describe the Virgin would be too daring.

At the beginning of canto XXXII, Bernard analyzes the hierarchy of souls beneath Mary, whom he calls Queen of Heaven, along with the different measures of grace allocated to those saved by repentance as adults and to those who owe salvation only to their baptism as infants. The two main divisions of souls in the Celestial Rose include equal populations of souls from the Old Testament and those from the New Testament. A vertical row of Old Testament women on one side of the rose (Mary, Eve, Rachel, Sarah, Rebecca, Judith, Ruth) and of New Testament men on the other (Saint John the Baptist, Saint Francis, Saint Benedict, Saint Augustine) divides it between souls who believed in Christ's coming and those who believed in the Christ who had already come. Among those from Old Testament times are Adam and Moses at Mary's left, and Saint Anne at the Baptist's right; among the New Testament figures are Saint Peter and Saint John the Evangelist at Mary's right, Beatrice on Rachel's right, and Saint Lucy on the Baptist's left. Dante includes all three of the women involved in his salvation (*Inferno* II). The lower half of the rose is filled with children, saved through baptism, circumcision, or their parents' faith. The white rose becomes a symbol of the purity and worth of the blessed.

In canto XXXIII, Saint Bernard intercedes directly with the Virgin Mary to ask that the Pilgrim be granted a personal vision of God. He can find God only through contemplation and grace. Instinctively, Dante looks into the light, which overwhelms his speech, memory, and sight (XXXIII: 49–105), and yet, as his vision seems to gain in power, the Poet claims his words and memory fail. The memory of the legendary ship Argo from 2,500 years before is clearer, he says, than this present moment of his vision. The Virgilian echoes of this last canto emphasize the fleeting, dreamlike nature of the visionary experience, and the Poet prays that God will help him capture "a single sparkle of [His] glory . . . [to] bequeath unto the future people" (XXXIII: 71–72).

The light no longer blinds the Pilgrim, for he sees anew with the eyes of mystical contemplation. His vision of God comes in the form of a book, a symbol of the unity of a creation that has a single source and of the most profound knowledge. In a contrapuntal movement, Dante uses all his poetic powers to convey the idea of the infinite diversity of the universe, but his vision of God as a book represents the extraordinary unity of a cosmos in which the multitude of diverse parts are gathered together. Dante's image of the book partakes of the language of poetry and the language of Scholastic philosophy. God is a book in which all of the separate pages represent everything that exists in the universe—the universe in its infinite diversity and complexity. The divine good that shines down and penetrates all parts of the universe is gathered back together in the "book," where "the good, which object is of will, / Is gathered all in this" (XXXIII: 103–104). The Pilgrim's feeling of joy assures him that he has seen the universal form in which there is a fusion of all things (XXXIII: 91–93). The image of a book that contains everything also represents his "sacred poem," with its extraordinary synthesis of classical and medieval poetry, belief, and learning.

Finally, Dante attempts to adapt the mystery of the Trinity into the visual, geometric pattern dominant throughout the *Comedy*—the circle. In the light the Pilgrim sees three rainbowlike colored rings, the second adorned with the human form and color, a reference to the Incarnation (XXX: 109–132). In a union of three in one, the three circles are equal, with the second reflecting the first (the Son reflecting the Father) and the third (the Spirit) representing the fire of love breathed forth from both Father and Son. In a final flash of enlightenment, the poem ends (XXXIII: 133–145). Although the poetic imagination fails, the Pilgrim feels like "a wheel that equally is moved," motivated by "The Love which moves the sun and the other stars" (XXXIII: 145).

In these last lines, Dante recaptures the central concepts, themes, and images of the *Comedy*: the poetic imagination that gives substance to the perfection, order, and interconnectedness of God's cosmos as well as God's power and the love that moves all things in harmony. His love for Beatrice has been transformed—through her eyes. In Dante's time, the eyes were thought to be the pathway to the heart and soul, and it was through the eyes that Cupid's arrow flew. Now Beatrice's eyes, in Platonic fashion, have led him beyond the beauty of her earthly and heavenly forms to God and to that "Love which moves the sun and the other stars."

Although heaven typically has no well-defined features in the Bible, except for the description in the Book of Revelation, Dante's poetic imagination has given it form and substance. At the Fourth Council of the Lateran in 1215, incomprehensibility was listed among God's characteristics. Hence, Dante attempts to sustain doctrine while providing a poetic picture of the Trinity. Central to the poetry and theology of *Paradiso* are the mysteries of the Christian faith that transcend human understanding. Dante finds a way to make these mysteries accessible to human powers of perception with his narrative fiction of the journey of spiritual growth. Rhetorically, this canticle is full of paradoxes of different types that prepare the reader for the mystery of the Poet's final vision of God.

Dante's journey through the light of God's glory is a journey of enlightenment in every sense of the word. Throughout *Purgatorio*, he is again exposed to the natural light of day, but in *Paradiso*, the souls appear to him in the brightness of eternity. In this light, he learns through his discussions with Beatrice and the various souls who come to him in celebration of his increasing wisdom; he also learns through more poetic means, with motions, especially dancing, music, and great, shining geometric configurations. Each sphere figures forth its meaning in new images, metaphors, similes, and even words. In the end, of course, the poetic variety itself represents the diversity of God's universe as well as its unity in God's love, which "moves the sun and the other stars." These words, the last of which ends all three canticles, bring a sense of closure to this poetic masterpiece.

Paradiso, the last of the three canticles of *The Divine Comedy*, represents the climax of the poetic narrative and of the Pilgrim's journey through the afterlife. By the end of *Paradiso*, Dante the Poet, looking back on his journey, describes it as a movement from time to eternity (XXXI: 38), from the everyday world of transient pleasures to the eternal realm of God that endures. The glory of God (I: 1) that he has seen throughout God's creation he now sees in its full splendor as the light of eternity, and he realizes that what he has seen before is but a dim reflection of that light. Eternity is experienced in the Empyrean by the heavenly company—God, the angels, the saved souls. It is not only Dante the Pilgrim, however, who has been transformed. So has Dante the Poet, who has overcome formidable challenges to his poetic powers and the ineffability of the divine. In creating a cosmic landscape for the afterlife, Dante draws on the knowledge and beliefs of his age, but he moves beyond the typical medieval allegories with his specific references to various branches of knowledge—physics, astronomy, biology, philosophy, and theology—and to literature. His historical references, especially to worldly violence and corruption, give the poem a realism that anchors it firmly in the world and in his own times. The paradoxical effects of juxtaposing the story of human corruption with a story of human salvation give the narrative great energy and pathos. Yet it is all placed within the context of a cosmic order governed by a love that offers perpetual hope to humanity.

Paradiso *and Allegory*

Dante constantly insists that what he saw in a journey through the afterlife was true. As Charles S. Singleton, one of Dante's greatest American interpreters, never tired of emphasizing, the key fiction of *The Divine Comedy* is that the poem is true. Dante wants his readers to believe that what they see, feel, and hear in his poem did actually occur. The work is not just an intellectual pastime for an exiled intellectual. Medieval literature is often described as a literature of allegory. In an allegorical reading of *Paradiso*, the reader would constantly be forced to identify characters with abstract ideas: Dante becomes Everyman, Beatrice becomes Revelation, and so forth. Everything in the poem would thus become a vast and impersonal puzzle. The reader's function would involve identifying what each of the characters stood for and observing the relationships and interplay among them. The result would be a lifting of the veil of allegory and a revealing or uncovering of the secret meaning underneath. That concealed meaning would of necessity involve an even more abstract kind of idea: love, death, evil, sin, heresy, treachery, and so forth.

However, such allegorical abstractions are simply not what Dante's great poem is all about. To understand Dante's position on allegory and historical truth, it is first necessary to understand that serious medieval thinkers (theologians, philosophers—not poets) considered poetry to be a fiction that did not tell the truth. Quite rightly, allegorical poems that used characters to represent abstract qualities could not be literally true and were considered "fables" in the pejorative sense. Dante wanted his reader—including serious thinkers—to consider his poem to be a true account of an actual journey. Even if the reader willfully suspends his or her disbelief in the reality of the poem's action and believes that this fantastical journey actually took place, a traditional allegorical poem would simply not serve his purposes. For such a poem would place more emphasis on abstract ideas than on the characters themselves.

The method that Dante employed in his work, and one that he suggests in a late letter to Cangrande della Scala, is quite different from the traditional allegory typical of works such as *The Romance of the Rose* or *The Pilgrim's Progress*. Contrary to the allegory of the poets, Dante accepted at least in part what was known as the allegory of the theologians. This involved bearing in mind four possible senses of a text: the historical or literal; the allegorical; the moral or tropological; and the anagogical. Such a method derived from reading Holy Scriptures, particularly the relationship between the historical and the allegorical senses. For example, in most Christian services regardless of the denomination, the ritual requires a reading of a passage from the Old Testament followed by, or juxtaposed to, a reading of a passage from the New Testament. In most cases, the Old Testament text prefigures or anticipates that of the New Testament, which fulfills or explains elements of the Old Testament.

The classic example of how these four senses operate may be taken from the event that Dante himself refers to in *Purgatorio* II: 46–47. There, an angelic boatman (the counterpart to the infernal Charon) delivers souls to the shore of Purgatory. As the souls arrive, they sing in Latin the words from the Vulgate *in exitu Israel de Aegypto* ("when Israel went out of Egypt," a biblical citation from Psalm 114). What are we to make of this moment in the poem? According to the four senses of the allegory of the theologians, we can read the passage in various ways. The event celebrated by the souls about to undergo purgation points us to the exodus of the Hebrews led by Moses. This event was and is historically and literally true. Leading the Hebrews out of captivity may, however, be explained allegorically as a prefiguration of Christ's redemption of lost souls, bringing mankind out of bondage to sin. In a real sense, then, Christ fulfills Moses and Moses prefigures or foreshadows Christ. This kind of figural interpretation is common to Christian thought. It explains why Job's suffering might be compared to Christ's passion, why Jonah's three days in the whale's belly was frequently compared to Christ's resurrection three days after the Crucifixion, and why Abraham's sacrifice of Isaac could be viewed as a prefiguration of God's sacrifice of His son, Jesus. In the case of Jonah, Christ even refers to the story in the Bible, Matthew 12: 40, as a prefiguration of what will happen to him, and in the Gospels Christ consciously seeks to fulfill the prophecies of the Old Testament.

Such a "figural" realism, as the literary historian Erich Auerbach has labeled it, makes sense from a Christian point of view, and it is one kind of meaning that Dante certainly understood and employed on occasion in his poem, when another medieval poet might have employed traditional allegory. Another interesting example of this kind of figural realism may be demonstrated by an analysis of why Dante places Cato of Utica, a suicide and a pagan who died before the birth of Christ, in canto I of *Purgatorio* rather than either in canto XIII of *Inferno*, the spot reserved for suicides, or in the Limbo of the Virtuous Pagans. Applying the principles of figural realism, Auerbach has argued persuasively that Cato fulfills in the afterlife his historical identity on earth: Once the embodiment of love for political freedom, he now constitutes a figural symbol for the freedom of the immortal soul. Dante's counterintuitive treatments of such pagans as Virgil or Cato point us to the final "house rule" of his poem. Our poet does not concern himself overly much with consistency. He makes the rules to fit his poetic design, not to satisfy logicians, philosophers, theologians, historians, or politicians. In Hell, he condemns popes to eternal damnation just as easily as he rewards Statius, a pagan poet we now consider far less a writer than Virgil, with eternal salvation.

Returning to the four senses of a text, the third and fourth senses—the moral, or tropological, and the anagogical sense—always seem more ambiguous. If we take our example from Exodus, the moral sense would refer to the soul of the individual Christian seeking an "exodus" from a life of sin in the present. The anagogical sense would refer to the end of time after the Last Judgment when the saved believe they will arrive in the Promised Land—for Christians, this is heaven and not the land of Israel. Frankly, Dante infrequently concerns himself with the third and fourth sense of a text, for he is most fascinated by suggesting ways in which historical events, ideas, or characters may suggest (foreshadow, prefigure) other interesting events, ideas, or characters. The best advice to the reader of *The Divine Comedy* in general and to *Paradiso* in particular is to pay attention to the literal sense of the poem. The greatest poetry in Dante resides in the literal sense of the work, its graphic descriptions of the sinners, their characters, and their punishments. In like manner, the greatest and most satisfying intellectual achievement of the poem comes from the reader's understanding (and not necessarily agreement with) Dante's complex view of morality, or the sinful world that God's punishment is designed to correct. In most cases, a concrete appreciation of the small details of his poem will almost always lead to surprising but satisfying discoveries about the universe Dante's poetry has created.

We read the classics because they offer us different perspectives on timeless questions. Very few people today who encounter *The Divine Comedy*, even Catholics, accept most of Dante's assumptions about the universe. We have gone from the Ptolemaic universe Dante understood through the Newtonian universe that overturned the classical and medieval world views and into the Einsteinian universe of black holes and relativity. In religion, we have experienced the complete schism of a single Christian church after the Reformation into many different Christian churches, and while Western society is clearly more secular in spirit than was the Florence of Dante's day, other non-Christian cultures seem to be returning to a religious fundamentalism not seen in the West for centuries. The confusing politics involving the petty squabbles of Guelph and Ghibelline have long since vanished and have been submerged since Dante's day by various kinds of political systems, most of which are far worse than those he experienced.

Perhaps Dante might recognize a similarity between the nascent capitalism of medieval Florence and our own contemporary multinational economic system. Both produced inordinate and unexpected quantities of wealth, although neither ever arrived at a fully equitable means of distributing it, and both economic systems have suffered periodic and frequent cyclical waves of boom and bust that sometimes threaten the lives and fortunes of those who depend on them. Dante would not have been surprised by the many religious, social, political, scientific, intellectual, or economic changes that have taken place since his times. He would only have been surprised if the characters that inhabit his *Comedy* seem dated, almost denizens of another planet. But, of course, Dante's characters are all too contemporary. It would not be difficult to compile a list of our acquaintances or colleagues and to place them in the appropriate places in Hell. More difficult, perhaps, would be a similar assignment of those we know to appropriate places in Purgatory or Paradise.

What explains our contemporary fascination with Dante is his attitude toward his characters. As members of a liberal, diverse, and tolerant culture typical of twenty-first-century democracies, at least in our ideals we tend to see everything and everyone from a variety of positive perspectives. We are asked to respect those with whom we disagree. The French maxim says it all—*tout comprendre, c'est tout pardoner* ("to understand all is to forgive all"). Dante stands entirely outside such a "civilized," politically correct perspective. For him, understanding does not imply justification, and Dante is the most judgmental of all poets. He believes that civilization involves understanding, an act of the intellect, but for Dante understanding leads inevitably to evaluation, judgment, and the assumption of a moral position based on very simple but immutable ethical and religious precepts. No situational ethics, no "I'm OK, you're OK," no automatic and naive acceptances of every point of view, no matter how ill-founded. His energy derives from moral indignation—indignation about the corruption of the Church, about the corruption of Florence and most Italian or European cities, about the weakness of the Holy Roman Empire, and about the general wretched state of humanity. But his genius is based on something even more precious and more unusual—his love for truth and his ability to express it in timeless poetic form.

JULIA CONAWAY BONDANELLA is Professor of Italian at Indiana University. In the past, she has served as President of the National Collegiate Honors Council and as Assistant Chairman of the National Endowment for the Humanities. Her publications include a book on Petrarch, *The Cassell Dictionary of Italian Literature*, and translations of Italian classics by Benvenuto Cellini, Niccolò Machiavelli, and Giorgio Vasari.

PETER BONDANELLA is Distinguished Professor of Comparative Literature and Italian at Indiana University and a past President of the American Association for Italian Studies. His publications include a number of translations of Italian classics, books on Italian literature, and studies of Italian cinema. His latest publication is *Hollywood Italians*, a history of images of Italian Americans in Hollywood films.

EMPYREAN   GOD   EMPYREAN

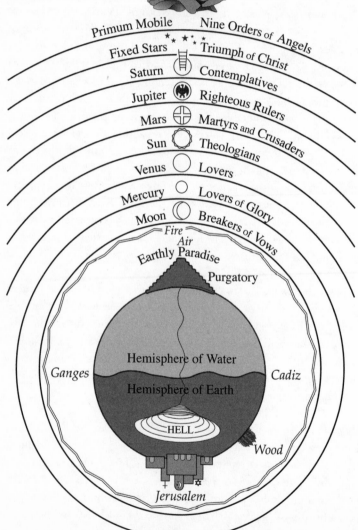

Primum Mobile   Nine Orders of Angels

Fixed Stars   Triumph of Christ

Saturn   Contemplatives

Jupiter   Righteous Rulers

Mars   Martyrs and Crusaders

Sun   Theologians

Venus   Lovers

Mercury   Lovers of Glory

Moon   Breakers of Vows

Fire

Air

Earthly Paradise   Purgatory

Ganges   Hemisphere of Water   *Cadiz*

Hemisphere of Earth

HELL

Wood

Jerusalem

THE PARADISO

CANTO I

THE glory of Him who moveth everything[1]
    Doth penetrate the universe, and shine
    In one part more and in another less.[2]
Within that heaven which most his light receives
    Was I,[3] and things beheld which to repeat   5
    Nor knows, nor can, who from above descends;[4]
Because in drawing near to its desire[5]
    Our intellect ingulphs itself so far,
    That after it the memory cannot go.
Truly whatever of the holy realm   10
    I had the power to treasure in my mind
    Shall now become the subject of my song.
O good Apollo,[6] for this last emprise*
    Make of me such a vessel of thy power
    As giving the beloved laurel asks![7]   15
One summit of Parnassus hitherto
    Has been enough for me, but now with both[8]
    I needs must enter the arena left.
Enter into my bosom, thou, and breathe
    As at the time when Marsyas[9] thou didst draw   20
    Out of the scabbard of those limbs of his.
O power divine, lend'st thou thyself to me
    So that the shadow of the blessed realm
    Stamped in my brain I can make manifest,
Thou'lt see me come unto thy darling tree,[10]   25
    And crown myself[11] thereafter with those leaves

---

*Enterprise; undertaking.

Of which the theme and thou shall make me worthy.
So seldom, Father, do we gather them
    For triumph or of Cæsar or of Poet,
    (The fault and shame of human inclinations,)   30
That the Peneian foliage should bring forth
    Joy to the joyous Delphic deity,[12]
    When any one it makes to thirst for it.
A little spark is followed by great flame;
    Perchance with better voices after me   35
    Shall prayer be made that Cyrrha may respond![13]
To mortal men by passages diverse
    Uprises the world's lamp; but by that one
    Which circles four uniteth with three crosses,
With better course and with a better star   40
    Conjoined it issues, and the mundane wax
    Tempers and stamps more after its own fashion.[14]
Almost that passage had made morning there
    And evening here,[15] and there was wholly white
    That hemisphere, and black the other part,   45
When Beatrice towards the left-hand side[16]
    I saw turned round, and gazing at the sun;
    Never did eagle[17] fasten so upon it!
And even as a second ray[18] is wont
    To issue from the first and reascend,   50
    Like to a pilgrim who would fain return,
Thus of her action, through the eyes infused
    In my imagination, mine I made,
    And sunward fixed mine eyes beyond our wont.[19]
There much is lawful which is here unlawful   55
    Unto our powers, by virtue of the place
    Made for the human species as its own.[20]
Not long I bore it, nor so little while
    But I beheld it sparkle round about
    Like iron that comes molten from the fire;[21]   60
And suddenly it seemed that day to day
    Was added, as if He who has the power
    Had with another sun the heaven adorned.

With eyes upon the everlasting wheels[22]
    Stood Beatrice all intent, and I, on her   65
    Fixing my vision from above removed,
Such at her aspect inwardly became
    As Glaucus, tasting of the herb that made him
    Peer of the other gods beneath the sea.[23]
To represent transhumanize in words   70
    Impossible were;[24] the example, then, suffice
    Him from whom Grace the experience reserves.[25]
If I was merely what of me thou newly
    Createdst, Love who governest the heaven,
    Thou knowest, who didst lift me with thy light![26]   75
When now the wheel,[27] which thou dost make eternal
    Desiring thee, made me attentive to it
    By harmony[28] thou dost modulate and measure,
Then seemed to me so much of heaven enkindled
    By the sun's flame,[29] that neither rain nor river   80
    E'er made a lake so widely spread abroad.
The newness of the sound and the great light
    Kindled in me a longing for their cause,
    Never before with such acuteness felt;
Whence she, who saw me as I saw myself,   85
    To quiet in me my perturbed mind,
    Opened her mouth, ere I did mine to ask,[30]
And she began: "Thou makest thyself so dull
    With false imagining, that thou seest not
    What thou wouldst see if thou hadst shaken it off.   90
Thou art not upon earth, as thou believest;
    But lightning, fleeing its appropriate site,
    Ne'er ran as thou, who thitherward returnest."[31]
If of my former doubt I was divested
    By these brief little words more smiled than spoken,   95
    I in a new one was the more ensnared;
And said: "Already did I rest content
    From great amazement; but am now amazed
    In what way I transcend these bodies light."[32]
Whereupon she, after a pitying sigh,   100

Her eyes directed tow'rds me with that look
　　A mother casts on a delirious child;
And she began: "All things[33] whate'er they be
　　Have order among themselves, and this is form,
　　That makes the universe resemble God.[34]　　　　105
Here do the higher creatures see the footprints
　　Of the Eternal Power, which is the end
　　Whereto is made the law already mentioned.[35]
In the order that I speak of are inclined
　　All natures, by their destinies diverse,　　　　110
　　More or less near unto their origin;[36]
Hence they move onward unto ports diverse
　　O'er the great sea of being; and each one
　　With instinct[37] given it which bears it on.
This bears away the fire towards the moon;　　　　115
　　This is in mortal hearts the motive power;
　　This binds together and unites the earth.
Nor only the created things that are
　　Without intelligence this bow[38] shoots forth,
　　But those that have both intellect and love.　　120
The Providence that regulates all this
　　Makes with its light the heaven forever quiet,
　　Wherein that turns which has the greatest haste.[39]
And thither now, as to a site decreed,
　　Bears us away the virtue of that cord　　　　125
　　Which aims its arrows at a joyous mark.[40]
True is it,[41] that as oftentimes the form
　　Accords not with the intention of the art,
　　Because in answering is matter deaf,
So likewise from this course doth deviate　　　　130
　　Sometimes the creature, who the power posesses,
　　Though thus impelled, to swerve some other way,
(In the same wise as one may see the fire
　　Fall from a cloud,[42]) if the first impetus
　　Earthward is wrested by some false delight.　　135
Thou shouldst not wonder more, if well I judge,
　　At thine ascent, than at a rivulet

6

From some high mount descending to the plain.[43]
Marvel it would be in thee, if deprived
　　Of hindrance, thou wert seated down below, 140
　　As if on earth the living fire were quiet."
Thereat she heavenward[44] turned again her face.

CANTO II

O YE, who in some pretty little boat,[1]
    Eager to listen, have been following
    Behind my ship, that singing sails along,
Turn back to look again upon your shores;
    Do not put out to sea, lest peradventure,   5
    In losing me, you might yourselves be lost.
The sea I sail has never yet been passed;[2]
    Minerva breathes, and pilots me Apollo,[3]
    And Muses nine point out to me the Bears.[4]
Ye other few who have the neck uplifted   10
    Betimes to th' bread of Angels upon which
    One liveth here and grows not sated by it,[5]
Well may you launch upon the deep salt-sea
    Your vessel, keeping still my wake before you
    Upon the water that grows smooth again.   15
Those glorious ones who unto Colchos passed
    Were not so wonder-struck as you shall be,
    When Jason they beheld a ploughman made![6]
The con-created* and perpetual thirst
    For the realm deiform† did bear us on,   20
    As swift almost as ye the heavens behold.
Upward gazed Beatrice, and I at her;
    And in such space perchance as strikes a bolt
    And flies, and from the notch unlocks itself,[7]
Arrived I saw me where a wondrous thing   25

*Innate; inborn.
†God's own realm (that is, the Empyrean).

Drew to itself my sight; and therefore she
From whom no care of mine could be concealed,
Towards me turning, blithe as beautiful,
Said unto me: "Fix gratefully thy mind
On God, who unto the first star[8] has brought us."   30
It seemed to me a cloud encompassed us,
Luminous, dense, consolidate and bright
As adamant on which the sun is striking.
Into itself did the eternal pearl[9]
Receive us, even as water doth receive   35
A ray of light,[10] remaining still unbroken.
If I was body, (and we here conceive not
How one dimension tolerates another,
Which needs must be if body enter body,)
More the desire should be enkindled in us   40
That essence to behold, wherein is seen
How God and our own nature were united.
There will be seen what we receive by faith,
Not demonstrated, but self-evident
In guise of the first truth that man believes.[11]   45
I made reply: "Madonna, as devoutly
As most I can do I give thanks to Him
Who has removed me from the mortal world.
But tell me what the dusky spots may be
Upon this body, which below on earth   50
Make people tell that fabulous tale of Cain?"[12]
Somewhat she smiled; and then, "If the opinion
Of mortals be erroneous," she said,
"Where'er the key of sense doth not unlock,
Certes, the shafts of wonder should not pierce thee   55
Now, forasmuch as, following the senses,
Thou seest that the reason has short wings.[13]
But tell me what thou think'st of it thyself."
And I: "What seems to us up here diverse,
Is caused, I think, by bodies rare and dense."[14]   60
And she: "Right truly shalt thou see immersed
In error thy belief, if well thou hearest

9

The argument that I shall make against it.
Lights[15] many the eighth sphere[16] displays to you
   Which in their quality and quantity[17]
   May noted be of aspects different.
If this were caused by rare and dense alone,
   One only virtue would there be in all
   Or more or less diffused, or equally.[18]
Virtues diverse must be perforce the fruits
   Of formal principles; and these, save one,
   Of course would by thy reasoning be destroyed.
Besides, if rarity were of this dimness
   The cause thou askest, either through and through
   This planet thus attenuate were of matter,
Or else, as in a body is apportioned
   The fat and lean, so in like manner this
   Would in its volume interchange the leaves.
Were it the former, in the sun's eclipse
   It would be manifest by the shining through
   Of light, as through aught tenuous interfused.
This is not so;[19] hence we must scan the other,
   And if it chance the other I demolish,
   Then falsified will thy opinion be.
But if this rarity go not through and through,
   There needs must be a limit, beyond which
   Its contrary prevents the further passing,
And thence the foreign radiance is reflected,
   Even as a color cometh back from glass,
   The which behind itself concealeth lead.
Now thou wilt say the sunbeam shows itself
   More dimly there than in the other parts,
   By being there reflected farther back.
From this reply experiment will free thee
   If e'er thou try it, which is wont to be
   The fountain to the rivers of your arts.
Three mirrors shalt thou take, and two remove
   Alike from thee, the other more remote
   Between the former two shall meet thine eyes.

65

70

75

80

85

90

95

Turned towards these, cause that behind thy back   100
    Be placed a light, illuming the three mirrors
    And coming back to thee by all reflected.
Though in its quantity be not so ample
    The image most remote, there shalt thou see
    How it perforce is equally resplendent.[20]   105
Now, as beneath the touches of warm rays
    Naked the subject of the snow remains
    Both of its former color and its cold,
Thee, thus remaining in thy intellect,
    Will I inform with such a living light,[21]   110
    That it shall tremble in its aspect to thee.
Within the heaven of the divine repose[22]
    Revolves a body, in whose virtue lies[23]
    The being of whatever it contains.
The following heaven,[24] that has so many eyes,   115
    Divides this being by essences diverse,
    Distinguished from it, and by it contained.
The other spheres,[25] by various differences,
    All the distinctions which they have within them
    Dispose unto their ends and their effects.   120
Thus do these organs of the world proceed,
    As thou perceivest now, from grade to grade;
    Since from above they take, and act beneath.[26]
Observe me well, how through this place I come
    Unto the truth thou wishest, that hereafter   125
    Thou mayst alone know how to keep the ford.[27]
The power and motion of the holy spheres,
    As from the artisan the hammer's craft,[28]
    Forth from the blessed motors must proceed.
The heaven,[29] which lights so manifold make fair,   130
    From the Intelligence profound, which turns it,
    The image takes, and makes of it a seal.[30]
And even as the soul within your dust
    Through members different and accommodated
    To faculties diverse expands itself,   135
So likewise this Intelligence diffuses

Its virtue multiplied among the stars,
    Itself revolving on its unity.
Virtue diverse doth a diverse alloyage
    Make with the precious body that it quickens,   140
    In which, as life in you, it is combined.
From the glad nature whence it is derived,
    The mingled virtue through the body shines,[31]
    Even as gladness through the living pupil.
From this proceeds whate'er from light to light   145
    Appeareth different, not from dense and rare:
    This is the formal principle that produces,
According to its goodness, dark and bright."[32]

CANTO III

$\mathcal{T}$HAT Sun,[1] which erst* with love my bosom warmed,[2]
    Of beauteous truth had unto me discovered,
    By proving and reproving,[3] the sweet aspect.[4]
And, that I might confess myself convinced
    And confident, so far as was befitting,   5
    I lifted more erect my head to speak.
But there appeared a vision, which withdrew me
    So close to it, in order to be seen,
    That my confession I remembered not.
Such as through polished and transparent glass,   10
    Or waters crystalline and undisturbed,
    But not so deep as that their bed be lost,
Come back again the outlines of our faces
    So feeble, that a pearl on forehead white
    Comes not less speedily unto our eyes;   15
Such saw I many faces prompt to speak,[5]
    So that I ran in error opposite[6]
    To that which kindled love 'twixt man and fountain.
As soon as I became aware of them,
    Esteeming them as mirrored semblances,   20
    To see of whom they were, mine eyes I turned,
And nothing saw,[7] and once more turned them forward
    Direct into the light of my sweet Guide,
    Who smiling kindled in her holy eyes.
"Marvel thou not," she said to me, "because   25
    I smile at this thy puerile conceit,

*Once; long ago.

Since on the truth it trusts not yet its foot,[8]
But turns thee, as 'tis wont, on emptiness.
    True substances are these which thou beholdest,
    Here relegate for breaking of some vow.[9]   30
Therefore speak with them, listen and believe;
    For the true light,[10] which giveth peace to them,
    Permits them not to turn from it their feet."
And I unto the shade that seemed most wishful
    To speak directed me, and I began,   35
    As one whom too great eagerness bewilders:
"O well-created spirit, who in the rays
    Of life eternal dost the sweetness taste
    Which being untasted ne'er is comprehended,
Grateful 'twill be to me, if thou content me   40
    Both with thy name and with your destiny."[11]
    Whereat she promptly and with laughing eyes:
"Our charity[12] doth never shut the doors
    Against a just desire, except as she
    Who wills that all her court be like herself.   45
I was a virgin sister[13] in the world;
    And if thy mind doth contemplate me well,
    The being more fair will not conceal me from thee,
But thou shalt recognize I am Piccarda,[14]
    Who, stationed here among these other blessed,   50
    Myself am blessed in the slowest sphere.[15]
All our affections, that alone inflamed
    Are in the pleasure of the Holy Ghost,
    Rejoice at being of his order formed;
And this allotment, which appears so low,   55
    Therefore is given us, because our vows
    Have been neglected and in some part void."
Whence I to her: "In your miraculous aspects
    There shines I know not what of the divine,
    Which doth transform you from our first conceptions.   60
Therefore I was not swift in my remembrance;
    But what thou tellest me now aids me so,
    That the refiguring is easier to me.

Canto III: Piccarda Donati, and Souls whose Vows had been broken

But tell me, ye who in this place are happy,
> Are you desirous of a higher place,[16]   65
> To see more or to make yourselves more friends?"

First with those other shades she smiled a little;
> Thereafter answered me so full of gladness,
> She seemed to burn in the first fire of love:

"Brother, our will is quieted by virtue   70
> Of charity, that makes us wish alone
> For what we have, nor gives us thirst for more.

If to be more exalted we aspired,
> Discordant would our aspirations be
> Unto the will of Him who here secludes us;[17]   75

Which thou shalt see finds no place in these circles,
> If being in charity is needful here,
> And if thou lookest well into its nature;

Nay, 'tis essential to this blest existence
> To keep itself within the will divine,   80
> Whereby our very wishes are made one;

So that, as we are station above station
> Throughout this realm, to all the realm 'tis pleasing,
> As to the King, who makes his will our will.

And his will is our peace;[18] this is the sea   85
> To which is moving onward whatsoever
> It doth create, and all that nature makes."

Then it was clear to me how everywhere
> In heaven is Paradise,[19] although the grace
> Of good supreme there rain not in one measure.   90

But as it comes to pass, if one food sates,
> And for another still remains the longing,
> We ask for this, and that decline with thanks,

E'en thus did I, with gesture and with word,
> To learn from her what was the web wherein   95
> She did not ply the shuttle to the end.[20]

"A perfect life and merit high in-heaven
> A lady o'er us,"[21] said she, "by whose rule
> Down in your world they vest and veil themselves,

That until death they may both watch and sleep   100

Beside that Spouse[22] who every vow accepts
    Which charity conformeth to his pleasure.
To follow her, in girlhood from the world
    I fled, and in her habit shut myself,
    And pledged me to the pathway of her sect.   105
Then men accustomed unto evil more
    Than unto good, from the sweet cloister tore me;
    God knows what afterward my life became.
This other splendor,[23] which to thee reveals
    Itself on my right side, and is enkindled   110
    With all the illumination of our sphere,
What of myself I say applies to her;
    A nun was she, and likewise from her head
    Was ta'en the shadow of the sacred wimple.
But when she too was to the world returned   115
    Against her wishes and against good usage,
    Of the heart's veil she never was divested.[24]
Of great Costanza this is the effulgence,
    Who from the second wind of Suabia[25]
    Brought forth the third and latest puissance."   120
Thus unto me she spake, and then began
    "Ave Maria" singing, and in singing
    Vanished, as through deep water something heavy.
My sight, that followed her as long a time
    As it was possible, when it had lost her   125
    Turned round unto the mark of more desire,[26]
And wholly unto Beatrice reverted;
    But she such lightnings flashed into mine eyes,
    That at the first my sight endured it not;
And this in questioning more backward made me.   130

CANTO IV

BETWEEN two viands, equally removed
 And tempting, a free man would die of hunger
 Ere either he could bring unto his teeth.
So would a lamb between the ravenings
 Of two fierce wolves stand fearing both alike;   5
 And so would stand a dog between two does.[1]
Hence, if I held my peace, myself I blame not,
 Impelled in equal measure by my doubts,
 Since it must be so, nor do I commend.
I held my peace; but my desire was painted   10
 Upon my face, and questioning with that
 More fervent far than by articulate speech.
Beatrice did as Daniel had done[2]
 Relieving Nebuchadnezzar from the wrath
 Which rendered him unjustly merciless,   15
And said: "Well see I how attracteth thee
 One and the other wish, so that thy care
 Binds itself so that forth it does not breathe.
Thou arguest, if good will be permanent,
 The violence of others, for what reason   20
 Doth it decrease the measure of my merit?[3]
Again for doubting furnish thee occasion
 Souls seeming to return unto the stars,
 According to the sentiment of Plato.[4]
These are the questions which upon thy wish   25
 Are thrusting equally; and therefore first
 Will I treat that which hath the most of gall.[5]

He of the Seraphim⁶ most absorbed in God,
    Moses, and Samuel, and whichever John
    Thou mayst select,⁷ I say, and even Mary,   30
Have not in any other heaven their seats,
    Than have those spirits that just appeared to thee,
    Nor of existence more or fewer years;
But all make beautiful the primal circle,
    And have sweet life in different degrees,⁸   35
    By feeling more or less the eternal breath.⁹
They showed themselves here, not because allotted
    This sphere has been to them, but to give sign
    Of the celestial which is least exalted.¹⁰
To speak thus is adapted to your mind,   40
    Since only through the sense it apprehendeth
    What then it worthy makes of intellect.
On this account the Scripture condescends
    Unto your faculties, and feet and hands
    To God attributes, and means something else;   45
And Holy Church under an aspect human
    Gabriel and Michael represents to you,
    And the other who made Tobit whole again.¹¹
That which Timæus argues of the soul
    Doth not resemble that which here is seen,   50
    Because it seems that as he speaks he thinks.¹²
He says the soul unto its star returns,
    Believing it to have been severed thence
    Whenever nature gave it as a form.
Perhaps his doctrine is of other guise   55
    Than the words sound, and possibly may be
    With meaning that is not to be derided.
If he doth mean that to these wheels return
    The honor of their influence and the blame,¹³
    Perhaps his bow doth hit upon some truth.   60
This principle ill understood once warped
    The whole world nearly,¹⁴ till it went astray
    Invoking Jove and Mercury and Mars.

The other doubt which doth disquiet thee
    Less venom has, for its malevolence   65
    Could never lead thee otherwhere from me.
That as unjust our justice should appear
    In eyes of mortals, is an argument
    Of faith, and not of sin heretical.[15]
But still, that your perception may be able   70
    To thoroughly penetrate this verity,
    As thou desirest, I will satisfy thee.
If it be violence when he who suffers
    Co-operates not with him who uses force,
    These souls were not on that account excused;   75
For will is never quenched unless it will,
    But operates as nature doth in fire,
    If violence a thousand times distort it.
Hence, if it yieldeth more or less, it seconds
    The force; and these have done so, having power   80
    Of turning back unto the holy place.[16]
If their will had been perfect, like to that
    Which Lawrence fast upon his gridiron held,[17]
    And Mutius made severe to his own hand,[18]
It would have urged them back along the road   85
    Whence they were dragged, as soon as they were free;
    But such a solid will is all too rare.
And by these words, if thou hast gathered them
    As thou shouldst do, the argument is refuted[19]
    That would have still annoyed thee many times.   90
But now another passage runs across
    Before thine eyes, and such that by thyself
    Thou couldst not thread it ere thou wouldst be weary.
I have for certain put into thy mind
    That soul beatified could never lie,[20]   95
    For it is ever near the primal Truth,
And then thou from Piccarda might'st have heard
    Costanza kept affection for the veil,
    So that she seemeth here to contradict me.
Many times, brother, has it come to pass,   100

That, to escape from peril, with reluctance
    That has been done it was not right to do,
E'en as Alcmæon[21] (who, being by his father
    Thereto entreated, his own mother slew)
    Not to lose pity pitiless became.   105
At this point I desire thee to remember
    That force with will commingles, and they cause
    That the offences cannot be excused.
Will absolute consenteth not to evil;
    But in so far consenteth as it fears,   110
    If it refrain, to fall into more harm.[22]
Hence when Piccarda uses this expression,
    She meaneth the will absolute, and I
    The other, so that both of us speak truth."[23]
Such was the flowing of the holy river   115
    That issued from the fount whence springs all truth;
    This put to rest my wishes one and all.
"O love of the first lover,[24] O divine,"
    Said I forthwith, "whose speech inundates me
    And warms me so, it more and more revives me,   120
My own affection is not so profound
    As to suffice in rendering grace for grace;
    Let Him, who sees and can, thereto respond.
Well I perceive that never sated is
    Our intellect unless the Truth illume it,   125
    Beyond which nothing true expands itself.
It rests therein, as wild beast in his lair,
    When it attains it;[25] and it can attain it;
    If not, then each desire would frustrate be.
Therefore springs up, in fashion of a shoot,[26]   130
    Doubt at the foot of truth; and this is nature,
    Which to the top from height to height impels us.[27]
This doth invite me, this assurance give me
    With reverence, Lady, to inquire of you
    Another truth, which is obscure to me.[28]   135
I wish to know if man can satisfy you
    For broken vows with other good deeds, so

That in your balance they will not be light."
Beatrice gazed upon me with her eyes
   Full of the sparks of love, and so divine,   140
   That, overcome my power, I turned my back
And almost lost myself[29] with eyes downcast.

CANTO V

*I*F in the heat of love I flame upon thee
    Beyond the measure that on earth is seen,
    So that the valor of thine eyes I vanquish,
Marvel thou not thereat; for this proceeds
    From perfect sight, which as it apprehends   5
    To the good apprehended moves its feet.[1]
Well I perceive how is already shining
    Into thine intellect the eternal light,
    That only seen enkindles always love;[2]
And if some other thing your love seduce,   10
    'Tis nothing but a vestige of the same,
    Ill understood,[3] which there is shining through.
Thou fain wouldst know if with another service
    For broken vow can such return be made
    As to secure the soul from further claim."[4]   15
This Canto thus did Beatrice begin;[5]
    And, as a man who breaks not off his speech,
    Continued thus her holy argument:
"The greatest gift that in his largess God
    Creating made, and unto his own goodness   20
    Nearest conformed, and that which he doth prize
Most highly, is the freedom of the will,
    Wherewith the creatures of intelligence
    Both all and only were and are endowed.[6]
Now wilt thou see, if thence thou reasonest,   25
    The high worth of a vow, if it be made
    So that when thou consentest God consents;

For, closing between God and man the compact,
>A sacrifice is of this treasure made,[7]
>Such as I say, and made by its own act.   30
What can be rendered then as compensation?[8]
>Think'st thou to make good use of what thou'st offered,
>With gains ill gotten thou wouldst do good deed.
Now art thou certain of the greater point;
>But because Holy Church in this dispenses,[9]   35
>Which seems against the truth which I have shown thee
Behoves thee still to sit awhile at table,
>Because the solid food which thou hast taken
>Requireth further aid for thy digestion.[10]
Open thy mind to that which I reveal,   40
>And fix it there within; for 'tis not knowledge,
>The having heard without retaining it.
In the essence of this sacrifice two things
>Convene together; and the one is that
>Of which 'tis made, the other is the agreement.   45
This last forevermore is cancelled not
>Unless complied with, and concerning this
>With such precision has above been spoken.[11]
Therefore it was enjoined upon the Hebrews[12]
>To offer still, though sometimes what was offered   50
>Might be commuted, as thou ought'st to know.
The other, which is known to thee as matter,
>May well indeed be such that one errs not
>If it for other matter be exchanged.
But let none shift the burden on his shoulder   55
>At his arbitrament, without the turning
>Both of the white and of the yellow key;[13]
And every permutation deem as foolish,
>If in the substitute the thing relinquished,
>As the four is in six,[14] be not contained.   60
Therefore whatever thing has so great weight
>In value that it drags down every balance,
>Cannot be satisfied with other spending.[15]

Canto V: The Host of Myriad Glowing Souls

Let mortals never take a vow in jest;
    Be faithful and not blind in doing that,   65
    As Jephthah[16] was in his first offering,
Whom more beseemed to say, 'I have done wrong,'
    Than to do worse by keeping; and as foolish
    Thou the great leader of the Greeks wilt find,
Whence wept Iphigenia her fair face,   70
    And made for her both wise and simple weep,[17]
    Who heard such kind of worship spoken of.
Christians, be ye more serious in your movements;
    Be ye not like a feather at each wind,
    And think not every water washes you.   75
Ye have the Old and the New Testament,
    And the Pastor of the Church who guideth you;[18]
    Let this suffice you unto your salvation.
If evil appetite[19] cry aught else to you,
    Be ye as men, and not as silly sheep,   80
    So that the Jew among you may not mock you.[20]
Be ye not as the lamb that doth abandon
    Its mother's milk, and frolicsome and simple
    Combats at its own pleasure with itself."
Thus Beatrice to me even as I write it;[21]   85
    Then all desireful turned herself again
    To that part where the world is most alive.[22]
Her silence and her change of countenance
    Silence imposed upon my eager mind,
    That had already in advance new questions;   90
And as an arrow that upon the mark
    Strikes ere the bowstring quiet hath become,
    So did we speed into the second realm.[23]
My Lady there so joyful I beheld,
    As into the brightness of that heaven she entered,   95
    More luminous thereat the planet grew;[24]
And if the star itself was changed and smiled,
    What became I, who by my nature am
    Exceeding mutable in every guise![25]
As, in a fish-pond which is pure and tranquil,   100

The fishes draw to that which from without
Comes in such fashion that their food they deem it;
So I beheld more than a thousand splendors[26]
Drawing towards us, and in each was heard:
"Lo, this is she who shall increase our love."[27]   105
And as each one was coming unto us,
Full of beatitude the shade was seen,[28]
By the effulgence clear that issued from it.
Think, Reader,[29] if what here is just beginning
No farther should proceed, how thou wouldst have   110
An agonizing need of knowing more;
And of thyself thou'lt see how I from these
Was in desire of hearing their conditions,
As they unto mine eyes were manifest.
"O thou well-born, unto whom Grace concedes   115
To see the thrones of the eternal triumph,[30]
Or ever yet the warfare be abandoned,[31]
With light that through the whole of heaven is spread
Kindled are we, and hence if thou desirest
To know of us, at thine own pleasure sate thee."   120
Thus by some one among those holy spirits
Was spoken, and by Beatrice: "Speak, speak
Securely, and believe them even as Gods."[32]
"Well I perceive how thou dost nest thyself
In thine own light,[33] and drawest it from thine eyes,   125
Because they coruscate* when thou dost smile,
But know not who thou art, nor why thou hast,
Spirit august, thy station in the sphere
That veils itself to men in alien rays."[34]
This said I in direction of the light   130
Which first had spoken to me; whence it became
By far more lucent than it was before.
Even as the sun, that doth conceal himself
By too much light, when heat has worn away
The tempering influence of the vapors dense,   135

*Flash; sparkle; glitter.

By greater rapture thus concealed itself
    In its own radiance[35] the figure saintly,
    And thus close, close enfolded[36] answered me
In fashion as the following Canto sings.

CANTO VI

AFTER that Constantine the Eagle turned
    Against the course of heaven,[1] which it had followed
    Behind the ancient who Lavinia took,[2]
Two hundred years and more[3] the bird of God[4]
    In the extreme of Europe held itself,   5
    Near to the mountains whence it issued first;
And under shadow of the sacred plumes
    It governed there the world from hand to hand,
    And, changing thus, upon mine own alighted.[5]
Cæsar I was, and am Justinian,[6]   10
    Who, by the will of primal Love I feel,
    Took from the laws the useless and redundant;
And ere unto the work I was attent,
    One nature to exist in Christ, not more,
    Believed, and with such faith was I contented.   15
But blessed Agapetus,[7] he who was
    The supreme pastor, to the faith sincere
    Pointed me out the way by words of his.
Him I believed, and what was his assertion
    I now see clearly, even as thou seest   20
    Each contradiction to be false and true.[8]
As soon as with the Church I moved my feet,
    God in his grace it pleased with this high task[9]
    To inspire me, and I gave me wholly to it,
And to my Belisarius[10] I commended   25
    The arms, to which was heaven's right hand so joined
    It was a signal that I should repose.
Now here to the first question terminates

My answer; but the character thereof
    Constrains me to continue with a sequel,[11]   30
In order that thou see with how great reason
    Men move against the standard sacrosanct,
    Both who appropriate and who oppose it.[12]
Behold how great a power has made it worthy
    Of reverence, beginning from the hour   35
    When Pallas died[13] to give it sovereignty.
Thou knowest it made in Alba[14] its abode
    Three hundred years and upward, till at last
    The three to three fought for it yet again.
Thou knowest what it achieved from Sabine wrong   40
    Down to Lucretia's sorrow,[15] in seven kings
    O'ercoming round about the neighboring nations;
Thou knowest what it achieved, borne by the Romans
    Illustrious against Brennus, against Pyrrhus,[16]
    Against the other princes and confederates.   45
Torquatus thence and Quinctius, who from locks
    Unkempt was named,[17] Decii and Febii,[18]
    Received the fame I willingly embalm;[19]
It struck to earth the pride of the Arabians,[20]
    Who, following Hannibal, had passed across   50
    The Alpine ridges, Po, from which thou glidest;[21]
Beneath it triumphed while they yet were young
    Pompey and Scipio,[22] and to the hill
    Beneath which thou wast born it bitter seemed;[23]
Then, near unto the time when heaven had willed   55
    To bring the whole world to its mood serene,
    Did Cæsar by the will of Rome assume it.
What it achieved from Var unto the Rhine,
    Isère beheld and Saône, beheld the Seine,
    And every valley whence the Rhone is filled;[24]   60
What it achieved[25] when it had left Ravenna,
    And leaped the Rubicon, was such a flight
    That neither tongue nor pen could follow it.
Round towards Spain it wheeled its legions; then
    Towards Durazzo, and Pharsalia smote[26]   65

That to the calid* Nile was felt the pain.²⁷
Antandros and the Simois, whence it started,²⁸
    It saw again, and there where Hector lies,
    And ill for Ptolemy then roused itself.²⁹
Thence came it like a thunder-bolt on Juba;   70
    Then wheeled itself again into your West,
    Where the Pompeian clarion it heard.³⁰
From what it wrought with the next standard-bearer
    Brutus and Cassius howl in Hell together,³¹
    And Modena and Perugia dolent† were;³²   75
Still doth the mournful Cleopatra weep
    Because thereof, who, fleeing from before it,³³
    Took from the adder sudden and black death.
With him it ran even to the Red Sea shore;
    With him it placed the world in so great peace,   80
    That unto Janus was his temple closed.³⁴
But what the standard that has made me speak
    Achieved before, and after should achieve
    Throughout the mortal realm that lies beneath it,
Becometh in appearance mean and dim,   85
    If in the hand of the third Cæsar³⁵ seen
    With eye unclouded and affection pure,
Because the living Justice that inspires me
    Granted it, in the hand of him I speak of,
    The glory of doing vengeance for its wrath.³⁶   90
Now here attend to what I answer thee;
    Later it ran with Titus to do vengeance
    Upon the vengeance of the ancient sin.³⁷
And when the tooth of Lombardy had bitten³⁸
    The Holy Church, then underneath its wings   95
    Did Charlemagne victorious succor her.
Now hast thou power to judge of such as those³⁹
    Whom I accused above, and of their crimes,
    Which are the cause of all your miseries.

*Hot.
†Sorrowful.

To the public standard one the yellow lilies   100
    Opposes, the other claims it for a party,[40]
    So that 'tis hard to see which sins the most.
Let, let the Ghibellines ply their handicraft
    Beneath some other standard; for this ever
    Ill follows he who it and justice parts.   105
And let not this new Charles e'er strike it down,
    He and his Guelfs, but let him fear the talons
    That from a nobler lion stripped the fell.*[41]
Already oftentimes the sons have wept
    The father's crime;[42] and let him not believe   110
    That God will change His scutcheon for the lilies.
This little planet doth adorn itself
    With the good spirits that have active been,
    That fame and honor might come after them;
And whensoever the desires mount thither,   115
    Thus deviating, must perforce the rays
    Of the true love less vividly mount upward.[43]
But in commensuration of our wages
    With our desert is portion of our joy,
    Because we see them neither less nor greater.   120
Herein doth living Justice sweeten so
    Affection in us, that forevermore
    It cannot warp to any iniquity.
Voices diverse make up sweet melodies;
    So in this life of ours the seats diverse   125
    Render sweet harmony among these spheres;[44]
And in the compass of this present pearl[45]
    Shineth the sheen of Romeo, of whom
    The grand and beauteous work was ill rewarded.
But the Provençals who against him wrought,   130
    They have not laughed, and therefore ill goes he
    Who makes his hurt of the good deeds of others.
Four daughters, and each one of them a queen,
    Had Raymond Berenger, and this for him

*Hide or skin of an animal.

Did Romeo, a poor man and a pilgrim;   135
And then malicious words incited him
    To summon to a reckoning this just man,
    Who rendered to him seven and five for ten.
Then he departed poor and stricken in years,
    And if the world could know the heart he had,   140
    In begging bit by bit his livelihood,[46]
Though much it laud him, it would laud him more."[47]

CANTO VII

*O*SANNA *sanctus Deus Sabaoth,*
    Superillustrans claritate tua
    Felices ignes horum malahoth!"[1]
In this wise, to its melody returning,
    This substance, upon which a double light   5
    Doubles itself,[2] was seen by me to sing,
And to their dance this and the others moved,
    And in the manner of swift-hurrying sparks
    Veiled themselves from me with a sudden distance.[3]
Doubting was I, and saying, "Tell her, tell her,"   10
    Within me, "tell her," saying, "tell my Lady,"
    Who slakes my thirst with her sweet effluences;[4]
And yet that reverence which doth lord it over
    The whole of me only by B and ICE,[5]
    Bowed me again like unto one who drowses.   15
Short while did Beatrice endure me thus;
    And she began, lighting me with a smile
    Such as would make one happy in the fire:
"According to infallible advisement,
    After what manner a just vengeance justly   20
    Could be avenged has put thee upon thinking,[6]
But I will speedily thy mind unloose;
    And do thou listen, for these words of mine
    Of a great doctrine will a present make thee.
By not enduring on the power that wills   25
    Curb for his good, that man who ne'er was born,
    Damning himself damned all his progeny;[7]
Whereby the human species down below

Lay sick for many centuries in great error,
    Till to descend it pleased the Word of God[8]   30
To where the nature, which from its own Maker
    Estranged itself, he joined to him in person
    By the sole act of his eternal love.
Now unto what is said direct thy sight;
    This nature when united to its Maker,   35
    Such as created, was sincere and good;[9]
But by itself alone was banished forth
    From Paradise, because it turned aside
    Out of the way of truth and of its life.
Therefore the penalty the cross held out,   40
    If measured by the nature thus assumed,
    None ever yet with so great justice stung,
And none was ever of so great injustice,[10]
    Considering who the Person was that suffered,
    Within whom such a nature was contracted.   45
From one act therefore issued things diverse;
    To God and to the Jews one death was pleasing;[11]
    Earth trembled[12] at it and the Heaven was opened.
It should no longer now seem difficult
    To thee, when it is said that a just vengeance   50
    By a just court was afterward avenged.
But now do I behold thy mind entangled
    From thought to thought within a knot, from which
    With great desire it waits to free itself.
Thou sayest, 'Well discern I what I hear;   55
    But it is hidden from me why God willed[13]
    For our redemption only this one mode.'
Buried remaineth, brother, this decree
    Unto the eyes of every one whose nature
    Is in the flame of love not yet adult.   60
Verily, inasmuch as at this mark
    One gazes long and little is discerned,[14]
    Wherefore this mode was worthiest will I say.
Goodness Divine, which from itself doth spurn
    All envy, burning in itself so sparkles   65

That the eternal beauties it unfolds.
Whate'er from this immediately distils
    Has afterwards no end, for ne'er removed
    Is its impression when it sets its seal.
Whate'er from this immediately rains down   70
    Is wholly free, because it is not subject
    Unto the influences of novel things.
The more conformed thereto, the more it pleases;
    For the blest ardor that irradiates all things
    In that most like itself is most vivacious.[15]   75
With all of these things has advantaged been
    The human creature; and if one be wanting,
    From his nobility he needs must fall.
'Tis sin alone which doth disfranchise him,[16]
    And render him unlike the Good Supreme,   80
    So that he little with its light is blanched,
And to his dignity no more returns,
    Unless he fill up where transgression empties
    With righteous pains for criminal delights.
Your nature when it sinned so utterly   85
    In its own seed, out of these dignities
    Even as out of Paradise was driven,
Nor could itself recover, if thou notest
    With nicest subtilty, by any way,
    Except by passing one of these two fords: 90
Either that God through clemency alone
    Had pardon granted, or that man himself
    Had satisfaction for his folly made.[17]
Fix now thine eye deep into the abyss
    Of the eternal counsel, to my speech   95
    As far as may be fastened steadfastly!
Man in his limitations had not power
    To satisfy, not having power to sink
    In his humility obeying then,
Far as he disobeying thought to rise;   100
    And for this reason man has been from power
    Of satisfying by himself excluded.[18]

Therefore it God behoved in his own ways
    Man to restore unto his perfect life,
    I say in one, or else in both of them.   105
But since the action of the doer is
    So much more grateful, as it more presents
    The goodness of the heart from which it issues,
Goodness Divine, that doth imprint the world,
    Has been contented to proceed by each[19]   110
    And all its ways to lift you up again;
Nor 'twixt the first day and the final night[20]
    Such high and such magnificent proceeding
    By one or by the other was or shall be;
For God more bounteous was himself to give   115
    To make man able to uplift himself,
    Than if he only of himself had pardoned;
And all the other modes were insufficient
    For justice, were it not the Son of God
    Himself had humbled[21] to become incarnate.   120
Now, to fill fully each desire of thine,
    Return I to elucidate one place,[22]
    In order that thou there mayst see as I do.
Thou sayst: 'I see the air, I see the fire,
    The water, and the earth, and all their mixtures   125
    Come to corruption,[23] and short while endure;
And these things notwithstanding were created';
    Therefore if that which I have said were true,
    They should have been secure against corruption.
The Angels, brother, and the land sincere   130
    In which thou art, created may be called
    Just as they are in their entire existence;
But all the elements which thou hast named,
    And all those things which out of them are made,
    By a created virtue are informed.[24]   135
Created was the matter which they have;
    Created was the informing influence
    Within these stars that round about them go.
The soul of every brute and of the plants[25]

By its potential temperament attracts   140
   The ray and motion of the holy lights;
But your own life[26] immediately inspires
   Supreme Beneficence, and enamors it
   So with herself, it evermore desires her.
And thou from this mayst argue furthermore   145
   Your resurrection, if thou think again
   How human flesh was fashioned at that time
When the first parents both of them were made."[27]

CANTO VIII

THE world used in its peril to believe
    That the fair Cypria delirious love[1]
    Rayed out, in the third epicycle turning;[2]
Wherefore not only unto her paid honor
    Of sacrifices and of votive cry   5
    The ancient nations in the ancient error,
But both Dione honored they and Cupid,[3]
    That as her mother, this one as her son,
    And said that he had sat in Dido's lap;[4]
And they from her, whence I beginning take,   10
    Took the denomination of the star
    That wooes the sun, now following, now in front.[5]
I was not ware of our ascending to it;
    But of our being in it gave full faith
    My Lady whom I saw more beauteous grow.[6]   15
And as within a flame a spark is seen,
    And as within a voice[7] a voice discerned,
    When one is steadfast, and one comes and goes,
Within that light beheld I other lamps[8]
    Move in a circle, speeding more and less,   20
    Methinks in measure of their inward vision.
From a cold cloud descended never winds,
    Or visible or not, so rapidly
    They would not laggard and impeded seem
To any one who had those lights divine   25
    Seen come towards us, leaving the gyration
    Begun at first in the high Seraphim.[9]
And behind those that most in front appeared

Sounded *"Osanna!"* so that never since
To hear again was I without desire.
Then unto us more nearly one approached,[10]   30
    And it alone began: "We all are ready
    Unto thy pleasure, that thou joy in us.
We turn around with the celestial Princes,
    One gyre and one gyration and one thirst,[11]   35
    To whom thou in the world of old didst say,
'*Ye who, intelligent, the third heaven are moving*';[12]
    And are so full of love, to pleasure thee
    A little quiet will not be less sweet."
After these eyes of mine themselves had offered   40
    Unto my Lady reverently, and she
    Content and certain of herself had made them,
Back to the light they turned, which so great promise
    Made of itself, and "Say, who art thou?" was
    My voice, imprinted with a great affection.   45
O how and how much I beheld it grow
    With the new joy that superadded was
    Unto its joys, as soon as I had spoken!
Thus changed, it said to me: "The world possessed me
    Short time below;[13] and, if it had been more,   50
    Much evil will be which would not have been.
My gladness keepeth me concealed from thee,
    Which rayeth round about me, and doth hide me
    Like as a creature swathed in its own silk.[14]
Much didst thou love me, and thou hadst good reason;   55
    For had I been below, I should have shown thee
    Somewhat beyond the foliage of my love.[15]
That left-hand margin, which doth bathe itself
    In Rhone, when it is mingled with the Sorgue,
    Me for its lord awaited[16] in due time,   60
And that horn of Ausonia, which is towned
    With Bari, with Gaeta and Catona,
    Whence Tronto and Verde[17] in the sea disgorge.
Already flashed upon my brow the crown
    Of that dominion which the Danube waters[18]   65

Canto VIII: Charles Martel addresses Dante and Beatrice

After the German borders it abandons;
  And beautiful Trinacria, that is murky
    'Twixt Pachino and Peloro, (on the gulf
    Which greatest scath from Eurus doth receive,[19])
Not through Typhœus, but through nascent sulphur,[20]   70
    Would have awaited her own monarchs still,
    Through me from Charles descended and from Rudolph
If evil lordship, that exasperates ever
    The subject populations, had not moved
    Palermo to the outcry of 'Death! death!'[21]   75
And if my brother could but this foresee,
    The greedy poverty of Catalonia[22]
    Straight would he flee, that it might not molest him;
For verily 'tis needful to provide,
    Through him or other, so that on his bark[23]   80
    Already freighted no more freight be placed.
His nature, which from liberal covetous
    Descended,[24] such a soldiery would need
    As should not care for hoarding in a chest."[25]
"Because I do believe the lofty joy   85
    Thy speech infuses into me, my Lord,
    Where every good thing doth begin and end
Thou seest as I see it, the more grateful
    Is it to me; and this too hold I dear,
    That gazing upon God thou dost discern it.   90
Glad hast thou made me; so make clear to me,
    Since speaking thou hast stirred me up to doubt,
    How from sweet seed can bitter issue forth."[26]
This I to him; and he to me: "If I
    Can show to thee a truth, to what thou askest   95
    Thy face thou'lt hold as thou dost hold thy back.[27]
The Good which all the realm thou art ascending
    Turns and contents, maketh its providence
    To be a power within these bodies vast;[28]
And not alone the natures are foreseen   100
    Within the mind that in itself is perfect,[29]
    But they together with their preservation.

For whatsoever thing this bow[30] shoots forth
    Falls foreordained unto an end foreseen,
    Even as a shaft directed to its mark.   105
If that were not, the heaven which thou dost walk
    Would in such manner its effects produce,
    That they no longer would be arts, but ruins.
This cannot be, if the Intelligences
    That keep these stars in motion are not maimed,   110
    And maimed the First who has not made them perfect.[31]
Wilt thou this truth have clearer made to thee?"
    And I: "Not so; for 'tis impossible
    That nature tire, I see, in what is needful."
Whence he again: "Now say, would it be worse   115
    For men on earth were they not citizens?"
    "Yes," I replied; "and here I ask no reason."
"And can they be so, if below they live not
    Diversely unto offices diverse?
    No, if your master writeth well for you."[32]   120
So came he with deductions to this point;
    Then he concluded: "Therefore it behoves
    The roots of your effects to be diverse.
Hence one is Solon born, another Xerxes,
    Another Melchisedec, and another he   125
    Who, flying through the air, his son did lose.[33]
Revolving Nature, which a signet is
    To mortal wax, doth practise well her art,
    But not one inn distinguish from another;[34]
Thence happens it that Esau differeth   130
    In seed from Jacob; and Quirinus comes
    From sire so vile that he is given to Mars.[35]
A generated nature its own way
    Would always make like its progenitors,
    If Providence divine were not triumphant.[36]   135
Now that which was behind thee is before thee;[37]
    But that thou know that I with thee am pleased,
    With a corollary will I mantle thee.[38]
Evermore nature, if it fortune find

Discordant to it, like each other seed   140
    Out of its region, maketh evil thrift;[39]
And if the world below would fix its mind
    On the foundation which is laid by nature,
    Pursuing that, 'twould have the people good.
But you unto religion wrench aside   145
    Him who was born to gird him with the sword,
    And make a king of him who is for sermons;
Therefore your footsteps wander from the road."[40]

CANTO IX

$\mathcal{B}$EAUTIFUL Clemence,[1] after that thy Charles
  Had me enlightened, he narrated to me
  The treacheries his seed should undergo;[2]
But said: "Be still[3] and let the years roll round";
  So I can only say, that lamentation   5
  Legitimate shall follow on your wrongs.
And of that holy light the life already
  Had to the Sun[4] which fills it turned again,
  As to that good which for each thing sufficeth.
Ah, souls deceived,[5] and creatures impious,   10
  Who from such good do turn away your hearts,
  Directing upon vanity your foreheads!
And now, behold, another of those splendors
  Approached me, and its will to pleasure me
  It signified by brightening outwardly.   15
The eyes of Beatrice, that fastened were
  Upon me, as before, of dear assent
  To my desire assurance gave to me.
"Ah, bring swift compensation to my wish,
  Thou blessed spirit," I said, "and give me proof 20
  That what I think in thee I can reflect!
Whereat the light, that still was new to me,
  Out of its depths, whence it before was singing,
  As one delighted to do good, continued:
"Within that region of the land depraved   25
  Of Italy, that lies between Rialto
  And fountain-heads of Brenta and of Piava,[6]
Rises a hill,[7] and mounts not very high,

Wherefrom descended formerly a torch[8]
    That made upon that region great assault.   30
Out of one root were born both I and it;
    Cunizza was I called, and here I shine
    Because the splendor of this star o'ercame me.[9]
But gladly to myself the cause I pardon
    Of my allotment, and it does not grieve me;   35
    Which would perhaps seem strong unto your vulgar.[10]
Of this so luculent* and precious jewel,[11]
    Which of our heaven is nearest unto me,
    Great fame remained; and ere it die away
This hundredth year shall yet quintupled be.[12]   40
    See if man ought to make him excellent,
    So that another life[13] the first may leave!
And thus thinks not the present multitude
    Shut in by Adige and Tagliamento,
    Nor yet for being scourged is penitent.   45
But soon 'twill be that Padua in the marsh
    Will change the water that Vicenza bathes,
    Because the folk are stubborn against duty;[14]
And where the Sile and Cagnano join[15]
    One lordeth it, and goes with lofty head,[16]   50
    For catching whom e'en now the net is making.
Feltro moreover of her impious pastor[17]
    Shall weep the crime, which shall so monstrous be
    That for the like none ever entered Malta.[18]
Ample exceedingly would be the vat   55
    That of the Ferrarese could hold the blood,
    And weary who should weigh it ounce by ounce,
Of which this courteous priest shall make a gift
    To show himself a partisan;[19] and such gifts
    Will to the living of the land conform.   60
Above us there are mirrors, Thrones you call them,
    From which shines out on us God Judicant,
    So that this utterance seems good to us."[20]

*Luminous; full of light.

Here it was silent, and it had the semblance
    Of being turned elsewhither, by the wheel   65
    On which it entered as it was before.
The other joy, already known to me,
    Became a thing transplendent in my sight,
    As a fine ruby smitten by the sun.[21]
Through joy effulgence is acquired above,   70
    As here a smile; but down below,[22] the shade
    Outwardly darkens, as the mind is sad.
"God seeth all things, and in Him, blest spirit,
    Thy sight is,"[23] said I, "so that never will
    Of his can possibly from thee be hidden;   75
Thy voice, then, that forever makes the heavens
    Glad, with the singing of those holy fires
    Which of their six wings make themselves a cowl,[24]
Wherefore does it not satisfy my longings?
    Indeed, I would not wait thy questioning   80
    If I in thee were as thou art in me."[25]
"The greatest of the valleys where the water
    Expands itself," forthwith its words began,
    "That sea excepted which the earth engarlands,[26]
Between discordant shores[27] against the sun   85
    Extends so far, that it meridian makes
    Where it was wont before to make the horizon.[28]
I was a dweller on that valley's shore
    'Twixt Ebro and Magra that with journey short
    Doth from the Tuscan part the Genoese.[29]   90
With the same sunset and same sunrise nearly
    Sit Buggia and the city whence I was,[30]
    That with its blood once made the harbor hot.[31]
Folco[32] that people called me unto whom
    My name was known; and now with me this heaven   95
    Imprints itself, as I did once with it;
For more the daughter of Belus never burned,
    Offending both Sichæus and Creusa,
    Than I, so long as it became my locks,
Nor yet that Rodophean, who deluded   100

Was by Demophoön, nor yet Alcides,

When Iole he in his heart had locked.[33]

Yet here is no repenting, but we smile,[34]

Not at the fault, which comes not back to mind,

But at the power which ordered and foresaw.   105

Here we behold the art that doth adorn

With such affection, and the good discover

Whereby the world above turns that below.[35]

But that thou wholly satisfied mayst bear

Thy wishes hence which in this sphere are born,   110

Still farther to proceed behoveth me.

Thou fain* wouldst know who is within this light

That here beside me thus is scintillating,

Even as a sunbeam in the limpid water.

Then know thou, that within there is at rest   115

Rahab, and being to our order joined,

With her in its supremest grade 'tis sealed.[36]

Into this heaven, where ends the shadowy cone

Cast by your world,[37] before all other souls

First of Christ's Triumph was she taken up.   120

Full meet it was to leave her in some heaven,

Even as a palm of the high victory[38]

Which he acquired with one palm and the other,

Because she favored the first glorious deed

Of Joshua upon the Holy Land,   125

That little stirs the memory of the Pope.[39]

Thy city, which an offshoot is of him

Who first upon his Maker turned his back,

And whose ambition is so sorely wept,

Brings forth and scatters the accursed flower   130

Which both the sheep and lambs hath led astray,

Since it has turned the shepherd to a wolf.[40]

For this the Evangel and the mighty Doctors

Are derelict, and only the Decretals

So studied that it shows upon their margins.[41]   135

*Gladly; with pleasure.

On this are Pope and Cardinals intent;
 Their meditations reach not Nazareth,[42]
 There where his pinions Gabriel unfolded;
But Vatican and the other parts elect
 Of Rome, which have a cemetery been   140
 Unto the soldiery that followed Peter,
Shall soon be free from the adulterer."[43]

CANTO X

Looking into his Son[1] with all the Love
    Which each of them eternally breathes forth,
    The primal and unutterable Power
Whate'er before the mind or eye revolves
    With so much order made, there can be none   5
    Who this beholds without enjoying it.
Lift up then, Reader,[2] to the lofty wheels
    With me thy vision straight unto that part
    Where the one motion on the other strikes,
And there begin to contemplate with joy   10
    That Master's art, who in himself so loves it
    That never doth his eye depart therefrom.
Behold how from that point goes branching off
    The oblique circle, which conveys the planets,
    To satisfy the world that calls upon them;   15
And if their pathway were not thus inflected,
    Much virtue in the heavens would be in vain,
    And almost every power below here dead.
If from the straight line distant more or less
    Were the departure, much would wanting be   20
    Above and underneath of mundane order.[3]
Remain now, Reader, still upon thy bench,
    In thought pursuing that which is foretasted,
    If thou wouldst jocund be instead of weary.
I've set before thee; henceforth feed thyself,   25
    For to itself diverteth all my care
    That theme whereof I have been made the scribe.[4]
The greatest of the ministers of nature,[5]

Who with the power of heaven the world imprints
    And measures with his light the time for us,   30
With that part which above is called to mind[6]
    Conjoined, along the spirals was revolving,
    Where each time earlier he presents himself;
And I was with him; but of the ascending
    I was not conscious,[7] saving as a man   35
    Of a first thought is conscious ere it come;
And Beatrice, she who is seen to pass
    From good to better, and so suddenly
    That not by time her action is expressed,
How lucent in herself must she have been!   40
    And what was in the sun, wherein I entered,
    Apparent not by color but by light,
I, though I call on genius, art, and practice,
    Cannot so tell that it could be imagined;
    Believe one can, and let him long to see it.   45
And if our fantasies too lowly are
    For altitude so great, it is no marvel,
    Since o'er the sun was never eye could go.[8]
Such in this place was the fourth family
    Of the high Father, who forever sates it,   50
    Showing how he breathes forth and how begets.[9]
And Beatrice began: "Give thanks, give thanks
    Unto the Sun of Angels, who to this
    Sensible one has raised thee by his grace!"
Never was heart of mortal so disposed   55
    To worship, nor to give itself to God
    With all its gratitude was it so ready,
As at those words did I myself become;
    And all my love was so absorbed in Him,
    That in oblivion Beatrice was eclipsed.[10]   60
Nor this displeased her; but she smiled at it
    So that the splendor of her laughing eyes
    My single mind on many things divided.[11]
Lights many saw I, vivid and triumphant,
    Make us a centre and themselves a circle,   65

More sweet in voice than luminous in aspect.
Thus girt about the daughter of Latona
    We sometimes see, when pregnant is the air,
    So that it holds the thread which makes her zone.[12]
Within the court of Heaven, whence I return,   70
    Are many jewels found, so fair and precious
    They cannot be transported from the realm;
And of them was the singing of those lights.
    Who takes not wings that he may fly up thither,
    The tidings thence may from the dumb await![13]   75
As soon as singing thus those burning suns
    Had round about us whirled themselves three times,
    Like unto stars neighboring the steadfast poles,
Ladies they seemed, not from the dance released,
    But who stop short, in silence listening   80
    Till they have gathered the new melody.[14]
And within one I heard[15] beginning: "When
    The radiance of grace, by which is kindled
    True love, and which thereafter grows by loving,
Within thee multiplied is so resplendent   85
    That it conducts thee upward by that stair,
    Where without reascending none descends,
Who should deny the wine out of his vial
    Unto thy thirst, in liberty were not
    Except as water which descends not seaward.   90
Fain wouldst thou know with what plants is enflowered
    This garland[16] that encircles with delight
    The Lady fair who makes thee strong for heaven.
Of the lambs was I of the holy flock
    Which Dominic conducteth by a road   95
    Where well one fattens if he strayeth not.
He who is nearest to me on the right
    My brother and master was; and he Albertus
    Is of Cologne, I Thomas of Aquinum.[17]
If thou of all the others wouldst be certain,   100
    Follow behind my speaking with thy sight
    Upward along the blessed garland turning.

That next effulgence issues from the smile
      Of Gratian, who assisted both the courts[18]
      In such wise that it pleased in Paradise.   105
The other which near by adorns our choir
      That Peter was who, e'en as the poor widow,
      Offered his treasure unto Holy Church.[19]
The fifth light, that among us is the fairest,
      Breathes forth from such a love, that all the world   110
      Below is greedy to learn tidings of it.[20]
Within it is the lofty mind, where knowledge
      So deep was put, that, if the true be true,
      To see so much there never rose a second.
Thou seest next the lustre of that taper.[21]   115
      Which in the flesh below looked most within
      The angelic nature and its ministry.
Within that other little light is smiling
      The advocate of the Christian centuries,
      Out of whose rhetoric Augustine was furnished.[22]   120
Now if thou trainest thy mind's eye along
      From light to light pursuant of my praise,
      With thirst already of the eighth thou waitest.
By seeing every good therein exults
      The sainted soul,[23] which the fallacious world   125
      Makes manifest to him who listeneth well;
The body whence 'twas hunted forth is lying
      Down in Cieldauro,[24] and from martyrdom
      And banishment it came unto this peace.
See farther onward flame the burning breath   130
      Of Isidore,[25] of Beda,[26] and of Richard
      Who was in contemplation more than man.[27]
This, whence to me returneth thy regard,
      The light is of a spirit unto whom
      In his grave meditations death seemed slow.   135
It is the light eternal of Sigier,
      Who, reading lectures in the Street of Straw,
      Did syllogize invidious verities."[28]
Then, as a horologe[29] that calleth us

What time the Bride of God is rising up   140
    With matins to her Spouse[30] that he may love her,
Wherein one part the other draws and urges,
    Ting! ting! resounding with so sweet a note,
    That swells with love the spirit well disposed,[31]
Thus I beheld the glorious wheel move round,   145
    And render voice to voice, in modulation
    And sweetness that can not be comprehended,
Excepting there where joy is made eternal.[32]

CANTO XI

O THOU insensate care of mortal men,
How inconclusive are the syllogisms
That make thee beat thy winds in downward flight![1]
One after laws and one to aphorisms
Was going, and one following the priesthood,   5
And one to reign by force or sophistry,
And one in theft, and one in state affairs,
One in the pleasures of the flesh involved
Wearied himself, one gave himself to ease;[2]
When I, from all these things emancipate,   10
With Beatrice above there in the Heavens
With such exceeding glory was received![3]
When each one had returned unto that point
Within the circle where it was before,
It stood as in a candlestick a candle;[4]   15
And from within the effulgence which at first
Had spoken unto me, I heard begin
Smiling while it more luminous became:
"Even as I am kindled in its ray,
So, looking into the Eternal Light,   20
The occasion of thy thoughts I apprehend.[5]
Thou doubtest, and wouldst have me to resift
In language so extended and so open
My speech, that to thy sense it may be plain,
Where just before I said,[6] 'where well one fattens,'   25
And where I said, 'there never rose a second';
And here 'tis needful we distinguish well.

The Providence, which governeth the world
  With counsel, wherein all created vision
  Is vanquished ere it reach unto the bottom,[7]   30
(So that towards her own Beloved[8] might go
  The bride of Him who, uttering a loud cry,[9]
  Espoused her with his consecrated blood,
Self-confident and unto Him more faithful,)
  Two Princes[10] did ordain in her behoof,*   35
  Which on this side and that might be her guide.
The one was all seraphical in ardor;
  The other by his wisdom upon earth
  A splendor was of light cherubical.
One will I speak of, for of both is spoken[11]   40
  In praising one, whichever may be taken,
  Because unto one end their labors were.
Between Tupino and the stream that falls
  Down from the hill elect of blessed Ubald,
  A fertile slope of lofty mountain hangs,   45
From which Perugia feels the cold and heat
  Through Porta Sole, and behind it weep
  Gualdo and Nocera their grievous yoke.[12]
From out that slope, there where it breaketh most
  Its steepness, rose upon the world a sun   50
  As this one doth sometimes from out the Ganges;[13]
Therefore let him who speaketh of that place,
  Say not Ascesi, for he would say little,
  But Orient, if he properly would speak.[14]
He was not yet far distant from his rising   55
  Before he had begun to make the earth
  Some comfort from his mighty virtue feel.
For he in youth his father's wrath incurred[15]
  For certain Dame, to whom, as unto death,
  The gate of pleasure no one doth unlock;[16]   60
And was before his spiritual court
  Et coram patre unto her united;[17]

*Behalf.

Then day by day more fervently he loved her.
She, reft* of her first husband,[18] scorned, obscure,
    One thousand and one hundred years and more,   65
    Waited without a suitor till he came.
Naught it availed to hear, that with Amyclas[19]
    Found her unmoved at sounding of his voice
    He who struck terror into all the world;
Naught it availed being constant and undaunted,   70
    So that, when Mary still remained below,[20]
    She mounted up with Christ upon the cross!
But that too darkly I may not proceed,
    Francis and Poverty for these two lovers
    Take thou henceforward in my speech diffuse.   75
Their concord and their joyous semblances,
    The love, the wonder, and the sweet regard,
    They made to be the cause of holy thoughts;
So much so that the venerable Bernard
    First bared his feet,[21] and after so great peace   80
    Ran, and, in running, thought himself too slow.
O wealth unknown! O veritable good!
    Giles bares his feet, and bares his feet Sylvester[22]
    Behind the bridegroom, so doth please the bride![23]
Then goes his way that father and that master,   85
    He and his Lady and that family[24]
    Which now was girding on the humble halter;[25]
Nor cowardice of heart weighed down his brow
    At being son of Peter Bernardone,
    Nor for appearing marvellously scorned;[26]   90
But regally his hard determination
    To Innocent he opened, and from him
    Received the primal seal[27] upon his Order.
After the people mendicant increased
    Behind this man, whose admirable life   95
    Better in glory of the heavens were sung,
Incoronated with a second crown[28]

*Bereft.

Was through Honorius by the Eternal Spirit
        The holy purpose of this Archimandrite.[29]
And when he had, through thirst of Martyrdom,   100
        In the proud presence of the Sultan preached
        Christ and the others who came after him,
And, finding for conversion too unripe[30]
        The folk, and not to tarry there in vain,
        Returned to fruit of the Italic grass,   105
On the rude rock 'twixt Tiber and the Arno
        From Christ did he receive the final seal,
        Which during two whole years his members bore.[31]
When He, who chose him unto so much good,
        Was pleased to draw him up to the reward   110
        That he had merited by being lowly,
Unto his friars, as to the rightful heirs,
        His most dear Lady did he recommend,
        And bade that they should love her faithfully;
And from her bosom the illustrious soul   115
        Wished to depart, returning to its realm,
        And for its body wished no other bier.[32]
Think now what man was he,[33] who was a fit
        Companion over the high seas to keep
        The bark of Peter[34] to its proper bearings.   120
And this man was our Patriarch; hence whoever
        Doth follow him as he commands can see
        That he is laden with good merchandise.
But for new pasturage his flock has grown
        So greedy, that it is impossible   125
        They be not scattered over fields diverse;
And in proportion as his sheep remote
        And vagabond go farther off from him,
        More void of milk return they to the fold.
Verily some there are that fear a hurt,   130
        And keep close to the shepherd; but so few,
        That little cloth doth furnish forth their hoods.[35]
Now if my utterance be not indistinct,
        If thine own hearing hath attentive been,

If thou recall to mind what I have said,   135
In part contented shall thy wishes be;
    For thou shalt see the plant that's chipped away,[36]
    And the rebuke that lieth in the words,
'Where well one fattens, if he strayeth not.'"[37]

Canto XII: The Rings of Glowing Souls

CANTO XII

Soon as the blessed flame[1] had taken up
        The final word to give it utterance,
        Began the holy millstone[2] to revolve,
And in its gyre had not turned wholly round,
        Before another in a ring[3] enclosed it,   5
        And motion joined to motion, song to song;
Song that as greatly doth transcend our Muses,
        Our Sirens,[4] in those dulcet clarions,
        As primal splendor that which is reflected.[5]
And as are spanned athwart a tender cloud   10
        Two rainbows parallel and like in color,
        When Juno to her handmaid[6] gives command,
(The one without born of the one within,
        Like to the speaking of that vagrant one
        Whom love consumed as doth the sun the vapors,)[7]   15
And make the people here, through covenant[8]
        God set with Noah, presageful of the world
        That shall no more be covered with a flood,
In such wise of those sempiternal* roses
        The garlands twain encompassed us about,   20
        And thus the outer to the inner answered.
After the dance, and other grand rejoicings,
        Both of the singing, and the flaming forth
        Effulgence with effulgence blithe and tender,
Together, at once, with one volition stopped,   25
        (Even as the eyes, that, as volition moves them,

*Ever or continuously; eternal.

Must needs together shut and lift themselves,)
Out of the heart of one of the new lights
 There came a voice,[9] that needle to the star[10]
 Made me appear in turning thitherward.   30
And it began: "The love that makes me fair
 Draws me to speak about the other leader,[11]
 By whom so well is spoken here of mine.
'Tis right, where one is, to bring in the other,
 That, as they were united in their warfare,   35
 Together likewise may their glory shine.
The soldiery of Christ, which it had cost
 So dear to arm again, behind the standard
 Moved slow and doubtful and in numbers few,
When the Emperor who reigneth evermore   40
 Provided for the host that was in peril,
 Through grace alone and not that it was worthy;[12]
And, as was said, he to his Bride brought succor
 With champions twain,[13] at whose deed, at whose word
 The straggling people were together drawn.   45
Within that region where the sweet west wind[14]
 Rises to open the new leaves, wherewith
 Europe is seen to clothe herself afresh,
Not far off from the beating of the waves,
 Behind which in his long career the sun   50
 Sometimes conceals himself from every man,
Is situate the fortunate Calahorra,
 Under protection of the mighty shield
 In which the Lion subject is and sovereign.[15]
Therein was born the amorous paramour   55
 Of Christian Faith, the athlete consecrate,[16]
 Kind to his own and cruel to his foes;
And when it was created was his mind
 Replete with such a living energy,
 That in his mother her it made prophetic.[17]   60
As soon as the espousals were complete
 Between him and the Faith at holy font,
 Where they with mutual safety dowered each other,

The woman, who for him had given assent,
    Saw in a dream[18] the admirable fruit   65
    That issue would from him and from his heirs;
And that he might be construed as he was,
    A spirit from this place went forth to name him
    With His possessive whose he wholly was.
Dominic was he called;[19] and him I speak of   70
    Even as of the husbandman whom Christ
    Elected to his garden[20] to assist him.
Envoy and servant sooth* he seemed of Christ,
    For the first love made manifest in him
    Was the first counsel[21] that was given by Christ.   75
Silent and wakeful many a time was he
    Discovered by his nurse upon the ground,
    As if he would have said, 'For this I came.'[22]
O thou his father, Felix verily!
    O thou his mother, verily, Joanna,   80
    If this, interpreted, means as is said![23]
Not for the world[24] which people toil for now
    In following Ostiense and Taddeo,
    But through his longing after the true manna,[25]
He in short time became so great a teacher,   85
    That he began to go about the vineyard,
    Which fadeth soon,[26] if faithless be the dresser;
And of the See, (that once was more benignant†
    Unto the righteous poor, not through itself,
    But him who sits there and degenerates,)[27]   90
Not to dispense or two or three for six,
    Not any fortune of first vacancy,
    Non decimas quæ sunt pauperum Dei,[28]
He asked for, but against the errant world
    Permission to do battle for the seed,[29]   95
    Of which these four and twenty plants[30] surround thee
Then with the doctrine and the will together,

---

*True; faithful; reliable.
†Benign.

With office apostolical[31] he moved,
 Like torrent[32] which some lofty vein out-presses;
And in among the shoots heretical   100
 His impetus with greater fury smote,
 Wherever the resistance was the greatest.[33]
Of him were made thereafter divers runnels,
 Whereby the garden catholic is watered,[34]
 So that more living its plantations stand.   105
If such the one wheel of the Biga was,
 In which the Holy Church itself defended
 And in the field its civic battle won,
Truly full manifest should be to thee
 The excellence of the other,[35] unto whom   110
 Thomas so courteous[36] was before my coming.
But still the orbit, which the highest part
 Of its circumference made, is derelict,
 So that the mould is where was once the crust.[37]
His family, that had straight forward moved   115
 With feet upon his footprints, are turned round
 So that they set the point upon the heel.[38]
And soon aware they will be of the harvest
 Of this bad husbandry, when shall the tares
 Complain the granary is taken from them.[39]   120
Yet say I, he who searcheth leaf by leaf
 Our volume through, would still some page discover
 Where he could read, 'I am as I am wont.'[40]
'Twill not be from Casal nor Acquasparta,
 From whence come such unto the written word 125
 That one avoids it, and the other narrows.[41]
Bonaventura of Bagnoregio's life
 Am I, who always in great offices
 Postponed considerations sinister.[42]
Here are Illuminato and Agostino,[43]   130
 Who of the first barefooted beggars were
 That with the halter[44] friends of God became.
Hugh of Saint Victor[45] is among them here,
 And Peter Mangiador,[46] and Peter of Spain,[47]

Who down below in volumes twelve is shining;   135
Nathan the seer,[48] and metropolitan
    Chrysostom, and Anselmus, and Donatus
    Who deigned to lay his hand to the first art;[49]
Here is Rabanus,[50] and beside me here
    Shines the Calabrian Abbot Joachim,[51]   140
    He with the spirit of prophecy endowed.
To celebrate so great a paladin[52]
    Have moved me the impassioned courtesy
    Of Fra* Tommaso, and his speech discreet;
And with me they have moved this company."   145

*Brother (from the Italian *frate*).

CANTO XIII

$\mathcal{L}$ET him imagine, who would well conceive
    What now I saw, and let him while I speak
    Retain the image as a steadfast rock,
The fifteen stars, that in their divers regions
    The sky enliven with a light so great   5
    That it transcends all clusters of the air;
Let him the Wain imagine unto which
    Our vault of heaven sufficeth night and day,
    So that in turning of its pole it fails not;
Let him the mouth imagine of the horn   10
    That in the point beginneth of the axis
    Round about which the primal wheel revolves,—[1]
To have fashioned of themselves two signs in heaven,
    Like unto that which Minos' daughter made,[2]
    The moment when she felt the frost of death;   15
And one to have its rays within the other,
    And both to whirl themselves in such a manner
    That one should forward go, the other backward;
And he will have some shadowing forth of that
    True constellation and the double dance   20
    That circled round the point at which I was;
Because it is as much beyond our wont,
    As swifter than the motion of the Chiana[3]
    Moveth the heaven that all the rest outspeeds.
There sang they neither Bacchus, nor Apollo,   25
    But in the divine nature Persons three,[4]
    And in one person the divine and human.

The singing and the dance fulfilled their measure,
  And unto us those holy lights gave heed,
  Growing in happiness from care to care.   30
Then broke the silence of those saints concordant
  The light[5] in which the admirable life
  Of God's own mendicant was told to me,
And said: "Now that one straw is trodden out
  Now that its seed is garnered up already,   35
  Sweet love invites me to thresh out the other.[6]
Into that bosom,[7] thou believest, whence
  Was drawn the rib to form the beauteous cheek[8]
  Whose taste to all the world is costing dear,
And into that which, by the lance transfixed,[9]   40
  Before and since, such satisfaction made
  That it weighs down the balance of all sin,
Whate'er of light it has to human nature
  Been lawful to possess was all infused
  By the same power that both of them created;   45
And hence at what I said above dost wonder,
  When I narrated that no second had
  The good which in the fifth light is enclosed.[10]
Now ope thine eyes to what I answer thee,
  And thou shalt see thy creed and my discourse   50
  Fit in the truth as centre in a circle.[11]
That which can die, and that which dieth not,[12]
  Are nothing but the splendor of the idea[13]
  Which by his love our Lord brings into being;
Because that living Light,[14] which from its fount[15]   55
  Effulgent flows, so that it disunites not
  From Him nor from the Love in them intrined,[16]
Through its own goodness reunites its rays
  In nine subsistences, as in a mirror,[17]
  Itself eternally remaining One.   60
Thence it descends to the last potencies,
  Downward from act to act becoming such
  That only brief contingencies[18] it makes;

And these contingencies I hold to be
    Things generated, which the heaven produces   65
    By its own motion, with seed and without.[19]
Neither their wax, nor that which tempers it,
    Remains immutable,[20] and hence beneath
    The ideal signet more and less shines through;
Therefore it happens, that the selfsame tree   70
    After its kind bears worse and better fruit,
    And ye are born with characters diverse.
If in perfection tempered were the wax,
    And were the heaven in its supremest virtue,
    The brilliance of the seal would all appear;   75
But nature gives it evermore deficient,
    In the like manner working as the artist,
    Who has the skill of art and hand that trembles.[21]
If then the fervent Love, the Vision clear,
    Of primal Virtue[22] do dispose and seal,   80
    Perfection absolute is there acquired.
Thus was of old the earth created worthy
    Of all and every animal perfection;
    And thus the Virgin was impregnate made;
So that thine own opinion I commend,   85
    That human nature never yet has been,
    Nor will be, what it was in those two persons.[23]
Now if no farther forth I should proceed,
    'Then in what way was he without a peer?'
    Would be the first beginning of thy words.[24]   90
But, that may well appear what now appears not,
    Think who he was, and what occasion moved him
    To make request, when it was told him, 'Ask.'
I've not so spoken that thou canst not see
    Clearly he was a king who asked for wisdom,   95
    That he might be sufficiently a king;[25]
'Twas not to know the number in which are
    The motors here above,[26] or if *necesse*[27]
    With a contingent e'er *necesse* make,
Non si est dare primum motum esse,[28]   100

Or if in semicircle can be made
  Triangle so that it have no right angle.[29]
Whence, if thou notest this and what I said,
  A regal prudence is that peerless seeing
  In which the shaft of my intention strikes.   105
And if on 'rose' thou turnest thy clear eyes,
  Thou'lt see that it has reference alone
  To kings who're many, and the good are rare.
With this distinction take thou what I said,
  And thus it can consist with thy belief   110
  Of the first father and of our Delight.[30]
And lead shall this be always to thy feet,
  To make thee, like a weary man, move slowly
  Both to the Yes and No thou seest not;
For very low among the fools is he   115
  Who affirms without distinction, or denies,
  As well in one as in the other case;
Because it happens that full often bends
  Current opinion in the false direction,
  And then the feelings bind the intellect.[31]   120
Far more than uselessly he leaves the shore,
  (Since he returneth not the same he went,)
  Who fishes for the truth, and has no skill;[32]
And in the world proofs manifest thereof
  Parmenides, Melissus, Brissus[33] are,   125
  And many who went on and knew not whither;
Thus did Sabellius, Arius,[34] and those fools
  Who have been even as swords unto the Scriptures
  In rendering distorted their straight faces.[35]
Nor yet shall people be too confident   130
  In judging, even as he is who doth count
  The corn in field or ever it be ripe.
For I have seen all winter long the thorn
  First show itself intractable and fierce,
  And after bear the rose upon its top;   135
And I have seen a ship direct and swift
  Run o'er the sea throughout its course entire,

To perish at the harbor's mouth at last.
Let not Dame Bertha nor Ser Martin think,
    Seeing one steal, another offering make,   140
    To see them in the arbitrament* divine;
For one may rise, and fall the other may."[36]

*Judgment.

CANTO XIV

$\mathcal{F}$ROM centre unto rim, from rim to centre,
    In a round vase the water moves itself,
    As from without 'tis struck or from within.
Into my mind upon a sudden dropped[1]
    What I am saying, at the moment when   5
    Silent became the glorious life of Thomas,
Because of the resemblance that was born
    Of his discourse and that of Beatrice,
    Whom, after him, it pleased thus to begin:
"This man has need (and does not tell you so,   10
    Nor with the voice, nor even in his thought)
    Of going to the root of one truth more.[2]
Declare unto him if the light wherewith
    Blossoms your substance shall remain with you
    Eternally the same that it is now;   15
And if it do remain, say in what manner,
    After ye are again made visible,
    It can be that it injure not your sight."[3]
As by a greater gladness urged and drawn
    They who are dancing in a ring sometimes   20
    Uplift their voices and their motions quicken;
So, at that orison* devout and prompt,
    The holy circles a new joy displayed
    In their revolving and their wondrous song.
Whoso lamenteth him that here[4] we die   25
    That we may live above, has never there[5]

*Prayer; request.

Seen the refreshment of the eternal rain.[6]
The One and Two and Three who ever liveth,
    And reigneth ever in Three and Two and One,
    Not circumscribed and all things circumscribing,   30
Three several times was chanted by each one[7]
    Among those spirits, with such melody
    That for all merit it were just reward;
And, in the lustre most divine of all
    The lesser ring, I heard a modest voice,   35
    Such as perhaps the Angel's was to Mary,[8]
Answer: "As long as[9] the festivity
    Of Paradise shall be, so long our love
    Shall radiate round about us such a vesture.
Its brightness is proportioned to the ardor,   40
    The ardor to the vision; and the vision
    Equals what grace it has above its worth.
When, glorious and sanctified, our flesh
    Is reassumed, then shall our persons be
    More pleasing by their being all complete;   45
For will increase whate'er bestows on us
    Of light gratuitous the Good Supreme,
    Light which enables us to look on Him;
Therefore the vision[10] must perforce increase,
    Increase the ardor which from that is kindled,   50
    Increase the radiance which from this proceeds.
But even as a coal that sends forth flame,
    And by its vivid whiteness overpowers it
    So that its own appearance it maintains,[11]
Thus the effulgence that surrounds us now   55
    Shall be o'erpowered in aspect by the flesh,
    Which still to-day the earth doth cover up;
Nor can so great a splendor weary us,
    For strong will be the organs of the body
    To everything which hath the power to please us."   60
So sudden and alert appeared to me
    Both one and the other choir to say Amen,
    That well they showed desire for their dead bodies;

Canto XIV: Dante and Beatrice translated to the sphere of Mars

Nor sole for them perhaps,[12] but for the mothers,
    The fathers, and the rest who had been dear   65
    Or ever they became eternal flames.
And lo! all round about of equal brightness
    Arose a lustre over what was there,
    Like an horizon that is clearing up.
And as at rise of early eve begin   70
    Along the welkin new appearances,
    So that the sight seems real and unreal,
It seemed to me that new subsistences
    Began there to be seen, and make a circle
    Outside the other two circumferences.   75
O very sparkling of the Holy Spirit,[13]
    How sudden and incandescent it became
    Unto mine eyes, that vanquished bore it not!
But Beatrice so beautiful and smiling
    Appeared to me, that with the other sights   80
    That followed not my memory I must leave her.
Then to uplift themselves mine eyes resumed
    The power, and I beheld myself translated
    To higher salvation with my Lady only.
Well was I ware that I was more uplifted   85
    By the enkindled smiling of the star,
    That seemed to me more ruddy than its wont.[14]
With all my heart, and in that dialect
    Which is the same in all, such holocaust
    To God I made as the new grace beseemed;[15]   90
And not yet from my bosom was exhausted
    The ardor of sacrifice, before I knew
    This offering was accepted and auspicious;
For with so great a lustre and so red
    Splendors appeared to me in twofold rays,[16]   95
    I said: "O Helios[17] who dost so adorn them!"
Even as distinct with less and greater lights
    Glimmers between the two poles of the world
    The Galaxy[18] that maketh wise men doubt,
Thus constellated in the depths of Mars,   100

Those rays described the venerable sign
     That quadrants joining in a circle make.[19]
Here doth my memory overcome my genius;
     For on that cross as levin* gleamed forth Christ,
     So that I cannot find ensample† worthy;   105
But he who takes his cross and follows Christ[20]
     Again will pardon me what I omit,
     Seeing in that aurora lighten Christ.
From horn to horn, and 'twixt the top and base,[21]
     Lights were in motion, brightly scintillating   110
     As they together met and passed each other;
Thus level and aslant and swift and slow
     We here behold, renewing still the sight,
     The particles of bodies long and short,
Across the sunbeam move, wherewith is listed   115
     Sometimes the shade, which for their own defence
     People with cunning and with art contrive.[22]
And as a lute and harp, accordant strung
     With many strings, a dulcet tinkling make
     To him by whom the notes are not distinguished,   120
So from the lights that there to me appeared
     Upgathered through the cross a melody,[23]
     Which rapt me, not distinguishing the hymn.
Well was I ware it was of lofty laud,
     Because there came to me, "Arise and conquer!"[24]   125
     As unto him who hears and comprehends not.
So much enamored I became therewith,
     That until then there was not anything
     That e'er had fettered me with such sweet bonds.
Perhaps my word appears somewhat too bold,[25]   130
     Postponing the delight of those fair eyes,
     Into which gazing my desire has rest;
But who bethinks him that the living seals
     Of every beauty grow in power ascending,[26]

*Lightning (archaic).
†Example.

And that I there had not turned round to those,   135
Can me excuse, if I myself accuse
    To excuse myself, and see that I speak truly:
    For here the holy joy is not disclosed,
Because it grows, ascending, more sincere.

CANTO XV

A will benign, in which reveals itself
    Ever the love that righteously inspires,
    As in the iniquitous, cupidity,
Silence imposed upon that dulcet lyre,
    And quieted the consecrated chords,   5
    That Heaven's right hand doth tighten and relax.[1]
How unto just entreaties shall be deaf
    Those substances, which, to give me desire
    Of praying them, with one accord grew silent?
'Tis well[2] that without end he should lament,   10
    Who for the love of thing that doth not last
    Eternally despoils him of that love!
As through the pure and tranquil evening air
    There shoots from time to time a sudden fire,
    Moving the eyes that steadfast were before,[3]   15
And seems to be a star that changeth place,
    Except that in the part where it is kindled
    Nothing is missed,[4] and this endureth little;
So from the horn that to the right extends
    Unto that cross's foot there ran a star   20
    Out of the constellation shining there;
Nor was the gem dissevered from its ribbon,
    But down the radiant fillet ran along,
    So that fire seemed it behind alabaster.[5]
Thus piteous did Anchises' shade[6] reach forward,   25
    If any faith our greatest Muse[7] deserve,
    When in Elysium he his son perceived.
"*O sanguis meus, O super infusa*

77

Gratia Dei, sicut tibi, cui
Bis unquam Cœli janua reclusa?"[8]   30
Thus that effulgence; whence I gave it heed;
    Then round unto my Lady turned my sight,
    And on this side and that was stupefied;
For in her eyes was burning such a smile[9]
    That with mine own methought I touched the bottom   35
    Both of my grace and of my Paradise!
Then, pleasant to the hearing and the sight,
    The spirit joined to its beginning things
    I understood not, so profound it spake;
Nor did it hide itself from me by choice,   40
    But by necessity; for its conception
    Above the mark of mortals set itself.
And when the bow of burning sympathy
    Was so far slackened, that its speech descended[10]
    Towards the mark of our intelligence,   45
The first thing that was understood by me
    Was, "Benedight be Thou, O Trine and One,[11]
    Who hast unto my seed so courteous been!"
And it continued: "Hunger long and grateful,
    Drawn from the reading of the mighty volume   50
    Wherein is never changed the white nor dark,[12]
Thou hast appeased, my son, within this light
    In which I speak to thee, by grace of her[13]
    Who to this lofty flight with plumage clothed thee.
Thou thinkest that to me thy thought doth pass   55
    From Him who is the first, as from the unit,
    If that be known, ray out the five and six;
And therefore who I am thou askest not,
    And why I seem more joyous unto thee
    Than any other of this gladsome crowd.   60
Thou think'st the truth; because the small and great
    Of this existence look into the mirror
    Wherein, before thou think'st, thy thought thou showest.[14]
But that the sacred love, in which I watch
    With sight perpetual, and which makes me thirst   65

With sweet desire, may better be fulfilled,
Now let thy voice secure and frank and glad
        Proclaim the wishes, the desire proclaim,
        To which my answer is decreed already."[15]
To Beatrice I turned me, and she heard   70
        Before I spake,[16] and smiled to me a sign,
        That made the wings of my desire increase;
Then in this wise began I: "Love and knowledge,
        When on you dawned the first Equality,
        Of the same weight for each of you became;   75
For in the Sun, which lighted you and burned
        With heat and radiance, they so equal are,
        That all similitudes are insufficient.
But among mortals will and argument,
        For reason that to you is manifest,   80
        Diversely feathered in their pinions are.
Whence I, who mortal am, feel in myself
        This inequality; so give not thanks,
        Save in my heart, for this paternal welcome.[17]
Truly do I entreat thee, living topaz!   85
        Set in this precious jewel as a gem,[18]
        That thou wilt satisfy me with thy name."
"O leaf of mine, in whom I pleasure took
        E'en while awaiting, I was thine own root!"[19]
        Such a beginning he in answer made me.   90
Then said to me: "That one from whom is named
        Thy race, and who a hundred years and more
        Has circled round the mount on the first cornice,
A son of mine and thy great-grandsire was;[20]
        Well it behoves thee that the long fatigue[21]   95
        Thou shouldst for him make shorter with thy works.
Florence, within the ancient boundary[22]
        From which she taketh still her tierce and nones,
        Abode in quiet, temperate and chaste.[23]
No golden chain she had, nor coronal,*   100

---

*Crown.

Nor ladies shod with sandal shoon, nor girdle
    That caught the eye[24] more than the person did.
Not yet the daughter at her birth struck fear
    Into the father, for the time and dower[25]
    Did not o'errun this side or that the measure.   105
No houses had she void of families,[26]
    Not yet had thither come Sardanapalus[27]
    To show what in a chamber can be done;
Not yet surpassed had Montemalo been
    By your Uccellatojo,[28] which surpassed   110
    Shall in its downfall be as in its rise.
Bellincion Berti saw I go begirt
    With leather and with bone, and from the mirror
    His dame depart without a painted face;[29]
And him of Nerli saw, and him of Vecchio,[30]   115
    Contented with their simple suits of buff,[31]
    And with the spindle and the flax their dames.
O fortunate women! and each one was certain
    Of her own burial-place, and none as yet
    For sake of France was in her bed deserted.[32]   120
One o'er the cradle kept her studious watch,
    And in her lullaby the language* used
    That first delights the fathers and the mothers;
Another, drawing tresses from her distaff,
    Told o'er among her family the tales   125
    Of Trojans and of Fesole and Rome.[33]
As great a marvel then would have been held
    A Lapo Salterello, a Cianghella,
    As Cincinnatus or Cornelia now.[34]
To such a quiet, such a beautiful   130
    Life of the citizen, to such a safe
    Community, and to so sweet an inn,
Did Mary give me, with loud cries invoked,[35]
    And in your ancient Baptistery at once
    Christian and Cacciaguida I became.[36]   135

---

*In this case, baby talk.

Moronto was my brother, and Eliseo;[37]
    From Val di Pado[38] came to me my wife,
    And from that place thy surname was derived.[39]
I followed afterward the Emperor Conrad,[40]
    And he begirt me of his chivalry,   140
    So much I pleased him with my noble deeds.
I followed in his train against that law's
    Iniquity, whose people doth usurp
    Your just possession, through your Pastor's fault.[41]
There by that execrable race was I   145
    Released from bonds of the fallacious world,
    The love of which defileth many souls,
And came from martyrdom unto this peace."[42]

Canto XVI: The Soul of Cacciaguida speaks of Florence

CANTO XVI

O THOU our poor nobility of blood,
    If thou dost make the people glory in thee
    Down here where our affection languishes,
A marvellous thing it ne'er will be to me;
    For there where appetite is not perverted,[1]   5
    I say in Heaven, of thee I made a boast!
Truly thou art a cloak that quickly shortens,
    So that unless we piece thee day by day
    Time goeth round about thee with his shears![2]
With *You*,[3] which Rome was first to tolerate,   10
    (Wherein her family[4] less perseveres,)
    Yet once again my words beginning made;
Whence Beatrice, who stood somewhat apart,
    Smiling, appeared like unto her who coughed[5]
    At the first failing writ[6] of Guenever.   15
And I began: "You are my ancestor,
    You give to me all hardihood to speak,
    You lift me so that I am more than I.
So many rivulets with gladness fill
    My mind, that of itself it makes a joy.   20
    Because it can endure this and not burst.
Then tell me, my beloved root ancestral,
    Who were your ancestors, and what the years
    That in your boyhood chronicled themselves?
Tell me about the sheepfold of Saint John,[7]   25
    How large it was, and who the people were
    Within it worthy of the highest seats."
As at the blowing of the winds a coal

Quickens to flame, so I beheld that light
  Become resplendent at my blandishments.   30
And as unto mine eyes it grew more fair,
  With voice more sweet and tender, but not in
  This modern dialect,[8] it said to me:
"From uttering of the *Ave*, till the birth
  In which my mother, who is now a saint,   35
  Of me was lightened who had been her burden,
Unto its Lion had this fire returned
  Five hundred fifty times and thirty more,
  To reinflame itself beneath his paw.[9]
My ancestors and I our birthplace had   40
  Where first is found the last ward of the city
  By him who runneth in your annual game.[10]
Suffice it of my elders to hear this;
  But who they were, and whence they thither came,
  Silence is more considerate than speech.   45
All those who at that time were there between
  Mars and the Baptist, fit for bearing arms,
  Were a fifth part of those who now are living;[11]
But the community, that now is mixed
  With Campi and Certaldo and Figghine,[12]   50
  Pure in the lowest artisan was seen.
O how much better 'twere to have as neighbors
  The folk of whom I speak, and at Galluzzo
  And at Trespiano[13] have your boundary,
Than have them in the town, and bear the stench   55
  Of Aguglione's churl, and him of Signa[14]
  Who has sharp eyes for trickery already.
Had not the folk, which most of all the world
  Degenerates, been a step-dame unto Cæsar,[15]
  But as a mother to her son benignant,   60
Some who turn Florentines, and trade and discount,
  Would have gone back again to Simifonte[16]
  There where their grandsires went about as beggars.
At Montemurlo still would be the Counts,
  The Cerchi in the parish of Acone,   65

Perhaps in Valdigrieve the Buondelmonti.[17]
Ever the intermingling of the people
    Has been the source of malady in cities,
    As in the body food it surfeits on;[18]
And a blind bull more headlong plunges down   70
    Than a blind lamb; and very often cuts
    Better and more a single sword than five.[19]
If Luni thou regard, and Urbisaglia,
    How they have passed away, and how are passing
    Chiusi and Sinigaglia after them,[20]   75
To hear how races waste themselves away,
    Will seem to thee no novel thing nor hard,
    Seeing that even cities have an end.
All things of yours have their mortality,
    Even as yourselves; but it is hidden[21] in some   80
    That a long while endure, and lives are short;
And as the turning of the lunar heaven[22]
    Covers and bares the shores without a pause,
    In the like manner fortune doth with Florence.
Therefore should not appear a marvellous thing   85
    What I shall say of the great Florentines
    Of whom the fame is hidden in the Past.
I saw the Ughi, saw the Catellini,
    Filippi, Greci, Ormanni, and Alberichi,[23]
    Even in their fall illustrious citizens;   90
And saw, as mighty as they ancient were,
    With him of La Sannella him of Arca,
    And Soldanier, Ardinghi, and Bostichi.[24]
Near to the gate that is at present[25] laden
    With a new felony of so much weight   95
    That soon it shall be jetsam from the bark,[26]
The Ravignani were, from whom descended
    The County Guido, and whoe'er the name
    Of the great Bellincione since hath taken.[27]
He of La Pressa[28] knew the art of ruling   100
    Already, and already Galigajo
    Had hilt and pommel gilded in his house.[29]

Mighty already was the Column Vair,[30]
    Sacchetti, Giuochi, Fifant, and Barucci,
    And Galli,[31] and they who for the bushel blush.[32]   105
The stock from which were the Calfucci[33] born
    Was great already, and already chosen
    To curule chairs the Sizii and Arrigucci.[34]
O how beheld I those who are undone
    By their own pride![35] and how the Balls Gold[36]   110
    Florence enflowered in all their mighty deed
So likewise did the ancestors of those
    Who evermore, when vacant is your church,
    Fatten by staying in consistory.[37]
The insolent race, that like a dragon follows   115
    Whoever flees, and unto him that shows
    His teeth or purse is gentle as a lamb,
Already rising was, but from low people;
    So that it pleased not Ubertin Donato
    That his wife's father should make him their kin.[38]   120
Already had Caponsacco to the Market
    From Fesole descended[39] and already
    Giuda and Infangato[40] were good burghers.
I'll tell a thing incredible, but true;
    One entered the small circuit by a gate   125
    Which from the Della Pera took its name![41]
Each one that bears the beautiful escutcheon
    Of the great baron whose renown and name
    The festival of Thomas keepeth fresh,[42]
Knighthood and privilege from him received;   130
    Though with the populace unites himself
    To-day the man who binds it with a border.[43]
Already were Gualterotti and Importuni;
    And still more quiet would the Borgo be[44]
    If with new neighbors[45] it remained unfed.   135
The house from which is born your lamentation,[46]
    Through just disdain that death among you brought
    And put an end unto your joyous life,
Was honored in itself and its companions.

O Buondelmonte, how in evil hour   140
    Thou fled'st the bridal at another's promptings!
Many would be rejoicing who are sad,
    If God had thee surrendered to the Ema[47]
    The first time that thou camest to the city.
But it behoved the mutilated stone   145
    Which guards the bridge, that Florence should provide
    A victim in her latest hour of peace.[48]
With all these families, and others with them,
    Florence beheld I in so great repose, .
    That no occasion had she whence to weep;   150
With all these families beheld so just
    And glorious her people, that the lily
    Never upon the spear was placed reversed,[49]
Nor by division was vermilion made."[50]

CANTO XVII

As came to Clymene, to be made certain
  Of that which he had heard against himself,
  He who makes fathers chary* still to children,¹
Even such was I, and such was I perceived
  By Beatrice and by the holy light   5
  That first on my account had changed its place.²
Therefore my Lady said to me: "Send forth
  The flame of thy desire, so that it issue
  Imprinted well with the internal stamp;
Not that our knowledge may be greater made   10
  By speech of thine, but to accustom thee
  To tell thy thirst, that we may give thee drink."³
"O my beloved tree,⁴ (that so dost lift thee,
  That even as minds terrestrial perceive
  No triangle containeth two obtuse,   15
So thou beholdest the contingent things
  Ere in themselves they are, fixing thine eyes
  Upon the point in which all times are present,)⁵
While I was with Virgilius conjoined
  Upon the mountain that the souls doth heal,   20
  And when descending into the dead world,
Were spoken to me of my future life
  Some grievous words,⁶ although I feel myself
  In sooth foursquare against the blows of chance.⁷
On this account my wish would be content   25
  To hear what fortune is approaching me,

*Wary.

Because foreseen an arrow comes more slowly."[8]
Thus did I say unto that selfsame light[9]
    That unto me had spoken before; and even
    As Beatrice willed was my own will confessed.   30
Not in vague phrase, in which the foolish folk
    Ensnared themselves of old, ere yet was slain
    The Lamb of God[10] who taketh sins away,
But with clear words and unambiguous
    Language responded that paternal love,   35
    Hid and revealed by its own proper smile:
"Contingency, that outside of the volume
    Of your materiality extends not,
    Is all depicted in the eternal aspect.
Necessity however thence it takes not,   40
    Except as from the eye, in which 'tis mirrored,
    A ship that with the current down descends.[11]
From thence, e'en* as there cometh to the ear
    Sweet harmony from an organ, comes in sight
    To me the time that is preparing for thee.   45
As forth from Athens went Hippolytus,
    By reason of his step-dame false and cruel,
    So thou from Florence must perforce depart.[12]
Already this is willed, and this is sought for;
    And soon it shall be done by him who thinks it,   50
    Where every day the Christ is bought and sold.[13]
The blame shall follow the offended party
    In outcry as is usual; but the vengeance
    Shall witness to the truth[14] that doth dispense it.
Thou shalt abandon everything beloved   55
    Most tenderly, and this the arrow is
    Which first the bow of banishment shoots forth.
Thou shalt have proof how savoreth of salt
    The bread of others, and how hard a road
    The going down and up another's stairs.[15]   60
And that which most shall weigh upon thy shoulders

*Even.

Will be the bad and foolish company[16]
    With which into this valley thou shalt fall;
For all ingrate, all mad and impious
    Will they become against thee; but soon after   65
    They, and not thou, shall have the forehead scarlet.[17]
Of their bestiality their own proceedings
    Shall furnish proof; so 'twill be well for thee
    A party to have made thee by thyself.
Thine earliest refuge and thine earliest inn   70
    Shall be the mighty Lombard's courtesy,
    Who on the Ladder bears the holy bird,[18]
Who such benign regard shall have for thee
    That 'twixt you twain, in doing and in asking,
    That shall be first which is with others last.[19]   75
Him shalt thou see, him who was so impressed
    At his nativity by this strong star,
    That wonderful shall his achievements be.
Not yet the people are aware of him
    Through his young age, since only nine years yet[20]   80
    Around about him have these wheels revolved.
But ere the Gascon cheat the noble Henry,[21]
    Some sparkles of his virtue shall appear
    In caring not for silver nor for toil.[22]
So recognized shall his magnificence   85
    Become hereafter, that his enemies
    Will not have power to keep mute tongues about it.
On him rely, and on his benefits;
    By him shall many people be transformed,
    Changing condition rich and mendicant;[23]   90
And written in thy mind thou hence shalt bear
    Of him, but shalt not say it"—and things he said
    Incredible to those who shall be present.
Then added: "Son, these are the commentaries[24]
    On what was said to thee; behold the snares   95
    That are concealed behind few revolutions;[25]
Yet would I not thy neighbors thou shouldst envy,[26]
    Because thy life into the future reaches

Beyond the punishment of their perfidies."
When by its silence showed that sainted soul   100
 That it had finished putting in the woof
 Into that web which I had given it warped,[27]
Began I, even as he who yearneth after,
 Being in doubt, some counsel from a person
 Who seeth, and uprightly wills, and loves: 105
"Well see I, father mine, how spurreth on
 The time towards me such a blow to deal me
 As heaviest is to him who most gives way.
Therefore with foresight it is well I arm me,
 That, if the dearest place[28] be taken from me,   110
 I may not lose the others[29] by my songs.
Down through the world of infinite bitterness,[30]
 And o'er the mountain,[31] from whose beauteous summit
 The eyes of my own Lady lifted me,
And afterward through heaven from light to light,   115
 I have learned that which, if I tell again,
 Will be a savor of strong herbs[32] to many.
And if I am a timid friend to truth,
 I fear lest I may lose my life with those
 Who will hereafter call this time the olden."[33]   120
The light in which was smiling my own treasure
 Which there I had discovered, flashed at first[34]
 As in the sunshine doth a golden mirror;
Then made reply: "A conscience overcast
 Or with its own or with another's shame,   125
 Will taste forsooth the tartness of thy word;
But ne'ertheless, all falsehood laid aside,
 Make manifest thy vision utterly,
 And let them scratch wherever is the itch;[35]
For if thine utterance shall offensive be   130
 At the first taste, a vital nutriment
 'Twill leave thereafter, when it is digested.
This cry of thine shall do as doth the wind,
 Which smiteth most the most exalted summits,
 And that is no slight argument of honor.[36]   135

Therefore are shown to thee within these wheels,
  Upon the mount and in the dolorous valley,
  Only the souls that unto fame are known;[37]
Because the spirit of the hearer rests not,
  Nor doth confirm its faith by an example   140
  Which has the root of it unknown and hidden,
Or other reason that is not apparent."[38]

CANTO XVIII

Now was alone rejoicing in its word
    That soul beatified,[1] and I was tasting
    My own, the bitter tempering with the sweet,[2]
And the Lady who to God was leading me
    Said: "Change the thought; consider that I am   5
    Near unto Him[3] who every wrong disburdens."
Unto the loving accents of my comfort
    I turned me round, and then what love I saw
    Within those holy eyes I here relinquish;
Not only that my language I distrust,   10
    But that my mind cannot return so far
    Above itself, unless another[4] guide it.
Thus much upon that point can I repeat,
    That, her again beholding, my affection
    From every other longing was released.   15
While the eternal pleasure, which direct
    Rayed upon Beatrice, from her fair face
    Contented me with its reflected aspect,
Conquering me with the radiance of a smile,
    She said to me, "Turn thee about and listen;   20
    Not in mine eyes alone is Paradise."[5]
Even as sometimes here do we behold
    The affection in the look, if it be such
    That all the soul is rapt away by it,
So, by the flaming of the effulgence holy   25
    To which I turned, I recognized therein
    The wish of speaking to me somewhat farther.
And it began: "In this fifth resting-place

Upon the tree that liveth by its top,
    And aye bears fruit, and never loseth leaf,[6]   30
Are blessed spirits that below, ere yet
    They came to Heaven, were of such great renown
    That every Muse therewith would affluent be.
Therefore look thou upon the cross's horns;[7]
    He whom I now shall name will there enact   35
    What doth within a cloud its own swift fire."[8]
I saw athwart the Cross a splendor drawn
    By naming Joshua,[9] even as he did it,
    Nor noted I the word before the deed;
And at the name of the great Maccabee[10]   40
    I saw another move itself revolving,
    And gladness was the whip unto that top.
Likewise for Charlemagne and for Orlando,[11]
    Two of them my regard attentive followed
    As followeth the eye its falcon flying.   45
Guglielmo[12] afterward, and Renouard,[13]
    And the Duke Godfrey,[14] did attract my sight
    Along upon that Cross, and Robert Guiscard.[15]
Then, moved and mingled with the other lights,[16]
    The soul that had addressed me showed how great   50
    An artist 'twas among the heavenly singers.
To my right side I turned myself around,
    My duty to behold in Beatrice
    Either by words or gesture signified;
And so translucent I beheld her eyes,   55
    So full of pleasure, that her countenance
    Surpassed its other and its latest wont.
And as, by feeling greater delectation,
    A man in doing good from day to day
    Becomes aware his virtue is increasing,   60
So I became aware that my gyration
    With heaven together had increased its arc,[17]
    That miracle[18] beholding more adorned.
And such as is the change, in little lapse
    Of time, in a pale woman, when her face   65

Canto XVIII: The Blessed Souls circling to form Letters

Is from the load of bashfulness unladen,[19]
Such was it in mine eyes, when I had turned,
    Caused by the whiteness of the temperate star,[20]
    The sixth, which to itself had gathered me.
Within that Jovial torch[21] did I behold   70
    The sparkling of the love which was therein
    Delineate our language to mine eyes.[22]
And even as birds uprisen from the shore,
    As in congratulation o'er their food,
    Make squadrons of themselves, now round, now long,   75
So from within those lights the holy creatures
    Sang flying to and fro, and in their figures
    Made of themselves now D, now I, now L.[23]
First singing they to their own music moved;
    Then one becoming of these characters,   80
    A little while they rested and were silent.
O divine Pegasea,[24] thou who genius
    Dost glorious make, and render it long-lived,
    And this through thee the cities and the kingdoms,
Illume me with thyself, that I may bring   85
    Their figures out as I have them conceived!
    Apparent be thy power in these brief verses!
Themselves then they displayed in five times seven
    Vowels and consonants; and I observed
    The parts as they seemed spoken unto me.   90
Diligite justitiam, these were
    First verb and noun of all that was depicted;
    Qui judicatis terram[25] were the last.
Thereafter in the M of the fifth word[26]
    Remained they so arranged, that Jupiter   95
    Seemed to be silver there with gold inlaid.
And other lights I saw descend where was
    The summit of the M, and pause there singing
    The good, I think, that draws them to itself.
Then, as in striking upon burning logs   100
    Upward there fly innumerable sparks,[27]
    Whence fools are wont to look for auguries,

More than a thousand lights seemed thence to rise,
　　　And to ascend, some more, and others less,
　　　Even as the Sun that lights them had allotted;　　　　　105
And, each one being quiet in its place,
　　　The head and neck beheld I of an eagle
　　　Delineated by that inlaid fire.
He who there paints has none to be his guide;
　　　But Himself guides; and is from Him remembered　　　110
　　　That virtue which is form unto the nest.
The other beatitude, that contented seemed
　　　At first to bloom a lily on the M,[28]
　　　By a slight motion followed out the imprint.
O gentle star![29] what and how many gems　　　　　115
　　　Did demonstrate to me, that all our justice
　　　Effect is of that heaven which thou ingemmest!
Wherefore I pray the Mind, in which begin
　　　Thy motion and thy virtue, to regard
　　　Whence comes the smoke that vitiates thy rays;[30]　　　120
So that a second time it now be wroth
　　　With buying and with selling in the temple[31]
　　　Whose walls were built with signs and martyrdoms![32]
O soldiery of heaven, whom I contemplate,
　　　Implore for those who are upon the earth　　　　　125
　　　All gone astray after the bad example!
Once 'twas the custom to make war with swords;
　　　But now 'tis made by taking here and there
　　　The bread the pitying Father shuts from none.[33]
Yet thou, who writest but to cancel,[34] think　　　　　130
　　　That Peter and that Paul, who for this vineyard[35]
　　　Which thou art spoiling died, are still alive!
Well canst thou say: "So steadfast my desire
　　　Is unto him who willed to live alone,
　　　And for a dance was led to martyrdom,　　　　　135
That I know not the Fisherman nor Paul."[36]

Canto XIX: The Blessed Souls forming an Eagle in the Sky

CANTO XIX

$\mathcal{A}$PPEARED before me with its wings outspread
    The beautiful image[1] that in sweet fruition
    Made jubilant the interwoven souls;
Appeared a little ruby each, wherein
    Ray of the sun was burning so enkindled   5
    That each into mine eyes refracted it.
And what it now behoves me to retrace
    Nor voice has e'er reported, nor ink written,
    Nor was by fantasy e'er comprehended;
For speak I saw, and likewise heard, the beak,   10
    And utter with its voice both *I* and *My*,
    When in conception it was *We* and *Our*.[2]
And it began: "Being just and merciful[3]
    Am I exalted here unto that glory
    Which cannot be exceeded by desire;   15
And upon earth I left my memory
    Such, that the evil-minded people there
    Commend it, but continue not the story."
So doth a single heat from many embers
    Make itself felt, even as from many loves   20
    Issued a single sound[4] from out that image.
Whence I thereafter: "O perpetual flowers
    Of the eternal joy, that only one
    Make me perceive your odors manifold,
Exhaling, break within me the great fast   25
    Which a long season has in hunger held me,
    Not finding for it any food on earth.[5]
Well do I know, that if in heaven its mirror

Justice Divine another realm doth make,
    Yours apprehends it not through any veil.   30
You know how I attentively address me
    To listen; and you know what is the doubt[6]
    That is in me so very old a fast."
Even as a falcon, issuing from his hood,[7]
    Doth move his head, and with his wings applaud him,   35
    Showing desire, and making himself fine,
Saw I become that standard, which of lauds
    Was interwoven of the grace divine,
    With such songs[8] as he knows who there rejoices.
Then it began: "He who a compass turned[9]   40
    On the world's outer verge, and who within it
    Devised so much occult and manifest,
Could not the impress of his power so make
    On all the universe, as that his Word
    Should not remain in infinite excess.   45
And this makes certain that the first proud being,[10]
    Who was the paragon of every creature,
    By not awaiting light fell immature.
And hence appears it, that each minor nature
    Is scant receptacle unto that good   50
    Which has no end, and by itself is measured
In consequence our vision, which perforce
    Must be some ray of that intelligence
    With which all things whatever are replete,
Cannot in its own nature be so potent,   55
    That it shall not its origin discern
    Far beyond that which is apparent to it.[11]
Therefore into the justice sempiternal
    The power of vision that your world receives;
    As eye into the ocean, penetrates;   60
Which, though it see the bottom near the shore;
    Upon the deep perceives it not, and yet
    'Tis there, but it is hidden by the depth.
There is no light but comes from the serene
    That never is o'ercast,[12] nay, it is darkness   65

Or shadow of the flesh, or else its poison.
Amply to thee is opened now the cavern[13]
   Which has concealed from thee the living justice
   Of which thou mad'st such frequent questioning.
For saidst thou: 'Born a man is on the shore   70
   Of Indus, and is none who there can speak
   Of Christ,[14] nor who can read, nor who can write;
And all his inclinations and his actions
   Are good, so far as human reason sees,
   Without a sin in life or in discourse: 75
He dieth unbaptized and without faith;
   Where is this justice that condemneth him?
   Where is his fault, if he do not believe?'
Now who art thou, that on the bench wouldst sit
   In judgment at a thousand miles away,   80
   With the short vision of a single span?[15]
Truly to him who with me subtilizes,
   If so the Scripture were not over you,[16]
   For doubting there were marvellous occasion.
O animals terrene,* O stolid minds,   85
   The primal will, that in itself is good,
   Ne'er from itself, the Good Supreme, has moved.
So much is just as is accordant with it;
   No good created draws it to itself,
   But it, by raying forth, occasions that."   90
Even as above her nest goes circling round
   The stork when she has fed her little ones,
   And he who has been fed looks up at her,
So lifted I my brows, and even such
   Became the blessed image,[17] which its wings   95
   Was moving, by so many counsels urged.
Circling around it sang, and said: "As are
   My notes to thee, who dost not comprehend them,
   Such is the eternal judgment to you mortals."[18]
Those lucent splendors of the Holy Spirit   100

---

*Earthly; terrestrial.

Grew quiet then, but still within the standard[19]
    That made the Romans reverend to the world.
It recommenced: "Unto this kingdom never
    Ascended one who had not faith in Christ,[20]
    Before or since he to the tree was nailed.   105
But look thou, many crying are, 'Christ, Christ!'
    Who at the judgment shall be far less near
    To him than some shall be who knew not Christ.
Such Christians shall the Ethiop condemn,
    When the two companies shall be divided,   110
    The one forever rich, the other poor.[21]
What to your kings may not the Persians[22] say,
    When they that volume opened[23] shall behold
    In which are written down all their dispraises?
There shall be seen, among the deeds of Albert,[24]   115
    That which erelong shall set the pen in motion,
    For which the realm of Prague shall be deserted.
There shall be seen the woe that on the Seine
    He brings by falsifying of the coin,
    Who by the blow of a wild boar shall die.[25]   120
There shall be seen the pride that causes thirst,
    Which makes the Scot and Englishman so mad[26]
    That they within their boundaries cannot rest;
Be seen the luxury and effeminate life
    Of him of Spain,[27] and the Bohemian,[28]   125
    Who valor never knew and never wished;
Be seen the Cripple of Jerusalem,
    His goodness represented by an I,
    While the reverse an M shall represent;[29]
Be seen the avarice and poltroonery   130
    Of him who guards the Island of the Fire,
    Wherein Anchises finished his long life;
And to declare how pitiful he is
    Shall be his record in contracted letters
    Which shall make note of much in little space.[30]   135
And shall appear to each one the foul deeds
    Of uncle and of brother[31] who a nation

So famous have dishonored, and two crowns.[32]
And he of Portugal[33] and he of Norway[34]
    Shall there be known, and he of Rascia too,   140
    Who saw in evil hour the coin of Venice.[35]
O happy Hungary,[36] if she let herself
    Be wronged no farther! and Navarre the happy,
    If with the hills that gird her she be armed![37]
And each one may believe that now, as hansel*   145
    Thereof, do Nicosìa and Famagosta
    Lament and rage because of their own beast,
Who from the others' flank departeth not."[38]

---

*Also spelled "handsel." First example of anything, giving an indication of what is to follow.

CANTO XX

WHEN he who all the world illuminates[1]
    Out of our hemisphere so far descends
    That on all sides the daylight is consumed,
The heaven, that erst* by him alone was kindled,[2]
    Doth suddenly reveal itself again   5
    By many lights, wherein is one resplendent.
And came into my mind this act of heaven,
    When the ensign of the world and of its leaders
    Had silent in the blessed beak become;
Because those living luminaries all,   10
    By far more luminous, did songs begin[3]
    Lapsing and falling from my memory.
O gentle Love,[4] that with a smile dost cloak thee,
    How ardent in those sparks didst thou appear,
    That had the breath alone of holy thoughts!   15
After the precious and pellucid crystals,
    With which begemmed the sixth light[5] I beheld,
    Silence imposed on the angelic bells,
I seemed to hear the murmuring of a river[6]
    That clear descendeth down from rock to rock,   20
    Showing the affluence of its mountain-top.
And as the sound upon the cithern's neck[7]
    Taketh its form, and as upon the vent
    Of rustic pipe the wind that enters it,
Even thus, relieved from the delay of waiting,   25
    That murmuring of the eagle mounted up

*First.

Along its neck, as if it had been hollow.
There it became a voice, and issued thence
 From out its beak, in such a form of words
 As the heart waited for wherein I wrote them.[8]   30
"The part in me which sees and bears the sun[9]
 In mortal eagles," it began to me,
 "Now fixedly must needs be looked upon;
For of the fires of which I make my figure,
 Those whence the eye doth sparkle in my head   35
 Of all their orders the supremest are.[10]
He who is shining in the midst as pupil
 Was once the singer of the Holy Spirit,
 Who bore the ark from city unto city;[11]
Now knoweth he the merit of his song,   40
 In so far as effect of his own counsel,
 By the reward which is commensurate.
Of five, that make a circle for my brow,
 He that approacheth nearest to my beak
 Did the poor widow for her son console;[12]   45
Now knoweth he how dearly it doth cost
 Not following Christ, by the experience
 Of this sweet life and of its opposite.
He who comes next in the circumference
 Of which I speak, upon its highest arc,   50
 Did death postpone by penitence sincere;
Now knoweth he that the eternal judgment
 Suffers no change, albeit worthy prayer
 Maketh below to-morrow of to-day.[13]
The next who follows, with the laws and me,   55
 Under the good intent that bore bad fruit
 Became a Greek by ceding to the pastor;[14]
Now knoweth he how all the ill deduced
 From his good action is not harmful to him,
 Although the world thereby may be destroyed.[15]   60
And he whom in the downward arc thou seest
 Guglielmo was, whom the same land deplores
 That weepeth Charles and Frederick[16] yet alive;

Now knoweth he how heaven enamored is
    With a just king; and in the outward show 65
    Of his effulgence he reveals it still.
Who would believe, down in the errant world,
    That e'er the Trojan Ripheus[17] in this round
    Could be the fifth one of the holy lights?
Now knoweth he enough of what the world 70
    Has not the power to see of grace divine,
    Although his sight may not discern the bottom."
Like as a lark that in the air expatiates,
    First singing and then silent with content
    Of the last sweetness that doth satisfy her, 75
Such seemed to me the image of the imprint
    Of the eternal pleasure,[18] by whose will
    Doth everything become the thing it is.
And notwithstanding to my doubt I was
    As glass is to the color that invests it,[19] 80
    To wait the time in silence it endured not,
But forth from out my mouth, "What things are these?"
    Extorted with the force of its own weight;
    Whereat I saw great joy of coruscation.*[20]
Thereafterward with eye still more enkindled 85
    The blessed standard[21] made to me reply,
    To keep me not in wonderment suspended:
"I see that thou believest in these things
    Because I say them, but thou seest not how;
    So that, although believed in, they are hidden. 90
Thou doest as he doth who a thing by name
    Well apprehendeth, but its quiddity[22]
    Cannot perceive, unless another show it.
Regnum cælorum suffereth violence[23]
    From fervent love, and from that living hope 95
    That overcometh the Divine volition;
Not in the guise that man o'ercometh man,
    But conquers it because it will be conquered,

*Flash, gleam, or ray of light.

And conquered conquers by benignity.

The first life of the eyebrow and the fifth[24]   100

      Cause thee astonishment, because with them

      Thou seest the region of the angels painted.

They passed not from their bodies, as thou thinkest,

      Gentiles, but Christians in the steadfast faith

      Of feet that were to suffer and had suffered.[25]   105

For one from Hell, where no one e'er turns back

      Unto good will, returned unto his bones,

      And that of living hope was the reward,—

Of living hope, that placed its efficacy

      In prayers to God made to resuscitate him,   110

      So that 'twere possible to move his will.

The glorious soul concerning which I speak,

      Returning to the flesh, where brief its stay,

      Believed in Him who had the power to aid it;

And, in believing, kindled to such fire   115

      Of genuine love, that at the second death[26]

      Worthy it was to come unto this joy.

The other one, through grace, that from so deep

      A fountain wells that never hath the eye

      Of any creature reached its primal wave,   120

Set all his love below on righteousness;

      Wherefore from grace to grace did God unclose

      His eye to our redemption yet to be,

Whence he believed therein, and suffered not

      From that day forth the stench of paganism,   125

      And he reproved therefor the folk perverse.[27]

Those Maidens three, whom at the right-hand wheel

      Thou didst behold, were unto him for baptism

      More than a thousand years before baptizing.[28]

O thou predestination, how remote   130

      Thy root is from the aspect of all those

      Who the First Cause do not behold entire![29]

And you, O mortals! hold yourselves restrained[30]

      In judging; for ourselves, who look on God,

      We do not know as yet all the elect;   135

And sweet to us is such a deprivation,
>Because our good in this good is made perfect,
>That whatsoe'er God wills, we also will."[31]
After this manner by that shape divine,
>To make clear in me my short-sightedness,   140
>Was given to me a pleasant medicine;
And as good singer a good lutanist
>Accompanies with vibrations of the chords,
>Whereby more pleasantness the song acquires,
So, while it spake, do I remember me   145
>That I beheld both of those blessed lights,[32]
>Even as the winking of the eyes concords,
Moving unto the words their little flames.

CANTO XXI

ALREADY on my Lady's face mine eyes
    Again were fastened, and with these my mind,
    And from all other purpose was withdrawn;
And she smiled not; but "If I were to smile,"
    She unto me began, "thou wouldst become   5
    Like Semele, when she was turned to ashes.[1]
Because my beauty, that along the stairs
    Of the eternal palace[2] more enkindles,
    As thou hast seen, the farther we ascend,
If it were tempered not, is so resplendent   10
    That all thy mortal power in its effulgence
    Would seem a leaflet that the thunder crushes.
We are uplifted to the seventh splendor,
    That underneath the burning Lion's breast[3]
    Now radiates downward mingled with his power.   15
Fix in direction of thine eyes the mind,
    And make of them a mirror for the figure
    That in this mirror[4] shall appear to thee."
He who could know what was the pasturage
    My sight had in that blessed countenance,   20
    When I transferred me to another care,
Would recognize how grateful was to me
    Obedience unto my celestial escort,
    By counterpoising one side with the other.[5]
Within the crystal which, around the world   25
    Revolving, bears the name of its dear leader,
    Under whom every wickedness lay dead,[6]

Colored like gold, on which the sunshine gleams,
    A stairway I beheld to such a height
    Uplifted, that mine eye pursued it not.   30
Likewise beheld I down the steps descending
    So many splendors,[7] that I thought each light
    That in the heaven appears was there diffused.
And as accordant with their natural custom
    The rooks together at the break of day   35
    Bestir themselves to warm their feathers cold;
Then some of them fly off without return,
    Others come back to where they started from,
    And others, wheeling round, still keep at home;
Such fashion[8] it appeared to me was there   40
    Within the sparkling that together came,
    As soon as on a certain step it struck,
And that which nearest unto us remained
    Became so clear, that in my thought I said,
    "Well I perceive the love thou showest me;   45
But she, from whom I wait the how and when
    Of speech and silence, standeth still; whence I
    Against desire do well if I ask not."
She thereupon, who saw my silentness
    In the sight of Him who seeth everything,[9]   50
    Said unto me, "Let loose thy warm desire."
And I began: "No merit of my own
    Renders me worthy of response from thee;
    But for her sake who granteth me the asking,
Thou blessed life that dost remain concealed   55
    In thy beatitude, make known to me
    The cause which draweth thee so near my side;
And tell me why is silent in this wheel
    The dulcet symphony of Paradise,[10]
    That through the rest below sounds so devoutly."   60
"Thou hast thy hearing mortal as thy sight,"[11]
    It answer made to me; "they sing not here,
    For the same cause that Beatrice has not smiled.
Thus far adown the holy stairway's steps

Canto XXI: The Angels descending the Heavenly Ladder

Have I descended but to give thee welcome   65
    With words, and with the light that mantles me;
Nor did more love cause me to be more ready,[12]
    For love as much and more up there is burning,
    As doth the flaming manifest to thee.
But the high charity,[13] that makes us servants   70
    Prompt to the counsel which controls the world,
    Allotteth here, even as thou dost observe."
"I see full well," said I, "O sacred lamp!
    How love unfettered in this court sufficeth
    To follow the eternal Providence;   75
But this is what seems hard for me to see,
    Wherefore predestinate wast thou alone
    Unto this office from among thy consorts."[14]
No sooner had I come to the last word,
    Than of its middle made the light a centre,   80
    Whirling itself about[15] like a swift millstone.
Then answer made the love that was therein:
    "On me directed is a light divine,
    Piercing through this in which I am embosomed,[16]
Of which the virtue with my sight conjoined   85
    Lifts me above myself so far, I see
    The supreme essence from which this is drawn
Hence comes the joyfulness with which I flame,
    For to my sight, as far as it is clear,
    The clearness of the flame I equal make.[17]   90
But that soul in the heaven which is most pure,
    That Seraph which his eye on God most fixes,
    Could this demand of thine not satisfy;[18]
Because so deeply sinks in the abyss
    Of the eternal statute[19] what thou askest,   95
    From all created sight it is cut off.
And to the mortal world, when thou returnest,
    This carry back, that it may not presume
    Longer tow'rd such a goal to move its feet.
The mind, that shineth here, on earth doth smoke;   100
    From this observe how can it do below

That which it cannot though the heaven assume it?"
Such limit did its words prescribe to me,
        The question I relinquished, and restricted
        Myself to ask it humbly who it was.[20]   105
"Between two shores of Italy[21] rise cliffs,
        And not far distant from thy native place,
        So high, the thunders far below them sound,
And form a ridge that Catria[22] is called,
        'Neath which is consecrate a hermitage[23]   110
        Wont to be dedicate to worship only."
Thus unto me the third speech[24] recommenced,
        And then, continuing, it said: "Therein
        Unto God's service I became so steadfast,
That feeding only on the juice of olives   115
        Lightly I passed away the heats and frosts,
        Contented in my thoughts contemplative.
That cloister used to render to these heavens
        Abundantly, and now is empty grown,
        So that perforce it soon must be revealed.[25] 120
I in that place was Peter Damiano;
        And Peter the Sinner was I[26] in the house
        Of Our Lady on the Adriatic shore.
Little of mortal life remained to me,
        When I was called and dragged forth to the hat 125
        Which shifteth evermore from bad to worse[27]
Came Cephas, and the mighty Vessel[28] came
        Of the Holy Spirit, meagre and barefooted,
        Taking the food of any hostelry.
Now some one to support them on each side[29]   130
        The modern shepherds need, and some to lead them,
        So heavy are they, and to hold their trains.
They cover up their palfreys with their cloaks,
        So that two beasts[30] go underneath one skin;
        O Patience, that dost tolerate so much!"   135
At this voice saw I many little flames
        From step to step descending and revolving
        And every revolution made them fairer.

Round about this one came they and stood still
    And a cry uttered of so loud a sound,[31]   140
    It here could find no parallel, nor I
Distinguished it, the thunder so o'ercame me.

CANTO XXII

O<small>PPRESSED</small> with stupor,[1] I unto my guide
    Turned like a little child who always runs
    For refuge there where he confideth most;
And she, even as a mother who straightway
    Gives comfort to her pale and breathless boy   5
    With voice whose wont it is to reassure him,
Said to me: "Knowest thou not thou art in heaven,
    And knowest thou not that heaven is holy all,
    And what is done here cometh from good zeal?
After what wise the singing would have changed thee   10
    And I by smiling, thou canst now imagine,
    Since that the cry has startled thee so much,[2]
In which if thou hadst understood its prayers
    Already would be known to thee the vengeance
    Which thou shalt look upon before thou diest.[3]   15
The sword above here smiteth not in haste
    Nor tardily,[4] howe'er it seem to him
    Who fearing or desiring waits for it.
But turn thee round towards the others now,
    For very illustrious spirits shalt thou see,   20
    If thou thy sight directest as I say."
As it seemed good to her mine eyes I turned,
    And saw a hundred spherules[5] that together
    With mutual rays each other more embellished.
I stood as one who in himself represses   25
    The point of his desire, and ventures not
    To question, he so feareth the too much.
And now the largest and most luculent[6]

Among those pearls came forward, that it might
Make my desire concerning it content. 30
Within it then I heard: "If thou couldst see
Even as myself the charity that burns
Among us, thy conceits would be expressed;
But, that by waiting thou mayst not come late
To the high end, I will make answer even 35
Unto the thought of which thou art so chary.
That mountain on whose slope Cassino stands
Was frequented of old upon its summit
By a deluded folk and ill-disposed;
And I am he who first up thither bore 40
The name of Him who brought upon the earth
The truth that so much sublimateth us.
And such abundant grace upon me shone
That all the neighboring towns I drew away
From the impious worship[7] that seduced the world. 45
These other fires, each one of them, were men
Contemplative, enkindled by that heat
Which maketh holy flowers and fruits spring up.
Here is Macarius, here is Romualdus,[8]
Here are my brethren, who within the cloisters 50
Their footsteps stayed and kept a steadfast heart."
And I to him: "The affection which thou showest
Speaking with me, and the good countenance
Which I behold and note in all your ardors,
In me have so my confidence dilated 55
As the sun doth the rose, when it becomes
As far unfolded as it hath the power.
Therefore I pray, and thou assure me, father,
If I may so much grace receive, that I
May thee behold with countenance unveiled."[9] 60
He thereupon: "Brother,[10] thy high desire
In the remotest sphere shall be fulfilled,
Where are fulfilled all others and my own.
There perfect is, and ripened, and complete,
Every desire; within that one alone 65

Is every part where it has always been;
For it is not in space, nor turns on poles,[11]
    And unto it our stairway[12] reaches up,
    Whence thus from out thy sight it steals away.
Up to that height the Patriarch Jacob saw it   70
    Extending its supernal* part, what time
    So thronged with angels it appeared to him.
But to ascend it now no one uplifts
    His feet from off the earth, and now my Rule
    Below remaineth for mere waste of paper.[13]   75
The walls that used of old to be an Abbey
    Are changed to dens of robbers, and the cowls
    Are sacks filled full of miserable flour.
But heavy usury is not taken up
    So much against God's pleasure as that fruit   80
    Which maketh so insane the heart of monks;
For whatsoever hath the Church in keeping
    Is for the folk that ask it in God's name,
    Not for one's kindred or for something worse.[14]
The flesh of mortals is so very soft,   85
    That good beginnings down below suffice not
    From springing of the oak to bearing acorns.[15]
Peter began with neither gold nor silver,
    And I with orison and abstinence,
    And Francis with humility his convent.   90
And if thou lookest at each one's beginning,
    And then regardest whither he has run,
    Thou shalt behold the white changed into brown.[16]
In verity the Jordan backward turned,
    And the sea's fleeing, when God willed, were more   95
    A wonder to behold, than succor here."[17]
Thus unto me he said; and then withdrew
    To his own band,[18] and the band closed together;
    Then like a whirlwind all was upward rapt.
The gentle Lady urged me on behind them   100

*Eternal.

Up o'er that stairway by a single sign,
    So did her virtue overcome my nature;[19]
Nor here below,[20] where one goes up and down
    By natural law, was motion e'er so swift
    That it could be compared unto my wing.[21]   105
Reader,[22] as I may unto that devout
    Triumph return, on whose account I often
    For my transgressions weep and beat my breast,—
Thou hadst not thrust thy finger in the fire
    And drawn it out again, before I saw   110
    The sign that follows Taurus,[23] and was in it.
O glorious stars, O light impregnated
    With mighty virtue, from which I acknowledge
    All of my genius, whatsoe'er it be,
With you was born,[24] and hid himself with you,   115
    He who is father of all mortal life,
    When first I tasted of the Tuscan air;
And then when grace was freely given to me
    To enter the high wheel which turns you round,
    Your region was allotted unto me.   120
To you devoutly at this hour my soul
    Is sighing, that it virtue may acquire
    For the stern pass that draws it to itself.
"Thou art so near unto the last salvation,"
    Thus Beatrice began, "thou oughtest now   125
    To have thine eyes unclouded and acute;
And therefore, ere thou enter farther in,
    Look down once more, and see how vast a world
    Thou hast already put beneath thy feet;
So that thy heart, as jocund as it may,   130
    Present itself to the triumphant throng
    That comes rejoicing through this rounded ether."
I with my sight returned through one and all
    The sevenfold spheres, and I beheld this globe
    Such that I smiled at its ignoble semblance;[25]   135
And that opinion I approve as best
    Which doth account it least;[26] and he who thinks

Of something else may truly be called just.
I saw the daughter of Latona shining
    Without that shadow,[27] which to me was cause   140
    That once I had believed her rare and dense.
The aspect of thy son, Hyperion,[28]
    Here I sustained, and saw how move themselves
    Around and near him Maia and Dione.[29]
Thence there appeared the temperateness of Jove   145
    'Twixt son and father,[30] and to me was clear
    The change that of their whereabout they make;
And all the seven[31] made manifest to me
    How great they are, and eke* how swift they are,
    And how they are in distant habitations.   150
The threshing-floor that maketh us so proud,[32]
    To me revolving with the eternal Twins,[33]
    Was all apparent made from hill to harbor!
Then to the beauteous eyes[34] mine eyes I turned.

*Also; likewise.

CANTO XXIII

E VEN as a bird,[1] 'mid the beloved leaves,
 Quiet upon the nest of her sweet brood
 Throughout the night, that hideth all things from us,
Who, that she may behold their longed-for looks
 And find the food wherewith to nourish them,   5
 In which, to her, grave labors grateful are,
Anticipates the time on open spray
 And with an ardent longing waits the sun,
 Gazing intent as soon as breaks the dawn:
Even thus my Lady standing was, erect   10
 And vigilant, turned round towards the zone
 Underneath which the sun displays less haste;[2]
So that beholding her suspense and wistful,
 Such I became as he is who desiring
 For something yearns, and hoping is appeased.   15
But brief the space from one When[3] to the other;
 Of my awaiting, say I, and the seeing
 The welkin* grow resplendent more and more.
And Beatrice exclaimed: "Behold the hosts
 Of Christ's triumphal march, and all the fruit   20
 Harvested by the rolling of these spheres!"[4]
It seemed to me her face was all aflame;
 And eyes she had so full of ecstasy
 That I must needs pass on without describing.
As when in nights serene of the full moon   25
 Smiles Trivia among the nymphs eternal[5]

*Curved vault of the sky; upper air.

Who paint the firmament through all its gulfs,
Saw I, above the myriads of lamps,
  A Sun that one and all of them enkindled,[6]
  E'en as our own doth the supernal sights,   30
And through the living light transparent shone
  The lucent substance[7] so intensely clear
  Into my sight, that I sustained it not.[8]
O Beatrice, thou gentle guide and dear!
  To me she said: "What overmasters thee   35
  A virtue is from which naught shields itself.
There are the wisdom and the omnipotence[9]
  That oped* the thoroughfares 'twixt heaven and earth,[10]
  For which there erst† had been so long a yearning."
As fire from out a cloud unlocks itself,   40
  Dilating so it finds not room therein,
  And down, against its nature, falls to earth,[11]
So did my mind, among those aliments
  Becoming larger, issue from itself,
  And that which it became cannot remember.[12]   45
"Open thine eyes, and look at what I am:[13]
  Thou hast beheld such things, that strong enough
  Hast thou become to tolerate my smile."
I was as one who still retains the feeling
  Of a forgotten vision, and endeavors   50
  In vain to bring it back into his mind,
When I this invitation heard, deserving
  Of so much gratitude, it never fades
  Out of the book that chronicles the past.[14]
If at this moment sounded all the tongues   55
  That Polyhymnia and her sisters made
  Most lubrical with their delicious milk,
To aid me, to a thousandth of the truth
  It would not reach,[15] singing the holy smile
  And how the aspect it illumed.   60

*Opened.
†Once; first; originally.

And therefore, representing Paradise,
 The sacred poem must perforce leap over,
 Even as a man who finds his way cut off;[16]
But whoso thinketh of the ponderous theme,
 And of the mortal shoulder laden with it,   65
 Should blame it not, if under this it tremble.
It is no passage for a little boat[17]
 This which goes cleaving the audacious prow,
 Nor for a pilot who would spare himself.
"Why doth my face so much enamor thee,   70
 That to the garden fair thou turnest not,
 Which under the rays of Christ is blossoming?[18]
There is the Rose[19] in which the Word Divine[20]
 Became incarnate; there the lilies are
 By whose perfume the good way was discovered."[21]   75
Thus Beatrice; and I, who to her counsels
 Was wholly ready, once again betook me
 Unto the battle of the feeble brows.[22]
As in the sunshine, that unsullied streams
 Through fractured cloud, ere now a meadow of flowers   80
 Mine eyes with shadow covered o'er have seen,
So troops of splendors manifold I saw
 Illumined from above with burning rays,
 Beholding not the source of the effulgence.
O power benignant that dost so imprint them!   85
 Thou didst exalt thyself to give more scope
 There to mine eyes, that were not strong enough.[23]
The name of that fair flower[24] I e'er invoke
 Morning and evening utterly enthralled
 My soul to gaze upon the greater fire.   90
And when in both mine eyes depicted were
 The glory and greatness of the living star[25]
 Which there excelleth, as it here excelled,
Athwart the heavens a little torch descended
 Formed in a circle like a coronal,   95
 And cinctured it, and whirled itself about it.
Whatever melody most sweetly soundeth

On earth,[26] and to itself most draws the soul,
    Would seem a cloud that, rent asunder, thunders,
Compared unto the sounding of that lyre   100
    Wherewith was crowned the sapphire beautiful,[27]
    Which gives the clearest heaven its sapphire hue.
"I am Angelic Love, that circle round
    The joy sublime which breathes from out the womb
    That was the hostelry of our Desire;[28]   105
And I shall circle, Lady of Heaven, while
    Thou followest thy Son, and mak'st diviner
    The sphere supreme,[29] because thou enterest there."
Thus did the circulated melody
    Seal itself up; and all the other lights   110
    Were making to resound the name of Mary.
The regal mantle of the volumes all
    Of that world, which most fervid is and living
    With breath of God and with his works and ways,[30]
Extended over us its inner border,   115
    So very distant, that the semblance of it
    There where I was not yet appeared to me.[31]
Therefore mine eyes did not possess the power
    Of following the incoronated flame,
    Which mounted upward near to its own seed.[32]   120
And as a little child, that towards its mother
    Stretches its arms, when it the milk has taken,
    Through impulse kindled into outward flame,
Each of those gleams of whiteness upward reached[33]
    So with its summit, that the deep affection   125
    They had for Mary was revealed to me.
Thereafter they remained there in my sight,
    Regina cœli[34] singing with such sweetness,
    That ne'er from me has the delight departed.
O, what exuberance is garnered up   130
    Within those richest coffers, which had been
    Good husbandmen for sowing here below![35]
There they enjoy and live upon the treasure
    Which was acquired while weeping in the exile

Of Babylon, wherein the gold was left.[36]

There triumpheth, beneath the exalted Son

    Of God and Mary,[37] in his victory,

        Both with the ancient council and the new,[38]

He who doth keep the keys of such a glory.

CANTO XXIV

O company elect to the great supper
    Of the Lamb benedight,[1] who feedeth you
    So that forever full is your desire,

If by the grace of God this man foretaste
    Something of that which falleth from your table,[2]   5
    Or ever death prescribe to him the time,

Direct your mind to his immense desire,[3]
    And him somewhat bedew;[4] ye drinking are
    Forever at the fount whence comes his thought."

Thus Beatrice; and those souls beatified   10
    Transformed themselves to spheres on steadfast poles,
    Flaming intensely in the guise of comets.

And as the wheels in works of horologes
    Revolve so that the first to the beholder
    Motionless seems, and the last one to fly,[5]   15

So in like manner did those carols,[6] dancing
    In different measure, of their affluence
    Give me the gauge,[7] as they were swift or slow.

From that one[8] which I noted of most beauty
    Beheld I issue forth a fire so happy   20
    That none it left there of a greater brightness;

And around Beatrice three several times
    It whirled itself with so divine a song,
    My fantasy repeats it not to me;[9]

Therefore the pen skips, and I write it not,   25
    Since our imagination for such folds,
    Much more our speech, is of a tint too glaring.[10]

"O holy sister mine, who us implorest

With such devotion, by thine ardent love
    Thou dost unbind me from that beautiful sphere!"   30
Thereafter, having stopped, the blessed fire
    Unto my Lady did direct its breath,
    Which spake in fashion as I here have said.
And she; "O light eterne* of the great man
    To whom our Lord delivered up the keys"   35
    He carried down of this miraculous joy,
This one examine on points light and grave,
    As good beseemeth thee, about the Faith
    By means of which thou on the sea didst walk.[12]
If he love well, and hope well, and believe,   40
    From thee 'tis hid not; for thou hast thy sight
    There where depicted everything is seen.
But since this kingdom has made citizens
    By means of the true Faith, to glorify it
    'Tis well he have the chance to speak thereof."   45
As baccalaureate arms himself, and speaks not
    Until the master doth propose the question,[13]
    To argue it, and not to terminate it,
So did I arm myself with every reason,
    While she was speaking, that I might be ready   50
    For such a questioner and such profession.
"Say, thou good Christian; manifest thyself;
    What is the Faith?" Whereat I raised my brow
    Unto that light wherefrom was this breathed forth.
Then turned I round to Beatrice, and she   55
    Prompt signals made to me that I should pour
    The water forth from my internal fountain.[14]
"May grace, that suffers me to make confession."
    Began I, "to the great centurion,[15]
    Cause my conceptions all to be explicit!"   60
And I continued: "As the truthful pen,
    Father, of thy dear brother[16] wrote of it,
    Who put with thee Rome into the good way,

*Eternal.

Faith is the substance of the things we hope for,
    And evidence of those that are not seen;   65
    And this appears to me its quiddity."[17]
Then heard I: "Very rightly thou perceivest,
    If well thou understandest why he placed it
    With substances and then with evidences."[18]
And I thereafterward: "The things profound,   70
    That here vouchsafe to me their apparition,
    Unto all eyes below are so concealed,
That they exist there only in belief,
    Upon the which is founded the high hope,
    And hence it takes the nature of a substance.   75
And it behoveth us from this belief
    To reason without having other sight,
    And hence it has the nature of evidence."
Then heard I: "If whatever is acquired
    Below by doctrine were thus understood,   80
    No sophist's subtlety would there find place."[19]
Thus was breathed forth from that enkindled love;
    Then added: "Very well has been gone over
    Already of this coin the alloy and weight;[20]
But tell me if thou hast it in thy purse?"[21]   85
    And I: "Yes, both so shining and so round,[22]
    That in its stamp there is no peradventure."*
Thereafter issued from the light profound
    That there resplendent was: "This precious jewel,[23]
    Upon the which is every virtue founded,[24]   90
Whence hadst thou it?" And I: "The large outpouring
    Of Holy Spirit, that hath been diffused
    Upon the ancient parchments and the new,[25]
A syllogism is, which proved it to me
    With such acuteness, that, compared therewith,   95
    All demonstration seems to me obtuse."
And then I heard: "The ancient and the new
    Postulates, that to thee are so conclusive,

*No chance, question, or doubt.

Why dost thou take them for the word divine?"
And I: "The proofs, which show the truth to me,   100
Are the works subsequent, whereunto Nature
Ne'er heated iron yet, nor anvil beat."[26]
'Twas answered me: "Say, who assureth thee
That those works ever were? the thing itself
That must be proved, naught else to thee affirms it."[27]   105
"Were the world to Christianity converted,"
I said, "withouten miracles, this one
Is such, the rest are not its hundredth part:[28]
Because that poor and fasting thou didst enter
Into the field to sow there the good plant,   110
Which was a vine and has become a thorn!"[29]
This being finished, the high, holy Court
Resounded through the spheres, "One God we praise!"[30]
In melody that there above is chanted.
And then that Baron,[31] who from branch to branch,   115
Examining, had thus conducted me,
Till the extremest leaves we were approaching,
Again began: "The Grace that dallying
Plays with thine intellect thy mouth has opened,
Up to this point, as it should opened be,   120
So that I do approve what forth emerged;
But now thou must express what thou believest,
And whence to thy belief it was presented."[32]
"O holy father, spirit who beholdest
What thou believedst so that thou o'ercamest,   125
Towards the sepulchre, more youthful feet,"[33]
Began I, "thou dost wish me in this place
The form to manifest of my prompt belief,
And likewise thou the cause thereof demandest.
And I respond: In one God I believe,   130
Sole and eterne,* who moveth all the heavens
With love and with desire, himself unmoved;[34]
And of such faith not only have I proofs

*Eternal.

Physical and metaphysical,[35] but gives them
    Likewise the truth that from this place rains down   135
Through Moses, through the Prophets and the Psalms,
    Through the Evangel, and through you, who wrote
    After the fiery Spirit sanctified you;[36]
In Persons three eterne believe, and these
    One essence I believe, so one and trine[37]   140
    They bear conjunction both with *sunt* and *est.*
With the profound condition and divine
    Which now I touch upon, doth stamp my mind
    Ofttimes the doctrine evangelical.
This the beginning is, this is the spark.   145
    Which afterwards dilates to vivid flame,[38]
    And, like a star in heaven, is sparkling in me."
Even as a lord who hears what pleaseth him
    His servant straight embraces, gratulating
    For the good news as soon as he is silent;   150
So, giving me its benediction, singing,
    Three times encircled me,[39] when I was silent,
    The apostolic light, at whose command
I spoken had, in speaking I so pleased him.

CANTO XXV

I F e'er it happen that the Poem Sacred,[1]
    To which both heaven and earth have set their hand,
    So that it many a year[2] hath made me lean,
O'ercome the cruelty that bars me out
    From the fair sheepfold, where a lamb I slumbered,   5
    An enemy to the wolves[3] that war upon it,
With other voice forthwith, with other fleece
    Poet will I return, and at my font
    Baptismal will I take the laurel crown;[4]
Because into the Faith that maketh known   10
    All souls to God there entered I, and then
    Peter for her sake[5] thus my brow encircled.
Thereafterward towards us moved a light
    Out of that band whence issued the firstfruits[6]
    Which of his vicars Christ behind him left,   15
And then my Lady, full of ecstasy,
    Said unto me: "Look, look! behold the Baron
    For whom below Galicia is frequented."[7]
In the same way as, when a dove alights
    Near his companion, both of them pour forth,   20
    Circling about and murmuring, their affection,
So one beheld I by the other[8] grand
    Prince glorified to be with welcome greeted,
    Lauding the food[9] that there above is eaten.
But when their gratulations were complete,   25
    Silently *coram me*[10] each one stood still,
    So incandescent it o'ercame my sight.
Smiling thereafterwards, said Beatrice:

"Illustrious life, by whom the benefactions
    Of our Basilica[11] have been described,   30
Make Hope resound within this altitude;
    Thou knowest as oft thou dost personify it
    As Jesus to the three gave greater clearness."——[12]
"Lift up thy head, and make thyself assured;
    For what comes hither from the mortal world   35
    Must needs be ripened in our radiance."
This comfort came to me from the second fire;[13]
    Wherefore mine eyes I lifted to the hills,[14]
    Which bent them down before with too great weight.
"Since, through his grace, our Emperor[15] wills that thou   40
    Shouldst find thee face to face, before thy death,
    In the most secret chamber, with his Counts,[16]
So that, the truth beholden of this court,
    Hope, which below there rightfully enamors
    Thereby thou strengthen in thyself and others,   45
Say what it is, and how is flowering with it
    Thy mind, and say from whence it came to thee."[17]
    Thus did the second light[18] again continue.
And the Compassionate,[19] who piloted
    The plumage of my wings in such high flight,   50
    Did in reply anticipate me thus:
"No child whatever the Church Militant
    Of greater hope possesses, as is written
    In that Sun which irradiates all our band;
Therefore it is conceded him from Egypt   55
    To come into Jerusalem to see,[20]
    Or ever yet his warfare be completed.
The two remaining points, that not for knowledge
    Have been demanded, but that he report
    How much this virtue unto thee is pleasing,   60
To him I leave; for hard he will not find them,
    Nor of self-praise; and let him answer them;
    And may the grace of God in this assist him!"
As a disciple,[21] who his teacher follows,
    Ready and willing, where he is expert,   65

That his proficiency may be displayed,
  "Hope,²² said I, "'is the certain expectation
    Of future glory, which is the effect
    Of grace divine and merit precedent.
From many stars this light comes unto me;²³   70
  But he instilled it first into my heart
    Who was chief singer unto the chief captain.²⁴
'*Sperent in te,*' in the high Theody²⁵
  He sayeth, 'those who know thy name'; and who
    Knoweth it not, if he my faith possess?   75
Thou didst instil me, then, with his instilling
  In the Epistle,²⁶ so that I am full,
    And upon others rain again your rain."
While I was speaking, in the living bosom
  Of that combustion quivered an effulgence,   80
    Sudden and frequent, in the guise of lightning;²⁷
Then breathed: "The love wherewith I am inflamed
  Towards the virtue still which followed me
    Unto the palm and issue of the field,²⁸
Wills that I breathe to thee that thou delight   85
  In her;²⁹ and grateful to me is thy telling
    Whatever things Hope promises to thee."³⁰
And I: "The ancient Scriptures and the new
  The mark establish, and this shows it me,
    Of all the souls whom God hath made his friends.   90
Isaiah saith, that each one garmented
  In his own land shall be with twofold garments,³¹
    And his own land is this delightful life.
Thy brother, too,³² far more explicitly,
  There where he treateth of the robes of white,   95
    This revelation manifests to us."
And first, and near the ending of these words,
  "*Sperent in te*"³³ from over us was heard,
    To which responsive answered all the carols³⁴
Thereafterward a light among them brightened,   100
  To that, if Cancer one such crystal had,
    Winter would have a month of one sole day.³⁵

And as uprises, goes, and enters the dance
    A winsome maiden, only to do honor
    To the new bride, and not from any failing,   105
Even thus did I behold the brightened splendor
    Approach the two,[36] who in a wheel revolved
    As was beseeming to their ardent love.
Into the song and music there it entered;
    And fixed on them my Lady kept her look,   110
    Even as a bride silent and motionless.
"This is the one who lay upon the breast
    Of our own Pelican;[37] and this is he
    To the great office[38] from the cross elected."
My Lady thus; but therefore none the more   115
    Did move her sight from its attentive gaze
    Before or afterward these words of hers.
Even as a man who gazes, and endeavors
    To see the eclipsing of the sun a little,
    And who, by seeing, sightless doth become,[39]   120
So I became before that latest fire,
    While it was said, "Why dost thou daze thyself
    To see a thing which here hath no existence?
Earth in the earth my body is, and shall be
    With all the others there, until our number   125
    With the eternal proposition tallies.[40]
With the two garments in the blessed cloister
    Are the two lights alone that have ascended:[41]
    And this shalt thou take back into your world."
And at this utterance the flaming circle   130
    Grew quiet, with the dulcet intermingling
    Of sound that by the trinal breath[42] was made,
As to escape from danger or fatigue
    The oars that erst were in the water beaten
    Are all suspended at a whistle's sound.   135
Ah, how much in my mind was I disturbed,
    When I turned round to look on Beatrice,
    That her I could not see,[43] although I was
Close at her side and in the Happy World!

Canto XXVI: St. John examines Dante concerning Love

CANTO XXVI

WHILE I was doubting for my vision quenched,
    Out of the flame refulgent that had quenched it
    Issued a breathing, that attentive made me,
Saying: "While thou recoverest the sense
    Of seeing which in me thou hast consumed,   5
    'Tis well that speaking thou shouldst compensate it.
Begin then, and declare to what thy soul
    Is aimed, and count it for a certainty,
    Sight is in thee bewildered and not dead;[1]
Because the Lady, who through this divine   10
    Region conducteth thee, has in her look
    The power the hand of Ananias[2] had."
I said: "As pleaseth her, or soon or late
    Let the cure come to eyes that portals were
    When she with fire I ever burn with entered.[3]   15
The Good, that gives contentment to this Court,
    The Alpha and Omega is of all
    The writing that love reads me low or loud."[4]
The selfsame voice,[5] that taken had from me
    The terror of the sudden dazzlement,   20
    To speak still farther put it in my thought;
And said: "In verity with finer sieve
    Behoveth thee to sift; thee it behoveth
    To say who aimed thy bow at such a target."[6]
And I: "By philosophic arguments,   25
    And by authority[7] that hence descends,
    Such love must needs imprint itself in me;
For Good, so far as good, when comprehended

Doth straight enkindle love, and so much greater
As more of goodness in itself it holds;   30
Then to that Essence (whose is such advantage
That every good which out of it is found
Is nothing but a ray of its own light)
More than elsewhither must the mind be moved
Of every one, in loving, who discerns   35
The truth in which this evidence is founded.[8]
Such truth he to my intellect reveals
Who demonstrates to me the primal love
Of all the sempiternal substances.[9]
The voice reveals it of the truthful Author,   40
Who says to Moses, speaking of Himself,
'I will make all my goodness pass before thee.'[10]
Thou too revealest it to me, beginning
The loud Evangel,[11] that proclaims the secret
Of heaven to earth above all other edict."   45
And I heard say: "By human intellect
And by authority concordant with it,
Of all thy loves reserve for God the highest.
But say again if other cords[12] thou feelest,
Draw thee towards Him, that thou mayst proclaim   50
With how many teeth this love is biting thee."[13]
The holy purpose of the Eagle of Christ[14]
Not latent was, nay, rather I perceived
Whither he fain would my profession[15] lead.
Therefore I recommenced: "All of those bites   55
Which have the power to turn the heart to God
Unto my charity have been concurrent.
The being of the world, and my own being,
The death which He endured that I may live,
And that which all the faithful hope, as I do,   60
With the forementioned vivid consciousness
Have drawn me from the sea of love perverse,
And of the right have placed me on the shore.[16]
The leaves, wherewith embowered is all the garden
Of the Eternal Gardener, do I love   65

As much as he has granted them of good."[17]
As soon as I had ceased, a song most sweet[18]
 Throughout the heaven resounded, and my Lady
 Said with the others, "Holy, holy, holy!"
And as at some keen light one wakes from sleep   70
 By reason of the visual spirit that runs
 Unto the splendor passed from coat to coat,[19]
And he who wakes abhorreth what he sees,
 So all unconscious is his sudden waking,
 Until the judgment cometh to his aid,   75
So from before mine eyes did Beatrice
 Chase every mote with radiance of her own,[20]
 That cast its light a thousand miles and more.
Whence better after than before I saw,
 And in a kind of wonderment I asked   80
 About a fourth light that I saw with us.
And said my Lady: "There within those rays
 Gazes upon its Maker the first soul
 That ever the first virtue did create."[21]
Even as the bough that downward bends its top   85
 At transit of the wind, and then is lifted
 By its own virtue, which inclines it upward,
Likewise did I, the while that she was speaking,
 Being amazed, and then I was made bold
 By a desire to speak wherewith I burned.   90
And I began: "O apple, that mature
 Alone hast been produced, O ancient father,
 To whom each wife is daughter and daughter-in-law,
Devoutly as I can I supplicate thee
 That thou wouldst speak to me; thou seest my wish; 95
 And I, to hear thee quickly, speak it not."
Sometimes an animal, when covered, struggles
 So that his impulse needs must be apparent,
 By reason of the wrappage following it;
And in like manner the primeval soul   100
 Made clear to me athwart its covering
 How jubilant it was to give me pleasure.[22]

Then breathed: "Without thy uttering it to me,
    Thine inclination better I discern
    Than thou whatever thing is surest to thee;   105
For I behold it in the truthful mirror,[23]
    That of Himself all things parhelion* makes,
    And none makes Him parhelion of itself.[24]
Thou fain wouldst hear how long ago[25] God placed me
    Within the lofty garden, where this Lady   110
    Unto so long a stairway thee disposed.
And how long to mine eyes it was a pleasure,
    And of the great disdain the proper cause,
    And the language that I used and that I made.
Now, son of mine, the tasting of the tree   115
    Not in itself was cause of so great exile,
    But solely the o'erstepping of the bounds.[26]
There, whence thy Lady moved Virgilius,
    Four thousand and three hundred and two circuits[27]
    Made by the sun, this Council[28] I desired;   120
And him I saw return to all the lights
    Of his highway[29] nine hundred times and thirty,[30]
    Whilst I upon the earth was tarrying.
The language that I spake was quite extinct
    Before that in the work interminable   125
    The people under Nimrod were employed;[31]
For nevermore result of reasoning
    (Because of human pleasure that doth change,
    Obedient to the heavens) was durable.[32]
A natural action is it that man speaks;   130
    But whether thus or thus, doth nature leave
    To your own art,[33] as seemeth best to you.
Ere I descended[34] to the infernal anguish,
    El was on earth the name of the Chief Good,[35]
    From whom comes all the joy that wraps me round;   135
Eli he then was called,[36] and that is proper,
    Because the use of men is like a leaf[37]

*Reflection.

On bough, which goeth and another cometh.
Upon the mount that highest o'er the wave
    Rises[38] was I, in life or pure or sinful,   140
    From the first hour to that which is the second,
As the sun changes quadrant, to the sixth."[39]

Canto XXVII: The Heavenly Host singing Gloria in Excelsis

CANTO XXVII

GLORY be to the Father, to the Son,
 And Holy Ghost!" all Paradise began,[1]
 So that the melody inebriate made me.
What I beheld seemed unto me a smile
 Of the universe;[2] for my inebriation   5
 Found entrance through the hearing and the sight.
O joy! O gladness inexpressible!
 O perfect life of love and peacefulness!
 O riches without hankering secure!
Before mine eyes were standing the four torches[3]   10
 Enkindled, and the one that first had come[4]
 Began to make itself more luminous;
And even such in semblance it became
 As Jupiter would become, if he and Mars
 Were birds, and they should interchange their plumes.[5]   15
That Providence, which here distributeth
 Season and service, in the blessed choir
 Had silence upon every side imposed.[6]
When I heard say: "If I my color change,
 Marvel not at it; for while I am speaking   20
 Thou shalt behold all these their color change.
He who usurps upon the earth my place,
 My place, my place,[7] which vacant has become[8]
 Before the presence of the Son of God,
Has of my cemetery made a sewer   25
 Of blood and stench, whereby the Perverse One,[9]
 Who fell from here, below there is appeased!"[10]
With the same color[11] which, through sun adverse,

Painteth the clouds at evening or at morn,
　　Beheld I then the whole of heaven suffused.　　　　30
And as a modest woman, who abides
　　Sure of herself, and at another's failing,
　　From listening only, timorous becomes,
Even thus did Beatrice change countenance;
　　And I believe in heaven was such eclipse,　　　　35
　　When suffered the supreme Omnipotence;[12]
Thereafterward proceeded forth his words
　　With voice so much transmuted from itself,
　　The very countenance was not more changed.[13]
"The spouse of Christ[14] has never nurtured been　　　40
　　On blood of mine, of Linus and of Cletus,[15]
　　To be made use of in acquest of* gold;
But in acquest of this delightful life
　　Sixtus and Pius, Urban and Calixtus,[16]
　　After much lamentation, shed their blood.　　　　45
Our purpose was not, that on the right hand
　　Of our successors should in part be seated
　　The Christian folk, in part upon the other;
Nor that the keys which were to me confided
　　Should e'er become the escutcheon on a banner,　　　50
　　That should wage war on those who are baptized;
Nor I be made the figure of a seal
　　To privileges venal and mendacious,
　　Whereat I often redden and flash with fire.[17]
In garb of shepherds the rapacious wolves　　　55
　　Are seen from here above o'er all the pastures!
　　O wrath of God, why dost thou slumber still?
To drink our blood the Caorsines and Gascons[18]
　　Are making ready. O thou good beginning,
　　Unto how vile an end must thou needs fall!　　　60
But the high Providence, that with Scipio
　　At Rome the glory of the world defended,
　　Will speedily bring aid,[19] as I conceive;

*In search of.

And thou, my son, who by thy mortal weight
    Shalt down return again, open thy mouth;[20]   65
    What I conceal not, do not thou conceal."
As with its frozen vapors downward falls
    In flakes our atmosphere, what time the horn
    Of the celestial Goat doth touch the sun,
Upward in such array saw I the ether   70
    Become, and flaked with the triumphant vapors,
    Which there together with us had remained.[21]
My sight was following up their semblances,
    And followed till the medium, by excess,
    The passing farther onward took from it;   75
Whereat the Lady, who beheld me freed
    From gazing upward, said to me: "Cast down
    Thy sight, and see how far thou art turned round."
Since the first time that I had downward looked,
    I saw that I had moved through the whole arc   80
    Which the first climate makes from midst to end;[22]
So that I saw the mad track of Ulysses
    Past Gades,[23] and this side, well nigh the shore
    Whereon became Europa a sweet burden.[24]
And of this threshing-floor[25] the site to me   85
    Were more unveiled, but the sun was proceeding
    Under my feet, a sign and more removed.[26]
My mind enamored,[27] which is dallying
    At all times with my Lady, to bring back
    To her mine eyes was more than ever ardent.   90
And if or Art or Nature has made bait
    To catch the eyes and so possess the mind,
    In human flesh or in its portraiture,
All joined together would appear as naught
    To the divine delight which shone upon me   95
    When to her smiling face I turned me round.
The virtue that her look endowed me with
    From the fair nest of Leda[28] tore me forth,
    And up into the swiftest heaven[29] impelled me.
Its parts exceeding full of life and lofty   100

Are all so uniform, I cannot say
>> Which Beatrice selected for my place.[30]
But she, who was aware of my desire,
>> Began, the while she smiled so joyously
>> That God seemed in her countenance to rejoice: 105
"The nature of that motion, which keeps quiet
>> The centre, and all the rest about it moves,
>> From hence begins as from its starting point.
And in this heaven there is no other Where
>> Than in the Mind Divine,[31] wherein is kindled 110
>> The love that turns it, and the power it rains.
Within a circle light and love embrace it,[32]
>> Even as this doth the others, and that precinct
>> He who encircles it alone controls.
Its motion is not by another meted, 115
>> But all the others measured are by this,
>> As ten is by the half and by the fifth.[33]
And in what manner time in such a pot
>> May have its roots, and in the rest its leaves,[34]
>> Now unto thee can manifest be made. 120
O covetousness, that mortals dost ingulf
>> Beneath thee so, that no one hath the power
>> Of drawing back his eyes from out thy waves!
Full fairly blossoms in mankind the will;
>> But the uninterrupted rain converts 125
>> Into abortive wildings the true plums.[35]
Fidelity and innocence are found
>> Only in children; afterwards they both
>> Take flights or e'er the cheeks with down are covered.
One, while he prattles still, observes the fasts, 130
>> Who, when his tongue is loosed, forthwith devours
>> Whatever food under whatever moon;
Another, while he prattles, loves and listens
>> Unto his mother, who when speech is perfect
>> Forthwith desires to see her in her grave. 135
Even thus is swarthy made the skin so white
>> In its first aspect of the daughter fair

Of him who brings the morn, and leaves the night.[36]
Thou, that it may not be a marvel to thee,
    Think that on earth there is no one who governs;   140
    Whence goes astray the human family.
Ere January be unwintered wholly
    By the centesimal on earth neglected,[37]
    Shall these supernal circles roar so loud
The tempest that has been so long awaited   145
    Shall whirl the poops about where are the prows;
    So that the fleet shall run its course direct,[38]
And the true fruit shall follow on the flower."[39]

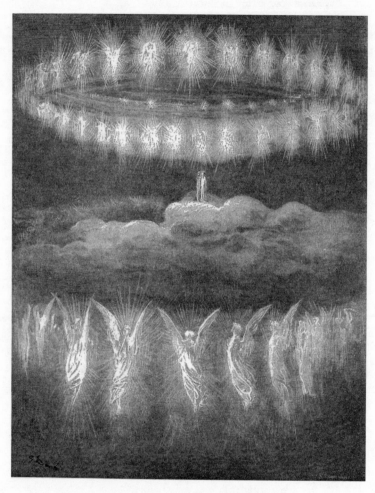

Canto XXVIII: The Sparkling Circles of the Heavenly Host

CANTO XXVIII

$\mathcal{A}$FTER the truth against the present life
    Of miserable mortals was unfolded
    By her who doth imparadise my mind,[1]
As in a looking-glass a taper's flame
    He sees who from behind is lighted by it,   5
    Before he has it in his sight or thought,
And turns him round to see if so the glass
    Tell him the truth, and sees that it accords
    Therewith as doth a music with its metre,
In similar wise my memory recollecteth   10
    That I did, looking into those fair eyes,
    Of which Love made the springs to ensnare me.[2]
And as I turned me round, and mine were touched
    By that which is apparent in that volume,[3]
    Whenever on its gyre we gaze intent,   15
A point beheld I, that was raying out
    Light so acute,[4] the sight which it enkindles
    Must close perforce before such great acuteness.
And whatsoever star seems smallest here[5]
    Would seem to be a moon, if placed beside it   20
    As one star with another star is placed.
Perhaps at such a distance as appears
    A halo cincturing* the light that paints it,
    When densest is the vapor that sustains it,
Thus distant round the point a circle of fire[6]   25

*Circling; belting.

So swiftly whirled, that it would have surpassed
    Whatever motion soonest girds the world;
And this was by another circumcinct,*
    That by a third, the third then by a fourth,
    By a fifth the fourth, and then by a sixth the fifth;   30
The seventh followed thereupon in width
    So ample now, that Juno's messenger[7]
    Entire would be too narrow to contain it.
Even so the eighth and ninth; and every one
    More slowly moved, according as it was   35
    In number distant farther from the first.
And that one had its flame most crystalline
    From which less distant was the stainless spark,
    I think because more with its truth imbued.
My Lady, who in my anxiety   40
    Beheld me much perplexed, said: "From that point
    Dependent is the heaven and nature all.[8]
Behold that circle most conjoined to it,[9]
    And know thou, that its motion is so swift
    Through burning love whereby it is spurred on."   45
And I to her: "If the world were arranged
    In the order which I see in yonder wheels,
    What's set before me would have satisfied me;
But in the world of sense we can perceive
    That evermore the circles are diviner   50
    As they are from the centre more remote[10]
Wherefore if my desire is to be ended
    In this miraculous and angelic temple,
    That has for confines only love and light,
To hear behoves me still how the example   55
    And the exemplar go not in one fashion,
    Since for myself in vain I contemplate it."
"If thine own fingers unto such a knot
    Be insufficient, it is no great wonder,
    So hard hath it become for want of trying."   60

*Girded round; cinctured.

My Lady thus; then said she: "Do thou take
    What I shall tell thee, if thou wouldst be sated,
    And exercise on that thy subtlety.
The circles corporal are wide and narrow
    According to the more or less of virtue[11]   65
    Which is distributed through all their parts.
The greater goodness works the greater weal,*
    The greater weal the greater body holds,
    If perfect equally are all its parts.
Therefore this one which sweeps along with it   70
    The universe sublime,[12] doth correspond
    Unto the circle which most loves and knows.
On which account, if thou unto the virtue
    Apply thy measure, not to the appearance
    Of substances that unto thee seem round,   75
Thou wilt behold a marvellous agreement,
    Of more to greater, and of less to smaller,
    In every heaven, with its Intelligence."
Even as remaineth splendid and serene
    The hemisphere of air, when Boreas   80
    Is blowing from that cheek where he is mildest,[13]
Because is purified and resolved the rack†
    That erst disturbed it, till the welkin‡ laughs
    With all the beauties of its pageantry;
Thus did I likewise, after that my lady   85
    Had me provided with her clear response,
    And like a star in heaven the truth was seen.
And soon as to a stop her words had come,
    Not otherwise does iron scintillate
    When molten, than those circles scintillated.   90
Their coruscation§ all the sparks repeated,[14]
    And they so many were, their number makes
    More millions than the doubling of the chess.[15]

*Good; benefit.
†Impurity.
‡Heaven.
§Flash, gleam, or ray of light.

I heard them sing hosanna choir by choir
    To the fixed point which holds them at the *Ubi*,[16]   95
    And ever will, where they have ever been.
And she, who saw the dubious meditations
    Within my mind, "The primal circles," said,
    "Have shown thee Seraphim and Cherubim.[17]
Thus rapidly they follow their own bonds,   100
    To be as like the point as most they can,
    And can as far as they are high in vision.
Those other Loves,[18] that round about them go,
    Thrones of the countenance divine are called,
    Because they terminate the primal Triad.[19]   105
And thou shouldst know that they all have delight
    As much as their own vision penetrates
    The Truth, in which all intellect finds rest.
From this it may be seen how blessedness
    Is founded in the faculty which sees,   110
    And not in that which loves, and follows next;[20]
And of this seeing merit is the measure,[21]
    Which is brought forth by grace, and by good will;
    Thus on from grade to grade doth it proceed.
The second Triad, which is germinating[22]   115
    In such wise in this sempiternal spring,
    That no nocturnal Aries despoils,[23]
Perpetually hosanna warbles forth
    With threefold melody, that sounds in three
    Orders of joy, with which it is intrined.[24]   120
The three Divine[25] are in this hierarchy,
    First the Dominions, and the Virtues next;
    And the third order is that of the Powers.
Then in the dances[26] twain penultimate
    The Principalities and Archangels wheel;   125
    The last is wholly of angelic sports.[27]
These orders upward all of them are gazing,[28]
    And downward so prevail, that unto God
    They all attracted are and all attract.
And Dionysius[29] with so great desire   130

To contemplate these Orders set himself,
    He named them and distinguished them as I do.
But Gregory afterwards dissented from him;
    Wherefore, as soon as he unclosed his eyes
    Within this heaven, he at himself did smile.[30]   135
And if so much of secret truth a mortal
    Proffered on earth, I would not have thee marvel,
    For he who saw it here revealed it to him,[31]
With much more of the truth about these circles."

CANTO XXIX

Aт what time both the children of Latona,[1]
    Surmounted by the Ram and by the Scales,
    Together make a zone of the horizon,
As long as from the time the zenith holds them
    In equipoise, till from that girdle both   5
    Changing their hemisphere disturb the balance.[2]
So long, her face depicted with a smile,
    Did Beatrice keep silence while she gazed
    Fixedly at the point[3] which had o'ercome me.
Then she began: "I say, and I ask not   10
    What thou dost wish to hear, for I have seen it
    Where centres every When and every *Ubi*.[4]
Not to acquire some good unto himself,
    Which is impossible, but that his splendor
    In its resplendency may say, '*Subsisto*,'[5]   15
In his eternity outside of time,
    Outside all other limits, as it pleased him,
    Into new Loves[6] the Eternal Love unfolded.
Nor as if torpid did he lie before;[7]
    For neither after nor before proceeded   20
    The going forth of God upon these waters.
Matter and Form[8] unmingled and conjoined
    Came into being that had no defect,[9]
    E'en as three arrows from a three-stringed bow.[10]
And as in glass, in amber, or in crystal   25
    A sunbeam flashes so, that from its coming
    To its full being is no interval,
So from its Lord did the triform effect

Ray forth into its being all together,
    Without discrimination of beginning.   30
Order was con-created and constructed
    In substances, and summit of the world
    Were those wherein the pure act was produced.[11]
Pure potentiality[12] held the lowest part;
    Midway bound potentiality with act[13]   35
    Such bond that it shall never be unbound.
Jerome has written unto you of angels
    Created a long lapse of centuries[14]
    Or ever yet the other world was made;
But written is this truth in many places   40
    By writers of the Holy Ghost,[15] and thou
    Shalt see it, if thou lookest well thereat.
And even reason seeth it somewhat,[16]
    For it would not concede that for so long
    Could be the motors without their perfection.   45
Now dost thou know both where and when these Loves
    Created were, and how; so that extinct
    In thy desire already are three fires.[17]
Nor could one reach, in counting, unto twenty
    So swiftly, as a portion of these angels   50
    Disturbed the subject of your elements.[18]
The rest remained,[19] and they began this art[20]
    Which thou discernest, with so great delight
    That never from their circling do they cease.
The occasion of the fall was the accursed   55
    Presumption of that One,[21] whom thou hast seen
    By all the burden of the world constrained.
Those whom thou here beholdest modest were
    To recognize themselves as of that goodness
    Which made them apt for so much understanding;   60
On which account their vision was exalted
    By the enlightening grace[22] and their own merit,
    So that they have a full and steadfast will.
I would not have thee doubt, but certain be,
    'Tis meritorious to receive this grace,[23]   65

According as the affection opens to it.
Now round about in this consistory
    Much mayst thou contemplate, if these my words
    Be gathered up, without all further aid.
But since upon the earth, throughout your schools,   70
    They teach that such is the angelic nature
    That it doth hear, and recollect, and will,[24]
More will I say, that thou mayst see unmixed
    The truth that is confounded there below,[25]
    Equivocating in such like prelections.   75
These substances, since in God's countenance
    They jocund were, turned not away their sight[26]
    From that wherefrom not anything is hidden;
Hence they have not their vision intercepted
    By object new, and hence they do not need   80
    To recollect, through interrupted thought.
So that below, not sleeping, people dream,
    Believing they speak truth, and not believing;
    And in the last is greater sin and shame.[27]
Below you do not journey by one path   85
    Philosophizing; so transporteth you
    Love of appearance and the thought thereof.
And even this above here is endured
    With less disdain, than when is set aside
    The Holy Writ, or when it is distorted.   90
They think not there how much of blood it costs
    To sow it in the world, and how he pleases
    Who in humility keeps close to it.
Each striveth for appearance, and doth make
    His own inventions; and these treated are   95
    By preachers, and the Evangel holds its peace.
One sayeth that the moon did backward turn,
    In the Passion of Christ, and interpose herself
    So that the sunlight reached not down below;
And lies; for of its own accord the light   100
    Hid itself; whence to Spaniards and to Indians,[28]
    As to the Jews, did such eclipse respond.

Florence has not so many Lapi and Bindi
  As fables such as these,[29] that every year
  Are shouted from the pulpit back and forth,   105
In such wise that the lambs,[30] who do not know,
  Come back from pasture fed upon the wind,
  And not to see the harm doth not excuse them.
Christ did not to his first disciples say,
  'Go forth, and to the world preach idle tales,'   110
  But unto them a true foundation gave;
And this so loudly sounded from their lips,
  That, in the warfare to enkindle Faith,
  They made of the Evangel shields and lances.[31]
Now men go forth with jests and drolleries   115
  To preach, and if but well the people laugh,
  The hood puffs out,[32] and nothing more is asked.
But in the cowl there nestles such a bird,[33]
  That, if the common people were to see it,
  They would perceive what pardons[34] they confide in,   120
For which so great on earth has grown the folly,
  That, without proof of any testimony,
  To each indulgence they would flock together.
By this Saint Anthony his pig doth fatten,[35]
  And many others, who are worse than pigs,   125
  Paying in money without mark of coinage.[36]
But since we have digressed abundantly,[37]
  Turn back thine eyes forthwith to the right path,
  So that the way be shortened with the time.
This nature doth so multiply itself   130
  In numbers, that there never yet was speech
  Nor mortal fancy that can go so far.[38]
And if thou notest that which is revealed
  By Daniel, thou wilt see that in his thousands
  Number determinate is kept concealed.[39]   135
The primal light, that all irradiates it,
  By modes as many is received therein,
  As are the splendors wherewith it is mated.
Hence, inasmuch as on the act conceptive

The affection followeth, of love the sweetness 140
  Therein diversely fervid is or tepid.[40]
The height behold now and the amplitude[41]
  Of the eternal power, since it hath made
  Itself so many mirrors,[42] where 'tis broken,
One in itself remaining as before." 145

CANTO XXX

$\mathcal{P}$ERCHANCE six thousand miles remote from us[1]
    Is glowing the sixth hour, and now this world
    Inclines its shadow almost to a level,
When the mid-heaven begins to make itself
    So deep to us, that here and there a star   5
    Ceases to shine so far down as this depth,
And as advances bright exceedingly
    The handmaid of the sun,[2] the heaven is closed
    Light after light to the most beautiful;[3]
Not otherwise the Triumph,[4] which forever   10
    Plays round about the point that vanquished me,
    Seeming enclosed by what itself encloses,[5]
Little by little from my vision faded;
    Whereat to turn mine eyes on Beatrice
    My seeing nothing and my love constrained me.   15
If what has hitherto been said of her
    Were all concluded in a single praise,
    Scant would it be to serve the present turn.[6]
Not only does the beauty I beheld
    Transcend ourselves, but truly I believe   20
    Its Maker only may enjoy it all.
Vanquished do I confess me by this passage
    More than by problem of his theme was ever
    O'ercome the comic or the tragic poet;[7]
For as the sun the sight that trembles most,   25
    Even so the memory of that sweet smile
    My mind depriveth of its very self.
From the first day[8] that I beheld her face

In this life, to the moment of this look,
 The sequence of my song has ne'er been severed;   30
But now perforce this sequence must desist
 From following her beauty with my verse,
 As every artist at his uttermost.[9]
Such as I leave her to a greater fame
 Than any of my trumpet, which is bringing   35
 Its arduous matter to a final close,
With voice and gesture of a perfect leader
 She recommenced: "We from the greatest body
 Have issued to the heaven that is pure light;[10]
Light intellectual replete with love,   40
 Love of true good replete with ecstasy,
 Ecstasy that transcendeth every sweetness.
Here shalt thou see the one host and the other[11]
 Of Paradise, and one in the same aspects[12]
 Which at the final judgment thou shalt see."[13]   45
Even as a sudden lightning[14] that disperses
 The visual spirits, so that it deprives
 The eye of impress from the strongest objects
Thus round about me flashed a living light,
 And left me swathed around with such a veil   50
 Of its effulgence, that I nothing saw.
"Ever the Love which quieteth this heaven
 Welcomes into itself with such salute,
 To make the candle ready for its flame."[15]
No sooner had within me these brief words   55
 An entrance found, than I perceived myself
 To be uplifted over my own power,
And I with vision new rekindled me,
 Such that no light whatever is so pure
 But that mine eyes were fortified against it.[16]   60
And light I saw in fashion of a river
 Fulvid with its effulgence, 'twixt two banks
 Depicted with an admirable Spring.
Out of this river issued living sparks,
 And on all sides sank down into the flowers,   65

Like unto rubies that are set in gold;[17]
And then, as if inebriate with the odors,
    They plunged again into the wondrous torrent,
    And as one entered issued forth another.
"The high desire, that now inflames and moves thee   70
    To have intelligence of what thou seest,
    Pleaseth me all the more, the more it swells.
But of this water it behoves thee drink
    Before so great a thirst in thee be slaked."
    Thus said to me the sunshine of mine eyes;   75
And added: "The river and the topazes
    Going in and out, and the laughing of the herbage,
    Are of their truth foreshadowing prefaces;[18]
Not that these things are difficult in themselves,
    But the deficiency is on thy side,   80
    For yet thou hast not vision so exalted."
There is no babe that leaps so suddenly
    With face towards the milk, if he awake
    Much later than his usual custom is,
As I did, that I might make better mirrors[19]   85
    Still of mine eyes, down stooping to the wave
    Which flows that we therein be better made.
And even as the penthouse of mine eyelids
    Drank of it, it forthwith appeared to me
    Out of its length to be transformed to round.   90
Then as a folk who have been under masks
    Seem other than before, if they divest
    The semblance not their own they disappeared in,
Thus into greater pomp were changed for me
    The flowerets and the sparks, so that I saw   95
    Both of the Courts of Heaven[20] made manifest.
O splendor of God! by means of which I saw
    The lofty triumph of the realm veracious,
    Give me the power to say how it I saw!
There is a light above, which visible   100
    Makes the Creator unto every creature,
    Who only in beholding Him has peace,

And it expands itself in circular form
    To such extent, that its circumference
    Would be too large a girdle for the sun.[21]   105
The semblance of it is all made of rays
    Reflected from the top of Primal Motion,
    Which takes therefrom vitality and power.
And as a hill in water at its base
    Mirrors itself, as if to see its beauty   110
    When affluent most in verdure and in flowers,
So, ranged aloft all round about the light,
    Mirrored I saw in more ranks than a thousand
    All who above there have from us returned
And if the lowest row collect within it   115
    So great a light, how vast the amplitude
    Is of this Rose in its extremest leaves![22]
My vision in the vastness and the height
    Lost not itself, but comprehended all[23]
    The quantity and quality of that gladness.   120
There near and far nor add nor take away;
    For there where God immediately doth govern,
    The natural law in naught is relevant.
Into the yellow of the Rose Eternal[24]
    That spreads, and multiplies, and breathes an odor   125
    Of praise unto the ever-vernal Sun,
As one who silent is and fain would speak,
    Me Beatrice drew on, and said: "Behold
    Of the white stoles[25] how vast the convent is!
Behold how vast the circuit of our city!   130
    Behold our seats so filled to overflowing,
    That here henceforward are few people wanting![26]
On that great throne whereon thine eyes are fixed
    For the crown's sake already placed upon it,
    Before thou suppest[27] at this wedding feast   135
Shall sit the soul (that is to be Augustus
    On earth) of noble Henry, who shall come
    To redress Italy[28] ere she be ready.
Blind covetousness,[29] that casts its spell upon you,

Has made you like unto the little child,   140
     Who dies of hunger and drives off the nurse.
And in the sacred forum then shall be
     A Prefect such, that openly or covert
     On the same road he will not walk with him.[30]
But long of God he will not be endured   145
     In holy office; he shall be thrust down
     Where Simon Magus is for his deserts,
And make him of Alagna lower go!"[31]

Canto XXXI: The Saintly Throng in the Form of a Rose

CANTO XXXI

IN fashion then as of a snow-white rose[1]
    Displayed itself to me the saintly host,
    Whom Christ in his own blood had made his bride,
But the other host,[2] that flying sees and sings
    The glory of Him who doth enamor it,   5
    And the goodness that created it so noble,
Even as a swarm of bees,[3] that sinks in flowers
    One moment, and the next returns again
    To where its labor is to sweetness turned,
Sank into the great flower, that is adorned   10
    With leaves so many, and thence reascended
    To where its love abideth evermore.[4]
Their faces had they all of living flame,
    And wings of gold, and all the rest so white
    No snow unto that limit doth attain.   15
From bench to bench, into the flower descending,
    They carried something of the peace and ardor[5]
    Which by the fanning of their flanks they won.
Nor did the interposing 'twixt the flower
    And what was o'er it of such plenitude   20
    Of flying shapes impede the sight and splendor;[6]
Because the light divine so penetrates
    The universe, according to its merit,
    That naught can be an obstacle against it.
This realm secure and full of gladsomeness,   25
    Crowded with ancient people and with modern,[7]
    Unto one mark had all its look and love.[8]
O Trinal Light, that in a single star[9]

Sparkling upon their sight so satisfies them,
  Look down upon our tempest here below![10]   30
If the barbarians, coming from some region
  That every day by Helice is covered,
  Revolving with her son whom she delights in,
Beholding Rome and all her noble works,
  Were wonder-struck, what time the Lateran   35
  Above all mortal things was eminent,—[11]
I who to the divine had from the human,
  From time unto eternity, had come,
  From Florence to a people just and sane,
With what amazement must I have been filled!   40
  Truly between this and the joy, it was
  My pleasure not to hear, and to be mute.
And as a pilgrim who delighteth him
  In gazing round the temple of his vow,
  And hopes some day to retell how it was,[12]   45
So through the living light my way pursuing
  Directed I mine eyes o'er all the ranks,
  Now up, now down, and now all round about.
Faces I saw of charity persuasive,
  Embellished by His light and their own smile,   50
  And attitudes adorned with every grace.
The general form of Paradise already
  My glance had comprehended as a whole,
  In no part hitherto remaining fixed,
And round I turned me with rekindled wish   55
  My Lady to interrogate of things
  Concerning which my mind was in suspense.
One thing I meant, another answered me;
  I thought I should see Beatrice, and saw
  An Old Man habited like the glorious people.[13]   60
O'erflowing was he in his eyes and cheeks
  With joy benign, in attitude of pity
  As to a tender father is becoming.
And "She, where is she?" instantly I said;
  Whence he: "To put an end to thy desire,   65

Me Beatrice hath sent from mine own place,
And if thou lookest up to the third round
    Of the first rank,[14] again shalt thou behold her
    Upon the throne her merits have assigned her."
Without reply I lifted up mine eyes,   70
    And saw her, as she made herself a crown
    Reflecting from herself[15] the eternal rays.
Not from that region which the highest thunders
    Is any mortal eye so far removed,
    In whatsoever sea it deepest sinks,   75
As there from Beatrice my sight; but this
    Was nothing unto me; because her image
    Descended not to me by medium blurred.
"O Lady, thou in whom my hope is strong,
    And who for my salvation didst endure   80
    In Hell[16] to leave the imprint of thy feet,
Of whatsoever things I have beheld,
    As coming from thy power and from thy goodness
    I recognize the virtue and the grace.
Thou from a slave hast brought me unto freedom,[17]   85
    By all those ways, by all the expedients,
    Whereby thou hadst the power of doing it.
Preserve towards me thy magnificence,
    So that this soul of mine, which thou hast healed,
    Pleasing to thee be loosened from the body."   90
Thus I implored; and she, so far away,
    Smiled, as it seemed, and looked once more at me;
    Then unto the eternal fountain turned.[18]
And said the Old Man holy: "That thou mayst
    Accomplish perfectly thy journeying,   95
    Whereunto prayer and holy love have sent me,
Fly with thine eyes all round about this garden;
    For seeing it will discipline thy sight
    Farther to mount along the ray divine.
And she, the Queen of Heaven, for whom I burn   100
    Wholly with love, will grant us every grace,
    Because that I her faithful Bernard am."[19]

As he who peradventure from Croatia
    Cometh to gaze at our Veronica,
      Who through its ancient fame is never sated,   105
But says in thought, the while it is displayed,
    "My Lord, Christ Jesus, God of very God,
      Now was your semblance made like unto this?"
Even such was I while gazing at the living
    Charity of the man, who in this world   110
      By contemplation tasted of that peace.[20]
"Thou son of grace, this jocund life," began he,
    "Will not be known to thee by keeping ever
      Thine eyes below here on the lowest place;
But mark the circles to the most remote,[21]   115
    Until thou shalt behold enthroned the Queen
      To whom this realm is subject and devoted."
I lifted up mine eyes, and as at morn
    The oriental part of the horizon
      Surpasses that wherein the sun goes down,   120
Thus, as if going with mine eyes from vale
    To mount, I saw a part in the remoteness
      Surpass in splendor all the other front.[22]
And even as there, where we await the pole
    That Phaeton drove badly,[23] blazes more   125
      The light, and is on either side diminished,
So likewise that pacific oriflamme[24]
    Gleamed brightest in the centre, and each side
      In equal measure did the flame abate.
And at that centre, with their wings expanded,   130
    More than a thousand jubilant Angels saw I.
      Each differing in effulgence and in kind.[25]
I saw there at their sports and at their songs
    A beauty smiling,[26] which the gladness was
      Within the eyes of all the other saints;   135
And if I had in speaking as much wealth
    As in imagining, I should not dare[27]
      To attempt the smallest part of its delight.

Bernard, as soon as he beheld mine eyes
    Fixed and intent upon its fervid fervor,   140
    His own with such affection turned to her
That it made mine more ardent to behold.

CANTO XXXII

$\mathcal{A}$BSORBED in his delight, that contemplator
    Assumed the willing office of a teacher,[1]
    And gave beginning to these holy words:
"The wound that Mary closed up and anointed,[2]
    She at her feet who is so beautiful,   5
    She is the one who opened it and pierced it,[3]
Within that order which the third seats make
    Is seated Rachel,[4] lower than the other,
    With Beatrice, in manner as thou seest.[5]
Sarah, Rebecca, Judith,[6] and her who was   10
    Ancestress of the Singer, who for dole
    Of the misdeed said, '*Miserere mei*,'[7]
Canst thou behold from seat to seat descending
    Down in gradation, as with each one's name
    I through the Rose go down from leaf to leaf.[8]   15
And downward from the seventh row, even as
    Above the same, succeed the Hebrew women,[9]
    Dividing all the tresses of the flower;
Because, according to the view which Faith
    In Christ hath taken, these are the partition   20
    By which the sacred stairways are divided.
Upon this side, where perfect is the flower
    With each one of its petals, seated are
    Those who believed in Christ who was to come.
Upon the other side, where intersected   25
    With vacant spaces[10] are the semicircles,
    Are those who looked to Christ already come.
And as, upon this side, the glorious seat

Of the Lady of Heaven, and the other seats
    Below it, such a great division make,   30
So opposite doth that of the great John,"
    Who, ever holy, desert and martyrdom
    Endured, and afterwards two years in Hell.
And under him thus to divide were chosen
    Francis, and Benedict, and Augustine,"   35
    And down to us the rest from round to round.
Behold now the high providence divine;
    For one and other aspect of the Faith
    In equal measure shall this garden fill."
And know that downward from that rank which cleaves   40
    Midway the sequence of the two divisions,
    Not by their proper merit are they seated;
But by another's under fixed conditions;
    For these are spirits one and all assoiled
    Before they any true election had."   45
Well canst thou recognize it in their faces,
    And also in their voices puerile,
    If thou regard them well and hearken to them.
Now doubtest thou, and doubting thou art silent;
    But I will loosen for thee the strong bond   50
    In which thy subtile fancies hold thee fast.
Within the amplitude of this domain
    No casual point can possibly find place,
    No more than sadness can, or thirst, or hunger;
For by eternal law has been established   55
    Whatever thou beholdest, so that closely
    The ring is fitted to the finger here."
And therefore are these people, festinate*
    Unto true life, not *sine causa*" here
    More and less excellent among themselves.   60
The King, by means of whom this realm reposes
    In so great love and in so great delight

---

*Hurried.

That no will ventureth to ask for more,
In his own joyous aspect every mind
    Creating, at his pleasure dowers with grace   65
    Diversely; and let here the effect suffice.[17]
And this is clearly and expressly noted
    For you in Holy Scripture, in those twins
    Who in their mother had their anger roused.
According to the color of the hair,[18]   70
    Therefore, with such a grace the light supreme
    Consenteth that they worthily be crowned.
Without, then, any merit of their deeds,
    Stationed are they in different gradations,
    Differing only in their first acuteness.[19]   75
'Tis true that in the early centuries,
    With innocence, to work out their salvation
    Sufficient was the faith of parents only.[20]
After the earlier ages were completed,
    Behoved it that the males by circumcision[21]   80
    Unto their innocent wings should virtue add;
But after that the time of grace had come
    Without the baptism absolute of Christ,[22]
    Such innocence below there was retained.
Look now into the face that unto Christ[23]   85
    Hath most resemblance; for its brightness only
    Is able to prepare thee to see Christ."
On her did I behold so great a gladness
    Rain down, borne onward in the holy minds[24]
    Created through that altitude to fly,   90
That whatsoever I had seen before
    Did not suspend me in such admiration,
    Nor show me such similitude of God.
And the same Love that first descended there,
    "*Ave Maria, gratia plena,*"[25] singing,   95
    In front of her his wings expanded wide.
Unto the canticle divine responded[26]
    From every part the court beatified,
    So that each sight became serener for it.

"O holy father, who for me endurest   100
      To be below here, leaving the sweet place
      In which thou sittest by eternal lot,
Who is the Angel[27] that with so much joy
      Into the eyes is looking of our Queen,
      Enamored so that he seems made of fire?"   105
Thus I again recourse had to the teaching
      Of that one who delighted him in Mary[28]
      As doth the star of morning[29] in the sun.
And he to me: "Such gallantry and grace
      As there can be in Angel and in soul,   110
      All is in him; and thus we fain would have it;
Because he is the one who bore the palm[30]
      Down unto Mary, when the Son of God
      To take our burden on himself decreed.
But now come onward with thine eyes, as I   115
      Speaking shall go, and note the great patricians[31]
      Of this most just and merciful of empires.
Those two[32] that sit above there most enraptured,
      As being very near unto Augusta,[33]
      Are as it were the two roots of this Rose.   120
He who upon the left is near her placed
      The father is, by whose audacious taste
      The human species so much bitter tastes.
Upon the right thou seest that ancient father
      Of Holy Church, into whose keeping Christ   125
      The keys committed of this lovely flower.
And he who all the evil days beheld,[34]
      Before his death, of her the beauteous bride
      Who with the spear and with the nails was won,
Beside him sits, and by the other rests   130
      That leader[35] under whom on manna lived
      The people ingrate, fickle, and stiff-necked.
Opposite Peter seest thou Anna[36] seated,
      So well content to look upon her daughter,
      Her eyes she moves not while she sings Hosanna.   135
And opposite the eldest household father

Lucìa sits,[37] she who thy Lady moved
　　When to rush downward thou didst bend thy brows.
But since the moments of thy vision fly,
　　Here will we make full stop, as a good tailor　　　　　140
　　Who makes the gown according to his cloth,
And unto the first Love will turn our eyes,[38]
　　That looking upon Him thou penetrate
　　As far as possible through his effulgence.[39]
Truly, lest peradventure thou recede,　　　　　145
　　Moving thy wings believing to advance,
　　By prayer behoves it that grace be obtained;
Grace from that one who has the power to aid thee;[40]
　　And thou shalt follow me with thy affection
　　That from my words thy heart turn not aside."　　　　　150
And he began this holy orison.[41]

CANTO XXXIII

THOU Virgin Mother,[1] daughter of thy Son,
 Humble and high beyond all other creature,
 The limit fixed of the eternal counsel,
Thou art the one who such nobility
 To human nature gave, that its Creator   5
 Did not disdain to make himself its creature,
Within thy womb rekindled was the love,
 By heat of which in the eternal peace
 After such wise this flower has germinated.
Here unto us thou art a noonday torch   10
 Of charity, and below there among mortals
 Thou art the living fountain-head of hope.
Lady, thou art so great, and so prevailing,
 That he who wishes grace, nor runs to thee,
 His aspirations without wings would fly.   15
Not only thy benignity gives succor
 To him who asketh it, but oftentimes
 Forerunneth of its own accord the asking.
In thee compassion is, in thee is pity,
 In thee magnificence; in thee unites   20
 Whate'er of goodness is in any creature.
Now doth this man, who from the lowest depth
 Of the universe as far as here has seen
 One after one the spiritual lives,[2]
Supplicate thee through grace for so much power   25
 That with his eyes he may uplift himself
 Higher towards the uttermost salvation.
And I, who never burned for my own seeing

More than I do for his, all of my prayers
    Proffer to thee, and pray they come not short,   30
That thou wouldst scatter from him every cloud
    Of his mortality so with thy prayers,
    That the Chief Pleasure³ be to him displayed.
Still farther do I pray thee, Queen, who canst
    Whate'er thou wilt, that sound thou mayst preserve
    After so great a vision⁴ his affections.   35
Let thy protection conquer human movements;
    See Beatrice and all the blessed ones
    My prayers to second clasp their hands to thee!"⁵
The eyes beloved and revered of God,   40
    Fastened upon the speaker, showed to us
    How grateful unto her are prayers devout;
Then unto the Eternal Light they turned,⁶
    On which it is not credible could be
    By any creature bent an eye so clear.   45
And I, who to the end of all desires
    Was now approaching, even as I ought
    The ardor of desire within me ended.
Bernard was beckoning unto me, and smiling,
    That I should upward look; but I already   50
    Was of my own accord⁷ such as he wished;
Because my sight, becoming purified,
    Was entering more and more into the ray,
    Of the High Light which of itself is true.
From that time forward what I saw was greater   55
    Than our discourse,⁸ that to such vision yields,
    And yields the memory unto such excess.
Even as he is who seeth in a dream,
    And after dreaming the imprinted passion
    Remains, and to his mind the rest returns not,   60
Even such am I, for almost utterly
    Ceases my vision,⁹ and distilleth yet
    Within my heart the sweetness born of it;
Even thus the snow is in the sun unsealed,
    Even thus upon the wind in the light leaves   65

Were the soothsayings of the Sibyl lost.[10]
O Light Supreme, that dost so far uplift thee
    From the conceits of mortals, to my mind
    Of what thou didst appear re-lend a little,
And make my tongue of so great puissance,   70
    That but a single sparkle of thy glory[11]
    It may bequeath unto the future people;
For by returning to my memory somewhat,
    And by a little sounding in these verses,
    More of thy victory shall be conceived!   75
I think the keenness of the living ray
    Which I endured[12] would have bewildered me,
    If but mine eyes had been averted from it;
And I remember that I was more bold
    On this account to bear, so that I joined   80
    My aspect with the Glory Infinite.[13]
O grace abundant, by which I presumed
    To fix my sight upon the Light Eternal,
    So that the seeing I consumed therein!
I saw that in its depth far down is lying   85
    Bound up with love together in one volume,
    What through the universe in leaves is scattered;
Substance, and accident, and their operations,
    All interfused together in such wise
    That what I speak of is one simple light.[14]   90
The universal fashion of this knot[15]
    Methinks I saw, since more abundantly
    In saying this I feel that I rejoice.
One moment is more lethargy to me,
    Than five and twenty centuries to the emprise   95
    That startled Neptune with the shade of Argo![16]
My mind in this wise wholly in suspense,
    Steadfast, immovable, attentive gazed,
    And evermore with gazing grew enkindled.
In presence of that light one such becomes,   100
    That to withdraw therefrom for other prospect
    It is impossible he e'er consent;

Because the good, which object is of will,[17]
     Is gathered all in this, and out of it
     That is defective which is perfect there.   105
Shorter henceforward will my language fall
     Of what I yet remember, than an infant's
     Who still his tongue doth moisten at the breast.[18]
Not because more than one unmingled semblance
     Was in the living light on which I looked,   110
     For it is always what it was before;
But through the sight, that fortified itself
     In me by looking, one appearance only
     To me was ever changing as I changed.
Within the deep and luminous subsistence   115
     Of the High Light appeared to me three circles,
     Of threefold color and of one dimension,
And by the second seemed the first reflected
     As Iris is by Iris,[19] and the third
     Seemed fire that equally from both is breathed.   120
O how all speech is feeble and falls short
     Of my conceit, and this to what I saw
     Is such, 'tis not enough to call it little![20]
O Light Eterne, sole in thyself that dwellest,
     Sole knowest thyself, and, known unto thyself   125
     And knowing, lovest and smilest on thyself![21]
That circulation, which being thus conceived
     Appeared in thee as a reflected light,
     When somewhat contemplated by mine eyes,
Within itself, of its own very color   130
     Seemed to me painted with our effigy,[22]
     Wherefore my sight was all absorbed therein.
As the geometrician, who endeavors
     To square the circle, and discovers not,
     By taking thought, the principle he wants,   135
Even such was I at that new apparition;
     I wished to see how the image to the circle
     Conformed itself, and how it there finds place;
But my own wings were not enough for this,

Had it not been that then there smote my mind   140
    A flash of lightning,[23] wherein came its wish.
Here vigor failed the lofty fantasy:[24]
    But now was turning my desire and will,[25]
    Even as a wheel that equally is moved,
The Love which moves the sun and the other stars.   145

Endnotes

In the notes to this edition of Paradiso *all quotations from the Bible are from the King James Version.*

CANTO I

1. (p. 3) *The glory of Him who moveth everything:* As the following verses of this first canto make clear, the glory of God (Him) is primarily God's light. Here Dante the Poet describes God as the Prime Mover in the Universe, the source of all other motion in it—an important aspect of Aristotelian and Scholastic philosophy. Dante's references to light will be one of the distinguishing characteristics of his poetry in the *Paradiso,* and indeed, the very last line of the poem will conclude that this light, this divine glory, is "the Love which moves the sun and the other stars" (XXXIII: 145).

2. (p. 3) *and shine / In one part more and in another less:* The Poet underscores a fundamental tenet of Scholastic philosophy as he declares that the light of God differs according to the greater or lesser capacity of each thing to contain it. Dante also discusses this idea in *Il Convivio (The Banquet)* III: vii: 2, and in his *Epistolam X ad Canem Grandem della Scala (The Letter to Cangrande).*

3. (p. 3) *Within that heaven . . . Was I:* The Poet declares that he was in the Empyrean, which, in the realm of Dante's scientific ideas, is the highest sphere of the Ptolemaic universe and the dwelling place of God and the Blessed. Thus the Poet is saying that he has already traveled to the end of his journey and is now relating, to the extent that human mental and literary capacities are able, what he saw there.

4. (p. 3) *which to repeat / Nor knows, nor can, who from above descends:* Classical rhetoricians refer to this passage as the "topos [theme] of ineffability or inexpressibility," as it is the Poet's declaration that it would be

impossible to describe adequately and fully the visions he has been privileged to enjoy in the Empyrean. What the Poet is about to describe is now in the past, and the impossibility of adequate description of Paradise will become one of his most convincing descriptions of this place throughout the third canticle.

5. (p. 3) *its desire:* That is, the vision of God is the object of the intellect's desire (an idea identified with Saint Thomas Aquinas and Scholastic theology).

6. (p. 3) *O good Apollo:* Lines 13–36, as Dante himself suggests in the *Epistolam X ad Canem Grandem della Scala*, may be considered as an exordium, or prologue, to the entire canticle. Following the tradition of poets (as opposed to orators) in including some form of invocation in a prologue, the Poet invokes not just the classical Muses (as he has done earlier in *Inferno* II: 7 and *Purgatorio* I: 8) but also Apollo, the Greek and Roman god of light, healing, poetry, and prophecy, and the father of the Muses.

7. (p. 3) *the beloved laurel asks!:* The Poet begs Apollo to grant him the power to merit the crown of laurel or bay leaf that was bestowed only upon great poets or conquering warriors. The "beloved laurel" also refers to the mythological tale of Daphne, who was loved and pursued by Apollo and was changed into a laurel. The source of this myth is Ovid's *Metamorphoses* I: 452–567.

8. (p. 3) *now with both:* According to Lucan (*Pharsalia* III: 173), the Mount of Parnassus had two peaks: Nisa, sacred to the Muses, and Cyrrha, sacred to Apollo. Because of the difficulty in committing to poetry what the Poet has observed in Paradise, he will now need all the help he can obtain—he will require the inspiration of both peaks of Parnassus, rather than the single peak he implies inspired the poetry of *Inferno* and *Purgatorio,* the subjects of which were simpler to relate.

9. (p. 3) *Marsyas:* In Ovid's *Metamorphoses* VI: 382–400, Dante would have read the description of the fate of a satyr of Phrygia who found a discarded flute and with great presumption challenged Apollo's musical ability with his lyre. When the Muses judged that Apollo had won the contest, Apollo punished Marsyas by tying him to a tree and pulling him out of his skin while he was still alive. Dante thus prays to Apollo to give him the same poetic skill that the god mustered up to vanquish his opponent. In some sense, he is also asking that his poetic

talents be freed from all earthly or human limitations in order to be capable of describing his heavenly experiences (a form of separating the mind and the body, perhaps a mystic experience that can be communicated to others).

10. (p. 3) *thy darling tree:* That is, the laurel.

11. (p. 4) *crown myself:* Here and in *Paradiso* XXV: 1–9, Dante declares his belief that his poetic talent and his *Divine Comedy* qualify him for the laurel crown of the master poet. Note that he speaks of crowning himself, not of being crowned; Dante was never very modest about his talent.

12. (p. 4) *the Peneian foliage . . . the joyous Delphic deity:* Laurel is called "Peneian" here because Daphne was the daughter of the river god Peneus, who was changed into a laurel by her father at her bequest while she fled from an aroused Apollo. Dante calls Peneus the "Delphic deity" because he had a temple and an oracle at Delphi, beneath Mount Parnassus.

13. (p. 4) *Perchance with better voices after me / Shall prayer be made that Cyrrha may respond!:* Feigning modesty after speaking of crowning himself poet laureate, the Poet now expresses hope that if his inspiration is insufficient, perhaps his attempt will inspire someone else to describe Paradise with Apollo's help. Cyrrha, one of the peaks of Parnassus, refers to Apollo himself.

14. (p. 4) *To mortal men by passages diverse / Uprises the world's lamp . . . after its own fashion:* Dante refers to the time (Wednesday, April 13, 1300) and the season (the vernal equinox) when the Pilgrim journeyed through Paradise. Similar statements requiring some knowledge of astronomy were made in *Inferno* II: 1–5 and *Purgatorio* I: 13, 115–117. A diagram best describes what he means here (see next page).

15. (p. 4) *morning there / And evening here:* At noon on the day of the vernal equinox, earth's southern hemisphere would be lit (therefore "morning there") while the northern hemisphere would be dark (therefore "evening here"). Although a dark northern hemisphere and a lighted southern hemisphere would be impossible in a system with the sun in the center of the universe, Dante obviously believes it is possible in the Ptolemaic system of the universe with the earth at its center. The reader should keep in mind that in Dante's fiction the Pilgrim entered Hell in the evening and his journey through Purgatory

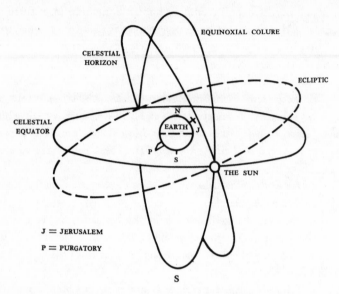

The "world's lamp" (l. 38) is the sun, which rises at different points (l. 37, "by passages diverse") on the horizon at various times of the year. The four circles (l. 39, "circles four") are the equinoctial colure, the celestial horizon, the celestial equator, and the ecliptic, while the "three crosses" of l. 39 are formed at the point where the four circles intersect. When the sun rises in this fashion, it is associated with the most desirable constellation, Aries, because the sun was said to be in Aries when God created the universe. Four circles and three crosses suggest a number of important things to Dante: the four cardinal virtues (prudence, fortitude, temperance, and justice); the three theological virtues (faith, hope, and charity); the trinity; and the cross. The intersection of these seven virtues is a good omen for salvation, the reward held out by Paradise. Finally, the sun is the perfect symbol for divine illumination. The wax of the world (the "mundane wax" of l. 41) is warmed by the sunlight of the approaching summer season, just as God's goodwill shines upon His creation.

commenced at dawn. Now the Pilgrim will begin his ascent to Paradise at high noon, the time when the sun is most resplendent.

16. (p. 4) *When Beatrice towards the left-hand side:* At the end of *Purgatorio*, Beatrice had been facing east, but she now turns to her left (that is, northward) to face the sun.

17. (p. 4) *Never did eagle:* It was commonly held during Dante's day that only the eagle could stare directly into the sun, as Beatrice does here.

18. (p. 4) *And even as a second ray:* In ll. 49–54, the Poet compares a scientific observation (how light reflects back to its source) with a pilgrim's desire to return home again. In a larger sense, this is what occurs during the Pilgrim's journey to Paradise: The mind returns to God.

19. (p. 4) *fixed mine eyes beyond our wont:* The Pilgrim imitates Beatrice and stares into the sun.

20. (p. 4) *the place / Made for the human species as its own:* The Pilgrim remains at this point in the Garden of Eden, and his ability to perceive more light than is normal results from his recent purification and return to the primal state of innocence that existed before the Fall.

21. (p. 4) *But I beheld it sparkle round . . . from the fire:* The blazing sparks the Pilgrim perceives underscore the fact that he has begun his journey upward toward the heavens. As yet, the Pilgrim is not aware of the fact that he is soaring through space upward, so he believes that the increased illumination results from God adding a second sun to the sky. In addition to increased light, there is also decreased weight, for throughout the poem Dante has associated purification with weighing less. From Hell through Purgatory, motion was impeded by gravity, but now the Pilgrim has been freed from such terrestrial bounds. At this time, the Pilgrim is rising through the Sphere of Air above the earthly Paradise and approaches the Sphere of Fire, a region thought to encircle earth between the Sphere of Air and the Sphere of the Moon.

22. (p. 5) *the everlasting wheels:* These are the eternal spheres of the Ptolemaic universe.

23. (p. 5) *As Glaucus . . . beneath the sea:* Ovid's *Metamorphoses* XIII: 904–968 describes how a fisherman noticed that the fish he caught revived and jumped back into the sea when they were placed upon a certain herb, and when he ate some of the herb, he was transformed into a sea-god. In like manner, as the Pilgrim gazes upon Beatrice, he begins to experience a transformation preparing him for Paradise and eventual immortality.

24. (p. 5) *To represent transhumanize in words / Impossible were:* Dante the Poet notes that it would be impossible to describe adequately "in words" (the original line is in Latin, *per verba*) the process of going beyond the human that Dante the Pilgrim is now experiencing. In this first canto, Dante has constantly underlined such transformation by several references to Ovid's *Metamorphoses,* the most famous classical text about human change available to him. Dante combines such ideas from classical antiquity with the mystical tradition of Christianity.

25. (p. 5) *Grace the experience reserves:* Dante notes that a true comprehension of this "transhumanizing" experience will come only through God's grace.

26. (p. 5) *If I was merely . . . lift me with thy life!:* Dante the Poet is uncertain if he rose bodily toward Paradise or rose with his soul alone. In *Purgatorio* XXV: 67–75, Statius explained to the Pilgrim that God breathed the soul into the body after all else had been created. The "Love who governest the heaven" refers to God (l. 74) while "thy light" (l. 75) refers to Beatrice. The Poet must be referring to Saint Paul's description of a similar experience in the Bible, 2 Corinthians 12: 3–4, where the Apostle refuses to specify whether or not the body and soul are united in a mystical vision of Paradise. The reader should recall the Pilgrim's remark in *Inferno* II: 32, "I not Aeneas am, I am not Paul": In spite of his expressed fears, he has already followed Aeneas through the underworld, and now he is about to follow Paul toward Paradise.

27. (p. 5) *the wheel:* The great eternal wheel or sphere is the Primum Mobile, the outermost sphere of the universe through which one must pass before entering the Empyrean, God's abode. Its motion was said to have derived from the love of God, since every part of the material universe is eager to come into contact with the Empyrean. Dante discusses this Aristotelian notion in *Il Convivio* II: iii: 9.

28. (p. 5) *harmony:* While a number of classical thinkers (Pythagoras and Plato among them) held that the motion of the heavenly spheres produced a kind of harmonious music, Aristotle rejected this idea in *De coelo* II: 9. Dante's source is probably Cicero's *De Republica* VI: xviii, 18–19, known as the *Somnium Scipionis* (*Dream of Scipio*) and widely read in the Middle Ages through the commentary of Macrobius.

29. (p. 5) *By the sun's flame:* Dante believed that a Sphere of Fire existed beyond earth's Sphere of Air. The Pilgrim has now risen into this realm. It was there, supposedly, that lightning was formed (see l. 115 in this canto: "This bears away the fire towards the moon").

30. (p. 5) *ere I did mine to ask:* Beatrice and the other souls in Paradise all have the ability to read the Pilgrim's mind and will frequently resolve his doubts before they are expressed.

31. (p. 5) *"But lightning . . . who thitherward returnest":* Just as lightning moves from the Sphere of Fire downward toward earth, the Pilgrim is moving more quickly than lightning toward Paradise, returning to the soul's home. Beatrice realizes the Pilgrim believes he is still on earth, so sudden is his transformation.

32. (p. 5) *"In what way I transcend these bodies light"*: The Pilgrim is obviously concerned about how he is actually rising through the heavens—whether by body or soul or both—since he seems to be defying the basic laws of physics. No answer is ever supplied to this question in Dante's poem.

33. (p. 6) *"All things . . . ."*: From here through l. 141, the penultimate line of the canto, Beatrice offers a complicated explanation of how the Pilgrim is able to ascend from earth to Paradise, providing in the process an important statement about the universe that combines Dante's understanding of the cosmos and how a providential order informs it.

34. (p. 6) *"order among themselves . . . the universe resemble God"*: Because there is a complete order and harmony in the universe as created by God, the form of the material universe is cast in the image of God its Maker.

35. (p. 6) *"Here do the higher creatures . . . Whereto is made the law already mentioned"*: God teleologically organizes the universe, and He is the final cause of its order, the end toward which all things move. His "footprints" (l. 106) may be discerned throughout creation. The "higher creatures"—men, the angels, the Blessed—possess the faculty to contemplate God's harmony and order.

36. (p. 6) *"In the order . . . near unto their origin"*: All things in the universe obey a motive force, which is love, but in a hierarchical fashion. Those most perfect (those "inclined . . . by their destinies diverse," ll. 109–110) will be closest to God, while those less perfect will be farther away.

37. (p. 6) *"O'er the great sea of being . . . With instinct"*: Everything in the universe seeks by instinct its natural position in the cosmic hierarchy, moved by a response to a kind of desire toward its proper position. Dante thus affirms what modern scholars have defined as the Great Chain of Being, but he calls it here "the great sea of being," where different ships head for diverse ports according to their natures and their rightful place in this hierarchical order.

38. (p. 6) *"this bow"*: Because Beatrice's explanation of the cosmos and man's place in it is teleological—stressing the end or purpose of all things—her metaphorical comparison of this system to archery and the aiming of a bow at a target is appropriate. God is thus an archer who aims each creature at its own proper position in the hierarchy. He does so with a bow that stands for love, the motive power of the universe.

39. (p. 6) *"the heaven ... the greatest haste"*: The reference is to the Empyrean, the final resting place of the blessed in their contemplation of God. The sphere "which has the greatest haste," or moves the swiftest, is the Primum Mobile, and it is contained within the Empyrean, which is characterized by quiet.

40. (p. 6) *"a joyous mark"*: As befits a teleological conception of the universe, God aims us at Himself because of His natural love, and thus He is a happy target.

41. (p. 6) *"True is it ...."*: In ll. 127–135, Beatrice addresses one of the most vexing of all theological and philosophical questions—that of free will versus determinism. Since some souls obviously do not return to God after He has aimed them at Himself, can He be at fault? God (now implicitly compared to an artist, perhaps a potter), whose intentions are always good, may not fully realize the object He creates because the matter or material with which he works, like defective potter's clay, may be "deaf" to the artist's intention (l. 129). Thus the fault lies with the material and not with the artist.

42. (p. 6) *"from a cloud"*: Just as lightning falls to earth from the skies, even though its natural inclination is to rise up, so too man may exercise free will and divert what should be the normal course toward God.

43. (pp. 6–7) *"Thou should not wonder more ... to the plain"*: Beatrice tells the Pilgrim that he should no more wonder that what is purified must ascend toward God than he would be amazed by the fact that water runs downhill.

44. (p. 7) *she heavenward:* After her long philosophical and theological discourse, which admits of no arguments or questions, Beatrice's heaven-directed face provides a natural conclusion to her argument and also implies that the Pilgrim will follow her gaze and rise with her to heaven. Beatrice's turn toward heaven will be immediately followed in the first 21 lines of the second canto by one of the most interesting addresses to the reader in Dante's entire poem.

CANTO II

1. (p. 8) *O ye, who in some pretty little boat . . . . :* Lines 1–21 interrupt the picture of Dante the Pilgrim following Beatrice's gaze toward heaven and include an important address to the reader of the poem by Dante the Poet. In *Purgatorio* I: 1–6, the Poet compared his poetic skill to a small boat ("the little vessel of my genius," as he puts it) that is traversing strange waters and appeals to the Muses for assistance. Now (ll. 8–9), not only the nine Muses but also Minerva, Apollo, and Beatrice assist him in the far more difficult task of recounting the vision of Paradise. Note that the Reader is in a little boat and Dante the Poet is in a larger one.

2. (p. 8) *has never yet been passed:* No other poet has ever attempted to cross such waters—a metaphor for Dante's description of difficult theological questions that had rarely been treated in epic poetry before.

3. (p. 8) *Minerva . . . Apollo:* Minerva was the goddess of wisdom, while Apollo was the god of poetry. In the poetry of the *Paradiso*, wisdom and poetry go hand in hand (indeed, without wisdom, it is virtually impossible to understand the poem fully).

4. (p. 8) *the Bears:* Dante means the pole of the northern hemisphere but identifies this direction by reference to the two "she-bears"—Ursa Major and Ursa Minor, the Big Bear (Big Dipper) and the Little Bear (Little Dipper). The North Star is contained in Ursa Minor.

5. (p. 8) *th' bread of Angels . . . not sated by it:* This biblical expression is taken from Psalms 78: 25, or the Wisdom of Solomon 16:20 in the Apocrypha. According to Dante in *Il Convivio* I: i: 7, the bread of the angels is wisdom obtained by the knowledge of God. Man grows "not sated" by this food because he is incapable of ever grasping totally the meaning of God, and his desire to do so is constantly unsatisfied.

6. (p. 8) *Colchos . . . a ploughman made:* Colchos, or Colchis, the kingdom of King Aetes, was the destination of Jason and his Argonauts in search of the Golden Fleece. Among the tasks the King obliged Jason to perform was to plow a field with wild bulls and to plant a field with serpent's teeth from which armed men would spring (Ovid's *Metamorphoses* VII: 102–158). Jason has already been encountered in *Inferno* XVIII: 86–96. The Poet means to imply that the Pilgrim's journey toward Paradise will be even more amazing than Jason's search for the Golden Fleece.

7. (p. 8) *as strikes a bolt . . . unlocks itself:* Earlier in canto I, the Pilgrim's rapid ascent had been compared to a bolt of lightning; now it is compared to the instant a crossbow's bolt flies through the air and strikes its target. However, the Poet reverses the order of the three events required to shoot a crossbow—"strikes," "flies," "unlocks," rather than "unlocks," "flies," "strikes"—emphasizing their virtual simultaneity and therefore incredible speed (a technique ancient rhetoricians called *hysteron proteron,* or "the last placed first"). Another interesting instance of this device is at *Paradiso* XXII: 109.

8. (p. 9) *"the first star":* The moon, in the Ptolemaic system, is the first star or planet, and the first Beatrice and the Pilgrim reach as they ascend toward Paradise.

9. (p. 9) *Luminous, dense . . . the eternal pearl:* By comparing the realm of the moon to both a diamond and a pearl, the Pilgrim wishes to emphasize that the moon is formed of actual matter and is not simply a cloudlike substance. By his comparison of the moon to a diamond lit by the sun's rays (l. 33), the Pilgrim also reveals that he believes that its surface is completely smooth. Some centuries later, Galileo's telescope would reveal that the moon's topography is certainly not diamondlike and smooth.

10. (p. 9) *even as water doth receive / A ray of light:* The Pilgrim seems to be thinking of himself as a corporeal entity and is surprised at the way one solid body (the moon) could take into itself another solid body (the Pilgrim), while both bodies remain intact. He thus enters the moon in corporeal form in the same mysterious way as light enters water.

11. (p. 9) *How God and our own nature were united . . . the first truth that man believes:* Christ's simultaneous human and divine nature may be considered, in physical terms, as analogous to the question of how two bodies manage to occupy the same space at the same time. The Pilgrim provides the answer to this question: The human and divine nature of Christ is demonstrated only by faith, and not by reason (l. 43) or by first principles or axioms (the "first truth").

12. (p. 9) *"that fabulous tale of Cain?":* In *Inferno* XX: 126 the Poet has already referred to the medieval belief that Cain, with a bush of thorns, was exiled to the moon for killing his brother Abel (Cain in the Moon was thus what we call the Man in the Moon). The Pilgrim asks Beatrice about this belief because from earth, dark marks on the moon (that is,

Cain and his thorns) are visible, even though he has just described the moon as a heavenly body that is diamondlike in its smoothness.

13. (p. 9) *"following the senses . . . reason has short wings":* Even with sensory knowledge, human reason is fallible.

14. (p. 9) *"by bodies rare and dense":* The Pilgrim explains moon spots by varying density: dense bodies reflect the sun's light, while in bodies with less density, the sun's rays shine through without reflecting, causing dark spots to appear to those observing from earth. This explanation follows an argument Dante employed earlier, in *Il Convivio* II: xiii: 9; there, Dante had followed a theory originally put forward by Averroës (1126–1198), an influential Arab explicator of Aristotle's philosophy who was much studied in Dante's times. Beatrice will now refute Averroës's views.

15. (p. 10) *"Lights":* These are the stars.

16. (p. 10) *"the eighth sphere":* This is the Sphere of the Fixed Stars, the eighth heaven counting upward from the moon. This area is where the various constellations are found and is located between the ninth sphere (the Primum Mobile) and the seventh sphere (the Sphere of Saturn).

17. (p. 10) *"quality and quantity":* That is, the quality, or color, and quantity, or intensity, of their light.

18. (p. 10) *"If this were caused . . . or equally":* Beatrice argues that the Sphere of the Fixed Stars shows many stars that are different in the quality and quantity of their light, and these differences must be explained in the same way as the moon spots. But if the differences resulted solely from the greater or lesser density of the stars, it would follow that all stars would have a single specific virtue or nature. Beatrice argues subsequently (ll. 70 ff.) that the fixed stars each have different virtues based on different formal principles. She accepts the Scholastic view that the formal principle, or substantial form, constitutes the various virtues of bodies, while the material principle, or primary matter, is the same in all bodies. The formal principle is the active principle that determines the specific form of any given thing.

19. (p. 10) *"Besides, if rarity . . . This is not so":* Beatrice turns from rejecting the Pilgrim's theory philosophically to a rejection of it in physical terms. First, she suggests that the explanation might be that the stars resemble meat, which has layers of fat and lean (l. 77). This is an

interesting comparison, since she also mentions the volume of a book with its leaves—not a printed book, of course, but a book made from parchment produced from animal skins (one side of which would be paler than the other, since one side would have had hair on it). In fact, medieval books made from parchment would alternate the sides of pages, so that when opened, the book would display two like pages (either two made from the hairy side of the hide or two made from the fleshy side of the hide). Beatrice rejects such an explanation, because we do not see the sun's rays shining through the "thin" parts of the moon during an eclipse (ll. 79–82).

20. (pp. 10–11) *"Now thou wilt say the sunbeam shows itself . . . equally resplendent"*: Beatrice proposes that the Pilgrim perform a scientific experiment, since experimentation is the source of learning or knowledge, the "rivers of your arts" (l. 96). Three mirrors should be arranged (see diagram below) so that two are equally distant from the Pilgrim and one is between them but farther away, and a light source should be placed behind him. The more distant mirror will cast back a light equal in brightness but inferior in size to the other two lights. This simulates a distribution of thick and thin material on the moon upon which the sun's rays strike.

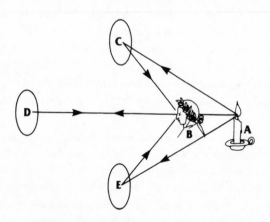

A lamp behind back (sun)
B person in experiment
C, D, E mirrors
C, E equidistant (outer surface of moon)
D more distant (center of moon)

21. (p. 11) *"Now, as beneath the touches of warm rays . . . living light"*: By refuting the Pilgrim's false ideas, Beatrice will purge his mind of error, just as the sun strips snow of its cold and whiteness, filling him with the "living light" of truth.

22. (p. 11) *"the heaven of the divine repose"*: This is the Empyrean, God's dwelling. To explain the moon spots, Beatrice turns to the tenth and highest heaven.

23. (p. 11) *"Revolves a body, in whose virtue lies"*: This is the Primum Mobile, the Ninth or Crystalline Heaven, that revolves within the Empyrean and contains the entire universe. Beatrice holds that the Primum Mobile derives a "virtue," or power, from the Empyrean, which contains it, and that the Primum Mobile in turn transmits this power to the material universe lying within it. Thus all power ultimately flows from God.

24. (p. 11) *"The following heaven"*: This is the eighth heaven, or the Sphere of the Fixed Stars, in which the constellations differentiate and distribute these powers or virtues through the planetary spheres to earth.

25. (p. 11) *"The other spheres"*: The other seven planetary spheres beneath the Primum Mobile and the Sphere of the Fixed Stars are, in ascending degree of importance: (1) the moon; (2) Mercury; (3) Venus; (4) the sun; (5) Mars; (6) Jupiter; (7) Saturn.

26. (p. 11) *"from above they take, and act beneath"*: Each sphere takes its power from God above and influences man below.

27. (p. 11) *"how to keep the ford"*: In a military metaphor, Beatrice tells the Pilgrim that after being properly instructed in the truth of the matter at hand, he should be capable of defending the ford himself (presumably the ford of the river of truth).

28. (p. 11) *"The power and motion . . . As from the artisan the hammer's craft"*: Just as the blacksmith determines the motion of his hammer and the shape of his art, the "blessed motors," or the nine angelic orders (l. 127), influence each sphere. These angelic orders were distributed throughout the universe, and each was associated with one of the nine realms under the Empyrean: (1) Moon / Angels; (2) Mercury / Archangels; (3) Venus / Powers; (4) Sun / Principalities; (5) Mars / Virtues; (6) Jupiter / Dominions; (7) Saturn / Thrones; (8) Fixed Stars / Cherubim; (9) Primum Mobile / Seraphim. We shall soon

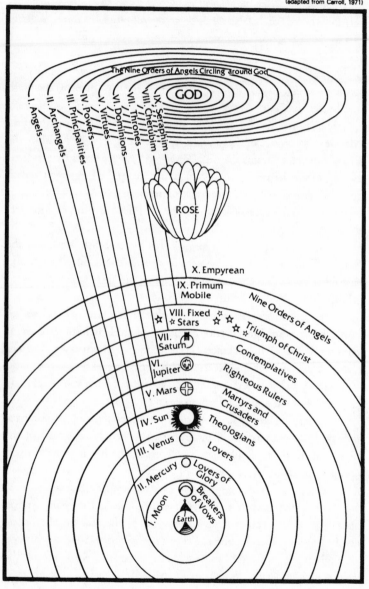

The Nine Orders of Angels Circling around God

GOD

I. Angels
II. Archangels
III. Principalities
IV. Powers
V. Virtues
VI. Dominions
VII. Thrones
VIII. Cherubim
IX. Seraphim

ROSE

X. Empyrean

IX. Primum Mobile

Nine Orders of Angels

VIII. Fixed Stars

Triumph of Christ

VII. Saturn

Contemplatives

VI. Jupiter

Righteous Rulers

V. Mars

Martyrs and Crusaders

IV. Sun

Theologians

III. Venus

Lovers

II. Mercury

Lovers of Glory

I. Moon

Breakers of Vows

Earth

discover that these nine realms are also associated with different personalities. See the diagram on facing page.

29. (p. 11) *"The heaven"*: This is the Sphere of the Fixed Stars (the eighth heaven).

30. (p. 11) *"the Intelligence profound . . . makes of it a seal"*: The angelic order that is associated with the Sphere of the Fixed Stars is the Cherubim. This eighth heaven receives from the mind of the presiding Cherubim, or "Intelligence," the power from God through the Primum Mobile. Taking God's image from above, the heaven makes itself the seal that impresses His image below in much the same way as an image is pressed upon hot wax by a seal.

31. (pp. 11–12) *"within your dust . . . mingled virtue through the body shines"*: "Dust" is a reference to the human body. Beatrice explains that the same way as the human soul distributes its power throughout the body, where it becomes differentiated according to the nature of the part that receives it, the undifferentiated power of God is distributed through the heavenly spheres and becomes differentiated when it combines with the qualities associated with them, producing a "mingled virtue."

32. (p. 12) *"From this proceeds whate'er from light to light . . . dark and bright"*: Appropriately enough, Beatrice concludes her explanation with a discussion of light. Each heavenly body emits light in accordance with its "mingled virtue," which is differentiated because of the different qualities of the angelic orders in each sphere. The Pilgrim must abandon his reliance upon sensory experience to understand the moon spots in favor of this more complicated explanation. Thus the dark spots on the moon result from the different mingling of virtue in different places on the moon. It should be noted that the Pilgrim's simple and initial question about moon spots, expressed first in terms of the rarity and density of matter, has been transformed into an explanation of spiritual causality that turns into an explanation of the divine plan of the entire universe. Beatrice's lesson in celestial physics with a Christian, Scholastic twist becomes a fitting introduction to the geography of Paradise.

CANTO III

1. (p. 13) *That sun:* The reference is to Beatrice.

2. (p. 13) *erst with love my bosom warmed:* In his *La Vita Nuova* (*The New Life*) II, Dante speaks of his love for Beatrice when he was only

nine years of age. The Poet mentions this youthful love in *Purgatorio* XXX: 41–42.

3. (p. 13) *proving and reproving:* Beatrice both provides proofs of her views, which are true, and disproves the views of the Pilgrim, which are in error.

4. (p. 13) *the sweet aspect:* That is, the sweet aspect of the truth concerning the spots on the moon.

5. (p. 13) *But there appeared a vision . . . faces prompt to speak:* The Pilgrim suddenly forgets his desire to confess his error to Beatrice upon seeing a strange sight, what appears to him to be faces that are so pale they look as if they are reflections on glass or perhaps on clear but shallow waters (ll. 10–11). The contrast between the color of the faces and the medium through which they are reflected is so slight that, the Pilgrim says, the contrast could be compared to the difference between a pearl and the milk-white brow of a woman who might wear the pearl (ll. 13–15).

6. (p. 13) *I ran in error opposite:* The Pilgrim is so startled that he makes a mistake that is the opposite of that of Narcissus, who mistook his reflection in a pool of water for an actual person and fell in love with himself, as told in Ovid's *Metamorphoses* III: 407–510. The Pilgrim, on the contrary, mistakes real faces for reflections. Narcissus is also mentioned in *Inferno* XXX: 128.

7. (p. 13) *And nothing saw:* In the experiment with mirrors described in canto II, turning around to find a light source, one would have found a candle, but here the Pilgrim turns to find the source of the pale reflections and discovers that there is no light source.

8. (pp. 13–14) *"I smile . . . on the truth it trusts not yet its foot":* The Pilgrim's thought is childish and therefore mistaken ("thy puerile conceit" of l. 26), and the thought does not yet trust its foot, or support.

9. (p. 14) *"True substances . . . some vow":* Beatrice affirms that the faces the Pilgrim sees are not mere reflections and informs him that they are real souls who have been "relegated" here because they have broken some vow. The Pilgrim will speak with only one group of the inconstant—nuns who have broken their vows—but one must assume that there are other forms of inconstancy represented by figures in this space. The Sphere of the Moon is an appropriate place for such people, since the moon, by virtue of its constantly changing shape, has

always been a symbol of inconstancy. The idea that the souls of this section of Paradise have been "relegated" here may suggest that they abide in this place, but we shall learn in canto IV: 28–63 that this is not the case.

10. (p. 14) *"the true light"*: The reference is to God.

11. (p. 14) *"with thy name and with your destiny"*: Longfellow's translation accurately reports the Italian of this line, employing the second person singular form of address ("thy") to refer specifically to the person's name and the second person plural form of address ("your") to inquire about all of the souls gathered in the Sphere of the Moon.

12. (p. 14) *"Our charity"*: The soul replies that the love, or charity, that is in her is incapable of rejecting a just request; in this sense, God's court (all of the blessed surrounding Him) is like God.

13. (p. 14) *"virgin sister"*: This is a nun.

14. (p. 14) *"I am Piccarda"*: Dante knew Piccarda Donati, since she was a relative of his wife, Gemma Donati. The Pilgrim has already encountered other members of the Donati family in the afterlife: her brother Forese Donati in *Purgatorio* XXIII: 48, and her brother Corso Donati, a man partially responsible for Dante's banishment from Florence, in *Purgatorio* XXIV: 82. According to early commentators on Dante's poem, Corso forced Piccarda to leave a convent so he could marry her off to a Florentine named Rossellini della Tosa. The Pilgrim was informed in *Purgatorio* XXIV: 10–15 that Piccarda was already "on high Olympus" (in Paradise); this information is now verified by her very presence.

15. (p. 14) *"the slowest sphere"*: In Dante's universe, proximity to the Empyrean and to God determines the speed of the rotation of each heavenly sphere. The Sphere of the Moon is the most distant from God and therefore turns the slowest.

16. (p. 16) *"Are you desirous of a higher place"*: The Pilgrim naturally assumes that souls assigned to this rather lowly spot would wish to be transferred to a higher level of blessedness. He will soon receive an explanation of why this is not the case.

17. (p. 16) *"that makes us wish alone . . . who here secludes us"*: One of the miraculous characteristics of Paradise is that God has created it in such a way that souls are as blessed as they can be, as blessed as their capacity allows them to be. As Piccarda explains, if this were not the

case, it would mean that God's will and the wills of the Blessed were not in harmony.

18. (p. 16) *"And his will is our peace":* This line, one of the most beautiful in the entire poem, expresses quite simply but concisely the idea that every soul among the blessed is attracted by the power of God's love and wishes to be in harmony with it.

19. (p. 16) *"everywhere / In heaven is Paradise":* No matter what their rank or location, all souls among the blessed are as blessed as they can be; therefore, there is no substantial difference in beatitude.

20. (p. 16) *"But as it comes to pass, if one food sates . . . She did not ply the shuttle to the end":* The Poet employs a double metaphor, one about food and another about weaving. His curiosity about the explanation of how all souls are equally blessed in Paradise is first compared to eating a meal and thinking about the next course while being satiated with the course that comes before the expected one. The second metaphor compares the weaver's shuttle to Piccarda's unfulfilled vow, itself implicitly compared to the web of cloth through which the shuttle never passed and therefore remained unfinished, like her vow.

21. (p. 16) *"A lady o'er us":* Saint Clare (1194–1253) was from a noble family of Assisi, like her spiritual leader, Saint Francis. In 1212 she founded the first Franciscan convent for women, the Order of the Poor Clares, and the group was confirmed by Pope Gregory IX in 1247. Pope Alexander IV canonized her in 1255. Piccarda informs the Pilgrim that Saint Clare is also in Paradise—obviously no surprise, but the Pilgrim never encounters her in his journey.

22. (p. 17) *"that Spouse":* The reference is to Christ, the true bridegroom of every nun.

23. (p. 17) *"This other splendor":* Piccarda now refers to another soul who remains unnamed until l. 118: Empress Costanza, or Constance (1154–1198), daughter of Roger II, king of Naples and Sicily; wife of Holy Roman Emperor Henry VI, son of the Emperor Frederick I Barbarossa; and the mother of Frederick II. Dante follows a popular belief that Constance was forced to leave a convent to marry in 1185, but this is a legend with no basis in historical fact.

24. (p. 17) *"the shadow of the sacred wimple . . . never was divested":* Even though Constance was stripped of her nun's wimple, or veil, this was only the shadow of her sacred and true wimple, worn only in her heart.

25. (p. 17) *"the second wind of Suabia":* Suabia is Swabia, a duchy in Germany. The Swabian rulers related to Constance are called "winds" because they ruled briefly but violently. The first wind is Frederick I Barbarossa; the second is Henry VI; and the third is Frederick II.

26. (p. 17) *unto the mark of more desire:* That is, toward Beatrice, whose appearance has now become even more dazzling than before— a process that will continue throughout the Pilgrim's journey toward God.

CANTO IV

1. (p. 18) *Between two viands . . . between two does:* The Pilgrim considers two doubts that have arisen in his mind from Piccarda's conversation in the last canto. Before defining what his doubts are, he provides three examples of the effect they have on him. The first comparison likens him to a man with free will (the "free man" of l. 2) forced to choose between two equidistant and equally appetizing dishes and rendered so immobile by the choice that he starves before he can make a decision. This imaginary dilemma (it is difficult to conceive of a man starving with two delectable dishes before him) was a popular topic of argument in the medieval period and may be traced back to classical versions of the dilemma in both Aristotle's *De caelo* II: 13: 295b and Ovid's *Metamorphoses* V: 165–166. One popular version of the dilemma was called the paradox of Buridan's Ass (named after the Rector of the University of Paris, Jean Buridan): Finding itself between two bundles of hay, an ass might starve before deciding which to eat. *Summa theologica* I–II, q. 13, a. 6, Saint Thomas Aquinas touches on this problem in his discussion of the will and refutes the idea that the will may be paralyzed between two equal choices. The other two comparisons—a lamb between two wolves not knowing which to fear the most (ll. 4–5) and a dog failing to choose which of two deer to eat (l. 6)—all must be referred back to Piccarda's dilemma: Her choice was between death and marriage, and faced with this choice, she broke her vows, thereby refuting the paralysis implied in the paradox of Buridan's Ass.

2. (p. 18) *Beatrice did as Daniel had done:* The biblical Daniel (in Daniel 2) not only interpreted Nebuchadnezzar's dream but divined its contents without being told of it by the Babylonian king. So too

Beatrice divines the Pilgrim's two doubts and begins to respond to each of them.

3. (p. 18) *"One and the other wish . . . the measure of my merit"*: The Pilgrim's first doubt is: If Piccarda's goodwill to keep her vows was constant, how can her brother's violent enforcement of her marriage lessen her merit? Thus the Pilgrim implicitly believes that Piccarda's location in Paradise represents a lesser merit because of its distance from the Empyrean.

4. (p. 18) *"Souls seeming to return unto the stars / According to the sentiment of Plato"*: The Pilgrim's second doubt is: According to Plato's *Timaeus*, each soul is assigned to a star, an idea contrary to Christian theology and rejected by Saint Thomas of Aquinas in *Summa theologica* III, suppl., q. 97, a. 5. The fact that Piccarda and Constance are associated with the moon causes the Pilgrim to wonder if Plato was correct. The *Timaeus* was the only Platonic dialogue known to Dante's times, through an incomplete Latin translation by a Christian bishop named Calcidius in the fourth or fifth century, but Plato's ideas were also encountered in other writings that survived during the Middle Ages or through Aristotle's works. The Council of Constantinople in A.D. 540 pronounced Plato's idea as heretical, affirming that God created every soul at the time of its bodily birth.

5. (p. 18) *"the most of gall"*: Plato's view of the soul is the most galling, since it contains an unacceptable theological concept, and this fact moves Beatrice to deal with it first.

6. (p. 19) *"the Seraphim"*: The highest order of the angels, the Seraphim, was closest to God in the Empyrean.

7. (p. 19) *"whichever John / Thou mayst select"*: Beatrice tells the Pilgrim that her information about the location of the blessed concerns not only John the Baptist but also John the Evangelist, and all the other characters the Pilgrim may encounter in Paradise.

8. (p. 19) *"But all make beautiful . . . sweet life in different degrees"*: God resides in the Empyrean, the "primal circle" of l. 34, where the blessed and all the various orders of angels see Him in direct vision (the source of their blessedness) and abide there. Thus the blessed enjoy their eternal life there, and Plato's idea that they are associated with different stars or planets is incorrect. Once again, the concept that must be understood here is that all souls are eternal and are eternally blessed in a

single heaven, but they differ in terms of the capacity of beatitude they can absorb. The Pilgrim will witness the truth of this apparently contradictory situation at the end of the poem. It is likely that this concept comes from the notion in the Bible, John 14: 2, that "in my Father's house are many mansions," since Saint Thomas Aquinas interprets the term "mansions" as various degrees of happiness in *Summa theologica* III, suppl., q. 93, a. 2, 3. There is thus no Platonic connection between the soul and the Sphere of the Moon.

9. (p. 19) *"the eternal breath"*: This is the breath of life from God, which different souls experience to different degrees.

10. (p. 19) *"but to give sign / Of the celestial which is least exalted"*: In order to show the Pilgrim the different degrees of the souls' beatitude, Dante presents the souls in order of their rank in the Empyrean (where they actually reside), but he distributes them throughout the various spheres of the cosmos for dramatic and didactic purposes. Otherwise he would have been forced to jump immediately to the Empyrean to converse with them all rather than taking a longer journey. The souls in the Sphere of the Moon occupy the position farthest from God. The fact that souls pop up in different places (and are not all encountered in one leap into the Empyrean) makes the journey through Paradise a much more interesting trip for the Pilgrim, and for his reader as well. Thus in the poem, the reader will gradually move up a kind of ladder toward God by stages, not jump into the Empyrean in a single bound. The Poet's invention of this scheme allows a parallel to the similarly progressive schemes through Hell and Purgatory.

11. (p. 19) *"only through the sense . . . made Tobit whole again"*: According to Aristotle as well as the Scholastic philosophers, theological verities can be understood only by passing through the senses as images (an important consideration for any poet, who deals in concrete images of abstract ideas). Of course, since Dante leaves open the question of whether or not the Pilgrim travels bodily through Paradise, he leaves unanswered as well how the Pilgrim could have sensory experience. Beatrice cites several examples of this communication of spiritual truths through images: (1) ascribing human features to God (ll. 43–45); and (2) presenting in human form the three Archangels Gabriel, Michael, and Raphael (l. 49: "the other who made Tobit whole again," or restored Tobit's sight, as reported in the apocryphal book of Tobit: 11: 1–15).

12. (p. 19) *"as he speaks he thinks"*: Beatrice refers here to Timaeus, the chief interlocutor in the Platonic dialogue entitled *Timaeus,* who she says speaks literally, not figuratively. Taken literally, Timaeus' remarks are unacceptable to Christian doctrine, but Dante (and Beatrice) leave open the question of whether or not his remarks may be taken figuratively or symbolically. There may be, therefore, some wiggle room for the acceptance of the astrological notion that heavenly bodies influence humanity. As she says, Plato's views may be filled "with meaning that is not to be derided" (l. 57) and may "hit upon some truth" (l. 60). Clearly, Dante is reluctant to dismiss such an important classical philosopher's views on metaphysics.

13. (p. 19) *The honor of their influence and the blame:* Astrology, the belief that the stars influence human beings, was a fundamental aspect of medieval thought and informs much of the structure of *Paradiso.* There is clearly some relationship between the kinds of souls in each step of the Pilgrim's journey and the various heavenly bodies associated with their different locations. In *Paradiso* XXII: 112–123, for example, the Pilgrim will associate his poetic genius with the constellation of Gemini, under which he was born.

14. (p. 19) *"once warped / The whole world nearly"*: In ancient times, virtually the entire world (with the exception of the Hebrews, who worshiped only one God) practiced idolatry based on the assumption that the heavenly bodies exerted divine influence over humanity.

15. (p. 20) *"The other doubt . . . sin heretical"*: Beatrice now returns to the Pilgrim's initial doubt about divine justice, which she describes as less poisonous (l. 65), because it will not lead to heretical thoughts. The Pilgrim wonders if Piccarda and Constance were rightly placed among the Inconstant when they were forced to break their vows against their will. This kind of doubt, unlike the kind of heretical position about Plato's *Timaeus* that was outlawed by the Council of Constantinople in A.D. 540, is an "argument of faith" (ll. 68–69), since such doubt in itself implies a belief in divine justice, not a belief in heresy.

16. (p. 20) *"For will . . . the holy place"*: Beatrice maintains that when human will remains resolute, it refuses to yield to external force, just as fire shows a natural bent to rise upward, no matter what kind of wind blows it. Thus Piccarda and Constance always had the capability

of returning to the convent, just as fire continues to burn upward after being diverted by another force.

17. (p. 20) *"Lawrence fast upon his gridiron held"*: With the example of Saint Lawrence, Dante begins the citation of paired Christian and classical figures. Saint Lawrence, martyred during the reign of Emperor Valerian in A.D. 258, was grilled alive for refusing to reveal to Roman officials where church treasures were located. He was said to have mocked his torturers by telling them that his body was done on one side and could be turned over. His will, obviously, was more perfect than that of either Piccarda or Constance. As Saint Thomas Aquinas argued in *Summa theologica* I–II, q. 6, a. 4, resp., a man may be dragged by force but he cannot be dragged of his own will.

18. (p. 20) *"Mutius made severe to his own hand"*: According to Livy's *History of Rome* II: xii: 1–16, Gaius Mucius attempted to assassinate Lars Porsena, who was besieging Rome, but failed and was captured. Sentenced to be burned alive, Mucius thrust his right hand into the flames and told Porsena that other Romans remained who would eventually kill him. Porsena was so impressed by Mucius' bravery that he freed him and made peace with the Romans, and thereafter Mucius was known as Mucius Scaevola ("Left-handed"). Dante mentions this famous example of Roman republican virtue in both *Il Convivio* IV: v: 13 and *De Monarchia (Monarchy)* II: v: 14.

19. (p. 20) *"the argument is refuted"*: Beatrice disposes of the Pilgrim's doubts by making a distinction common to Scholastic philosophy (see Saint Thomas Aquinas, *Summa theologica* I–II, q. 6, a. 4–6) that is based upon Aristotle's *Nicomachean Ethics* III: i: 1109b–1110a. The Absolute Will cannot will evil, but the Conditional Will can be coerced by violence and may consent to a lesser harm to avoid a greater one (the case with Piccarda and Constance). This distinction between different kinds of will shall now be clarified in ll. 91–114.

20. (p. 20) *"soul beatified could never lie"*: Given the fact that a blessed soul is incapable of lying, how can there be a contradiction between what Piccarda says about Constance (that she remained a nun in her heart) and Beatrice's argument? Beatrice once again reads the Pilgrim's thoughts to understand that he still has doubts.

21. (p. 21) *"Alcmaeon"*: As reported in Statius' *Thebaid* IV: 187–213, the soothsayer Amphiaraus foresaw that he would die in the attack

upon Thebes and concealed himself to avoid this fate. But his wife, Eriphyle, was bribed with a golden necklace to reveal her husband's hiding place, and Amphiaraus was forced to go to war, knowing he would die. Before he left, Amphiaraus asked his son Alcmaeon to take revenge, and Alcmaeon eventually killed his mother. Dante has already mentioned Alcmaeon's story in *Purgatorio* XII: 50–51, and he placed Amphiaraus in *Inferno* XX: 31–34. The story is mentioned both in Aristotle's third book of his *Nicomachean Ethics* and in the commentary of Saint Thomas Aquinas on this work, *In decem libros Ethicorum ad Nicomachum expositio* III, lect. 2, n. 395, so Dante obviously followed the argument very closely in his readings.

22. (p. 21) *"Will absolute consenteth not to evil . . . to fall into more harm"*: Absolute Will can never agree to do evil, but the Conditional Will may consent to a lesser evil to avoid a great one.

23. (p. 21) *"both of us speak truth"*: Since Piccarda referred to the Absolute Will while Beatrice meant the Conditional Will, their positions are not contradictory: Only her Conditional Will agreed to break her vows of chastity, while her Absolute Will remained steadfast.

24. (p. 21) *the holy river . . . "the first lover"*: God is the source of "the holy river / That issued from the fount whence springs all truth" and He is also the "first lover."

25. (p. 21) *"Our intellect unless the Truth illume it . . . wild beast in his lair, / When it attains it"*: Man's desire for knowledge is inborn, and the intellect cannot rest until it acquires the ultimate knowledge—that is, the Truth of God. Dante compares the Truth of God to a lion's den and the human mind to a wild beast that must be contained inside it.

26. (p. 21) *"If not, then each desire would frustrate be . . . fashion of a shoot"*: That is, each desire would be in vain. Aristotelian and Scholastic philosophy held that nothing in the universe was without a goal or purpose or was in vain. All things have a natural desire to know, just as a plant grows up shoot after shoot from its root.

27. (p. 21) *"to the top from height to height impels us"*: Nature compels the journey upward toward the highest reaches of the universe. In like manner, the Pilgrim will move from heaven to heaven until he reaches God at the end of his adventure.

28. (p. 21) *"Another truth, which is obscure to me"*: The Pilgrim now has another doubt that comes up naturally after the explanation by Beatrice of the two kinds of will. This time he has a question about the nature of vows, and he will be answered in canto V. The earlier metaphor of the human mind and the lion's den implied that the human mind, like a wild beast, would be restless until it achieved ultimate illumination (possible only by the truth of God). Consequently, it is only natural that the more the Pilgrim learns from Beatrice, the more doubts arise, since he has not yet achieved this absolute knowledge.

29. (p. 22) *almost lost myself:* Beatrice will explain why the sight of her in canto V overcomes the Pilgrim.

CANTO V

1. (p. 23) *"If in the heat of love . . . move its feet":* Beatrice explains to the Pilgrim that she will become more beautiful and more radiant as they ascend through the heavenly spheres, a radiance that derives from perfected vision (l. 5, "perfect sight") that enables her to understand God.

2. (p. 23) *"the eternal light . . . always love":* The light of God is already kindling love and spiritual illumination in the Pilgrim.

3. (p. 23) *"your love seduce . . . Ill understood":* Human love can become fixed on some earthly object, because all objects contain something of God's light. But naturally, this may lead to our being "seduced" into loving some unworthy object through an act of will.

4. (p. 23) *"Thou fain wouldst know . . . from further claim":* Beatrice repeats the question the Pilgrim had at the end of the last canto: Can anything be done to make up for broken vows?

5. (p. 23) *This Canto thus did Beatrice begin:* Here Dante the Poet intervenes in the narrative of Dante the Pilgrim.

6. (p. 23) *"freedom of the will . . . are endowed":* Only the angelic orders and humanity (the "creatures of intelligence" of l. 23) have received the precious gift of free will.

7. (pp. 23–24) *"The high worth of a vow . . . of this treasure made":* God accepts only serious vows, not frivolous or evil ones. God's acceptance of a vow constitutes a pact that becomes like a "sacrifice" (l. 29) or an offering of that free will.

8. (p. 24) *"What can be rendered then as compensation?":* The implied answer is that nothing can be offered in compensation for the sacrifice of free will implicit in making a pact with God, since free will is God's greatest gift to humanity and is unequaled by anything else.

9. (p. 24) *"because Holy Church in this dispenses"*: Beatrice now must explain the apparent contradiction that arises from the fact that the Church may give dispensations, releasing people from their vows.

10. (p. 24) *"for thy digestion"*: Dante employs the metaphor of eating and digesting food for the acquisition of knowledge. The Pilgrim must not only hear Beatrice's explanation but also remember it, since knowledge comes from retaining the information, just as merely swallowing food does not guarantee digestion.

11. (p. 24) *"two things . . . has above been spoken"*: Beatrice explains the two things that are involved when an individual "sacrifices" his free will in a compact or vow with God. The first is the thing promised (ll. 44–45, "that / Of which 'tis made")—for example, chastity—while the second is the act of agreement (l. 45), in which man's free will has been sacrificed.

12. (p. 24) *"enjoined upon the Hebrews"*: In the Bible, Leviticus 27, the Hebrews are obligated to make ritual sacrifices, but under certain conditions, these sacrifices can be altered.

13. (p. 24) *"The other . . . yellow key"*: The individual making the vow without destroying the contract may change the specific subject matter of the vow, such as poverty or chastity. But this can be done not by arbitrary decision but only (ll. 56–57) with "the turning / Both of the white and of the yellow key." As the reader has already learned from *Purgatorio* IX: 117–129, the white or silver key represents the priest's judgment that the desire to be released from a vow is legitimate, while the yellow or gold key symbolizes his power to bring about the release.

14. (p. 24) *"As the four is in six"*: One thing promised in a vow cannot be replaced by a lesser thing, just as the number 6 is greater than the number 4 and contains the 4.

15. (p. 24) *whatever thing has so great weight . . . Cannot be satisfied with other spending:* In the specific cases of Piccarda and Constance, their free will was offered as their sacrifice and nothing can balance that gift. Yet they are saved and therefore they must have been forgiven.

16. (p. 26) *"As Jephthah"*: In the Bible, Judges 11: 30–34 recounts the story of the Hebrew Jephthah, who promises to sacrifice to Jehovah the first person who greets him at his door if he can defeat the Ammonites in battle. Having done so and returned home, his only daughter greets him. This is a clear example of a hasty vow.

17. (p. 26) *"the great leader of the Greeks . . . wise and simple weep"*: The Poet adds another example of a hasty vow: the story of how Agamemnon vowed to sacrifice to Diana the most beautiful creature born that year in his kingdom, and that turned out to be his daughter Iphigenia. Dante certainly did not know of this story from Greek tragedy or from Homer. Various other versions of the story are mentioned in Virgil's *Aeneid* II: 116–119 and Ovid's *Metamorphoses* XII: 24–34, but Dante most likely had in mind the mention of this hasty vow in Cicero's *On Duties* III: 95.

18. (p. 26) *"Christians, be ye more serious . . . Pastor of the Church who guideth you"*: Unlike the Hebrews or the ancient Greeks, Christians guarantee salvation without hasty vows. Vows should be made only on the most serious of occasions, and as l. 75 suggests, a bit of holy water cannot remove the obligations incurred by making a vow. Christians have both the Old and the New Testament as well as the guidance of the pope ("the Pastor of the Church") to guarantee their salvation; indeed, the pope does have the power to unbind the obligations incurred by vows.

19. (p. 26) *"If evil appetite"*: If something or someone other than the Old and New Testaments or the pope offers release from a serious vow, this is a choice that should be avoided. Here Dante no doubt refers to some corrupt friars who might offer such dispensations for money. An early commentator suggested that the Friars of Saint Anthony absolved people from vows for a fee (they are mentioned later in *Purgatorio* XXIX: 124–126).

20. (p. 26) *"So that the Jew among you may not mock you"*: As the Jews are held to a strict observance of their religious vows, hasty vows by Christians and the subsequent desire to rescind such ill-advised vows would hold Christians up to ridicule by the Jews.

21. (p. 26) *Thus Beatrice to me even as I write it*: Earlier in l. 16 and later in l. 139, as well as here, the Poet stresses an image of Dante as a scribe writing down exactly what Beatrice has said to him.

22. (p. 26) *where the world is most alive*: Upward toward the Empyrean, God's abode. Beatrice's gaze upward here, as elsewhere, signals the continuation of the Pilgrim's travels, now toward the Sphere of Mercury, the "second realm" of l. 93.

23. (p. 26) *And as an arrow . . . we speed into the second realm*: Earlier in *Paradiso* I: 119 and 125–126, as well as in *Paradiso* II: 22–25, the Poet employed a metaphor involving, respectively, a bow and arrow and a crossbow, both intended to stress speed; here the speed of the Pilgrim's ascent with Beatrice is so rapid that it is compared to the flight of an arrow, which strikes its target while the bowstring is still quivering.

24. (p. 26) *More luminous thereat the planet grew:* Beatrice radiates so much joy that Mercury increases the brilliance of the light of its sphere when she enters that space. This should not take place, since the heavens were supposed to be immutable.

25. (p. 26) *And if the star itself . . . mutable in every guise!:* If the supposedly immutable planet Mercury grew brighter (figuratively, "smiled," as in l. 97) when Beatrice arrived, then Dante asks his reader to consider how much more he, a changeable mortal, was affected by Beatrice's splendor.

26. (p. 27) *more than a thousand splendors:* These are the souls, already called "splendors" in *Paradiso* III: 109. We learn only later, in *Paradiso* VI: 112–114, that these souls in their earthly existence sought honor and fame.

27. (p. 27) *"Lo, this is she who shall increase our love":* In *Purgatorio* XV: 67–75, the Pilgrim had been told that love increases in Paradise when the number of souls there increases.

28. (p. 27) *Full of beatitude the shade was seen:* In this second heaven, the outline of the body may still be faintly discerned in the "splendors," although we will see in ll. 133–139 that the soul's joy may be so intense that its radiance hides this corporeal outline.

29. (p. 27) *Think, Reader:* So begins another of the Poet's wonderful addresses to his reader. In this address, Dante draws a parallel between his reader's desire to know more about this sphere and Dante the Pilgrim's thirst to learn more when he visited this realm.

30. (p. 27) *"O thou well-born . . . To see the thrones of the eternal triumph":* The Pilgrim is addressed by one of the souls, who realizes that he has been given special permission through Divine Grace to see "the thrones of the eternal triumph," or the condition of souls in Paradise.

31. (p. 27) *"ever yet the warfare be abandoned":* The reference is to the warfare of life (see the Bible, Job 7: 1, where life is described as enforced labor or forced military service). Dante the Pilgrim still experiences this warfare, while the souls of the elect have passed beyond this concern.

32. (p. 27) *"believe them even as Gods":* Beatrice's seemingly blasphemous remark follows Saint Thomas Aquinas' belief that the blessed partake of divinity, as he explains in *Summa theologica* I, q. 13, a. 9.

33. (p. 27) *"nest thyself / In thine own light":* The Pilgrim makes it clear that he discerns the elements of the human form within the radiant light that the "splendors" emit; the souls "nestle down" in their own light, as will become even clearer in the last two verses of this canto. In canto VIII: 54, this kind of nestling is compared to that of the silk worm.

34. (p. 27) *"in the sphere / That veils itself to men in alien rays":* Because Mercury is so close to the sun, it is often obscured by the greater light of that more powerful sphere and is not easily visible from earth.

35. (pp. 27–28) *By too much light . . . In its own radiance:* While Mercury is often difficult to see because of the sun's light, the sun itself is difficult to see because of the intensity of its light. Often, mortals can see the sun only when it is shrouded in vapors. In like manner, the features of the "splendor" who has addressed the Pilgrim (as yet unnamed until the next canto) are hidden by its "own radiance."

36. (p. 28) *close, close enfolded:* Several commentators have noted that the original Italian of this line, with its repetition of the adjective (*chiusa, chiusa*), seems to imitate the "nestling down" of the soul inside its radiance.

CANTO VI

1. (p. 29) *"After that Constantine . . . Against the course of heaven":* When the Emperor Constantine (who reigned from A.D. 306 to 337) moved the seat of the Roman Empire from Rome to Byzantium (later Constantinople), the imperial eagle, symbol of the empire, was moved eastward. This move was against the westward course of the sun in the heavens and for Dante was in the wrong direction.

2. (p. 29) *"the ancient who Lavinia took":* Aeneas married Lavinia, who became the mother of the Roman race. Aeneas, in contrast to Constantine, moved from east to west.

3. (p. 29) *"Two hundred years and more":* Constantine reigned from 306 to 337, while the speaker (the Emperor Justinian) reigned from 527 to 565. The period 337 between 527 is less than two hundred years, but it has been suggested that Dante may have followed the chronology his teacher Brunetto Latini employed in his *Trésor,* which dated the transfer from Rome to Byzantium as 333 and the accession of Justinian as 539.

4. (p. 29) *"the bird of God":* Dante has the speaker refer to the Roman eagle as God's bird because he believed that the Roman Empire was a divinely inspired human institution.

5. (p. 29) *"whence it issued first . . . upon mine own alighted":* By moving to Byzantium, a city near the ancient site of Troy (the birthplace of Aeneas), the eagle had returned to its origins. Eventually the eagle passed from hand to hand from emperor to emperor until it reached the soul speaking to the Pilgrim, the Emperor Justinian. He established his own government back in Italy in the town of Ravenna, and for Dante the return of the eagle to Italy would have been a positive event.

6. (p. 29) *"Justinian":* Justinian I was born in Illyricum in 483, married Empress Theodora in 525, and ruled from 527 until 565. His most lasting achievement was the establishment of a commission of jurists who compiled the *Codex Justinianus* (529; the Justinian code), a collection of the valid edicts promulgated by Roman emperors after Hadrian; subsequently, another commission revised rulings of classical Roman lawyers, editing out all irrelevant or confusing texts, resulting in the *Digesta* or *Pandectae,* one of the four books of the code. Less lasting were the military triumphs of Belisarius, his great general (see l. 25).

7. (p. 29) *"One nature . . . But blessed Agapetus":* As Justinian admits when he says, "One nature to exist in Christ, not more," he once adhered to the Eutychian heresy (named for Eutyches, a priest in Constantinople), also called the Monophysite heresy—the belief that Christ was divine but not human. Contemporary scholars of Justinian believe it was his wife, Theodora, and not Justinian who had such views. According to Dante's account, Agapetus I, pope from 535 to 536, converted Justinian back to the orthodox view of Christ.

8. (p. 29) *"Each contradiction to be false and true":* Justinian now sees the orthodox view of Christ's dual nature as clearly as the Pilgrim accepts the logical "law of contradictories." This is the fundamental Aristotelian principle in logic that two propositions—one positive and the other negative—cannot both be true at the same time. One statement must be true and the other must be false.

9. (p. 29) *"this high task"*: Justinian's Roman legal codes.

10. (p. 29) *"to my Belisarius"*: Justinian's general (c.505–565) overthrew the Vandal kingdom in North Africa, conquered Italy from the Ostrogoths, and allowed Justinian to establish the exarchate of Ravenna. (An exarchate was a term employed for a province in the Byzantine Empire and was ruled by an exarch—a prefect or governor.)

11. (pp. 29–30) *"the first question . . . a sequel"*: Justinian responds to the Pilgrim's request (*Paradiso* V: 127) to identify himself, and he continues with a "sequel," an account of the history of the Roman Empire.

12. (p. 30) *"Both who appropriate and who oppose it"*: As will become clear from Justinian's account of imperial history, he rejects both the Ghibellines (who supposedly support the empire) and the Guelphs (who reject the empire), the two major political factions of Dante's day. Indeed, the dominant political struggle of Dante's era was between forces owing allegiance to the pope (the Guelphs) and those supporting the Holy Roman Emperor (the Ghibellines); references to the Guelphs and Ghibellines occur throughout the three canticles.

13. (p. 30) *"When Pallas died"*: Pallas, son of the Latin king Evander, was killed by Turnus while fighting to help Aeneas (Virgil, *Aeneid* X: 479–489). Subsequently, Aeneas gained a new kingdom for his Trojans by killing Turnus.

14. (p. 30) *"Alba"*: The kingdom of Aeneas was not immediately centered in Rome but in Lavinium; Ascanius, son of Aeneas, subsequently transferred the kingdom to Alba Longa, where it remained for some three centuries until Alba fell to Rome during the reign of Tullus Hostilius (670–638 B.C; the fall was the result of the victory of one set of triplet brothers, the Horatii from Rome, over another set of triplet brothers from Alba Longa, the Curiatii. When the three brothers from Rome slew the three brothers from Alba Longa, Rome was effectively turned into a major power on the Italian peninsula. For a discussion of this Roman republican mythology in Western culture, see Peter Bondanella, *The Eternal City: Roman Images in the Modern World* (Chapel Hill: University of North Carolina Press, 1987).

15. (p. 30) *"from Sabine wrong / Down to Lucretia's sorrow"*: Romulus, the founder of the city of Rome, kidnapped Sabine women to marry the men of his city. Subsequently, Rome grew in power through seven kings until the last king, Tarquinius Superbus, raped Lucretia, who killed herself in shame, causing the revolution of the "First Brutus" and the establishment of the Roman Republic in 510 B.C.

16. (p. 30) *"against Brennus, against Pyrrhus"*: Brennus led the Gauls who besieged the Roman Capitol in 390 B.C. King Pyrrhus of Epirus waged war against Rome until his defeat at Beneventum in 275 B.C. His costly victories explain the term "pyrrhic victory."

17. (p. 30) *"Torquatus thence and Quinctius . . . unkempt was named"*: Titus Manlius Torquatus was a distinguished Roman soldier who served as dictator twice and as consul three times between 353 and 340 B.C. Lucius Quintius Cincinnatus was the Roman hero summoned from his farm to become dictator, saving Rome from one of her many enemies. The American city of Cincinnati was named after him; like George Washington, Cincinnatus was the archetypal republican hero. He held total power but relinquished it for the good of the republic. His name, as Dante notes, was based on the Latin word *cincinnus*, which means curly or disheveled.

18. (p. 30) *"Decii and Fabii"*: These were two important Roman patrician families from which many great Roman leaders and statesmen sprang.

19. (p. 30) *"embalm"*: The term is used here in the sense of "preserve" or "protect."

20. (p. 30) *"the Arabians"*: Dante means here the Carthaginians of Hannibal, not the Arabs who occupied North Africa in his day. Hannibal (247–c.183 B.C.), Rome's greatest military opponent, fought Rome almost to defeat in the Second Punic War—first in Spain, then crossing the Alps into Italy. He was finally defeated by Scipio Africanus in 202 B.C.

21. (p. 30) *"Po, from which thou glidest"*: That is, "from which you, River Po, descend."

22. (p. 30) *"yet were young / Pompey and Scipio"*: Pompey (Gnaeus Pompeius Magnus, 106–48 B.C.), a member of the first triumvirate with Crassus and Julius Caesar, was defeated by Caesar at the battle of Pharsalia in 48 B.C. Scipio Africanus the Elder (c.235–c.183 B.C.) first won fame as a young man of seventeen by saving his father's life in battle; later, in 202 B.C., he defeated Hannibal at the battle of Zama in North Africa.

23. (p. 30) *"to the hill / Beneath which thou wast born it bitter seemed"*: Justinian suddenly turns from Roman history to refer to the hill of Fiesole,

overlooking Dante's native city of Florence. In Dante's time it was believed that the Roman conspirator Catiline took refuge in Fiesole, causing the city to be destroyed by a Roman army (a bitter memory).

24. (p. 30) *"from Var unto the Rhine, / Isère beheld and Saône, beheld the Seine . . . the Rhone is filled"*: These are references to various rivers associated with the Gallic Wars of Julius Caesar.

25. (p. 30) *"What it achieved"*: When Julius Caesar crossed the Rubicon River, a small stream between Ravenna and Rimini, he crossed the boundary between Cisalpine Gaul and Italy. This action was illegal and began his civil war against the forces of Pompey.

26. (p. 30) *"Durazzo, and Pharsalia smote"*: Caesar first defeated Pompey at Dyrrachium (Durazzo in Italian; a city on the Adriatic Sea, it is now called Durrës) and then finally crushed him at Pharsalia in Thessaly.

27. (p. 31) *"to the calid Nile was felt the pain"*: Pompey fled to Egypt, the land of the Nile River, where he was murdered after the defeat at Pharsalia.

28. (p. 31) *"Antandros and the Simois, whence it started"*: Aeneas left his native Troy for Italy from Antandros, a coastal town located near the River Simois. Thus the symbolic history of the Roman eagle effectively began here. When Caesar pursued Pompey, according to Lucan's *Pharsalia* IX: 961–999, he stopped to visit Hector's burial place near the ruins of Troy.

29. (p. 31) *"And ill for Ptolemy then roused itself"*: It is important to remember that Justinian's long speech refers to the history of the Roman eagle, which here rouses itself to Ptolemy's bad fortune. Ptolemy XII was king of Egypt from 45 to 47 B.C., sharing power with his sister, Cleopatra. She joined forces with Julius Caesar to depose Ptolemy, who drowned while attempting to escape. Ptolemy may have had something to do with Pompey's murder after he fled to Egypt after his defeat at Pharsalia.

30. (p. 31) *"like a thunder-bolt on Juba . . . the Pompeian clarion it heard"*: The Roman eagle, in Caesar's hands, then struck Juba, king of Numidia (one of Pompey's allies) in 46 B.C. Caesar subsequently defeated an army raised by Pompey's sons in Spain at the battle of Munda (the army was raised by the "Pompeian clarion," or trumpet).

31. (p. 31) *"the next standard-bearer . . . howl in Hell together"*: The standard-bearer is Augustus, the second standard-bearer after Julius

Caesar, who with Marc Antony defeated Brutus and Cassius at the battle of Philippi in 42 B.C. In *Inferno* XXXIV: 64–67 Dante consigns Brutus and Cassius to the bottom of Hell. While Brutus is here described as howling like a dog in Hell, Dante's description of him in *Inferno* stresses the fact that he never says a word.

32. (p. 31) *"Modena and Perugia dolent were"*: Marc Antony was defeated by Augustus at Modena in 43 B.C. before forming a brief alliance with Augustus. Antony's brother Lucius was defeated at Perugia by Augustus in 41 B.C.

33. (p. 31) *"the mournful Cleopatra . . . fleeing from before it"*: After Caesar's death, Cleopatra became Marc Antony's mistress. But after Antony's defeat by Augustus at the battle of Actium in 31 B.C., Cleopatra fled from the scene (here she is described as "fleeing from before it," meaning the imperial eagle of Rome).

34. (p. 31) *"even to the Red Sea shore . . . unto Janus was his temple closed"*: With Augustus, the imperial eagle reached the shores of the Red Sea in Egypt. Because Augustus established an era of peace, he was able to close the gates to the temple of the god Janus, custodian of the universe, kept open during wartime because prayers to Janus were thought to bring about good endings.

35. (p. 31) *"in the hand of the third Caesar"*: The third Caesar is Tiberius, emperor of Rome when Christ was crucified, marking what Dante would have considered to be the apogee of the Roman eagle's historical journey. Dante believed that it was part of a divine plan for the Crucifixion to occur during what he believed to be the universal Roman rule over the then-known world, since this enabled the sin of Adam to be expiated for all mankind.

36. (p. 31) *"in the hand of him I speak of, / The glory of doing vengeance for its wrath"*: The Roman Empire, in the hands of Tiberius, received the glory of fulfilling God's divine plan by wreaking vengeance upon Christ, the Son of God, to expiate the sin of Adam. The death of the Son of God placates God's wrath for Adam's original transgression and reconciles Him with the human race. God chose the Roman Empire to perform this task in the person of Pontius Pilate; by so doing, God implicitly recognized the legitimacy of the Roman Empire. Dante also discusses this question in *De Monarchia* II: xi.

37. (p. 31) *"Now here attend to what I answer thee . . . Upon the vengeance*

of the ancient sin": Titus, son of Vespasian, ruled as emperor from A.D. 79 to 81. In A.D. 70, while his father ruled, Titus destroyed Jerusalem. Dante believes that he did so to avenge the death of Christ at the hands of the Jews, an idea he probably found in Paulus Orosius' *A History Against the Pagans* VII: iii: 8; ix, 9. The Pilgrim will encounter this author in the Sphere of the Sun (*Paradiso* X: 119). Placing the blame for the death of Christ on the Jews has always been one of the explanations for European anti-Semitism. But other important theological questions are raised here. There is, first of all, the question of free will: If God willed this Crucifixion, did the Jews have any choice in the matter, and can any decision taken without the possibility of choice result in guilt? Then there is the question of the blame that might be shared with the Romans, who are absolved of any guilt in Christian tradition. Basically, Dante seems to believe that in spite of the fact that the Crucifixion of Christ was necessary to redeem mankind, the Jews were guilty of condemning an innocent man. The Romans, on the contrary, through Pontius Pilate's hand washing, merely carried out the request of the Jewish religious officials and thus incurred no moral guilt.

38. (p. 31) *"And when the tooth of Lombardy had bitten"*: In A.D. 773, Pope Adrian I called Charlemagne (who, for Dante, represented the Roman Empire, even though he was not crowned until A.D. 800) to dethrone King Desiderius, the Lombard.

39. (p. 31) *"of such as those"*: This is a reference to the Ghibellines and Guelphs, mentioned earlier in l. 33.

40. (p. 32) *"the yellow lilies . . . for a party"*: The Guelphs supported France and employed their standard (the golden fleur de lis), while the Ghibellines employed the standard of the imperial eagle. But Dante believes that the imperial standard must support justice, not merely a partisan sect.

41. (p. 32) *"And let not this new Charles . . . stripped the fell"*: Charles II of Naples (1248–1309), son of Charles of Anjou (mentioned in *Purgatorio* XX: 79) was leader of the Guelphs supporting the Church against the Ghibelline supporters of the Empire. Charles II was the father of Charles Martel, who appears in *Paradiso* VIII. Justinian warns Charles II that the imperial eagle has stripped the hide ("fell") off nobler rulers than he.

42. (p. 32) *"oftentimes the sons have wept / The father's crime"*: Justinian warns Charles II that his offspring may pay for his mistakes. In fact, in *Paradiso* VIII: 49–84, we shall learn of the misfortunes of Charles Martel.

43. (p. 32) *"This little planet . . . less vividly mount upward"*: The "little planet" is Mercury. Justinian now begins to answer the Pilgrim's second question (*Paradiso* V: 127–129), explaining that the souls dwelling in this section of Paradise did good works motivated not only by the love of God but also by their desire for earthly fame and honor (l. 114). Because they did not direct their actions completely toward the true goal, God's love, their radiance is less than it might have otherwise been.

44. (p. 32) *"we see them neither less nor greater . . . sweet harmony among these spheres"*: The joy these spirits experience comes from there being an exact match between their merit and their reward. As a result, they have no envy (l. 123, "iniquity") of those who have a greater capacity in other spheres for beatitude, and they therefore participate in the harmonious existence of the souls in the heavenly spheres (l. 126).

45. (p. 32) *"this present pearl"*: This is the Sphere of Mercury (in *Paradiso* II: 34, the moon was also referred to as a pearl).

46. (p. 33) *"Romeo . . . his livelihood"*: Justinian now introduces us to the figure of Romeo di Veilleneuve (1170–1250), the minister of Ramón Berenguer IV, count of Provence. Dante the Poet recounts the tale of a man whose nobility and service goes as unappreciated as his own public service, which resulted in exile from his native Florence. Romeo arranged the affairs of the Count well and set up important dynastic marriages for his four daughters (l. 133): Margaret married King Louis IX of France (Saint Louis); Eleanor married Henry III of England; Sancha married Henry's brother, Richard of Cornwall; and Beatrice married Charles of Anjou. The legend makes Romeo "a poor man and a pilgrim" (l. 135) as he arrives at Ramón's court. The word *romeo* was applied generically to pilgrims, since they most often headed toward Rome. Members of Ramón's Provençal ruling class were jealous of Romeo and accused him of mismanagement (l. 137), even though he had, as Longfellow translates the line, rendered to Raymond twelve (seven plus five) for ten—that is, given better than he had received. Obviously hurt by the unfair treatment he has received from his lord, Romeo left the court and lived the rest of his life begging as a poor man (l. 141). The jealous courtiers were punished for their deeds (l. 131, "They have not laughed"), since Beatrice's marriage to Charles of Anjou in 1246 eventually led to the much harsher Angevin rule of Provence.

47. (p. 33) *"it would laud him more"*: Romeo's goodness of heart is even greater than what can be imagined by those who know about his fate.

CANTO VII

1. (p. 34): "Osanna . . . malahoth!": The words sung by Justinian and the other souls are a combination of Latin and Hebrew. Longfellow's own translation of them reads as follows: "Hosanna, Holy God of Sabaoth, illuminating with thy brightness the happy fires of these realms." The three Hebrew words mixed with the Latin are *osanna* ("o save," the shout of the crowd that greeted Jesus when he entered Jerusalem on Palm Sunday as reported in the Bible by Matthew 21: 9); *sabaoth* ("hosts"); and *malahoth* (a mistake for *mamlacoth*, "realms" or "kingdoms"). Dante knew no Hebrew, and scholars have suggested that his mistaken spelling of *mamlacoth* results from copying the word from Saint Jerome's preface to the Latin Vulgate. The happy fires (*felices ignes*) are the illuminated souls.

2. (p. 34) *a double light / Doubles itself:* Dante invents a verb (*s'addua*) based on the number 2; elsewhere in *Paradiso*, he does something similar with verbs using the numbers 3 (IX: 40) and 5 (XIII: 57). Numerous explanations have been given for the double lights: They may represent Justinian's historical role as lawgiver and emperor; the powers of natural intelligence and divine grace; or the illumination by God's light of the soul's light.

3. (p. 34) *with a sudden distance:* After their heavenly dance, the souls return to their dwelling place in the Empyrean. It should be kept in mind that the Pilgrim is being shown these souls as an act of love in various places according to their capacity for beatitude: They are actually somewhere else (that is, in the Empyrean). See note 10 to Canto IV.

4. (p. 34) *"Tell her, tell her" . . . sweet effluences:* The Pilgrim addresses his own thoughts and is anxious for Beatrice to answer yet another doubt that arises in his mind, since she usually quenches his thirst for the truth with the sweet drops, or "effluences" of the truth.

5. (p. 34) *only by B and ICE:* The Italian for this line is *per Be e per ice.* "Be" represents the Italian pronunciation of the first letter of Beatrice's name (B); "ice" is the last part of her name; Bice is a shortened version of her name in Italian. The Pilgrim is filled with such reverence for Beatrice's name that one must imagine how much more reverent he is in the presence of the heavenly, resplendent version of the mortal woman he once loved.

6. (p. 34) *"After what manner a just vengeance justly / Could be avenged has put thee upon thinking":* Because Beatrice has the power to read the Pilgrim's thoughts correctly, she forms his doubt, which concerns Justinian's reference to Titus in *Paradiso* VI: 92–93 as the man who was divinely appointed to "do vengeance / Upon the vengeance of the ancient sin." The Pilgrim wonders why the Crucifixion was avenged with the destruction of Jerusalem and the diaspora of the Jews if it was also the just vengeance for Adam's original sin.

7. (p. 34) *"that man who ne'er was born . . . all his progeny":* Adam was created directly by God, not born of woman. Beatrice follows Christian doctrine in asserting that in "damning himself" Adam "damned all his progeny."

8. (p. 35) *"the Word of God":* Christ, the Son of God, came to humanity in the form of the second person of the Holy Trinity.

9. (p. 35) *"When united to its Maker . . . sincere and good":* Human nature in Christ ("when united to its Maker") was pure and unsullied by sin, just as Adam's original nature was before the Fall. But Adam had free will, so his original sin sullied his originally pure human nature. In effect, Adam exiled himself from the Garden of Eden.

10. (p. 35) *"so great justice . . . of so great injustice":* Christ assumed human nature, and the Crucifixion was just in that it was necessary for the Son of God to expiate the original sin of Adam. At the same time, as Christ remained God in the form of the second person of the Trinity, his death was an injustice, and thus the Jews are responsible for this outrage to his divinity. Here Dante repeats an argument advanced by Saint Thomas Aquinas in *Summa theologica* III, q. 46, a. 12 ad 3.

11. (p. 35) *"To God and to the Jews one death was pleasing":* The Crucifixion pleased God because it was part of a divinely organized scheme to redeem mankind and the original sin of Adam. It also pleased the Jews, but for entirely different and evil reasons, and therefore the Jews must be held accountable for their deed. Again, Dante follows Saint Thomas Aquinas in *Summa theologica* III, q. 47, a. r., resp.

12. (p. 35) *"Earth trembled"*: According to the Bible, Matthew 27: 51, when Christ died on the cross "the veil of the temple was rent in twain from the top to the bottom; and the earth did quake, and the rocks rent."

13. (p. 35) *"But now do I behold . . . 'hidden from me why God willed' "*: Once again Beatrice reads the Pilgrim's mind and outlines another question he has, this time a knotty one: Why did God select this particular method of redeeming mankind, and why did he take on human form and suffer death on the cross when he could have easily done this in another way?

14. (p. 35) *"in the flame of love not yet adult . . . little is discerned"*: The Pilgrim fails to understand the kind of infinite love that moved God to sacrifice himself for mankind because he has not matured or ripened in the love that makes such understanding possible. As Beatrice points out immediately afterward, men try to discern the answers to such weighty theological questions without the proper spiritual enlightenment.

15. (p. 36) *"the eternal beauties it unfolds . . . itself is most vivacious"*: God creates angels and men's souls, "the eternal beauties," in the same way the hot fire sends out sparks. They are immortal and free of the influences of secondary causes (the "novel things" of l. 72). God's love shines forth from all things, but most of all from those things—angels or men—who most resemble Him (l. 75).

16. (p. 36) *"With all of these things . . . sin alone which doth disfranchise him"*: Men's souls have been "advantaged," or endowed, with immortality, free will, and likeness to God, and it is sin that takes away man's endowments, changing his God-like nature to something corrupted.

17. (p. 36) *"one of these two fords . . . his folly made"*: Beatrice offers only two possibilities for mankind to regain the endowments that Adam's original sin lost: Either God simply pardons mankind (ll. 91–92) or mankind expiates its sin (l. 92–93).

18. (p. 36) *"had not power . . . himself excluded"*: Beatrice explains the impossibility of mankind's expiation of original sin by the fact that the original sin was that of pride, and mankind is incapable of humbling itself.

19. (p. 37) *"in his own ways... to proceed by each":* God's ways are mercy and justice, and as Beatrice declares in l. 105, to redeem mankind He had to choose either mercy or justice or a combination of the two qualities. She states in l. 110 that God decided to employ both methods.

20. (p. 37) *"'twixt the first day and the final night":* That is, between the first day of creation and Judgment Day. Dante actually inverted the two terms of beginning and end in the original Italian (*Né tra l'ultima notte e 'l primo die*), a form of *hysteron proteron* ("the last placed first"), a rhetorical figure mentioned earlier in canto II, endnote 7. It is strange that Longfellow's usually careful translation overlooks this poetic effect here.

21. (p. 37) *"Himself had humbled":* The Incarnation of Christ, in which God became human, was the only act of humility that could atone for Adam's original sin.

22. (p. 37) *"one place":* Beatrice needs now to explain the difference between direct creation by God (l. 67) and creation by secondary causes (ll. 72–73).

23. (p. 37) *"and all their mixtures / Come to corruption":* Again reading the Pilgrim's mind, Beatrice states that all the elements making up the sublunary world (air, fire, water, earth) are corruptible, a fact that is seemingly in contradiction with what Beatrice said earlier in ll. 67–72. The Pilgrim wonders why these elements are not eternal as well.

24. (p. 37) *"The Angels, brother, and the land sincere... created virtue are informed":* Beatrice distinguishes between direct creation of the angels and the heavenly spheres (the spot where the Pilgrim is at the moment) and secondary creation, such that of plants and animals, which are "informed" by a created virtue but are not created directly by God.

25. (p. 37) *"the informing influence... the soul of every brute and of the plants":* The "informing influence" of the stars gives life to the animals and plants. But since this kind of soul is not created by God Himself, it is mortal, unlike the immortal soul of man.

26. (p. 38) *"But your own life":* God breathes life into the immortal soul and thus directly creates each human soul. See *Purgatorio* XXV: 70–75 for the earlier description of the soul's creation by God.

27. (p. 38) *"the first parents both of them were made":* Because God directly created the bodies of both Adam and Eve, the resurrection of the body and the immortality of the soul will, on Judgment Day, return the primal couple ("the first parents") to their former condition.

CANTO VIII

1. (p. 39) *in its peril ... the fair Cypria delirious love:* This reference is to Venus, called so because she was born on Cypress. The ancient world believed that Venus inspired delirious or "mad" love, and when men believed in such idolatrous gods before Christianity offered humankind redemption by Grace, they were in peril of the true God's wrathful punishment for false beliefs.

2. (p. 39) *the third epicycle turning:* According to the Ptolemaic system of the universe, planets possessed not only orbital motion but also epicyclical motion. The Sphere of Venus has a small revolving sphere attached to it that somehow carries the planet, and this small sphere is the planet's epicycle. See the diagram below.

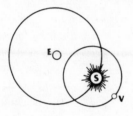

S (Sun), revolves around E (Earth)
The Sun carries with it V (Venus)
Venus revolves around the Sun in a small circle--that is, the epicycle.

3. (p. 39) *But both Dione honored they and Cupid:* Dione was the mother of Venus. Cupid was the son of Venus.

4. (p. 39) *in Dido's lap:* According to Virgil's *Aeneid* I: 657–660 and 715–719, Cupid often sat in Dido's lap in the form of Aeneas' young son Ascanius, and this was what caused her fatal passion for Aeneas.

5. (p. 39) *wooes the sun, now following, now in front:* When Venus is behind the sun (in the original Italian, Venus woos the "nape" of the sun), the planet is the evening star (Hesperus): when Venus is in front of the sun (in the original Italian, Venus woos the sun's "brow"), the planet is the morning star (Lucifer).

6. (p. 39) *I was not ware of our ascending to it ... more beauteous grow:* The Pilgrim suddenly realized that he and Beatrice have ascended to the next

sphere, the Sphere of Venus. The proof of their ascent lies in the fact that once again, Beatrice becomes more and more radiant as she ascends.

7. (p. 39) *And as with a flame . . . And as within a voice:* The Pilgrim encounters lights, souls who have descended from the Empyrean to greet the two travelers. Line 21 implies that even though the lights dance in a circle here, they retain their "inward vision" of God in the Empyrean. They are compared in a double simile to the sparks within a flame (l. 16) and then to the distinguishable sound of one voice within a chorus of several voices (ll. 17–18).

8. (p. 39) *other lamps:* These are the lights who now appear to the Pilgrim in the Sphere of Venus.

9. (p. 39) *in the high Seraphim:* That is, they come from the Empyrean with the Seraphim, the highest order of angels.

10. (p. 40) *one approached:* Although this soul never identifies itself by name, it is clear from what he says in ll. 32–84 that he is Charles Martel (1271–1295), first son of Charles II of Anjou and Mary, daughter of the King of Hungary. Charles died at the age of twenty-four, but he visited Florence in 1294 and most likely met Dante then. This Charles Martel must not be confused with the more famous Charles Martel, king of the Franks (c.688–741).

11. (p. 40) *"the celestial Princes . . . one thirst":* These are the Principalities, the order of angels associated with the third Sphere of Venus. The souls turn in complete harmony with the Principalities.

12. (p. 40) *" 'Ye who, intelligent, the third heaven are moving' ":* Charles Martel cites to the Pilgrim the first verse of the first *canzone* discussed in book II of Dante's *Il Convivio*. In that work, Dante identifies the angels who turn the third heaven by their intellection as the Thrones, not the Principalities (see *Il Convivio* II: v: 13).

13. (p. 40) *"Short time below":* Charles died at the age of twenty-four.

14. (p. 40) *"a creature swathed in its own silk":* Charles describes himself concealed in the radiance of his happiness as being similar to a silk worm inside the silk it has spun.

15. (p. 40) *"had I been below . . . the foliage of my love":* Had Charles lived longer, he would have shown to the Pilgrim the proof of his love for him.

16. (p. 40) *"That left-hand margin . . . Me for its lord awaited":* Provence lies on the left bank of the Rhone below the Sorgue; Charles Martel would have inherited this province from Charles II.

17. (p. 40) *"that horn of Ausonia . . . Tronto and Verde"*: Ausonia is a name for Italy employed by Latin poets. Ausonia's horn refers to the Kingdom of Naples and Apulia, in what is now southern Italy; the towns of Bari, Gaeta, and Catona, and the Rivers Tronto and Verde are located there.

18. (p. 40) *"Of that dominion which the Danube waters"*: The reference is to Hungary, through which the Danube flows; Charles became king (although in title only) of this dominion in 1290.

19. (p. 42) *"beautiful Trinacria . . . scath from Eurus doth receive"*: The reference is to Sicily. Cape Passero (Pachynus or Pachino) is at the southeastern point of Sicily, while Cape Faro (Pelorus or Peloro) is at the northeastern end of the island (l. 68). Eurus is the name given by the ancient world to the southeast wind, what we now call the sirocco, and the gulf in question (l. 69) is the Gulf of Catania.

20. (p. 42) *"Not through Typhoeus . . . sulphur"*: According to Ovid's *Metamorphoses* V: 346–356, the volcanic eruptions of Mount Etna were caused by the giant Typhoeus, who was buried under the mountain by Jupiter and who tried to free himself, causing the mountain to erupt. Here Dante rejects this explanation and declares it comes from the production of sulfur.

21. (p. 42) *" 'Death! death!' "*: The gist of Charles Martel's remarks in ll. 67–75 is this: The descendants of Charles I of Anjou (Charles Martel's grandfather) and Rudolf of Hapsburg (Charles Martel's father-in-law) would still be governing Sicily if it had not been for the Sicilian Vespers (1282), a revolt that was prompted by the misrule of Charles I of Anjou and that replaced his misgovernment with the rule of Peter III of Aragon.

22. (p. 42) *"my brother could but this foresee, / The greedy poverty of Catalonia"*: The King of Aragon held Charles Martel's brother Robert hostage for his father in Catalonia from 1288 to 1295. During this time, Robert gained a number of Spanish friends who became key figures in his administration of the Kingdom of Naples and Sicily after 1309, and they were famous for their greed. Because this event takes place nine years after the Pilgrim's journey to Paradise in 1300, Charles Martel's remarks form a prophecy about his brother's future problems.

23. (p. 42) *"his bark"*: This may be a reference to Robert's ship of state in Naples, which was already laden down with problems

("freight," l. 87). He did not need the additional trouble the avarice of his advisers brought about.

24. (p. 42) *"liberal covetous / Descended"*: Robert's stingy, or "covetous," nature descended from a more generous, or "liberal," nature, that of his father Charles II. This remark about how a generous nature can degenerate into a stingy one will provoke the Pilgrim's question in l. 93, the answer to which will be given in the remainder of the canto.

25. (p. 42) *"such a soldiery . . . hoarding in a chest"*: Robert needs administrators who will not hoard money in their coffers by misrule.

26. (p. 42) *"How from sweet seed can bitter issue forth"*: This important question from the Pilgrim follows a touching passage that testifies to Dante's respect and admiration for the young Charles Martel. The Pilgrim rejoices that Charles is in Paradise (l. 90), and Charles will now answer the Pilgrim's concerns about how it is possible for sweet seed to produce bitter fruit.

27. (p. 42) *"Thy face thou'lt hold as thou dost hold thy back"*: Charles states that if he is able to explain something to the Pilgrim, what has been unclear to him (what has been concealed behind his back) will now be clear (now in front of his face). When Charles finally completes his explanation in l. 136, he informs the Pilgrim, "Now that which was behind thee is before thee."

28. (p. 42) *"The Good . . . within these bodies vast"*: God, whose realm (the heavenly spheres) the Pilgrim is climbing, makes His Providence act as a power in these vast bodies—that is, the planets and stars.

29. (p. 42) *"Within the mind that in itself is perfect"*: In the perfect divine mind, the various natures and characters of individuals are foreseen or influenced by the heavenly bodies in a manner that reflects God's plan.

30. (p. 43) *"this bow"*: As in *Paradiso* I: 125–126, the Poet employs the metaphor of bow and arrow to underline the teleological principle informing God's universe. Created in accordance with God's will, the universe cannot do less than it is preordained to do.

31. (p. 43) *"but ruins . . . not made them perfect"*: If God's Providence did not inform the entire universe, the result would be chaos, not His Art. But this cannot be, since the angelic intelligences that turn the heavenly spheres by their intellection, as well as the First Intelligence (God), are not "maimed," or deficient (l. 110).

32. (p. 43) *"were they not citizens... your master writeth well for you"*: Here Dante follows the view of his "master," Aristotle, in arguing that man is by nature a social animal. In *Inferno* IV: 131, Aristotle is also called the "Master I beheld of those who know."

33. (p. 43) *"The roots of your effects to be diverse... his son did lose"*: The "roots," or dispositions, of men vary according to the influences radiating from the heavens. The Poet provides various examples of different dispositions: One may be born to be a lawgiver like Solon, the famous Athenian legislator of the seventh century B.C.; another may be a soldier like Xerxes, king of Persia in the fifth century B.C.; a third may be a priest like Melchisedec (Genesis 14: 18) in the Old Testament; and a fourth may be a mechanic like the mythical Daedalus, whose son Icarus was killed when he flew too close to the sun using waxen wings made by his father (see also *Inferno* XVII: 109–111).

34. (p. 43) *"Revolving Nature... from another"*: Nature, created by the power of the constantly turning heavenly spheres, acts as a stamp on the "mortal wax" (human beings) as a seal does in warming wax. However, such an operation takes no notice of the lineage (the "inn" of l. 129, in the sense of abode) of various individuals, so that birth does not guarantee nobility of character or greatness.

35. (p. 43) *"Thence happens... Mars"*: After declaring that heredity has no effect upon character, Charles Martel provides the Pilgrim with two examples: While Jacob and Esau were presumably similar because they were twins, in fact they were entirely different (see the Bible, Genesis 25: 21–27); Quirinus, another name for Romulus, the founder of Rome, was the son of a poor man but was nevertheless such a great hero that his fellow citizens could not believe his humble lineage and imagined that he was the son of the god Mars.

36. (p. 43) *"If Providence divine were not triumphant"*: God's divine Providence prevents the constant inheritance of the same traits from generation to generation.

37. (p. 43) *"Now that which was behind thee is before thee"*: As in ll. 95–96, Charles Martel returns to this convoluted manner of expressing how a question is first unclear (behind the Pilgrim's back) and then subsequently clarified (in front of the Pilgrim).

38. (p. 43) *"With a corollary will I mantle thee"*: Like a Scholastic philosopher adding one final point, a corollary, to his concluding argument, Charles Martel adds a comment as if he were placing a cloak over the Pilgrim's shoulders.

39. (pp. 43–44) *"Evermore nature ... maketh evil thrift"*: Nature, meaning here the natural disposition of any individual to a certain character, cannot be realized if it encounters contrary fortune, just as a seed cannot grow if it falls on unsuitable soil. Such discordance ends badly, "maketh evil thrift": Longfellow employs not the economic sense of the term but the more archaic sense of the English word—physical thriving or vigorous growth.

40. (p. 44) *"Him who was born ... your footsteps wander from the road"*: If men would allow their fellows to follow their natural dispositions, rather than forcing a man suitable to be a priest to be a soldier and vice versa, things on earth would be much different and would follow God's will.

CANTO IX

1. (p. 45) *Beautiful Clemence:* Scholars disagree on the identity of this lady. Some identify her with the wife of Charles Martel, Clemence of Habsburg, who died in 1295 at the age of twenty-seven in the same plague that killed her husband at the age of twenty-four. Others say she is Clemence of Anjou, daughter of Clemence of Habsburg and Charles Martel; this Clemence was born in 1293, married King Louis X of France in 1315, and died in 1328. If the woman is Clemence of Habsburg, the Pilgrim addresses a dead woman, although he may imagine that she is in Paradise with her husband.

2. (p. 45) *The treacheries his seed should undergo:* Charles Martel's son Robert became king of Hungary between 1308 and 1342, when he died. He was also heir to the throne of Naples, but his uncle, also named Robert (working with Pope Clement V), deposed him of that title and became King of Naples in 1309. Since the date of the Pilgrim's conversation with Charles Martel is supposed to be 1300, this future treachery is something of a prophecy.

3. (p. 45) *"Be still"*: Apparently Charles Martel has ordered the Pilgrim not to reveal these treacheries in the future.

4. (p. 45) *"to the Sun"*: That is, toward God.

5. (p. 45) *"Ah, souls deceived"*: The Poet aims his anger at those human beings who turn away from God toward the vanities of the world.

6. (p. 45) *"between Rialto / And fountain-heads of Brenta and of Piava"*: The soul is referring to the region between Venice (whose largest island is called Rialto) and the Alps, where the Rivers Brenta and Piave have their sources.

7. (p. 45) *"Rises a hill"*: The land of this soul's earthly birthplace is located in the March of Treviso, where her family's castle stood on the hill of Romano near the city of Bassano.

8. (p. 46) *"a torch"*: The torch that attacked the region is Azzolino III da Romano, a cruel Ghibelline tyrant of the region that the Pilgrim has already met in Hell (*Inferno* XII: 110). He is described as a torch, since it was said when he was born that his mother had dreamed she would give birth to a firebrand.

9. (p. 46) *"Out of one root . . . this star o'ercame me:* This spirit had the same parents as Azzolino, and as we learn immediately, she was his sister Cunizza da Romano (c.1198–c.1279), who married the Guelph leader Count Riccardo di San Bonfazio of Verona in 1222. Shortly thereafter she was either kidnapped or carried off by her lover, the troubadour Sordello (see *Purgatorio* VI–VIII, where the Pilgrim encounters this poet in Ante-Purgatory). Returning to her brother Azzolino's court, she reportedly ran off with a knight named Bonio, who died in the service of her brother. Then she married Aimerio, count of Breganze, and when he died, she married a man from Verona. Upon his death she married Salione Buzzacarini of Padua, Azzolino's astrologer. After outliving these four husbands, Cunizza moved to Florence and freed many of the slaves belonging to her father and brother, signing the documents of manumission in the home of Cavalcante de' Cavalcanti, the father of Dante's friend Guido. Dante places her in the heavenly Sphere of Venus for obvious reasons, given her love affairs and, as she reports, "because the splendor of this star o'ercame me" (l. 33). The fact that she is saved and her brother damned is yet another proof of how human dispositions vary.

10. (p. 46) *"does not grieve me . . . perhaps seem strong unto your vulgar"*: Cunizza has no remorse about her sins, since in the realm of the blessed, the waters of Lethe wash away all bitter memories, as the Poet explains at the end of *Purgatorio*. The vulgar, ordinary people will find this feeling difficult to understand.

11. (p. 46) *"luculent and precious jewel"*: Cunizza indicates a soul nearby who will be the next to speak. That soul is only named in l. 94 of the canto.

12. (p. 46) *"shall yet quintupled be"*: Employing a verb coined by the Poet (*s'incinqua*, meaning to "be fived"), Cunizza predicts that the fame of this as yet unnamed soul will endure for five times a century, or five hundred years from 1300.

13. (p. 46) *"another life"*: Cunizza is referring to life on earth, a life of early fame that must be abandoned for eternal life.

14. (p. 46) *"Shut in by Adige and Tagliamento . . . stubborn against duty"*: These two rivers make up the boundaries of the region known as the March of Treviso. This is a difficult passage, but most commentators believe these lines refer to the defeat of the Paduans outside Vicenza in 1314 by Dante's patron, Cangrande della Scala. The Paduans are described as "stubborn against duty" because they do not obey the imperial authority that Cangrande della Scala will reassert.

15. (p. 46) *"the Sile and Cagnano join"*: These two rivers join at Treviso; the Cagnanao is now known as the Botteniga.

16. (p. 46) *"One lordeth it, and goes with lofty head"*: This is Rizzardo da Camino, the son of the "good Gherardo" (*Purgatorio* XVI: 124), husband of Giovanna (*Purgatorio* VIII: 71) and son-in-law of "noble Judge Nino" (*Purgatorio* VIII: 53). Rizzardo ruled Treviso as a tyrant and members of the nobility, who despised his arrogance (his "lofty head" in l. 50), murdered him while he was playing chess.

17. (p. 46) *"Feltro moreover of her impious pastor"*: The impious shepherd of Feltro refers to Alessandro Novello of Treviso, bishop of Feltre. In 1314 he gave refuge to some thirty Ghibellines conspirators and betrayed them to the Guelph authorities in Ferrara, who had them executed.

18. (p. 46) *"none ever entered Malta"*: This reference is not to the island but to one of several prisons with this name at the time. The Poet is simply saying that the Bishop of Feltre's treachery was so foul that no criminal was ever sent to prison for anything worse.

19. (p. 46) *"That of the Ferrarese . . . a partisan"*: The Bishop was delighted to offer the gift of Ghibelline blood (l. 56) to prove his loyalty to the Guelph faction and in so doing is a partisan of the Guelphs.

20. (p. 46) *"mirrors . . . seems good to us"*: Cunizza here refers to the Thrones, the order of angelic intelligences that direct the Sphere of Saturn, the seventh sphere above the Pilgrim and Beatrice. God's judgments

shine down on Cunizza in the Sphere of Venus, and she can see mirrored in the Thrones the punishment that God has in store for the sinners she has described earlier. This harsh judgment seems "good," or satisfactory, to the souls there.

21. (p. 47) *"The other joy . . . ruby smitten by the sun":* This is the other soul mentioned in l. 37, who now advances to speak to the Pilgrim and is described as a "fine ruby."

22. (p. 47) *"Through joy effulgence is acquired above . . . but down below":* The Poet notes that joy causes the radiance of the souls to increase in Paradise ("above"), while in Hell or on earth (depending on one's reading of the words "down below"), the soul darkens.

23. (p. 47) *"and in Him, blest spirit, / Thy sight is":* In the original Italian (*e tuo veder s'inluia*), the Poet coins another verb from the pronoun "lui"—meaning, literally, as Longfellow notes in a gloss on the line, "thy sight *in-Hims-itself*." This is a clever means of saying that all souls in Paradise share God's vision, which is omniscient, so they can read the Pilgrim's thoughts just as God can. Mindreading is a condition of the blessed.

24. (p. 47) *"those holy fires . . . six wings make themselves a cowl":* In the Bible, Isaiah 6: 2, each of the Seraphim is said to have six wings.

25. (p. 47) *"If I in thee were as thou art in me":* This is another of the Poet's clever plays on words with coined verbs. Here, two verbs are created from the pronouns *tu* and *mi* (*s'io m'intuassi, come tu t'inmii*, or as Longfellow translates literally in his footnotes, "if I in'theed myself as thou in'meest thyself "). This kind of thing occurs thirteen times in *Paradiso*. The grammatical construction is an ingenious means for the Pilgrim to state that if he shared the ability to read minds with the souls in Paradise, he would answer a question before being asked.

26. (p. 47) *"The greatest of the valleys . . . the earth engarlands":* The Mediterranean Sea flows into the Atlantic ("where the water / Expands itself "), and was thought by medieval geographers to surround all dry land on earth and therefore to "garland" earth.

27. (p. 47) *"discordant shores":* This is varied, uneven.

28. (p. 47) *"it meridian makes / Where it was wont before to make the horizon":* The Mediterranean is so vast, running east against the sun, that if one stands at its west end (its meridian), the opposite end seems to be the horizon and vice versa.

29. (p. 47) *"'Twixt Ebro and Magra . . . part the Genoese":* The birth-place of the soul who is speaking, as yet unnamed, is Marseilles, mid-way between the mouths of the River Ebro in Spain and the River Magra in Italy. In Dante's time the River Magra divided Genoese ter-ritory from Tuscany.

30. (p. 47) *"Sit Buggia and the city whence I was":* Marseilles and Bougie, on the coast of North Africa, share practically the same meridian.

31. (p. 47) *"made the harbor hot":* In 49 B.C., Julius Caesar conquered Marseilles from Pompey's allies (see Lucan, *Pharsalia* III: 572–573).

32. (p. 47) *Folco:* Folco, or Folquet of Marseilles (c.1160–1231), was a Provençal troubadour who frequented a number of medieval courts and in later life became a Cistercian monk. As bishop of Toulouse he was instrumental in the persecution of the Albigensian heretics, an important biographical fact that Dante fails to mention. Dante praises one of Folquet's poems in *De Vulgari Eloquentia* II: vi: 6— "Tant m'abellis l'amoros pessamens," or "The cares of love so greatly delight me"—as one of the best examples of poetic rhetoric. Folquet is the only vernacular poet that is presented as being among the blessed in Paradise (excepting, of course, Dante himself, who is guar-anteed a place there by Beatrice and by virtue of the special dispensa-tion he has received to visit Paradise).

33. (pp. 47–48) *"the daughter of Belus . . . his heart had locked":* Folco says that the daughter of Belus, Dido, never burned with love more than he did when she offended both her dead husband, Sichaeus, and the dead wife of Aeneas, Creusa, with her passion. The flames of Folco's pas-sion lasted until he grew older (until his hair turned grey—"so long as it became my locks," l. 99). In like manner, continuing his references to other classical passions besides Dido's, Folco cites the story of Phyllis, princess of Rhodes ("that Rodophean," l. 100), who hanged herself when Demophoön, son of Theseus, did not appear at their wedding (Ovid, *Heroides* II: 147–148). He also mentions Hercules (Alcides), who lost his life because of his attraction to Iole, daughter of the King of Thessaly. The Poet has already mentioned Hercules' demise in *In-ferno* XII: 67–69.

34. (p. 48) *"Yet here is no repenting, but we smile":* As in Cunizza's declaration in ll. 33–36, Folco too does not repent of his sin, since the waters of the Lethe have removed the memory of it. Nevertheless the cleansed souls of Paradise have an objective understanding of the nature of their sin and of the justice of God's divine plan.

35. (p. 48) *"Whereby the world above turns that below":* God's affection wishes the return of every soul to its original heavenly home, and His Providence works through the operation of the heavenly spheres on the world below.

36. (p. 48) *"Rahab . . . supremest grade 'tis sealed":* Again reading the Pilgrim's mind, Folco informs him that the soul within the light next to him is Rahab, the harlot of Jericho who hid the two spies Joshua sent to explore the city and was the only resident to survive. As a result, she was "to our order joined" (l. 116)—she was assumed in the heavenly Sphere of Venus (an appropriate place for a prostitute) when Christ freed the virtuous Hebrews from Limbo after the Crucifixion in the Harrowing of Hell (see *Inferno* IV: 46–63, and note 38 just below). For Rahab in the Bible, see Joshua 2; Hebrews 11: 31; and James 2: 25. Rahab was the first of all the Virtuous Hebrews taken up, and she therefore became the brightest light ("supremest grade") in the Sphere of Venus.

37. (p. 48) *"the shadowy cone / Cast by your world":* It was believed that the shadow of earth extended in a cone shape that reached the Sphere of Venus.

38. (p. 48) *"a palm of the high victory":* The victory is Christ's Harrowing of Hell, the triumphant descent of Christ into Hell to bring salvation to the souls imprisoned there since the beginning of time. The Harrowing of Hell took place between the time of Christ's Crucifixion (thus the reference to "one palm and the other") and His Resurrection.

39. (p. 48) *"Of Joshua . . . little stirs the memory of the Pope":* Unlike Joshua, who conquered the land of Canaan, Pope Boniface VIII cares little about the liberation of the Holy Land from the infidels. Boniface was pope from 1294 to 1303, so he was pontiff in 1300, when the poem is set.

40. (p. 48) *"Thy city . . . to a wolf ":* Here begins an attack upon Dante's native city of Florence, called an offshoot, or plant, of the Devil (l. 128, "Who first upon his Maker turned his back"). The "accursed flower" refers to the lily stamped on one side of the Florentine florin, the gold coin that represented Florence's economic power. Greed is the reason that the shepherds (the pope and priests in general) have turned into greedy wolves, thereby leading their flocks of sheep and lambs (l. 131) astray.

41. (p. 48) *"the Evangel and the mighty Doctors . . . upon their margins"*: While the pope and his cardinals abandon the Gospels and the works of the great church doctors (leaving them "derelict," l. 134), they study only the Decretals—compilations of papal decrees that form general church law—not for edifying purposes but, instead, searching for financial gain to such an extent that their margins are soiled and worn out from constant use. Dante probably disliked the Decretals also because one of their compilations was done by the order of his arch villain, Pope Boniface VIII, in 1298.

42. (p. 49) *Nazareth:* This town in the Holy Land was the scene of the Annunciation, when the Angel Gabriel opened his wings in homage to Mary. Numerous Italian paintings immortalize this moment.

43. (p. 49) *"Vatican and the other parts elect . . . from the adulterer"*: The pope resided in the Lateran Palace during Dante's day, as popes had done since the fourth century, but the Vatican Hill on the right side of the Tiber was where Saint Peter's Basilica and the Vatican Palace were located. Since Saint Peter was martyred on the Vatican Hill, it was one of the most sacred places in the Holy City. The prophecy in the conclusion of the canto ("shall soon be free from the adulterer") may refer to the death of Pope Boniface VIII in 1303; to the Babylonian Captivity of the Church in 1305, when the pope moved to Avignon; or to a more general savior of Italy who will come in the future to restore imperial justice throughout the peninsula.

CANTO X

1. (p. 50) *Looking into his Son:* In a definition of the Holy Trinity, Dante explains that the love that God the Father ("the primal and unutterable Power" of l. 3) has for His Son produces the Holy Spirit through an act of creative love.

2. (p. 50) *Lift up then, Reader:* So Dante the Poet begins his address to his reader, an important moment in the poem that extends to l. 27. He invites the reader to contemplate the exacting order of God's universe. The "lofty wheels" (l. 7) of the heavenly bodies present the Pilgrim with a vision of order. Two motions are subsequently mentioned in l. 9 ("where the one motion on the other strikes"): the daily revolutions of the planets around earth that are parallel to the equator and the annual movement of the sun along its ecliptic, a movement that is oblique to the equator. Although moving in different directions, these two wheels cross at two points: in Aries at the spring equinox and in Libra at the autumnal equinox. The seasons are produced by the oblique motion of the sun (l. 14). It should be remembered that the Pilgrim takes his journey when the sun is in Aries.

3. (p. 50) *If from the straight line . . . of mundane order:* If the ecliptic, or zodiac, was not oblique but in a straight line, the influence of the heavenly bodies and the stars would be weakened and would be confined to a much smaller area of the globe.

4. (p. 50) *Remain now, Reader . . . made the scribe:* Realizing that his Reader will understand his astronomical references only with great difficulty, the Poet urges his audience to stay with him on the bench of the banquet table he is setting (l. 25) and where the Reader has already had a foretaste of the food he is providing (l. 23). But he tells the reader to "feed thyself," since the Poet has more important tasks at hand (l. 26–27).

5. (p. 50) *The greatest of the ministers of nature:* With this reference to the sun, the Poet informs us that the Pilgrim has reached the Sphere of the Sun, the fourth heaven.

6. (p. 51) *With that part which above is called to mind:* In l. 9, the Poet had mentioned that the point where the two motions cross is in Aries.

7. (p. 51) *And I was with him . . . I was not conscious:* The Pilgrim finds himself in the Sphere of the Sun almost without realizing it.

8. (p. 51) *And what was in the sun . . . never eye could go:* The Pilgrim is unable to discern the souls of the wise, the residents of this part of Paradise, because they are even brighter than the light of the sun. But as he goes on to explain in l. 48, the human eye cannot see anything brighter than the sun's light. Here, as elsewhere in the *Paradiso*, Dante makes the impossibility of accurate description serve as a poetic means of expressing the inexpressible.

9. (p. 51) *the fourth family . . . how begets:* The wise and learned theologians and philosophers that inhabit this realm of the sun contemplate

the generation of the Holy Trinity (l. 51, "how he breathes forth and how begets"), the mystery mentioned in the opening of the canto.

10. (p. 51) *the Sun of Angels . . . Beatrice was eclipsed:* The Sun of Angels is God. Only God could have been capable of eclipsing the thought of Beatrice in the Pilgrim's mind (l. 60).

11. (p. 51) *My single mind on many things divided:* The Pilgrim's mind is occupied by a number of compelling things: God, Beatrice, and the vision of the universe before him.

12. (p. 52) *the daughter of Latona . . . thread which makes her zone:* The reference is to Diana, the moon. The circle of light around Dante and Beatrice is thus compared to a halo around the moon, the "thread" of l. 69.

13. (p. 52) *The tidings thence may from the dumb await!:* The wonders of what the Pilgrim witnesses in this part of heaven are so amazing that only by acquiring the "wings" of the Poet and retracing the Pilgrim's steps could anyone who has not been graced with such a vision describe it accurately to others. The situation is thus compared to waiting for news ("tidings") from a man without a tongue ("from the dumb").

14. (p. 52) *Till they have gathered the new melody:* The spirits circle around the Pilgrim and Beatrice as if they were ladies dancing a particular form of round dance called a *ballata*, which features a ring of women dancers who, at the end of each stanza, wait for a leader to sing the stanza before they repeat the stanza as they circle around (the part of the dance called the *ripresa*). The celestial spirits pause in exactly such a fashion.

15. (p. 52) *one I heard:* We do not learn the identity of the soul who speaks until l. 99.

16. (p. 52) *"This garland":* The still unidentified speaker now compares the circle of spirits to a garland of flowers.

17. (p. 52) *"I Thomas of Aquinum":* The spirit finally identifies himself as Thomas Aquinas (1225–1274) of the Dominican Order (l. 95), who studied with Albertus Magnus (c.1200–1280) in Cologne before becoming the most important and influential of all Church doctors (that is, scholars) and the authority on Scholastic theology. Pope John XXII canonized him in 1323. His greatest work is *Summa theologica*, a summation of Church doctrine that is influenced heavily by the philosophy of Aristotle. See the diagram below for a schematic of the souls who revolve around Dante and Beatrice in a circle within another circle in cantos X and XII:

Double Circle of Souls

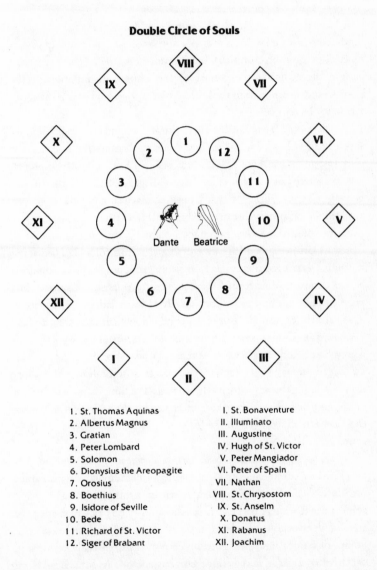

1. St. Thomas Aquinas
2. Albertus Magnus
3. Gratian
4. Peter Lombard
5. Solomon
6. Dionysius the Areopagite
7. Orosius
8. Boethius
9. Isidore of Seville
10. Bede
11. Richard of St. Victor
12. Siger of Brabant

I. St. Bonaventure
II. Illuminato
III. Augustine
IV. Hugh of St. Victor
V. Peter Mangiador
VI. Peter of Spain
VII. Nathan
VIII. St. Chrysostom
IX. St. Anselm
X. Donatus
XI. Rabanus
XII. Joachim

18. (p. 53) *"Gratian, who assisted both the courts":* Franciscus Gratianus, or Gratian, was the twelfth-century founder of the study of canon law

and an Italian who was famous for his *Decretum Gratiani,* an attempt to reconcile church and secular law. This explains why he is said to have "assisted both the courts."

19. (p. 53) *"That Peter was ... unto Holy Church":* This is Peter Lombard from Novara (c.1100–c.1160), author of a collection of "sentences," or opinions, of the Church fathers, entitled *Libri sententiarum quatuor.* He dedicates the preface to the Church in imitation of the poor widow mentioned in the Bible, Luke 21: 1–4, who gave a small offering to the temple.

20. (p. 53) *"The fifth light ... learn tidings of it":* This is King Solomon, son of King David. He is the "most fairest" because the book of the Old Testament attributed to his authorship (The Song of Solomon) was interpreted by Church fathers as an allegory of the mystical union between Christ and the Church. However, given some of the questionable things Solomon did during his earthly existence, some theologians questioned whether he might be among the blessed only after Christ's Harrowing of Hell (see endnote 38 to canto IX) rescued some virtuous pagans from eternal damnation. Saint Augustine maintained he was damned, while Saint Jerome argued the opposite position. Thus people in Dante's time would be "greedy to learn tidings" of his fate.

21. (p. 53) *"next the lustre of that taper":* The burning candle, or "taper," next to Solomon is Dionysius the Areopagite, the Athenian whom Saint Paul converted in Athens, as told in the Bible, Acts 17: 34. *De caelesti ierarchia (The Celestial Hierarchy),* a treatise dealing with the orders of the angels, was incorrectly attributed to him. Dante's treatment of the angelic orders in *Paradiso* is influenced by this Neoplatonic work that was actually written in the fifth or sixth century. (See note 29 in canto XXVIII.)

22. (p. 53) *"The advocate of the Christian centuries ... Augustine was furnished":* Most commentators identify this unnamed figure with Paulus Orosius, whose *A History Against the Pagans* argued that, contrary to what some ancient writers had claimed, Christianity had not worsened the state of the world. Paulus lived in the fifth century and was a contemporary of Saint Augustine. The influence of his work is also evident in canto VI of *Paradiso,* and as l. 120 emphasizes, Paulus influenced Saint Augustine. Strangely enough, Saint Augustine does not appear in this collection of Church theologians.

23. (p. 53) *"The sainted soul"*: This is Boethius (c.480–524), author of *The Consolation of Philosophy*, who was executed by Theodoric, king of the Ostrogoths. Boethius' book helped to spread knowledge of classical antiquity during the Middle Ages and was widely read, since Boethius was considered something of a Christian martyr. He was also known as Saint Severinus, although he was never canonized.

24. (p. 53) *"Cieldauro"*: This is the Church of Saint Peter in Ciel d'Oro ("with the golden ceiling") in Pavia, where Boethius was buried in the eighth century, years after his death.

25. (p. 53) *"Isidore"*: Saint Isidore of Seville (c.570–636) was one of the Church doctors and author of *Etymologiarum Libri XX*, an encyclopedic compendium of the period's scientific knowledge.

26. (p. 53) *"Beda"*: The so-called Venerable Bede was an Anglo-Saxon monk (c.673–735), a doctor of the Church, and the author of the *Ecclesiastical History of the English Nation*.

27. (p. 53) *"Richard . . . in contemplation more than man"*: Richard of Saint Victor (died 1173), English mystic and Scholastic theologian, was the author of many books, in particular one entitled *On Contemplation*, which explains l. 132.

28. (p. 53) *"Sigier . . . syllogize invidious verities"*: Siger of Brabant (c.1226–1284), was a professor at the University of Paris who lectured in the Latin Quarter in the Rue du Fouarre (the "Street of Straw" of l. 137). His presence is surprising, since his views on the immortality of the soul were eventually judged heretical and were in opposition to those more orthodox views identified with Saint Thomas Aquinas. Nevertheless, Saint Thomas here affirms that Siger syllogized (that is, demonstrated in Scholastic argument) "invidious," or enviable, truths. Here in death, two theological enemies are thus reconciled in Paradise. It is possible that Saint Thomas means to underscore the fact that other theologians were envious of the truths Siger set out so well in his works.

29. (p. 53) *as a horologe*: This is a tower clock.

30. (p. 54) *the Bride of God is rising up / With matins to her Spouse*: The Church is traditionally called the Bride of Christ, her spouse. The hour of matins is dawn.

31. (p. 54) *That swells with love the spirit well disposed*: The canto ends on an erotic note. Dante compares the sound and motion of the souls to a clock as it chimes the matins to listeners, but the movements may also have an amorous connotation, given the presence of a bride and groom.

32. (p. 54) *made eternal:* The very last line of the Italian original contains another coined word by Dante, *s'insempra*—from *sempre*, or "forever."

CANTO XI

1. (p. 55) *in downward flight!:* While movement upward is linked to contemplation, moving downward toward earthly things points to the pursuit of material, not spiritual, goals.

2. (p. 55) *One after laws . . . himself to ease:* The Poet contrasts the spiritual goals of Paradise with a number of earthly goals: in l. 4, the study of civil or canon law and of medicine (based upon the *Aphorisms* of Hippocrates, which along with a commentary on it by Galen, constituted the textbooks for the study of medicine in Dante's time); in l. 5, the study of theology; in l. 6, those who rule by force or fraud; in ll. 7–8, those who steal and work as politicians; and in l. 9, those who give themselves over to sensual pursuits or to the indolent life.

3. (p. 55) *When I . . . exceeding glory was received:* Unlike those who pursue the various professions for purely material ends listed in ll. 3–9, the Pilgrim has been freed from such material concerns by Beatrice and his journey to Paradise, and now the Poet exults in his freedom.

4. (p. 55) *as in a candlestick a candle:* The twelve spirits surrounding Dante and Beatrice now stand immobile, like twelve candles placed on a circular chandelier.

5. (p. 55) *"the effulgence . . . thoughts I apprehend":* This light is the soul of Thomas Aquinas, who understands the Pilgrim's doubts before they are spoken. Aquinas sees them directly through the mind of God as he looks into the "Eternal Light."

6. (p. 55) *"Where just before I said":* Thomas Aquinas understands that the Pilgrim has two doubts raised by his earlier remarks in canto X. The first doubt arises from X: 96 ("where well one fattens if he strayeth not"), where Aquinas refers to the path where lambs fatten well if they do not stray. This doubt will be discussed in canto XI. The second doubt arises from X: 114 ("there never rose a second") and concerns Thomas' assertion that Solomon was never equaled in wisdom. This doubt will be treated in canto XIII.

7. (p. 56) *"unto the bottom"*: Divine Providence governs the world in mysterious ways, and no amount of understanding will allow one to fathom its ways or get to the bottom of its intentions.

8. (p. 56) *"her own Beloved"*: This is Christ, the bridegroom of the Church.

9. (p. 56) *"the bride of Him who, uttering a loud cry"*: This is the Church, who metaphorically married Christ when He cried out on the cross "My God, my God, why hast thou forsaken me?" (see the Bible, Matthew 27: 46).

10. (p. 56) *"Two Princes"*: Providence instituted two leaders, founders of mendicant orders, to ensure that the Church would remain faithful to her bridegroom, Christ. The leaders will be identified as Saint Francis of Assisi, founder of the Franciscan Order; and Saint Dominic, founder of the Dominican Order. Saint Thomas Aquinas was a Dominican, but he now recounts the story of Saint Francis, the founder of the Franciscan Order, while the Franciscan Saint Bonaventure will later in canto XII return the favor by describing the life of Saint Dominic.

11. (p. 56) *"all seraphical in ardor ... both is spoken"*: Saint Francis is identified with the Seraphim, the highest order of angels, representing love, while Saint Dominic is identified with the Cherubim, the next highest order of angels, representing wisdom. Saint Thomas announces that he will only speak of "one" (l. 40), Saint Francis. Born Giovanni Francesco Bernardone, the son of a wealthy merchant, in 1181 or 1182, Francis led a pleasant and well-to-do life before changing his ways completely and embracing poverty while renouncing the worldly life. In 1223 Pope Honorius III recognized this group of like-minded Christians dedicated to returning life to its evangelic simplicity; in 1224 Francis received the stigmata (the wounds received by Christ on the cross). He died in 1226, and Pope Gregory IX canonized him two years later. It would be difficult to overestimate the impact this monk had upon medieval life.

12. (p. 56) *"Between Tupino ... grievous yoke"*: Dante now describes the geographical location of Assisi, where Saint Francis was born. The town is between the Topino and the Chiascio Rivers, and Ubaldo, the bishop of Gubbio, lived as a hermit on the "hill elect" nearby (l. 44). The "lofty mountain" in l. 45 is Mount Subasio, which reflects the sun's rays upon the town of Perugia. Porta Sole is the gate of Perugia that faces Assisi. Gualdo and Nocera are two towns that are controlled by Perugia and weep at their "grievous yoke."

13. (p. 56) *"a sun . . . out the Ganges"*: Saint Francis was often described as a sun. Here, the saint is compared to the real sun that arises from the Ganges River in the East.

14. (p. 56) *"Say not Ascesi . . . properly would speak"*: In Dante's times, the town of Assisi was known as Ascesi, which also can be translated as the past tense of the verb to rise, meaning "I have risen." According to the Poet, this may be suggestive of the rising sun, but the word Orient (l. 54) would be more accurate.

15. (p. 56) *"his father's wrath incurred"*: Francis renounced all worldly goods, including his garments. He stripped these off in 1207 in the presence of his father and the bishop, to whom his angry father had turned to protect his property.

16. (p. 56) *"For certain Dame . . . no one doth unlock"*: The Dame, or Lady, of l. 59 is Lady Poverty, to whom no one willingly opens or unlocks the door, since men normally fear poverty as much as death.

17. (p. 56) *"before his spiritual court / Et coram patre unto her united"*: At the episcopal court of Assisi, Francis renounced his inheritance "in the presence of his father." This is a Latin expression taken from the Vulgate version of the Bible, Matthew 10: 33. Francis therefore married Poverty.

18. (p. 57) *"She, reft of her first husband"*: Poverty's first husband was Christ, and she was forced to wait until Francis' appearance more than a thousand years later for another suitable groom. Note that Dante is saying here that the Church ignored Christ's preaching about poverty for virtually its entire history.

19. (p. 57) *"with Amyclas"*: In Lucan's *Pharsalia* V: 515–531, the Latin poet recounts the story of a poor fisherman named Amyclas, who remained unafraid at the sound of the warlike voice of Julius Caesar when the general appeared at his doorstep and demanded to be ferried across the Adriatic. Amyclas was fearless because he was poor and possessed no earthly goods and therefore had nothing to lose. Dante comments on this advantage of poverty in *Il Convivio* IV: 13: 12. Even with such an example, no one after Christ espoused poverty until Francis.

20. (p. 57) *"when Mary still remained below"*: Because Christ was cru-
cified naked, he died accompanied by Poverty even while his mother
Mary remained at the foot of the cross. The Italian text Longfellow
follows reads "She mounted up with Christ" (*salse,* meaning "she
climbed up") rather than the modern textual reading of *pianse,* "she
wept with Christ." Longfellow's version merely makes the meaning
clearer, but both versions of the text underline how Poverty was by
Christ's side at His death.

21. (p. 57) *"the venerable Bernard / First bared his feet"*: This is
Bernardo da Quintavalle, Francis' first convert. He was a wealthy mer-
chant of Assisi who threw away his shoes and raced to join Francis in
his marriage to Poverty. The Franciscans walked barefooted in imita-
tion of the Apostles, as told in the Bible, Luke 22: 35.

22. (p. 57) *"Giles . . . Sylvester"*: Giles, or Aegidius, was the third
convert of Francis. Sylvester was another early follower of Francis.

23. (p. 57) *"Behind the bridegroom, so doth please the bride!"*: Francis is
now the bridegroom and the bride is Poverty.

24. (p. 57) *"Then goes his way . . . He and his Lady and that family"*:
Francis, Poverty, and his followers go to Rome.

25. (p. 57) *"the humble halter"*: In a sign of humility, Francis and his
followers wore a simple rope rather than a belt.

26. (p. 57) *"At being son . . . appearing marvellously scorned"*: Even
though Francis' father, Peter Bernardone, was a merchant and not a
nobleman, Francis was unashamed of his origins. Nor was he dis-
turbed by the initially negative reception he received at the papal
court.

27. (p. 57) *"his hard determination . . . the primal seal"*: Even Pope Inno-
cent III found the Franciscan Rule governing Francis' order extremely
rigid ("his hard determination"), but the Pope verbally sanctioned the
Franciscan Order in 1209 or 1210 with his "primal seal."

28. (p. 57) *"a second crown"*: Pope Honorius III gave the second
and official sanction of the Franciscan Rule in 1223.

29. (p. 58) *"this Archimandrite"*: This term, taken from the vocabu-
lary of the Greek Orthodox Church, means "head of the fold," refer-
ring to supervision of monasteries.

30. (p. 58) *"In the proud presence of the Sultan . . . conversion too unripe"*:
In 1219 Francis and some of his followers accompanied the soldiers of

the Fifth Crusade to Egypt, where he preached before the sultan at the town of Damietta and was received by that ruler courteously. He was not, however, successful in converting the infidels (l. 103).

31. (p. 58) *"On the rude rock . . . two whole years his members bore"*: In 1224, while fasting on Mount Alvernia, between the River Arno and the River Tiber, Francis received from a Seraph the stigmata, the marks of Christ's five wounds on his hands, feet, and side. Francis retained the stigmata until his death two years later.

32. (p. 58) *"no other bier"*: Francis wanted his dead body to lie upon the ground naked, faithful to Poverty even in death.

33. (p. 58) *"what man was he"*: Saint Thomas now returns to Saint Dominic, the founder of the Dominican Order (their "Patriarch," l. 121), and continues to lament the degeneracy of his own order. In canto XII, the Poet will select the Franciscan Saint Bonaventure to denounce the degeneracy of the Franciscan Order. He also turns to answering the Pilgrim's first doubt about his earlier remark in X: 96.

34. (p. 58) *"The bark of Peter"*: This is the Church.

35. (p. 58) *"little cloth doth furnish forth their hoods"*: So few members of the Dominican Order follow Saint Dominic's example that it would take very little cloth to fashion their cowls.

36. (p. 59) *" 'the plant that's chipped away' "*: The Dominican Order has been chipped away by the degeneracy of its members.

37. (p. 59) *"Where well one fattens, if he strayeth not"*: Dominic repeats the line he delivered to the Pilgrim in X: 96 that caused his first doubt. The Dominicans (metaphorically described as Dominic's flock of faithful sheep) "fatten properly" and not degenerately if they obey his Rule and do not stray from it.

CANTO XII

1. (p. 61) *the blessed flame:* This is the soul of Saint Thomas Aquinas.

2. (p. 61) *the holy millstone:* This is the ring of the twelve spirits, primarily Dominicans.

3. (p. 61) *another in a ring:* Another circle of twelve other spirits, primarily Franciscans, now joins the first ring. The Wisdom of the Dominicans is in harmony with the Love of the Franciscans, and the two qualities are joined together.

4. (p. 61) *doth transcend our Muses, / Our Sirens:* The harmony generated by the motion of the two circles of spirits surpasses earth's poetry ("Our Muses") or earth's songs ("Our Sirens").

5. (p. 61) *As primal splendor that which is reflected:* This music is superior to that on earth, just as a direct beam of light is superior to a ray that is reflected from it.

6. (p. 61) *Two rainbows parallel . . . Juno to her handmaid:* Juno's handmaid was Iris, the personification of the rainbow who was regarded as the messenger of the gods. Juno was reported to appear in a double rainbow when she attended to her mistress.

7. (p. 61) *(The one without born of the one within . . . the sun the vapors,):* The outer part of a double rainbow might be thought of as an echo, or a reflection, of the inner part. Such an echo recalls to the Poet the "vagrant one" of l. 14, the wandering nymph Echo, who fell in love with Narcissus but lost her voice in grief when her love was not returned. See Ovid's *Metamorphoses* III: 356–401. The heat of love thus consumed her just as the heat of the sun consumes vapors.

8. (p. 61) *through covenant:* In biblical terms the rainbow represents the pact that God made with Noah not to destroy the world by flood ever again (see Genesis 9: 8–17).

9. (p. 62) *There came a voice:* This voice belongs to Saint Bonaventure (Giovanni di Fidanza, 1221–1274), and it will be identified only in l. 127. He became head of the Franciscan Order in 1257 and wrote a number of important works, including a biography of Saint Francis that Dante uses as one of his sources in canto XI. Pope Sixtus IV canonized him in 1482, and in the sixteenth century Sixtus V made him one of the doctors of the Church, with the title Doctor Seraphicus.

10. (p. 62) *that needle to the star:* When the Pilgrim turned toward the voice of Saint Bonaventure, he did so in the same way that the needle of a compass turns toward the North.

11. (p. 62) *"the other leader":* Saint Dominic. Bonaventure's description of Saint Dominic will now parallel Saint Thomas' narrative about Saint Francis.

12. (p. 62) *"The soldiery of Christ . . . Through grace alone and not that it was worthy":* The Poet now introduces military terms, in keeping with the militant image Saint Dominic had in regards to rooting out heresy and mistaken theological positions. The Christian army was rearmed by the blood of martyrs and by the standard (l. 38)—the cross, representing Christ's atonement for human sins. God ("the Emperor" of l. 40) provided this not because of human merit but because of Divine Grace alone.

13. (p. 62) *"as was said... With champions twain"*: In *Paradiso* XI: 35–39, Saint Thomas had already informed the Pilgrim that the two "champions" (Francis and Dominic) were brought forth by Divine Providence to assist the church (l. 43, "to his Bride brought succor").

14. (p. 62) *"that region where the sweet west wind"*: Spain is the country near the source of the west wind.

15. (p. 62) *"the fortunate Calahorra... the Lion subject is and sovereign"*: This is the Spanish town of Caleruega in Castile, whose rulers displayed coats of arms containing a lion below a castle and another lion above a castle (therefore, one lion subject and one lion sovereign). The town is deemed "fortunate" because it was Saint Dominic's birthplace.

16. (p. 62) *"the amorous paramour / Of Christian Faith, the athlete consecrate"*: Dominic is described as a lover of faith and a sacred athlete because he was devoted to the purity of theological doctrine and took part in the Albigensian Crusade against a heretical sect in southern France. He founded his Order of Preaching Friars in 1215; Pope Honorius III officially recognized the order in 1216. He died in Bologna in 1221 after moving his order from Toulouse to that Italian city and was canonized in 1234 by Pope Gregory IX. He was, in a sense, an athlete in his staunch defense of the faith.

17. (p. 62) *"in his mother her it made prophetic"*: According to tradition, Dominic's mother dreamed that she gave birth to a black-and-white dog with a torch in its mouth. Dominicans dressed in white robes with black trim and were known, because of their zeal (symbolized by the torch) as *Domini canes* ("hounds of the Lord").

18. (pp. 62–63) *"Between him and the Faith at holy font... Saw in a dream"*: Dominic's baptism is viewed as a marriage to Faith, just as Saint Francis married Poverty. Moreover, his godmother (l. 64, the woman who presents the child at the baptism and answers the priest in the child's behalf) dreamed that Dominic would be born with a star on his head that would illuminate the world.

19. (p. 63) *"Dominic was he called"*: Dominic's name was inspired by heaven and reflects the fact that the possessive adjective of *Dominus* in Latin is *Dominicus*, meaning "the Lord's."

20. (p. 63) *"husbandman whom Christ / Elected to his garden"*: Dominic's name is associated with the "husbandman," or keeper, of Christ's garden. Dante probably found this association in Jacopo da Varagine's *Aurea Legenda* 113 (*Golden Legend*), where the saint's life is discussed; this work was extremely popular and appeared around 1260. In ll. 71–75, the Poet does not rhyme Christ with any word but itself. Such a refusal to reduce the word to anything but a unique status is repeated in *Paradiso* XIV: 104–108, XIX: 104–108, and XXII: 83–87.

21. (p. 63) *"the first counsel"*: Christ's first counsel may be said to be contained in the first of the Beatitudes: "Blessed are the poor in spirit" (see the Bible, Matthew 5: 3). Therefore, Dante affirms that Dominic, like Francis, loved Poverty as much as he loved Wisdom and Learning.

22. (p. 63) *'For this I came'*: Dominic was said to have slept on the floor in imitation of Christ's humility, just as if he would have echoed the words of Christ in the Bible, Mark 1: 38: "For therefore came I forth."

23. (p. 63) *"Felix verily!... means as is said!"*: In the Middle Ages it was believed that names are the consequences of things they name (*nomina sunt consequentia rerum*)—that is, they connote qualities of the person who bears them. In fact, Dante says precisely this in *La Vita Nuova* XIII: 4). Thus Saint Dominic's father Felix was truly "felix"— "happy" or "blessed"—for having such a son; the name of Dominic's mother, Joanna or Giovanna, means in Hebrew "abounding in the grace of the Lord."

24. (p. 63) *"Not for the world"*: Dominic did not become a theologian for worldly gain.

25. (p. 63) *"Ostiense and Taddeo ... true manna"*: In becoming a Church doctor, Dominic is said to have followed the footsteps of Enrico da Susa, the theologian from Ostia (the town at the mouth of the Tiber), where Enrico served as cardinal bishop from 1261 until his death in 1271; and of Thaddeus Alderotti (c.1235–1295), a famous physician at the University of Bologna who wrote commentaries on Hippocrates and Galen. Both Enrico and Thaddeus became rich and famous, while Dominic studied only for the "true manna," or true knowledge.

26. (p. 63) *"the vineyard, / Which fadeth soon"*: The vineyard of the Lord, the Church, does not maintain its green color if it is neglected by its "dresser," or gardener.

27. (p. 63) *"of the See, (that once was more benignant . . . who sits there and degenerates,)"*: Dante is speaking of the papal chair, or Holy See. He means to say that the present pope, Boniface VIII, is less kind to the poor than one in his office should be, because of the degeneracy of the papacy under his rule. The office of the papacy is blameless, but not so the current occupant.

28. (p. 63) *"Not to dispense or two or three for six . . . pauperum Dei"*: Dominic, unlike other church figures, did not ask permission to dispense church wealth, withholding two or three of every six coins for himself. Nor did he (l. 92) seek any vacant benefice or ask "for the tithes that belong to God's poor" (*non decimas quæ sunt pauperum Dei*).

29. (p. 63) *"against the errant world . . . do battle for the seed"*: All Dominic asked was to do battle for the true faith ("the seed") against the heretics (the "errant world") during the Albigensian Crusade.

30. (p. 63) *"these four and twenty plants"*: The double garland surrounding the Pilgrim and Beatrice, it should be remembered, contains twenty-four spirits.

31. (p. 64) *"With office apostolical"*: Dominic's order gained the official sanction of Pope Honorius III in 1216.

32. (p. 64) *"Like torrent"*: Dominic's energetic actions against heresy are compared to the force of a torrent in flood.

33. (p. 64) *"Wherever the resistance was the greatest"*: This is probably southern France, site of the Albigensian Crusade.

34. (p. 64) *"divers runnels . . . the garden catholic is watered"*: The "divers runnels," or many other rivulets or streams, refer to Dominic's followers and to particular groups within the Dominican Order. Such rivulets would naturally water the garden of the Universal (that is, Catholic) Church.

35. (p. 64) *"the one wheel of the Biga . . . the other"*: The Biga is a two-wheeled chariot; one wheel is Saint Dominic, and the other Saint Francis.

36. (p. 64) *"Thomas so courteous"*: Saint Thomas (a Dominican) treated the life of Saint Francis as courteously as Saint Bonaventure (a Franciscan) has treated the life of Saint Dominic. On earth and throughout much of their interrelated history, the two orders were seen in conflict, but now they are in harmony in Paradise.

37. (p. 64) *"But still the orbit . . . once the crust"*: The track Saint Francis

established is no longer followed by the Franciscans, and like the Do-
minican Order, the Franciscan Order has become corrupted. As l. 114
underscores, bad wine leaves a mold rather than a crust in the barrel.

38. (p. 64) *"they set the point upon the heel"*: Dominic's followers are
now walking backward in the founder's footsteps, placing the points
of their feet into the heels of Dominic.

39. (p. 64) *"when shall the tares / Complain the granary is taken from
them"*: Tares, noxious weeds, are bundled up separately from the wheat
during a harvest and burned. Dante probably refers here to a passage
in the Bible, Matthew 13:30, "Gather ye together first the tares, and
bind them in bundles to burn them: but gather the wheat into my
barn." These lines may be a reference to the failure of corrupt Francis-
cans to enter Paradise, or they may be a more specific reference to
Pope John XXII's condemnation of the Spirituals in 1318. The Spiritu-
als were a radical group in the order who wanted an extremely strict
adherence to the vows of poverty. Ironically, it was the stupendous
success of the Franciscan Order that made it wealthy, since they at-
tracted gifts from those who admired their vow of poverty.

40. (p. 64) *"searcheth leaf by leaf / Our volume ... 'I am as I am wont'"*:
Dante compares the Franciscan Order to a volume and the individual
friars are the volume's leaves. It might be still possible, but very diffi-
cult, to find a page, or a friar, who could still declare: "I am still now
what I have always been"—that is, "I continue to follow the rules of
Saint Francis as they were originally established."

41. (p. 64) *"not be from Casal nor Acquasparta ... the other narrows"*:
Casal is a town with a monastery in northern Italy near Turin. The ref-
erence is to Ubertino da Casale (born in 1259), leader of the Spirituals,
who opposed the relaxation of the Franciscan Rule. He left the Fran-
ciscan Order upon the election of Pope John XXII and entered the
Benedictine Order in 1317. Acquasparta, a town in Umbria, refers to
Matteo of Acquasparta. Appointed general of the Franciscan Order
in 1287, he relaxed the discipline of the order, paving the way for the
abuses criticized in this canto. He died in 1302. Matteo "avoids" the
Rule, while Ubertino "narrows" it (l. 126).

42. (p. 64) *"Bonaventura of Bagnoregio's ... considerations sinister"*: Saint
Bonaventure, the speaker, finally identifies himself. He was from Ba-
gnoregio, near Orvieto, and as he describes himself, he "postponed

considerations sinister," or always kept temporal concerns as his last concern. This is appropriate, for he was also the author of an important treatise, *Itinerary of the Mind into God,* a book about contemplation.

43. (p. 64) *"Illuminato and Agostino":* Illuminato da Rieti, one of the earliest followers of Saint Francis, went with him to Egypt. Agostino joined the Order in 1210 and became its head in 1216. Saint Bonaventure thus begins listing twelve Franciscans with these two members of the original group.

44. (p. 64) *"the halter":* This is the rope cord, the symbol of the Franciscan Order.

45. (p. 64) *"Hugh of Saint Victor":* Hugh was a celebrated theologian and mystic of the twelfth century (therefore not a Franciscan) who resided in the abbey of Saint Victor in Paris and died in 1141. He was the author of many influential books, was frequently cited by Saint Thomas Aquinas, and numbered among his students Richard of Saint Victor and Peter Lombard, both of whom are in this second circle.

46. (p. 64) *"Peter Mangiador":* Petrus Comestor—"Peter the Book-Eater," so called because he devoured books—was from Troyes in France. He became chancellor of the University of Paris and died in 1179. His major work, *Historia scholastica,* a history of the early church, was much admired in the Middle Ages.

47. (p. 64) *"Peter of Spain":* Born c.1226 in Lisbon, Peter was elected to the papacy as Pope John XXI in 1276. He reigned only for several months before he was killed by the collapse of a palace wall in Viterbo. He was the author of a very popular manual of logic.

48. (p. 65) *"Nathan the seer":* This is the prophet Nathan, who in the Bible, 2 Samuel 12: 1–12, is sent by God to reproach David for harrying Bathsheba and causing the death of her husband, Uriah.

49. (p. 65) *"metropolitan / Chrysostom, and Anselmus, and Donatus . . . the first art":* Saint John Chrysostom, Greek father of the Church, was called "metropolitan" because he was a bishop with power over a province containing several dioceses. He was also known as "Golden Mouth" (the translation of his Greek surname) because of his fame as an orator. He was born in Antioch c.345 and died in 407. He was concerned with reform of the clergy and is thus an appropriate person to place in a canto concerned with the same problem. Anselm was archbishop of

Canterbury from 1093 to 1190 but came from Aosta, Italy. Pope Alexander VI eventually canonized him in 1494. Donatus was a fourth-century Roman rhetorician who wrote an important Latin grammar that was extremely popular in the Middle Ages. Grammar is one of the seven liberal arts, which in the Middle Ages were divided into the trivium (the lower division; the other two are rhetoric and logic) and the quadrivium (the higher division: arithmetic, music, geometry, and astronomy); grammar is the "first art," as l. 138 indicates.

50. (p. 65) *"Rabanus"*: Rabanus Maurus Magnentius, archbishop of Mainz (c.776–856), was author of numerous theological works and biblical commentaries.

51. (p. 65) *"Abbot Joachim"*: Joachim da Fiore (c.1132–1202) was a Calabrian mystic and a member of the Cistercian Order whose doctrines were extremely popular among the Franciscan Spirituals. Just as Saint Thomas Aquinas attacked the views of Siger of Brabant, so too did Saint Bonaventure attack the ideas of Joachim da Fiore. Now, in Paradise, these opponents are all reconciled.

52. (p. 65) *"so great a paladin"*: Saint Dominic is described as a warrior in keeping with his character as guardian of the true faith.

CANTO XIII

1. (p. 66) *Let him imagine . . . primal wheel revolves:* To describe the scene that unfolds before the Pilgrim, the Poet urges his reader to consider an unimaginable scene. His repetition of the word "imagine" three times in ll. 1–10 underscores Dante's attempt to render the impossibility for human imagination to achieve such a task. The twenty-four spirits must be compared to the brightest stars in the heavens. These stars include the fifteen brightest stars (l. 4) that were acknowledged to be so by Ptolemaic astronomy; these fifteen would be combined with the seven greatest stars in the Wain (l. 7)—the Great Bear (Ursa Major or the Big Dipper)—and with the last two stars of "the horn"—Ursa Minor or the Little Dipper (l. 10). This brings the total to twenty-four, the same number of stars as spirits in the two circles. The Pole, or North Star, at the opposite end of the Little Dipper is not included in the count, although it is the axis upon which the Primum Mobile, "the primal wheel" of l. 12, revolves.

2. (p. 66) *that which Minos' daughter made:* According to Ovid, in

Metamorphoses VIII: 174–182, when Ariadne, daughter of King Minos, died, the wreath she had worn at her wedding was changed into the constellation Corona Borealis (Northern Crown). Dante also mentions King Minos in *Inferno* V: 4.

3. (p. 66) *beyond our wont, / As swifter than the motion of the Chiana:* Expressing the experience of seeing the celestial dance of the two circles of brilliant souls in human terms is not possible ("beyond our wont"). Any attempt to do so would be as inadequate as saying the speed of the Primum Mobile (the swiftest part of the heavens) surpasses the speed of the Chiana River in Tuscany, a sluggish stream in Dante's times.

4. (p. 66) *neither Bacchus, nor Apollo . . . Persons three:* In the pagan era, those who worshiped Bacchus and Apollo sung their praises; now the heavenly spirits sing about the Trinity and the dual divine and human nature of Christ.

5. (p. 67) *The light:* This is Saint Thomas Aquinas, who recounted the narrative of God's mendicant ("beggar") saint, Francis. Now he speaks again.

6. (p. 67) *"to thresh out the other":* Now that Saint Thomas has answered one of the Pilgrim's doubts (X: 96: "Where well one fattens if he strayeth not") in canto XI, he is obliged to address the second doubt (X: 114: "there never rose a second"), about King Solomon's wisdom (see endnote 20 to canto X) . In declaring his willingness to do so, the philosopher employs language similar to that frequently used in the Gospels about separating the chaff from the wheat.

7. (p. 67) *"Into that bosom":* This is a reference to Adam.

8. (p. 67) *"the beauteous cheek":* This is a reference to Eve.

9. (p. 67) *"by the lance transfixed":* This is a reference to Christ.

10. (p. 67) *"no second had / The good which in the fifth light is enclosed":* Saint Thomas, ever reading the Pilgrim's mind, understands that the Pilgrim knows Adam and Christ were endowed with more knowledge than any other humans. Yet this fact seems to be in contradiction to the statement he made earlier in canto X: 114, claiming the person enclosed in the fifth light (King Solomon) had "no second." Basically, Saint Thomas' complicated response in ll. 52–87 follows Scholastic logic, defining Adam and Christ as direct creations of God, while Solomon was a secondary creation from Nature.

11. (p. 67) *"Fit in the truth as centre in a circle"*: Saint Thomas informs the Pilgrim that his reasoning and the Pilgrim's doubt will be reconciled, just as the center of a circle is located in a single specific point. The apparent contradiction will be, in short, resolved by Scholastic reasoning.

12. (p. 67) *"That which can die, and that which dieth not"*: Things that can die are the corruptible earthly things created by secondary causes, while things that cannot die are the incorruptible things created directly by God—the angels, the heavens, the human soul, and so forth.

13. (p. 67) *"nothing but the splendor of the idea"*: That is, everything created is only a reflection of God's idea.

14. (p. 67) *"that living Light"*: This is the Son of the Trinity, or the Word.

15. (p. 67) *"its fount"*: That is, the source, God the Father, the First Cause of everything created.

16. (p. 67) *"the Love in them intrined"*: The Love is the Holy Spirit, the third part of the Holy Trinity. Note that Dante invents a word here—*s'intrea* in the original Italian—rendered by Longfellow as "intrined" and meaning "threes itself," a reference to the Trinity.

17. (p. 67) *"nine subsistences, as in a mirror"*: These are the nine orders of the angels that reflect God's wisdom, as if in a mirror.

18. (p. 67) *"only brief contingencies"*: Contingencies are created by the passage of the divine, creating light as it descends through the orders of the angels to the sublunary world. Such contingencies are not eternal.

19. (p. 68) *"with seed and without"*: Animals and plants have seed, while minerals do not.

20. (p. 68) *"Neither their wax, nor that which tempers it, / Remains immutable"*: The corruptible material, the wax, may be imprinted imperfectly by the heavenly stamp, and since the imprint on the wax may vary due to the varying capacity of the material, there is vast diversity throughout creation. If primal matter were perfectly imprinted, perfection would be omnipresent but there would be no variety. Nature, the second cause (God is the first cause), thus resembles the artisan of ll. 77–78, whose hand may tremble.

21. (p. 68) *"hand that trembles"*: Any mistakes in the sublunary world are explained not by God's error but by mistakes that derive from Nature's downward transmission of the creative powers. Nature can make errors the way the trembling hand of an artist can make a mistake. The question of how Nature can create an imperfect world if it is a direct creation of God has not been answered.

22. (p. 68) *"If then the fervent Love, the Vision clear, / Of primal Virtue"*: If the entire Trinity—God or primal Virtue; fervent Love or the Holy Spirit; and the Vision clear, the Son—create something directly by stamping or sealing it on primal matter, that thing so created is perfect and immutable.

23. (p. 68) *"Thus was of old . . . in those two persons"*: In ll. 82–84, the Poet gives us two examples of direct and therefore perfect creations: Adam, created directly from the dust of earth, and Christ in His human aspect, conceived in Mary's womb. As Saint Thomas declares in l. 87, human nature has never reached the perfection of either Adam or Christ.

24. (p. 68) *" 'Then in what way was he without a peer?' / Would be the first beginning of thy words"*: Saint Thomas again reads the Pilgrim's mind, since he would obviously ask how it could be possible that earlier it was said that King Solomon was without peer in human nature, and now it is stated categorically that only Adam and Christ were without peer.

25. (p. 68) *"sufficiently a king"*: Solomon asked for specific practical wisdom that would assist him in governing—not for other more abstract sorts of wisdom that would be useful in other areas. These other areas are specified in ll. 97–102.

26. (p. 68) *"not to know the number . . . motors here above"*: In the first place, Solomon did not ask how many angels there were (angels being the heavenly "motors"), a subject that might be treated by philosophy or theology. The number of angels was supposed to be infinite.

27. (p. 68) *"or if necesse"*: Furthermore, Solomon did not ask for logical wisdom in order to respond to the question of whether an absolute or necessary premise (*necesse*) could produce a contingent or conditional conclusion. Plato, Aristotle, and Scholastic philosophers discussed this problem, and the answer was no.

28. (p. 68) *"Non si est dare primum motum esse"*: The question here, which the Poet presents in Latin as if it were part of a Scholastic argument, which it frequently was, is whether or not there exists a motion without a cause or a First Mover. Naturally, here the answer is that all motion depends upon God, the First or Prime Mover. This would be a problem for both philosophy and theology.

29. (p. 69) *"semicircle can be made . . . no right angle":* The final kind of wisdom Solomon did not demand is geometrical, whether it would be possible to inscribe a non-right-angled triangle within a semicircle (the answer is no, at least in the universe imagined by Euclid).

30. (p. 69) *"And if on 'rose' thou turnest thy clear eyes . . . the first father and of our Delight":* Saint Thomas reminds the Pilgrim of the line in *Paradiso* X: 114 ("never rose a second") that caused his doubt about Solomon's peerless status in terms of human wisdom. In l. 104, he has defined the kind of wisdom Solomon possesses as "regal prudence," or the kind of wisdom required to govern, not the other kinds of possible wisdoms. His conclusion, then, is that what he said earlier about Solomon and what he now says about Adam and Christ (l. 111) are not contradictory statements.

31. (p. 69) *"move slowly . . . feelings bind the intellect":* Saint Thomas warns the Pilgrim to avoid jumping to conclusions without having all the facts and to expect truth to be reached by making subtle distinctions, since emotions can often rule the intellect.

32. (p. 69) *"Far more than uselessly . . . fishes for the truth, and has no skill":* It is preferable to remain ignorant than to search for truth without the proper skills.

33. (p. 69) *"Parmenides, Melissus, Brissus":* Saint Thomas provides three examples of ancient philosophers whose views would not be supported by either Aristotelian or Scholastic philosophy and theology. Parmenides, born c.513 B.C. and founder of the Eleatic school of philosophy, falsely believed that all things come from the sun. His disciple Melissus believed that the motion visible in the universe was only apparent. Brissus (or Bryson) was cited by Aristotle as a man who attempted to square the circle with false geometrical methods.

34. (p. 69) *"Sabellius, Arius":* Sabellius was a heretic of the third century who rejected the orthodox doctrine of the Holy Trinity (the doctrine embraced by Dante in this particular canto), believing that the three parts of the Triune God were merely different names for a single God. Arius, who died in A.D. 336, was the father of the Arian heresy, which claimed that the Father and Son are not of "one substance." He advocated the position that the Son was the first being created and was inferior to the Father, and that the Holy Spirit was created by the power of the Son. This belief caused a great deal of controversy and was at the center of disputes about heresy within the Christian church for centuries. The Nicene Creed of A.D. 325 was, in large measure, a response to the Arian heresy. Sabellius and Arius were worse than believers in heresy: They were technically heresiarchs, or founders of heretical sects who persevered in their false and unortho-dox beliefs, leading other less intelligent Christians astray.

35. (p. 69) *"been even as swords . . . distorted their straight faces"*: Rather than reflecting the Scriptures properly, these foolish and heretical thinkers have reflected the truth in a distorted manner, as a sword blade would reflect the image of a face.

36. (p. 70) *"Let not Dame Bertha nor Ser Martin think . . . fall the other may"*: Using popular names of the period and adding the normally honorific titles of *Donna* (Dame, Lady, or Miss) and *Ser* (Sir or Mis-ter) to them, the Poet creates a sarcastic and disparaging opinion of popular judgment that can never understand the judgments of God. Even though men witness one man steal and another make a pious of-fering (l. 140), this does not mean that the thief ends up in Hell ("fall the other may") and the pious devotee ends up in Paradise ("one may rise"). Thus Solomon may well have sinned, but he is nevertheless in Paradise among the blessed, since mere human beings cannot fathom divine wisdom.

CANTO XIV

1. (p. 71) *From centre unto rim . . . my mind upon a sudden dropped:* The Pilgrim and Beatrice stand in the midst of two circles of souls, and the Pilgrim suddenly sees a parallel between this situation and a round container of water that, when struck, undulates from circumference to rim or from rim to circumference, depending upon whether the con-tainer is struck from outside or from inside. Due to their different lo-cations, Beatrice would speak from center to rim, while Saint Thomas would speak in the opposite direction.

2. (p. 71) *"This man . . . one truth more"*: Beatrice is now speaking, referring to the Pilgrim's need to learn "one truth more."

3. (p. 71) *"if the light wherewith . . . it injure not your sight"*: By reading the Pilgrim's mind as usual, Beatrice realizes that he wants to know if the light that surrounds the souls will be there forever, even after the resurrection of the body, and if so, will the eyes of the resurrected be

able to endure the radiance of such bright light? The resurrection of the body is implied by l. 17, where Beatrice speaks of the bodies being made visible once again after the Last Judgment, since Orthodox Christianity believes in the *bodily* resurrection.

4. (p. 71) *here:* That is, on earth.

5. (p. 71) *there:* That is, in heaven.

6. (p. 72) *refreshment of the eternal rain:* God's grace refreshes the souls in Paradise.

7. (p. 72) *The One and Two and Three . . . chanted by each one:* Once again, the souls celebrate the mystery of the Trinity.

8. (p. 72) *a modest voice . . . the Angel's was to Mary:* This modest voice coming from the brightest of the lights in the inner ring of souls belongs to King Solomon, precisely the person whose wisdom was the focus of canto XIII. Saint Thomas has previously described him in X: 109 as the brightest of the lights in that circle. Dante compares his voice to that of the Angel Gabriel at the Annunciation, as described in the Bible, Luke 1: 28.

9. (p. 72) *"As long as":* In ll. 37–60, Solomon informs the Pilgrim that the joy of Paradise is eternal, and the radiance of the souls is also eternal (ll. 37–39). However, the souls shall shine in proportion to the ardor of their love, which depends upon the strength of their vision, or understanding, of God, and this strength finally depends upon God's grace, not upon works or merit. The physical body will be perfect when it is resurrected, and quite naturally the power of sight will be improved so that the resurrected bodies may gaze upon the bright lights in heaven (l. 49).

10. (p. 72) *"Therefore the vision":* After discussing the interrelationship between ardor, vision, and radiance in ll. 40–43, Solomon now repeats himself, placing the three qualities in the proper order according to Christian doctrine: the understanding, or vision, of God produces the increased ardor of love that increases the brilliance of the radiance.

11. (p. 72) *"But even as a coal . . . its own appearance it maintains":* After the resurrection, the radiance of the blessed within their shining will seem like an intensely glowing coal within its own flame: The light within the coal (compared to the body) will be even greater than the brilliant light surrounding it (compared to the soul).

12. (p. 72) *Nor sole for them perhaps:* The souls desire to regain their

earthly bodies (something that takes place only before the Last Judgment) not because they miss their physical shapes but rather because they hope to be reunited with their loved ones then.

13. (p. 74) *a circle / Outside the other two circumferences. / O very sparkling of the Holy Spirit:* Suddenly a third circle of souls begins to form, the "very sparkling of the Holy Spirit." The three circles also underline the theme of the Holy Trinity.

14. (p. 74) *I beheld myself translated . . . more ruddy than its wont:* As the Pilgrim gazes once again at Beatrice, he is instantaneously lifted up to the fifth heaven, the Sphere of Mars. His move upward is defined (l. 84) as a move toward "higher salvation," since the next sphere implies a higher degree of blessedness. Mars seems redder upon his arrival as if to celebrate the presence of the Pilgrim.

15. (p. 74) *in that dialect . . . new grace beseemed:* The "dialect," the silent language of the heart, is a language common to all humanity. The Pilgrim offers a "holocaust"—offering or sacrifice—with this silent language. The "new grace" refers to his translation to the fifth heaven.

16. (p. 74) *in twofold rays:* The souls of the warrior saints intersect to form a cross of light that will be described in ll. 101–102. This cross contains the souls of the Christian warrior saints, an appropriate group of souls to be in the Sphere of Mars, the pagan god of warfare.

17. (p. 74) *"Helios":* In the original Italian text, the word is *Eliòs,* a fusion of the Greek word for God (*Helios*) and the Hebrew *Ely* (God). The Pilgrim is praising the beauty and glory of the vision before him, set out by God for his observation.

18. (p. 74) *The Galaxy:* This is the Milky Way, the subject of various theories about its composition from classical antiquity to Dante's time. Dante discusses these theories in *Il Convivio* II: 14: 5–8, where he correctly affirms that the Galaxy is composed of stars.

19. (p. 75) *the venerable sign / That quadrants joining in a circle make:* The lines describing the four quadrants of the circle form a Greek cross.

20. (p. 75) *gleamed forth Christ . . . follows Christ:* Once again, Dante refuses to rhyme Christ with any other word except itself (see also *Paradiso* XIX: 104–108 and XXII: 83–87).

21. (p. 75) *From horn to horn, and 'twixt the top and base:* That is, from arm to arm and from top to bottom of the cross.

22. (p. 75) *particles of bodies . . . with art contrive:* The movement of

the souls within the cross is compared to earthly particles, or specks of dust, floating in a beam of light that shines through some aperture into a shaded area that may be produced by things men make to protect themselves from the light (a curtain, for instance).

23. (p. 75) *through the cross a melody:* Now the power of music is added to the power of Beatrice's eyes to cause the Pilgrim to go into rapture.

24. (p. 75) *"Arise and conquer!":* This militant hymn is appropriate to the warrior saints in this section of Paradise.

25. (p. 75) *there was not anything . . . somewhat too bold:* The Pilgrim's claim (ll. 127–129) that the melody gives him greater pleasure than anything he has experienced before causes him to pause, since he suddenly realizes that this would mean it would give him more pleasure than the sight of Beatrice's eyes. This momentary self-accusation is set aside, however, in l. 135, where the Pilgrim reminds himself that he has not yet gazed into Beatrice's eyes in the Sphere of Mars.

26. (p. 75) *the living seals . . . grow in power ascending:* Beatrice's eyes (the "living seals") increase in brilliance as she and the Pilgrim ascend higher and higher in Paradise.

CANTO XV

1. (p. 77) *A will benign . . . tighten and relax:* Just as goodwill expresses itself in love, self-seeking or selfish love leads to iniquity. The Poet is saying that since the souls making up the Greek cross are of goodwill in harmony with God, they are generous and want to help the Pilgrim, so they fall silent. The lute and harp of XIV: 118 have now become a lyre whose strings are plucked by the hand of God—that is, the souls are attuned to God's will.

2. (p. 77) *'Tis well:* It is right that souls suffer eternal damnation in Hell if they ignore true eternal love for transient, material goals.

3. (p. 77) *a sudden fire . . . eyes that steadfast were before:* The sight of a shooting star or meteor, a "sudden fire," causes the spectator's eyes to move to follow the sudden sight.

4. (p. 77) *Nothing is missed:* No star is missing.

5. (p. 77) *So from the horn . . . behind alabaster:* One of the souls in the cross shoots past the right arm of the cross ("the horn") toward the Pilgrim, and is compared first to a gem on a ribbon as it travels in its

motion across the radial line that divides the circle into quadrants. It is also compared to a fire behind an alabaster screen, which would make it brighter than the material surrounding it (just as this spirit is apparently brighter than the light surrounding it).

6. (p. 77) *Thus piteous did Anchises' shade:* Dante compares the Pilgrim's encounter with this spirit to the encounter of Aeneas with his father, Anchises, in the Elysian Fields, as told in Virgil's *Aeneid* VI: 684–688. Just as Virgil's hero meets one of his ancestors in the other world, the Pilgrim is about to meet one of his own relatives in Paradise.

7. (p. 77) *our greatest Muse:* Virgil, for Dante the greatest of all pagan poets, inspires other poets just as the Muses do.

8. (pp. 77–78) *"O sanguis meus . . . janua reclusa?":* Longfellow's translation of these three Latin lines reads as follows: "O blood of mine! O grace of God infused / Superlative! To whom as unto thee / Were ever twice the gates of heaven unclosed?" These verses are extremely important for a number of reasons. First of all, the use of Latin for greeting the Pilgrim is unprecedented. As Latin is the official language of both the Church and of philosophy, it gives this encounter an especially solemn tone. Second, and perhaps most important, is the fact that the third line of the tercet referring to the gates of heaven being twice "unclosed" represents a guarantee of the Pilgrim's future salvation. Before Dante, only Saint Paul has been blessed with such an honor. The identity of the soul who tells the Pilgrim this is not specifically given in the text until l. 135, when the reader finally discovers that the speaker is Cacciaguida, Dante's great-great-grandfather, whose appearance in cantos XV–XVII marks an essential moment in the poem. Cacciaguida lived in the late eleventh and early twelfth century and did not have the advantage of being able to read Dante's great epic poem that did so much to create the Italian language, so it is not surprising to see that his first words are in Latin. Most of what is known about Cacciaguida comes from Dante's text, and this commentary will reveal it piecemeal, just as Cacciaguida reveals it to Dante and to his reader.

9. (p. 78) *turned my sight . . . in her eyes was burning such a smile:* For the first time in the Sphere of Mars, the Pilgrim gazes directly at Beatrice. The Pilgrim is amazed ("stupefied," l. 33) because the spirit addresses him as a blood relation, but Beatrice's smile is increasing in its radiance because she (with the usual foreknowledge) understands how much the Pilgrim will be delighted to meet one of his ancestors in heaven.

10. (p. 78) *Above the mark of mortals set itself . . . so far slackenend, that its speech descended:* Because the spirit has resided in Paradise for some time and has absorbed infinite wisdom and understanding by association with God, his first words to the Pilgrim are incomprehensible—his speech is like an arrow shot above the target employed by mortals. He must adjust to the Pilgrim's level of lower comprehension; in a continuation of the metaphor of bow and arrow, the bow of the spirit's comprehension must be "slackened."

11. (p. 78) *"O Trine and One":* The spirit thanks God for the arrival of his descendant, underscoring the fact of the Trinity once again, a consistent theme in *Paradiso*.

12. (p. 78) *"the mighty volume / Wherein is never changed the white nor dark":* Cacciaguida has been waiting for some time for his descendant's arrival, having read of his journey in the book of the future that can never be changed.

13. (p. 78) *"by grace of her":* This is Beatrice, who gives Dante the ability to ascend through the heavens.

14. (p. 78) *"From Him who is the first, as from the unit . . . thy thought thou showest":* Just as numbers such as 5 or 6 have their origin in the number 1, all knowledge derives from God, and as the Pilgrim's thoughts ray out, they are reflected from the mind of God to the minds of the blessed who are gazing upon God. Thus in l. 63, the Pilgrim's thoughts are already apparent to the blessed.

15. (p. 79) *"Now let thy voice . . . answer is decreed already":* Even though the soul already knows what the Pilgrim is going to ask and his answer is already prepared, he urges the Pilgrim to speak nevertheless.

16. (p. 79) *she heard / Before I spake:* As usual, Beatrice has foreknowledge of the Pilgrim's thoughts and gives her permission to him to ask his questions.

17. (p. 79) *"Love and knowledge . . . this paternal welcome":* In ll. 73–78, the Pilgrim answers his ancestor Cacciaguida with a reply designed to be as dignified as the special occasion demands. He notes that once the souls first saw the first Equality (God, in whom all qualities are balanced perfectly and therefore equally), love, or desire, and intelligence became equal in them. In like manner, light and heat (l. 77,

"heat and radiance") coexist equally in the sun. While the blessed thus have no desire that they are incapable of fulfilling with their intelligence, this is not the case among mortals, whose will and argument (in the sense of evidence) may not be equally matched. Thus in ll. 82–84 the Pilgrim states that while he might have the will to express his gratitude to the soul to whom he is speaking, he lacks the expressive means to do so. This entire passage represents one of Dante's most complicated ways of saying something that he stresses frequently in Paradise: Human powers of description fall short of the majesty and the mystery of the afterlife.

18. (p. 79) *"living topaz! / Set in this precious jewel as a gem":* Cacciaguida appears in the cross of souls as if he is a gem set in a band of jewelry; yellow topaz may be chosen here since it becomes red (the color of love) when heated.

19. (p. 79) *"O leaf of mine . . . I was thine own root!":* Cacciaguida declares he is the root of Dante's family tree, while the Pilgrim is a later descendant, only a recent leaf.

20. (p. 79) *"on the first cornice . . . great-grandsire was":* Cacciaguida informs the Pilgrim that his son, Dante's great-grandfather, is presently expiating the sin of Pride on the first ledge of the Mountain of Purgatory and should be prayed for to decrease his time there ("make shorter with thy works," l. 96). Apparently this sin seems to run in the family! This figure would be Alighiero, the first to bear Dante's family name, who is mentioned in a document dating back to 1189. The date given by Cacciaguida ("a hundred years and more," l. 92) probably indicates uncertainty about the actual date on the Poet's part.

21. (p. 79) *"the long fatigue":* The Reader should bear in mind the unpleasant punishment of the Proud—being forced to carry an enormous stone on one's back.

22. (p. 79) *"Florence, within the ancient boundary":* Here begins a long diatribe about the good old days in Florence before corruption set in, along with an account of various characters from recent Florentine history. The "ancient boundary" refers to the old city walls from the ninth century, which were situated more or less along the site of the original Roman walls. Florence still counted the church hours there because the Badia church (still standing) near the walls rang the canonical hours of tierce (the third hour, about 9 A.M.) and nones (the ninth hour, about 3 P.M.). Dante's home was located near the church.

23. (p. 79) *"quiet, temperate and chaste"*: Before the corruption of Dante's day set in, Florence was quiet (without internecine strife), moderate in its mode of living, and, above all, not lascivious in its customs.

24. (p. 80) *"girdle / That caught the eye"*: Most translators render the Italian phrase *non gonne contigiate* as embroidered, decorated, or lavish gowns.

25. (p. 80) *"Not yet the daughter . . . time and dower"*: Women did not yet marry at a very young age, nor were their dowries so huge that they threatened to impoverish a family's wealth.

26. (p. 80) *"No houses had she void of families"*: There were no enormous and ostentatious palaces too great for their inhabitants. It is also possible that this line refers to the empty homes left that way in Dante's time because of internal strife or bloodlines dying out.

27. (p. 80) *"Sardanapalus"*: This ancient king of Assyria was famous in antiquity for his lavish spending and effeminacy.

28. (p. 80) *"Not yet surpassed had Montemalo been / By your Uccellatojo"*: Montemalo (today Montemario) is the hill in Rome from which one first sees the Eternal City when approaching from the north. Monte Uccellatoio is the spot where one can first see Florence when approaching that city from Bologna. At the uncorrupted time Cacciaguida praises, Florence had not surpassed Rome in splendor and wealth. During the Middle Ages and through much of the early Renaissance, Rome was a relatively insignificant city with a very small population, while Florence became one of the world's largest and most powerful cities. Cacciaguida predicts that Florence's downfall will be even swifter than Rome's (a prediction that never came true).

29. (p. 80) *"Bellincion Berti . . . without a painted face"*: He was a member of the important Ravignani family in the twelfth century and the father of the "good Gualdrada" mentioned in *Inferno* XVI: 37. In that simple age, he wore a modest belt (plain leather with bone clasp), not one decorated with precious stones or metals. His wife also left the house without makeup on her face.

30. (p. 80) *"of Nerli saw, and him of Vecchio"*: The Nerli and the Vecchi (also known as the Vecchietti) were old Guelph families in the Florence of Caccaiguida's day.

31. (p. 80) *"simple suits of buff"*: These were simple garments made from unlined leather rather than leather covered or lined with expensive fabrics or furs.

32. (p. 80) *"O fortunate women!... her bed deserted"*: Florentine matrons were fortunate, for they were certain to be buried in their own churchyard, not in exile, and they were not yet abandoned by husbands who were off in France making money as merchants. Cacciaguida's lament reveals the intensely conservative views Dante held about economic change in his day: The aspects of communal life he criticizes here are precisely those that made Florence the most important Italian city of the late Middle Ages and the Renaissance, rivaled only by the splendor of Venice.

33. (p. 80) *"the tales... Fesole and Rome"*: These are legends told about the founding of Rome by the Trojans and the founding of Fiesole and Florence by the Romans.

34. (p. 80) *"As great a marvel... Cornelia now"*: Lapo Salterello was a corrupt lawyer and judge banished from Florence in 1302 along with Dante; Cianghella was a Florentine woman of very low morals, also contemporary with Dante. Cacciaguida declares that when Florence was uncorrupted, it would have been as surprising to find Lapo and Cianghella in the city as it would be today, in corrupt times, to find there such noble (and uncorrupted) Romans as Cincinnatus or Cornelia, mother of the two Gracchi tribunes. Cornelia is placed in Limbo (*Inferno* IV: 128) with other virtuous pagan women.

35. (p. 80) *"Mary give me, with loud cries invoked"*: Women in the pangs of childbirth appealed to the Virgin Mary.

36. (p. 80) *"Christian and Cacciaguida I became"*: The speaker finally gives his baptismal name to the Pilgrim. Cacciaguida was baptized in the same baptismal font that the Pilgrim admits to breaking in *Inferno* XIX: 16–20.

37. (p. 81) *"Moronto... Eliseo"*: We know nothing about these two brothers.

38. (p. 81) *"Val di Pado"*: This is the valley of the Po River. (Early glosses on this line by commentators on Dante's poem specified the place to be the city of Ferrara.)

39. (p. 81) *"thy surname was derived"*: Cacciaguida married Alighiera degli Alighieri; their son was named Alighiero, and his offspring took his Christian name as their surname.

40. (p. 81) *"the Emperor Conrad"*: This is Conrad III (1093–1152), who was crowned king of Saxony in Milan in 1128 and thereafter recognized as emperor. He led the Second Crusade (1147–1149) with the ruler of France.

41. (p. 81) *"that law's / Iniquity . . . your Pastor's fault"*: Law here means religion, referring to the Muslims who have usurped the rights of Christians to visit the Holy Land partly because of the indifference of the Roman papacy.

42. (p. 81) *"Released from bonds . . . from martyrdom unto this peace"*: Cacciaguida was killed in the Holy Land during the Second Crusade. His death is called "martyrdom" because he was fighting for the faith, and it was believed that Christians who died on a crusade in the Holy Land would go directly to heaven.

CANTO XVI

1. (p. 83) *our poor nobility of blood . . . there where appetite is not perverted*: The Pilgrim is unafraid to feel pride in his ancestry in Paradise (l. 5, "there"), contrasting that pride to the false pride that has ruined so many noble families on earth (l. 3, "down here"). Incidentally, it is only Dante's claim that establishes Cacciaguida's ascension to nobility (l. 2, "the people glory in thee"), thanks to his military service under Conrad III.

2. (p. 83) *Truly thou art a cloak . . . with his shears!*: Nobility is not really based solely on birth but must be fashioned continuously by good character, like a cloak that is pieced together every day before the scissors of time snips its fabric away.

3. (p. 83) *With You*: In addressing Cacciaguida, the Pilgrim employs the second person plural "you," the honorific form *voi*, rather than the more familiar *tu*, the singular "you." According to tradition, this form was first employed to address Julius Caesar. The word *voi* is also repeated in ll. 16–18. In *The Divine Comedy*, the Pilgrim employs the *voi* form a number of times: with Farinata and Cavalcante in *Inferno* X; with Brunetto Latini in *Inferno* XV: 80; with Pope Adrian V in *Purgatorio* XIX: 131; with Guido Guinizelli in *Purgatorio* XXVI: 112; and with Beatrice until the end of the poem, when he shifts to the familiar form *tu* in *Paradiso* XXXI: 80–90.

4. (p. 83) *her family*: That is, her people (the Romans). In Dante's day, the Romans were apparently less likely to employ the *voi* form than the *tu* form in their speech.

5. (p. 83) *unto her who coughed:* In the Old French romance of Lancelot of the Lake, the book that was so crucial a part of the tragic story of Paolo and Francesca in *Inferno* V: 127–138, the lady in waiting, Dame de Malehaut, coughed when she heard the clandestine exchange of lovers' vows to let Paolo and Francesca know that she was nearby.

6. (p. 83) *failing writ:* That is, recorded mistake or fault.

7. (p. 83) *the sheepfold of Saint John:* These are the Florentines, whose patron saint was Saint John the Baptist.

8. (p. 84) *but not in / This modern dialect:* While Cacciaguida's first words to the Pilgrim (*Paradiso* XV: 28–30) were in Latin, now he seems to be speaking the older vernacular Florentine dialect of his own day, not the Florentine that was spoken at the time the poem takes place (1300) and that Dante's poem reflects.

9. (p. 84) *"From uttering of the Ave ... beneath his paw":* The Florentines calculated the beginning of each year with the Annunciation (when the Angel Gabriel greeted the Virgin Mary with the "Ave Maria"), traditionally held to be March 25, exactly nine months before Christ's birth on December 25. Cacciaguida gives the date of his birth in ll. 34–39 in a very complicated manner. From the Annunciation to the time of his birth, Mars (l. 37, "this fire") returned 580 times to the constellation of Leo (l. 37, "its Lion"). One revolution of Mars was supposed to take about 687 days: Multiplying 580 revolutions by 687 days and then dividing that sum by the 365 days in a year results in a birth date of 1091. Cacciaguida died in the Second Crusade in 1147, so he was around fifty-six or fifty-seven years old at the time.

10. (p. 84) *"My ancestors and I our birthplace had ... in your annual game":* A horse race, or *palio*, was run each year in honor of Saint John's day (June 24), and at the beginning of the "last ward" or last district of the city (the Porto San Piero district) stood the home of the Elisei family, from which Cacciaguida probably was descended.

11. (p. 84) *"between / Mars and the Baptist ... who now are living":* Cacciaguida claims that in his day the population of the area between the old statue of Mars on the Arno River at the Ponte Vecchio and the Baptistry of San Giovanni in the center of Florence was only a fifth (l. 48, "a fifth part") of what it was in Dante's time, 1300.

12. (p. 84) *"Campi and Certaldo and Figghine"*: Campi, Certaldo, and Figline are small Tuscan towns within between 8 and 18 miles from Florence.

13. (p. 84) *"at Galluzzo / And at Trespiano"*: Galluzzo is about 2 miles outside the Porta Romana of Florence, in the direction of Rome; Trespiano is located about 3 miles outside Porto San Gallo, in the direction of Bologna.

14. (p. 84) *"Aguglione's churl, and him of Signa"*: These are references to Baldo d'Aguglione and to Fazio de' Marubaldini, from Signa. Aguglione was a powerful political leader who in 1311 drew up a list to recall a number of Guelph exiles from Florence but expressly excluded Dante's name. Marubaldini, whose village of Signa is about 10 miles west of Florence, was another political leader who enjoyed an unsavory reputation.

15. (p. 84) *"Had not the folk, which most of all the world / Degenerates, been a step-dame unto Caesar"*: If the men of the Church, who are more corrupt than anyone else in the world, had not been hostile (like a stepmother, a figure traditionally associated with bad treatment of stepchildren) to Caesar (representing the temporal power of the Holy Roman Empire), things would have been very different. The Church should instead have acted like a loving mother.

16. (p. 84) *"Some who turn Florentines . . . back again to Simifonte"*: Simifonte is a fortress in the Val d'Elsa, southwest of Florence, which was captured and destroyed by the Florentines in 1202 after a long siege. Dante's reference is apparently to some parvenu from that town who had come to corrupt Florence to make his fortune. Such immigrants would not have been welcomed in the purer days when Cacciaguida was living.

17. (pp. 84–85) *"At Montemurlo . . . the Buondelmonti"*: If things had remained in their uncorrupted state, the Conti Guidi (forced to sell their fortress to the Florentines in 1254) would continue to hold it; the Cerchi family would still live in the small parish of Acone rather than in Florence, where they quarreled with the noble Donati family; and the Buondelmonti family (important Guelph leaders) would still be living in their castle in the valley of the River Greve and would not have moved to Florence in 1135 and stirred up mischief there. All these families played a prominent role in the bitter strife in Florence between the Guelph and Ghibelline factions.

18. (p. 85) *"Ever the intermingling of the people . . . as in the body food it sur-feits on"*: Dante was no believer in mixing the classes or the races: New blood added to old could only cause mischief, just as food badly digested makes the body ill.

19. (p. 85) *"a single sword than five"*: Larger size does not determine good civil government or a better quality of life, and the aggressive political policies that caused Florence to expand through the Tuscan territory had only negative effects.

20. (p. 85) *"If Luni thou regard . . . Sinigaglia after them"*: Cacciaguida cites a number of cities that have or will be destroyed, including Luni (an ancient Etruscan city); Urbisaglia (the ancient Urbs Salvia in the Marches south of Ancona, already destroyed in Dante's day); Chiusi (halfway between Florence and Rome on the Via Cassia, a city that suffered from malaria); and Sinigaglia, now known as Senigallia, on the Adriatic northwest of Ancona, severely damaged during the internecine wars of Dante's time and ravaged by malaria.

21. (p. 85) *"even cities have an end . . . but it is hidden"*: Because human lives are relatively brief, men are not always aware of the fact that cities too die out, even if they endure for a longer period of time.

22. (p. 85) *"And as the turning of the lunar heaven"*: Just as the revolution of the moon causes tides to ebb and flow, so too the turning of Fortune's wheel will affect Florence, obviously in a negative manner, according to Cacciaguida. He will now list a number of distinguished Florentine families who are currently extinct or without any influence.

23. (p. 85) *"the Ughi, saw the Catellini, . . . and Alberichi"*: The Ughi, Catellini, Filippi, Greci, Ormanni, and the Alberichi are families that declined, disappeared, or were eclipsed by the passage of time. The Greci were once important enough to have a major street in the city, today's Borgo dei Greci, named after them.

24. (p. 85) *"With him of La Sannella him of Arca, / And Soldanier, Ardinghi, and Bostichi"*: These are more noble Florentine families that had fallen into disrepute or even extinction. "Him of Arca" refers to the dell'Arca family.

25. (p. 85) *"Near to the gate that is at present"*: According to most commentators, this is a reference to the Cerchi family, who bought a palace belonging to the Conti Guidi near the Porta San Piero. Dante considered the Cerchi (already mentioned in l. 65) guilty of fomenting civil unrest in Florence.

26. (p. 85) *"soon it shall be jetsam from the bark"*: Florence is the ship that shall soon throw overboard members of its community.

27. (p. 85) *"The Ravignani ... Of the great Bellincione since hath taken"*: The Ravignani is another old family that had become extinct by Dante's times. Its head in Cacciaguida's day was Bellincione Berti (already mentioned in *Paradiso* XV: 112), from whom the Conti Guido descended. The Conti Guidi had inherited the houses from the Ravignani with the marriage of Count Guido Guerra to the "good Gualdrada," daughter of Bellincione Berti. The son-in-law of Bellincione Berti, a member of the Donati family, took the name of Bellincione, making it his surname.

28. (p. 85) *"He of La Pressa"*: This is a Ghibelline family driven out of Florence in 1258.

29. (p. 85) *"Galigajo / Had hilt and pommel gilded in his house"*: Galigaio de' Galigai was a member of a Ghibelline family exiled in 1258. By Cacciaguida's day, the family had achieved knighthood, hence the reference to "hilt and pommel gilded."

30. (p. 86) *"the Column Vair"*: A strip of vair (squirrel hair or ermine) decorated the shield of the Pigli, another old family.

31. (p. 86) *"Sacchetti, Giuochi, Fifant, and Barucci, / And Galli"*: The Sacchetti, an ancient Guelph family, fled Florence after the Ghibelline victory at Montaperti in 1260; the Giuochi, Fifanti, and Barucci families were Ghibellines who were either exiled in 1258 or extinct by Dante's day. The Galli were Ghibellines whose homes were torn down in 1293.

32. (p. 86) *"they who for the bushel blush"*: This is a reference to the Chiaramontesi family, one of whom was responsible for an infamous scandal in the city's regulation of salt (see *Purgatorio* XII: 105).

33. (p. 86) *"the Calfucci"*: This Guelph family, extinct in Dante's time, included ancestors of the Donati, the family to which Dante's wife Gemma Donati belonged.

34. (p. 86) *"To curule chairs the Sizii and Arrigucci"*: A curule chair is a high civic office reserved for only the most important city officials. The Sizii and the Arrigucci were two ancient noble families who lived near the Duomo in the center of Florence and who fled the city after the victory of the Ghibellines at Montaperti in 1260.

35. (p. 86) *"those who are undone / By their own pride!"*: This is the Uberti family. The Pilgrim has already met Farinata degli Uberti in *Inferno* X; he was responsible for the Ghibelline victory at Montaperti.

36. (p. 86) *"the Balls Gold"*: The Lamberti family's coat of arms sported golden balls. According to *Inferno* XXVIII: 106, Mosca dei Lamberti had been responsible for the murder of Buondelmonte dei Buondelmonti by the Amidei family, the ultimate origin of the Guelph and Ghibelline feud in Florence.

37. (p. 86) *"when vacant is your church, / Fatten by staying in consistory"*: The Visdomini and Tosinghi families administered the revenues of the church whenever the Florentine bishopric was vacant. The Poet accuses them of growing fat on the revenues of their profits by helping to delay any appointments.

38. (p. 86) *"The insolent race... That his wife's father should make him their kin"*: This reference is to the Adimari family, Guelphs expelled from Florence in 1248. The clan was divided into three branches: the Argenti (one of them, Filippo Argenti, encounters the Pilgrim in *Inferno* VIII: 11–63); the Aldobrandi; and the Cavicciuli. One member of this last branch took possession of Dante's belongings after he was exiled and always worked to prevent his return, for obvious reasons. Cacciaguida declares that their origins were so base that Umbertino Donati, who had married one of Bellincione Berti's daughters, was upset that another daughter married into the Adimari clan (ll. 119–120).

39. (p. 86) *"Caponsacco to the Market / From Fesole descended"*: The Caponsacchi family from Fesole (Fiesole) was once one of the most important Ghibelline families in Florence. They were originally exiled in 1258, returned, joined the White faction of the Guelphs, and were again exiled in 1302. They settled in the old market quarter of the city.

40. (p. 86) *"Giuda and Infangato"*: These are two old Ghibelline families.

41. (p. 86) *"I'll tell a thing incredible... Which from the Della Pera took its name!"*: Cacciaguida believes the decline of the old Della Pera family was so precipitous that it is hard to believe that in Dante's time one of the city's minor gates, the Porta Peruzza, is named for them.

42. (p. 86) *"Each one that bears the beautiful escutcheon... The festival of*

Thomas keepeth fresh": When Marquis Hugh of Brandenburg (known in Italy as Ugo il Grande) came to Florence as Imperial Vicar of Emperor Otto III, he apparently conferred knighthood on six Florentine families (the Giandonati, Pulci, Nerli, Gangalandi, Alepri, and della Bella), all of whom employed versions of his coat of arms, which contained seven staves. Hugh died on Saint Thomas' Day (December 26) in 1006. On that day every year, prayers were offered for the salvation of his soul in the church of the Badia, which either he or his mother established.

43. (p. 86) *"with the populace unites himself . . . the man who binds it with a border"*: This is a reference to Giano della Bella, whose family had originally been knighted by Hugh. But in 1293, shortly before his exile in 1295, Giano introduced strict measures against the Florentine nobility. These Ordinances of Justice favored the merchant classes by excluding all patrician families from holding political office and refusing them the right to renounce their noble ancestry. Thus Giano tinged the original family coat of arms with a border of gold, signifying to Dante that he now sided with the lower classes.

44. (p. 86) *"Gualterotti and Importuni . . . more quiet would the Borgo be"*: These Guelph families who lived in the Borgo Santi Apostoli quarter near the city's center had declined greatly by Dante's times.

45. (p. 86) *"new neighbors"*: The new neighbors of the two families who had seen better days are the members of the Buondelmonti family. They came to live in the Borgo Santi Apostoli quarter after their castle in Montebuono was destroyed in 1135.

46. (p. 86) *"The house from which is born your lamentation"*: The feud between the Amidei and the Buondelmonti was thought to be the cause of Florentine civil conflict. Buondelmonte dei Buondelmonti was betrothed to one of the Amidei family but on his wedding day left her for one of the Donati clan. To avenge this insult, the Amidei assassinated him (see *Inferno* XXVIII: 103–111).

47. (p. 87) *"If God had thee surrendered to the Ema"*: Given the trouble Buondelmonte caused by jilting a member of the Amidei family, Florence would have been better off if he and all the Buondelmonti had been drowned in the River Ema, which the clan would have crossed making their way from their castle in the countryside to Florence.

48. (p. 87) *"But it behoved the mutilated stone . . . A victim in her latest hour of peace"*: During her last peace, it was appropriate that Florence offered

a victim (Buondelmonte) as a sacrifice to the broken statue of the pagan god of war, Mars. The statue was located at the Ponte Vecchio, and Buondelmonte was murdered here on Easter morning of 1216.

49. (p. 87) *"the lily / Never upon the spear was placed reversed":* During the subsequent conflicts between Guelphs and Ghibellines that followed the murder of Buondelmonte, the victors dishonored the standards of the defeated by dragging them in the dust. The lily was the symbol of the city of Florence.

50. (p. 87) *"Nor by division was vermilion made":* In 1251 the Guelphs reversed the Florentine colors from a white lily on a field of red to a red lily upon a field of white.

CANTO XVII

1. (p. 88) *"As came to Clymene . . . fathers chary still to children":* During his journey through Hell and Purgatory, the Pilgrim has learned some disturbing information about his future, and since Cacciaguida's main theme has been Florentines being driven into exile by internal strife, he is naturally interested in learning what his fate will be. In *Inferno* X: 130–132, the poet Virgil had told the Pilgrim that it would be Beatrice who would reveal his future. Some critics believe that between composing the first canticle and the last canticle, Dante the Poet changed his mind and replaced Beatrice with Cacciaguida as the one to perform this task. However, it is even more likely that the Poet has his beloved Virgil make an error in the first canticle, implicitly warning his readers that human reason is fallible when they remember Virgil's mistake. Here Dante compares the Pilgrim to Phaëthon, who went to ask his mother, Clymene, if he was really the son of Apollo, as he had always thought. She affirmed that he was and advised him to ask Apollo himself. During the course of that conversation, Apollo was convinced to let his son drive the chariot of the sun, which resulted in Phaëthon's death (see Ovid's *Metamorphoses* I: 750–761). The story teaches fathers to be reluctant in granting sons their wishes.

2. (p. 88) *the holy light . . . had changed its place:* This is Cacciaguida, whose change of place is noted in *Paradiso* XV: 19–24, when he descends to the foot of the cross of stars in the heavens.

3. (p. 88) *"Not that our knowledge . . . that we may give thee drink":* Beatrice informs the Pilgrim that he should speak, not to give her any information (since the souls in heaven already know everything he will say because they can read the mind of God), but rather because he needs to become accustomed to speaking his mind and eventually describing what he has seen to those back in the world of the living.

4. (p. 88) *"O my beloved tree"*: Cacciaguida is described by the Italian word *piota*, which means both "sole of the foot" (and therefore the foundation) and "root" (and therefore the beginning of the Pilgrim's family tree).

5. (p. 88) *"No triangle containeth two obtuse . . . in which all times are present,)"*: Just as earthly minds can grasp basic principles of geometry (such as the fact that two obtuse angles cannot be contained in a triangle), so too the blessed in heaven can see contingencies and causal things in the past, present, and future, because they share the vision of God.

6. (p. 88) *"While I was with Virgilius conjoined . . . Some grievous words"*: During his journey through Hell and Purgatory, the Pilgrim heard unsettling things ("grievous words") about his future from a number of characters: Farinata degli Uberti (*Inferno* X: 79–81); Brunetto Latini (*Inferno* XV: 61–72); Vanni Fucci (*Inferno* XXIV: 142–151); Corrado Malaspina (*Purgatorio* VIII: 133–139); and Oderisi da Gubbio (*Purgatorio* XI: 139–141).

7. (p. 88) *"foursquare against the blows of chance"*: The Pilgrim stands foursquare, like a perfect cube, against the blows of Fortune on every side.

8. (p. 89) *"Because foreseen an arrow comes more slowly"*: Future misfortunes of which the Pilgrim has been forewarned will be less shocking. But since the information comes from the mind of God, it will be impossible to avoid the "arrow" of fate by dodging it with this foreknowledge of its arrival.

9. (p. 89) *that selfsame light:* The reference is to Cacciaguida.

10. (p. 89) *"Not in vague phrase . . . ere yet was slain / The Lamb of God"*: Basing his prophecy upon the information obtained from the mind of God and not from an oracle or a sibyl of the pagan world—the tellers of fortunes before the coming of Christ (l. 33)—Cacciaguida's prediction of Dante's future will be as clear as a bell.

11. (p. 89) *"Contingency . . . with the current down descends"*: Cacciaguida denies that foreknowledge of contingency (things derived from secondary causes) implies necessity (an eternal, elementary fact, like a geometrical axiom), any more than the sight of a ship moving down a river stream gives the observer control over its direction. Freedom of the human will is thereby affirmed.

12. (p. 89) *"As forth from Athens went Hippolytus . . . thou from Florence must perforce depart"*: Phaedra, the stepmother of Hippolytus and wife of Theseus, fell in love with Hippolytus, who rejected her overtures. She then accused him of dishonoring her, forcing him to flee the city (Ovid's *Metamorphoses* XV: 497–505). In like manner, the innocent Dante will be forced into exile from Florence on January 27, 1302, a sentence reaffirmed on March 10, 1302.

13. (p. 89) *"Already this is willed . . . the Christ is bought and sold"*: Dante implies that Pope Boniface VIII ("by him who thinks it") had already planned the events leading to the exile of those belonging to his political faction in Florence, the Bianchi, or White Guelphs, in April 1300 (the date of Cacciaguida's prophecy). So Boniface was already set against Dante and his political allies when he went to Rome in October 1301 ("Where every day the Christ is bought and sold") to make an appeal to the papacy.

14. (p. 89) *"the vengeance / Shall witness to the truth"*: Truth punishes the guilty: The misfortunes of the Neri, or Black Guelph, faction after Dante's exile, as well as the humiliation of Pope Boniface VIII by the French monarch and his subsequent death in 1303, prove the innocence of Dante and his companions.

15. (p. 89) *"The going down and up another's stairs"*: Reversing the usual "up and down" motion (which implicitly refers to a single set of stairs), Dante's brilliant line here imitates the motion in exile between two different sets of stairs (down one and up another), suggesting the Pilgrim's tragic fate.

16. (p. 90) *"the bad and foolish company"*: The reference is to the Bianchi, or White Guelphs. After his exile, Dante basically broke with his companions and apparently had very little respect for them.

17. (p. 90) *"the forehead scarlet"*: They will be blushing because of their stupidity.

18. (p. 90) *"the mighty Lombard's courtesy . . . Ladder bears the holy bird"*: Dante will first receive the hospitality of one of the members of the Scaliger family of Verona, Bartolomeo della Scala (died 1304); Verona is in the Italian region of Lombardy. The family's coat of arms contained an imperial eagle on a golden ladder.

19. (p. 90) *"in asking, . . . first which is with others last":* The mighty Lombard will give before he is asked, while other less generous hosts will wait to be asked before giving.

20. (p. 90) *"his young age, since only nine years yet":* The young man in question is Cangrande della Scala, the younger brother of the mighty Lombard, Bartolomeo (1291–1329), who became lord of Verona from 1322 until his death. In an important Latin letter (*Epistolae* XIII), Dante dedicates *Paradiso* to him and discusses the nature of *The Divine Comedy*. Bartolomeo has also been identified with the Greyhound of *Inferno* I: 101–111, described by Virgil as a future savior of Italy. Cangrande would have been only nine years old at the fictional date of the Pilgrim's journey, 1300.

21. (p. 90) *"But ere the Gascon cheat the noble Henry":* Before 1312, Pope Clement V (Bertrand de Got), a Frenchman from Gascony, supported Emperor Henry VII and invited him to come to Italy. The French king, Philip IV, subsequently pressured Clement to oppose Henry's descent into Italy. In *Inferno* XIX: 82–87, the Poet attacks Pope Clement V as a simonist under the thumb of the French monarchy who moved the Holy See to Avignon away from its rightful place in Rome.

22. (p. 90) *"not for silver nor for toil":* Cangrande's magnanimity is reflected in his disdain for wealth and his indifference to hard work.

23. (p. 90) *"Changing condition rich and mendicant":* This is perhaps a reference to the Bible, Luke 1: 51–53, which speaks of sending the rich away hungry and feeding the beggars.

24. (p. 90) *"the commentaries":* These are clarifications or glosses on what has already been predicted. The Poet claims that he cannot reveal the information about Cangrande (l. 92, "but shalt not say it") because this figure is only nine years old and has yet to accomplish his great deeds in the future.

25. (p. 90) *"few revolutions":* Only a few revolutions of the sun— that is, only a few years, will pass before Dante's exile actually begins.

26. (p. 90) *"not thy neighbors thou shouldst envy":* Cacciaguida seems to promise not only that Dante will outlive his immediate enemies— such as Pope Boniface VIII and Corso Donati, an actual neighbor in the literal sense of the term—but that he will gain revenge on his enemies by winning eternal fame with his poetry.

27. (p. 91) *"finished putting in the woof ... I had given it warped"*: After responding to the Pilgrim's concerns (the warp of l. 102), Cacciaguida completes the weaving of the woof, producing the whole cloth of his prophecy. In weaving, the warp is the yarn arranged and ready for weaving; the woof is the thread that crosses the warp.

28. (p. 91) *"the dearest place"*: This is Florence.

29. (p. 91) *"the others"*: Other places of refuge in exile.

30. (p. 91) *"the world of infinite bitterness"*: The reference is to Hell.

31. (p. 91) *"the mountain"*: This is Purgatory.

32. (p. 91) *"a savor of strong herbs"*: The Pilgrim has learned many unpleasant, bitter, and even scandalous things during his encounters with the souls in the afterlife, and if some of these things he has learned are repeated on earth, he may well discover that it is difficult to find hospitality during his exile. One can well imagine what a relative of a person Dante the Poet has condemned to Hell might think of Dante's future poem!

33. (p. 91) *"a timid friend to truth ... the olden"*: Dante realizes that if he does not give a truthful account of what he has witnessed in the afterlife, he will be a "timid friend to truth" and will have betrayed his obligation to posterity—those who will look back on the year 1300 and call that period the "old days."

34. (p. 91) *"flashed at first"*: Cacciaguida glows brighter with the chance to answer the Pilgrim's concerns.

35. (p. 91) *"A conscience overcast ... And let them scratch wherever is the itch"*: In answer to the Pilgrim's concerns about telling the truth, Cacciaguida affirms that taking offense at Dante's descriptions of the characters he has encountered in the afterlife is actually a proof of a guilty conscience ("overcast"). He ends with a common proverb, an abrupt change of his normal noble tone.

36. (p. 91) *"the most exalted summits ... no slight argument of honor"*: Dante's attacks upon the mighty are similar to the strong winds that buffet the highest peaks, proof of his great courage.

37. (p. 92) *"Only the souls that unto fame are known"*: The exasperated first-time reader of Dante's poem, bogged down in the many historical and mythological notes required for a reading of this work, will certainly object that many of the characters encountered by the Pilgrim during his journey or mentioned by the interlocutors in the poem are anything but famous today.

38. (p. 92) *"that is not apparent"*: Cacciaguida believes that unless Dante's exemplary figures are well known and his arguments are crystal clear, his future readers will have trouble understanding his poem. It seems, on the contrary, that the difficulty of Dante's arguments and the obscurity of some of his characters have paradoxically increased interest and argument about his work. Intelligent readers remain fascinated by the complexity of a poem that seems to encompass an entire historical period, and they are not afraid to do a bit of hard work to comprehend so great work of literature.

CANTO XVIII

1. (p. 93) *That soul beatified:* In the original Italian, the Poet calls Cacciaguida *quello specchio beato,* or "that mirror beatified," since like a mirror, Cacciaguida reflects God's mind, as do all of the blessed.

2. (p. 93) *I was tasting / My own, the bitter tempering with the sweet:* Like Cacciaguida, the Pilgrim is considering his inner thoughts, contrasting those that are bitter (the news of his future exile) with those that are sweet (perhaps the future greatness of Cangrande della Scala, his future patron, and, of course, further proof of his eventual salvation).

3. (p. 93) *"Near unto Him":* Beatrice reminds the Pilgrim that she is near God and can intercede for him with God.

4. (p. 93) *"unless another":* The "other" in this case is God.

5. (p. 93) *"Turn thee about . . . Not in mine eyes alone is Paradise":* Beatrice orders the Pilgrim to turn back toward Cacciaguida and listen to him. She reminds the Pilgrim that Paradise is all around him, not just in her eyes. As we shall see immediately, Cacciaguida has not completed his message to the Pilgrim.

6. (pp. 93–94) *"In this fifth resting-place . . . and never loseth leaf ":* The Sphere of Mars is the fifth of ten tiers in the heavens, which are thought of as a tree whose crown is directly beneath the dwelling place of God (and therefore the tree derives its nourishment from its top, not its roots). The tree always produces fruit (blessedness) and never loses its leaves.

7. (p. 94) *"look thou upon the cross's horns":* In canto XIV, the Pilgrim learned that the souls of the Christian warriors had formed a cross.

He is now urged to view a spectacle that will begin forming on the four arms (horns) of the cross.

8. (p. 94) *"What doth within a cloud its own swift fire":* The Pilgrim is now offered a kind of medieval sound and light show, where the souls speed by the red background of the planet Mars, resembling flashes of lightning. In Dante's day, lightning was believed to come from the ignition of fire within a cloud.

9. (p. 94) *Joshua:* In the Old Testament, he is successor to Moses and conqueror of the Promised Land. Dante has mentioned Joshua previously in *Purgatorio* XX: 111 and *Paradiso* IX: 124–125.

10. (p. 94) *the great Maccabee:* This is Judas Maccabaeus, who resisted the attempts of the Syrian kings to destroy the Jewish religion. After purifying the Temple at Jerusalem in 165 or 164 B.C., he was slain in battle in 160 B.C. His life is described in one of the apocryphal books of the Bible, 1 Maccabees 3–5.

11. (p. 94) *for Charlemagne and for Orlando:* Pope Leo III crowned Charlemagne (742–814) emperor of the Holy Roman Empire in Rome in 800. Orlando, or Roland, was Charlemagne's nephew and one of the twelve peers of France who, according to legend and literary tradition, died at Roncesvalles in 778, killed by the Saracens because of the treachery of Ganelon.

12. (p. 94) *Guglielmo:* This is William, count of Orange, the hero of a number of Old French epics, who fought the Saracens in southern France.

13. (p. 94) *Renouard:* Guglielmo's lieutenant and also a literary figure, Renouard was reputed to be a Saracen who converted to Christianity.

14. (p. 94) *Duke Godfrey:* Godfrey of Bouillon was the leader of the First Crusade (1096) and the first Christian king of Jerusalem.

15. (p. 94) *Robert Guiscard:* This eleventh-century Norman conqueror took most of southern Italy and Sicily from the Saracens.

16. (p. 94) *moved and mingled with the other lights:* Cacciaguida now returns to take his place with the other souls. Dante the Poet has given one of his ancestors the greater part of five cantos in the canticle.

17. (p. 94) *my gyration / With heaven together had increased its arc:* As the Pilgrim moves from one sphere to another, he revolves with it in increasingly larger arcs. While gazing at Beatrice's ever more beautiful

smile, he becomes suddenly aware of having risen to the next and sixth Sphere of Jupiter.

18. (p. 94) *That miracle:* Beatrice.

19. (pp. 94, 96) *in a pale woman . . . the load of bashfulness unladen:* The Poet compares his move from the red Sphere of Mars to the white sphere of Jupiter to the disappearance of a blush from the face of a woman with a fair complexion. The figure of speech is meant to underline the quickness of the change from one sphere to the next.

20. (p. 96) *the temperate star:* In *Il Convivio* II: xiii: 25, Dante cites Ptolemy in declaring that Mars is hot and Saturn cold, and that Jupiter falls between them and is temperate.

21. (p. 96) *Jovial torch:* That is, belonging to the Sphere of Jove, but also jovial, as in joyful (the quality associated with this portion of heaven).

22. (p. 96) *Delineate our language to mine eyes:* That is, the souls will use human language, and in the following lines their shapes form specific letters of the alphabet to spell out a sentence.

23. (p. 96) *Sang flying to and fro . . . Made of themselves now D, now I, now L:* The souls now assemble themselves in such a fashion as to spell out the letters of a sentence (finally spelled out completely in ll. 91 and 93). Dante compares them to the flight of river birds (probably cranes) that have just fed themselves and have taken flight out of joy.

24. (p. 96) *O divine Pegasea:* Pegasus, the winged horse, was associated with the Muses, who drank from the spring created when the horse struck the earth with his hoof. Therefore, the Poet is appealing to the Muses here, not the horse!

25. (p. 96) Diligite justitiam . . . Qui judicatis terram: The Vulgate Latin phrase comes from one of the apocryphal books of the Bible (the Wisdom of Solomon 1: 1) and means "Love righteousness, ye that be judges of the earth." Thus we learn that the souls in the Sphere of Jupiter are the Just and that the principle of Justice is at the center of this realm. The sentence indeed contains thirty-five letters, as is noted in l. 88.

26. (p. 96) *in the M of the fifth word:* Several drawings are useful here to illustrate the kind of "sky-writing" that is being presented by the souls around the letter M of the Latin word *terram*, a figure that eventually will be transformed into the figure of the imperial eagle.

In l. 94, the reader must visualize a large, gothic M shaped approximately like this:

(1)

In l. 98, souls alight on the top of the letter M, changing its shape:

(2)

In l. 107, the letter undergoes more change with the addition of the eagle's neck and crest at the top:

(3)

In ll. 112–113, the souls who were left out of the formation of the eagle's neck and head come together to transform the legs of the letter M so that they resemble a heraldic lily (the fleur-de-lys), such as might be found on the coat of arms of the French royal family. Finally, in l. 114, souls not part of the neck and head shift position and form the wings and the body of the imperial eagle.

(4)

27. (p. 96) *striking upon burning logs . . . innumerable sparks:* It was believed at one time that fortunes could be told by reading the sparks shooting off a burning log.

28. (p. 97) *contented seemed / At first to bloom a lily on the M:* Many commentators see this temporary fleur-de-lys as the symbol of a French monarchy that only temporarily (with Charlemagne) restored the Holy Roman Empire but eventually lost that empire to the Germans. The M clearly stands for "monarchy," while the eagle is the imperial eagle of the Roman Empire.

29. (p. 97) *O gentle star!:* This is Jupiter, which is the gem of the Sphere of Jupiter.

30. (p. 97) *the smoke that vitiates thy rays:* As ll. 121–136 (the end of the canto), make clear, it is the avarice of the papacy that creates the metaphorical smoke preventing the proper administration of justice on earth.

31. (p. 97) *So that a second time . . . selling in the temple:* These lines recall the biblical passage in Matthew 21: 12–13, in which Christ drives the moneychangers from the Temple of Jerusalem. Clearly Dante hopes that God's anger will descend to cleanse the Church of avarice.

32. (p. 97) *signs and martyrdoms!:* The walls of the Temple (the Christian Church) were once constructed with miracles (signs) and martyrdoms, but now the Church engages in the traffic of selling sacraments, indulgences, and ecclesiastical offices.

33. (p. 97) *taking here and there / The bread the pitying Father shuts from none:* Rather than wage real wars, the papacy now wages war by denying the sacrament (the holy bread of the Eucharist) to those who are attacked with papal interdicts and excommunications.

34. (p. 97) *Yet thou, who writest but to cancel:* This is probably a reference to Pope John XXII, who excommunicated Dante's patron Cangrande della Scala in 1317. One of John's favorite means of raising money was first to excommunicate and then to cancel the excommunication for a fee; the abolition of excommunications was a major source of papal revenue.

35. (p. 97) *Peter and that Paul, who for this vineyard:* The two great founders of the Church ("this vineyard") are still alive in heaven, but they died for a church the papacy is destroying.

36. (p. 97) *"unto him who willed to live alone ... not the Fisherman nor Paul":* This is a very clever but difficult reference to Pope John's avarice. "Him who willed to live alone" is John the Baptist, martyred to please Salome, as told in the Bible, Matthew 14: 1–12. Pope John's mind is so intent on John the Baptist (meaning here not the actual saint but the image of John the Baptist on the golden florin, the Florentine coin that in Dante's day formed the common currency throughout Europe) that he has forgotten about the Fisherman (Saint Peter) and Saint Paul.

CANTO XIX

1. (p. 99) *The beautiful image:* The image is of the eagle.

2. (p. 99) *a little ruby each ... We and Our:* Although the eagle is composed of numerous souls, each of which seems like a small ruby, it will speak with one voice, reflecting the single nature of Justice. Thus, in l. 11, the eagle can utter both the singular words "I" and "my," stressing the unity of Justice, while in l. 12 it can also utter the words "we" and "our," speaking collectively for the just souls that form the eagle.

3. (p. 99) *"Being just and merciful":* Justice and piety should guide earth's rulers.

4. (p. 99) *a single heat . . . a single sound:* These are more images of the unity of justice.

5. (p. 99) *"Not finding for it any food on earth":* No mortal understanding can satiate the Pilgrim's hunger to know the nature of God's divine justice.

6. (p. 100) *"you know what is the doubt":* By now the Pilgrim understands the fact that in heaven, all souls have foreknowledge of his questions and doubts, because they partake of the divine mind of God. As will become evident, the Pilgrim's doubt or question is a request for the explanation of the nature of God's Justice, in particular a request about the fates of those who live in ignorance of Christ and who live without either baptism or faith: Will they or will they not be damned?

7. (p. 100) *Even as a falcon, issuing from his hood:* When hunting with a falcon, the bird is kept hooded until its target has been sighted.

8. (p. 100) *that standard . . . With such songs:* The eagle is now called a standard, or ensign, associating it with the banner of the Roman Empire. In response to the Pilgrim's question about divine justice, the eagle sings a song in praise of God before responding.

9. (p. 100) *"He who a compass turned":* The image of God employing a compass to measure creation comes from Proverbs 8: 27–29, and the eagle's response stresses God's infinity and the fact that it is impossible to create anything greater than He.

10. (p. 100) *"the first proud being":* Satan, or Lucifer, was the greatest of God's early creations, but even so, he was infinitely less than God Himself. The sin of pride caused him to rebel and try to equal God rather than ripening to maturity by absorbing the divine light from God.

11. (p. 100) *"our vision . . . beyond that which is apparent to it":* Human vision, or understanding, cannot fathom God's knowledge but is sufficiently strong to realize that human wisdom cannot penetrate God's mind.

12. (p. 100) *"There is no light . . . the serene / That never is o'ercast":* There is no truth ("light") except that which comes from God (the serene, clear sky of l. 65)—all else is error, ignorance, or vice.

13. (p. 101) *"the cavern":* Here, the cavern is a hiding place, a reference to the unfathomable depth of God's justice.

14. (p. 101) *"Of Indus, and is none who there can speak / Of Christ":* The eagle now speaks directly to the Pilgrim's query about the treatment of those who have not known Christ by taking as an example an inhabitant from the Indus River in northern India. For people of Dante's day, this region was virtually the end of the known world.

15. (p. 101) *"Now who art thou . . . of a single span?":* The answer given to the Pilgrim's unspoken inquiry by the eagle is a resounding rebuke for presumption. In fact, the Pilgrim's vision is compared to the length of a single hand or span. It must be admitted that this response is not a very satisfying theological explanation.

16. (p. 101) *"If so the Scripture were not over you":* The eagle then hastens to add that without the Scriptures to guide mankind, it would indeed be difficult to understand divine justice. The only true answer to the Pilgrim's question therefore lies in faith.

17. (p. 101) *The stork . . . Became the blessed image:* Just as the stork circles over its young, so too does the enormous figure of the eagle circle over the Pilgrim.

18. (p. 101) *"Such is the eternal judgment to you mortals":* God's justice is as inscrutable as the musical notes being sung by the eagle.

19. (p. 102) *still within the standard:* The souls making up the eagle stop but retain the shape of the imperial standard as the eagle begins to speak again.

20. (p. 102) *"who had not faith in Christ":* The eagle affirms that no one will be saved without faith in Christ. Lines 104, 106, and 108 make up another group of lines that employs the word *Cristo* as a rhyme only with itself (for others, see *Paradiso* XII: 71, 73, and 75, and XIV: 105, 106, and 108). The rhyme obviously stresses the importance of faith in Christ for human salvation.

21. (p. 102) *"But look thou . . . forever rich, the other poor":* In spite of the partisan tone of the eagle's first statement about the necessity for belief in Christ, its subsequent statements offer hope that just men of whatsoever faith may find some reward from God, since many who profess belief in Christ will be "far less near" (l. 107) to Christ than those who never knew Him. Even the heathens (l. 109; Dante uses the generic term "Ethiopians" for all pagans) will condemn such false Christians at the Day of Judgment, when the rich (the saved) will be separated from the poor (the damned). See the Bible, Matthew 25: 31–46.

22. (p. 102) *"the Persians"*: Like the Ethiopians of l. 109, Persians here are used to mean pagans in general.

23. (p. 102) *"that volume opened"*: This is God's Book of Judgment and is perhaps a reference to Revelation 20: 12.

24. (p. 102) *"Albert"*: Now the Poet begins a series of verses condemning Christian rulers of his day. The repetition of the phrase "There shall be seen" that opens each of the nine tercets must be understood to refer to God's Book of Judgment in l. 113. Albert I of Austria (ruled 1298–1308), the "German Albert" of *Purgatorio* VI: 97, invaded Bohemia and its capital of Prague in 1304, attacking the kingdom of Wenceslaus IV, who was his brother-in-law. The description of Albert's deeds is described in the future tense, since the date of the Pilgrim's conversation with the eagle, it must be remembered, is 1300.

25. (p. 102) *"Who by the blow of a wild boar shall die"*: This is a reference to the French King Philip IV, "the Fair," who died in 1314 after a hunting accident involving a wild boar; apparently the King was also accused of falsifying coins and debasing the currency of his realm to raise money.

26. (p. 102) *"the pride that causes thirst . . . Scot and Englishman so mad"*: This is a reference to the wars of English kings Edward I and Edward II against the Scots, led by William Wallace and Robert the Bruce.

27. (p. 102) *"him of Spain"*: This is Ferdinand IV, king of Castile and León from 1295 to 1312.

28. (p. 102) *"the Bohemian"*: This is Wenceslas IV (1270–1305).

29. (p. 102) *"the Cripple of Jerusalem . . . an M shall represent"*: Charles II of Naples ("The Lame") inherited the title king of Jerusalem. See other mentions of this figure in *Purgatorio* VII: 127–129 and XX: 79–81; and *Paradiso* XX: 63. The eagle is not above making a pun when referring to the letters I and M, which may connote the numbers 1 (Charles' one virtue, liberality) and 1,000 (his many vices).

30. (p. 102) *"the Island of the Fire . . . note of much in little space"*: The "Island of Fire" is Sicily, where Anchises (father of Aeneas) died in Virgil's *Aeneid*; therefore the reference is to Frederick II of Aragon (1272–1337), king of Sicily. He abandoned the Ghibelline cause after the death of Emperor Henry VII. Frederick is also mentioned in *Purgatorio* VII: 119. He is such an insignificant figure, according to Dante, that his deeds can be recorded by employing a kind of shorthand writing in a very brief space (ll. 134–135).

31. (p. 102) *"Of uncle and of brother"*: Frederick II's uncle was James, king of the Balearic Islands or Mallorca from 1262 to 1311; his brother, James II, was king of Sicily (1285) before Frederick and thereafter king of Aragon (1291–1327). See *Purgatorio* VII: 115–120.

32. (p. 103) *"two crowns"*: The reference is to the kingdoms of the Balearic Islands and Aragon.

33. (p. 103) *"he of Portugal"*: This is King Diniz, or Dionysius (1261–1325), whose historical reputation stands in contrast to Dante's condemnation here. Besides founding the first university in his country, in 1290, he was esteemed as an able and honest administrator, and his court was celebrated for its culture. A number of explanations have been advanced for Dante's negative attitude: the King's part in the suppression of the Templars; his infidelity to his wife; and his role in developing Portugal's economy instead of crusading against the infidels. But the fact remains that Dante's judgment is in sharp contrast with modern historical assessments of this ruler.

34. (p. 103) *"he of Norway"*: This is probably a reference to Kaakon V (1299–1319), whose reign was characterized by numerous wars with Denmark. Since Dante's knowledge of Scandinavia was extremely limited, his reference may well be to another and earlier ruler.

35. (p. 103) *"he of Rascia . . . the coin of Venice"*: This is Stephen Urosh II (1275–1321), ruler of the kingdom of Serbia, or Rascia, as it was then called (also the name of its capital in Dalmatia). He reportedly counterfeited Venetian currency.

36. (p. 103) *"O happy Hungary"*: In 1301, Caroberto, the son of the unfortunate Charles Martel (see *Paradiso* VIII), succeeded to the throne of Hungary after that country had suffered from a number of incompetent rulers.

37. (p. 103) *"Navarre the happy . . . hills that gird her she be armed!"*: If the kingdom of Narvarre could use the Pyrenees mountain range to protect herself against France, she would be happy. Navarre came under French rule in 1314.

38. (p. 103) *"as hansel / Thereof, do Nicosìa and Famagosta . . . others' flank departeth not"*: Nicosia and Famagusta, two cities in Cyprus, serve as warnings to Navarre of what is to follow (they are "hansels" of this future development) if Navarre comes under French rule. Here Dante alludes to the misrule in Cyprus by Henry II of Lusignan, who assumed the government of the island in 1285. In 1291, he was unsuccessful in his efforts to recapture the last Christian territory in the Holy Land from the Saracens, the city of Acre. After a period of conflict with his brother Amalric, Henry resumed his unhappy rule until his death in 1324. Here Dante describes him as a beast that keeps pace with the other evil rulers ("others' flank") whose terrible deeds he has previously described.

CANTO XX

1. (p. 104) *When he who all the world illuminates:* This is a reference to the sun.

2. (p. 104) *that erst by him alone was kindled:* In Dante's times, it was thought that the stars derived their illumination from the sun.

3. (p. 104) *By far more luminous, did songs begin:* The first four tercets of this canto represent a difficult description of celestial phenomena. The figure of the eagle has previously been speaking as a single, unified voice, although it is composed of many parts. The hymn that now breaks forth is not from the eagle but from the many beings that compose the eagle. The intensification of the individual lights composing the figure of the eagle reminds Dante of the brightness of the night sky as the stars retain the illumination from the sun.

4. (p. 104) *O gentle Love:* This is the love of the spirits for God, here expressed through the joy of light.

5. (p. 104) *the sixth light:* The planet Jupiter is in the sixth sphere.

6. (p. 104) *the murmuring of a river:* In ll. 19–30, the Pilgrim hears a number of different sounds: a flowing stream, the music of a lute and that of a flute, and finally a voice.

7. (p. 104) *the cithern's neck:* This is the neck of the lute, where the fingering is done.

8. (p. 105) *As the heart waited for wherein I wrote them:* The identities of some of the spirits in this part of heaven have been inscribed in the Pilgrim's memory (his heart).

9. (p. 105) *"The part in me which sees and bears the sun":* The "part" is the eagle's eye. In Dante's time, it was believed that the eagle trained its young to gaze at the sun. The eagle thus orders the Pilgrim to gaze into his eye. Because the imperial eagle was always displayed in profile in heraldic imagery, the Pilgrim will only see one eye of this symbolic beast that addresses him.

10. (p. 105) *"For of the fires of which I make my figure ... their orders the supremest are":* The spirits that form the eagle's body are of the highest rank, or value. The eagle will now describe the souls who make up his eye (a single soul: David) and his eyebrow (five souls: Trajan; Hezekiah; Constantine; William II of Sicily; and Rhipeus). See the diagram below.

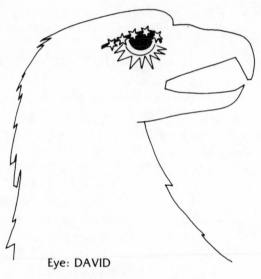

Eye: **DAVID**

Eyebrow: **TRAJAN**
         HEZEKIAH
         CONSTANTINE
         WILLIAM II of Sicily
         RHIPEUS
         (reading from right to left)

11. (p. 105) *"the singer of the Holy Spirit ... ark from city unto city":* The pupil of the eagle's eye is King David, the author of the Psalms (divinely inspired by the Holy Spirit) who moved the Ark of the Covenant to Jerusalem (l. 39). Dante describes David in detail in *Purgatorio* X: 55–69 as the second image of humility, derived from the Bible, 2 Samuel 6: 1–17. There, King David ("the humble Psalmist") is depicted as dancing before the Ark of the Covenant as he brings it into Jerusalem.

12. (p. 105) *the poor widow for her son console:* The closest spirit to the eagle's beak is the Roman Emperor Trajan (ruled A.D. 98–117). Dante has already described him in detail in *Purgatorio* X: 71–93 as a symbol of humility. According to legend, Trajan (a pagan, although he ruled after the birth of Christ) stopped on his way to battle and answered the pleas of a widow who had lost her son in his service. The legend appears in a life of Saint Gregory the Great written in the ninth century by John the Deacon and was often repeated in devotional literature and paintings. Gregory (born c.540, pope from 590 to 604) was widely believed by legend to have recalled Trajan to life from Hell so that he might repent. Saint Thomas Aquinas even discusses this belief (*Summa theologica* II, suppl., q. 71, a. 5 ad 5), suggesting that Trajan's punishment might only have been postponed. Dante places Trajan's soul in Paradise, just as he places other pagans he considers virtuous—Virgil, Cato, Statius, and Ripheus—in locations in the afterlife that orthodox Christians might find objectionable or impossible.

13. (p. 105) *"Did death postpone by penitence sincere . . . to-morrow of to-day":* When Hezekiah, king of Judah, fell ill (2 Kings 20: 1–6), he begged God to spare his life and was given fifteen extra years to live. Dante employs this story to underscore the efficacy of prayer, which can turn today into tomorrow, as he puts it in l. 54.

14. (p. 105) *"The next who follows . . . Became a Greek by ceding to the pastor":* In the *translatio Imperii,* or the transfer of imperial power, Emperor Constantine the Great (A.D. 274–337) ceded Rome to Pope Sylvester I and transferred the Empire to Byzantium. He thereby made himself, the eagle ("and me" in l. 55), and the laws Greek instead of Roman. Dante has already deplored the negative results of this Donation of Constantine in *Inferno* XIX: 115–117. In the fifteenth century, the Italian humanist Lorenzo Valla proved that the documents that purported to authenticate this transference of power were forgeries.

15. (p. 105) *"his good action . . . thereby may be destroyed":* Because Dante supported the re-establishment of the empire, he is careful not to fault Emperor Constantine for his actions, since he could not have foreseen the abuses that would follow from giving the papacy such temporal power. Constantine's favored status in Dante's mind is underscored by the fact that his spirit resides in the highest part of the arc that forms the eagle's eyebrow.

16. (p. 105) *"he whom in the downward arc thou seest . . . weepeth Charles and Frederick":* Guglielmo, or William II, king of Naples and Sicily from 1166 to 1189, was loved by his subjects and renowned for his generosity and patronage of religious institutions. The memory of his happy rule emphasizes the evil reigns of Charles and Frederick, the rulers who Dante attacks in *Paradiso* XIX: 127–135.

17. (p. 106) *"Who would believe . . . the Trojan Ripheus":* Dante found this Trojan hero, slain in the sack of Troy, in Virgil's *Aeneid* (II: 339, 394, 426–428), where he is described as one of the most righteous and just of the Trojans. Who would believe, asks the Poet rhetorically, that such a pagan could be placed in the Christian heaven? Of course, Dante particularly favored the Trojans because they were the ancestors of the Romans. But more than this, the presence of Ripheus in heaven underscores the mysterious ways by which God's divine justice operates. Dante follows legend and literature in saving Trajan, but his salvation of Ripheus is entirely his own invention. This figure represents a powerful proof that God was not unmindful of the fact that virtuous pagans existed.

18. (p. 106) *Like as a lark . . . Of the eternal pleasure:* The Poet compares his satisfaction at the explanation of God's inscrutable purpose in connection with the salvation of Ripheus or Trajan to the reaction of a person who enjoys the vision of a joyous skylark singing and soaring above him in the sky. God's "eternal pleasure" is justice.

19. (p. 106) *to my doubt I was / As glass is to the color that invests it:* The Pilgrim's doubts about the salvation of pagans shows forth, as a layer of paint shows through a plate of glass covering it.

20. (p. 106) *forth from out my mouth . . . great joy of coruscation:* As they anticipate the satisfaction of the Pilgrim's doubts about the salvation of the pagans (emphasized by his incredulous question of l. 82, "What things are these?"), the souls are filled with joy and their brilliance subsequently increases.

21. (p. 106) *The blessed standard:* This is the eagle, speaking now as a unity, not as a collection of different voices.

22. (p. 106) *its quiddity:* This word is a typical term in Scholastic philosophy: The quiddity of something is its "thingness" or "whatness"—that which causes a thing to be what it is. Although the Pilgrim understands the fact of the salvation of Trajan and Ripheus, he cannot fathom the essence of the reason this has occurred.

23. (p. 106) "*Regnum cœlorum suffereth violence*": The kingdom of heaven suffers violent assault (the Bible, Matthew 11: 12). Dante cites the line partially in Latin and partially in Italian, just as Longfellow's translation combines Latin and English. The original line of the Latin Vulgate is *regnum cœlorum vim patitur*. Further on in l. 98, the passage makes it clear that the kingdom of heaven endures the assault of love or of hope, either of which has the power to overcome God's will (l. 96), and His will allows itself to be conquered (l. 99) because of God's beneficence.

24. (p. 107) "*The first life of the eyebrow and the fifth*": This would be Trajan and Ripheus, respectively.

25. (p. 107) "*but Christians . . . were to suffer and had suffered*": The eagle informs the Pilgrim that neither Trajan nor Ripheus died as pagans but were Christians at their deaths. Trajan believed in Christ whose feet were nailed to the cross ("feet . . . had suffered"), while Ripheus, who died before Christ, believed in the future Christ whose feet would be treated in this fashion ("feet that were to suffer").

26. (p. 107) "*For one from Hell . . . the second death*": Following the legend of Saint Gregory the Great, Dante explains that goodwill alone (l. 107) is incapable of bringing a person back from the dead. Yet Trajan was resuscitated, thanks to Gregory's entreaties to God, and he could then be baptized and saved in a proper manner. When Trajan was brought back to life, it is not surprising that he believed "in Him who had the power to aid it" (l. 114), and as a result of this genuine belief in Christianity, at his second death (l. 116) he became worthy to ascend to heaven as if he had always been a Christian.

27. (p. 107) "*Wherefore from grace to grace did God unclose . . . reproved therefor the folk perverse*": God bestowed special grace upon Ripheus so he was capable of believing by an implicit faith. This is comparable to the grace God bestowed upon those special people who were harrowed from Hell when Christ descended to rescue virtuous pagans—Old Testament figures worthy of salvation.

28. (p. 107) "*Those Maidens three . . . a thousand years before baptizing*": The Pilgrim met these three personified theological virtues of faith, hope, and charity in the earthly Paradise at the summit of the Mountain of Purgatory (*Purgatorio* XXX: 121–129). They provide Ripheus' baptism. Thus both pagans obtained baptism, a rite required for salvation: Trajan after being resuscitated, and Ripheus after a special act of grace and the intervention of the three maidens, an act that took place a thousand years before baptism even existed. It was the baptism of Christ by John the Baptist that began this sacrament.

29. (p. 107) *"O thou predestination . . . do not behold entire!"*: The eagle underscores the inscrutability of God's divine plans and man's inability to fathom His plans completely, a position bolstered by the twin examples of Trajan and Ripheus.

30. (p. 107) *"hold yourselves restrained"*: The Pilgrim is admonished to withhold judgment, since even the elect in heaven cannot truly penetrate God's divine plan.

31. (p. 108) *"whatsoe'er God wills, we also will"*: The blessed souls are happy, since their wills have been completely surrendered to that of God. Note also that now the eagle speaks in the first person plural ("we"), since it reflects the view of the countless souls who represent God's divine justice.

32. (p. 108) *"a good lutanist / Accompanies . . . I beheld both of those blessed lights"*: While the eagle speaks, the lights of Trajan and Ripheus twinkle together as if they were a pair of eyes at the two ends of the arc forming the eagle's eyebrow—just as a lute player touches the strings to accompany the singer.

CANTO XXI

1. (p. 109) *"If I were to smile . . . Like Semele, when she was turned to ashes"*: According to Ovid's *Metamorphoses* III: 253–315, Semele (daughter of Cadmus and mother of Bacchus) asked to see her lover Jupiter in all his divine majesty; when he so revealed himself, she was burned to ashes. Beatrice's beauty would do the same to the Pilgrim if she smiled directly upon him.

2. (p. 109) *"the stairs / Of the eternal palace"*: Metaphorically, the various heavens, or spheres, through which Dante the Pilgrim passes are seen as if they were steps leading up an enormous staircase to God's palace, or the Empyrean.

3. (p. 109) *"the seventh splendor . . . underneath the burning Lion's breast"*: This is the seventh Sphere of Saturn, which, as l. 14 asserts, is aligned with the constellation of Leo (the Lion) during the fictional year of the Pilgrim's journey, 1300. As in other parts of heaven, the Pilgrim's arrival in a new sphere is instantaneous.

4. (p. 109) *"this mirror":* This is the planet Saturn.

5. (p. 109) *He who could know . . . counterpoising one side with the other:* The Poet means to say that a reader who can imagine how sweet it was to feast his eyes on Beatrice's beautiful face may understand how sweet it was to obey her even when he was obliged to turn away from her face (his first joy) for a second joy, that of obedience to her.

6. (p. 109) *within the crystal . . . every wickedness lay dead:* The crystal is the Sphere of Saturn. The god Saturn was supposed to have ruled during the Golden Age of mankind, which was perfect, when "every wickedness lay dead."

7. (p. 110) *A stairway . . . So many splendors:* The golden stairway is a symbol of contemplation, suitable to the part of heaven devoted to the contemplatives. For this stairway imagery Dante may be indebted to Jacob's ladder, described in the Bible, Genesis 28: 12. Unlike the eagle, which was composed of the souls of the blessed in the form of points of light, the stairway is a structure upon which the souls tread.

8. (p. 110) *The rooks together . . . Such fashion:* The contemplatives are compared to the rooks (European crows) that flock and then break up into flight. One of the souls increases in brightness when he approaches the Pilgrim and will later be identified in l. 121 as Peter Damian.

9. (p. 110) *Him who seeth everything:* This is God.

10. (p. 110) *draweth thee so near my side . . . why is silent in this wheel / The dulcet symphony of Paradise:* The Pilgrim asks two questions—why the soul draws nearer to his side and why the heavenly music has stopped. The questions will be answered in reverse order.

11. (p. 110) *"thy hearing mortal as thy sight":* The as-yet-unidentified soul tells the Pilgrim that just as Beatrice's smile is far too powerful for his mortal eyes, so too the heavenly music would overpower him if he heard it.

12. (p. 112) *"Nor did more love cause me to be more ready":* The soul explains that though he has greeted the Pilgrim, he does not have greater love to express than the other souls do. In other words, there is no personal connection that explains his descent to speak to the Pilgrim. In fact, the soul notes that there are others above him with far greater radiance (and therefore greater love).

13. (p. 112) *"the high charity":* God's love moves the souls to fulfill their tasks instinctively (in this case, greeting the Pilgrim).

14. (p. 112) *"Wherefore predestinate . . . among thy consorts":* The Pilgrim again returns to the problem of predestation, wondering why this particular soul was chosen to greet him.

15. (p. 112) *made the light a centre, / Whirling itself about:* As in other places in the other spheres of heaven, souls become brighter in their anxiety to respond to the Pilgrim's questions. In this case the soul spins around with joy over his assignment.

16. (p. 112) *"I am embosomed":* To express the idea of being enclosed or contained, Dante here invents a verb (*inventrarsi*), meaning literally (according to various translators) "I am embosomed," "I am enwombed," "I am embellied," or even "I embowel myself."

17. (p. 112) *"The clearness of the flame I equal make":* The soul declares that he matches the clarity of his flame, thus underlining that happiness depends upon clarity of spiritual vision, which is itself a result of divine grace.

18. (p. 112) *"That Seraph which his eye on God most fixes . . . this demand of thine not satisfy":* Even the Seraphim, the order of angels closest to God and highest in rank, cannot fathom God's design or explain predestination. Consequently, it is impossible for man to understand it perfectly.

19. (p. 112) *"the eternal statute":* This is a reference to that which God has eternally decreed.

20. (p. 113) *to ask it humbly who it was:* The Pilgrim finally gives up on the meaning of predestination and remains satisfied with learning the identity of the soul to whom he has spoken.

21. (p. 113) *"Between two shores of Italy":* That is, between the Adriatic and the Tyrrhenian Seas surrounding each side of the Italian peninsula.

22. (p. 113) *"Catria":* Monte Catria, one of the peaks of the Apennines, is near the border of Umbria and the Marches, close to the town of Gubbio.

23. (p. 113) *"a hermitage":* This is the monastery of Santa Croce di Fonte Avellana. The monastery belonged to the Camaldolese order, which Saint Romuald established in the early eleventh century.

24. (p. 113) *the third speech:* The soul has spoken to the Pilgrim two times previously (ll. 61–72 and ll. 83–102).

25. (p. 113) *"to render to these heavens / Abundantly . . . it soon must be* *revealed"*: Apparently the monastery used to send large numbers of monks to heaven but has subsequently fallen upon hard or corrupt times (the exact explanation is never clear).

26. (p. 113) *"Peter Damiano; / And Peter the Sinner was I"*: Bishop and church reformer, Peter Damian (1007–1072) entered the monastery at Fonte Avellana after studying in Faenza and Parma, where he became prior. He fought for church reform and in 1057 was appointed cardinal bishop of Ostia. He wrote a number of letters and treatises, including one that attacks homosexuality among the clergy and another that uses the image of the ladder of contemplation (picked up by Dante in this canto). Line 122 has created a great deal of scholarly controversy over whether Peter identifies himself to the Pilgrim with two different names (Peter Damiano and Peter the Sinner)—both Peters therefore being the same person—or whether the first Peter is Peter Damiano and the second Peter is a man whom some scholars have identified as Pietro degli Onesti, who died in 1119. Longfellow's translation follows the majority opinion—that the soul merely says he was known as Peter Damiano in the monastery of Fonte Avellana and as Peter the Sinner in another monastery, Santa Maria in Porto, near Ravenna on the Adriatic coast. Dante is, by this interpretation, not introducing another person.

27. (p. 113) *"dragged forth to the hat . . . from bad to worse"*: Peter was most unwilling to become a high officer of the church. Dante's reference to a cardinal's hat is an anachronism, since the office was not provided with a specific headpiece until Pope Innocent IV did so in 1252, almost two centuries after Peter's death. Peter's reference to things going from "bad to worse" in reference to cardinals is yet another instance of Dante condemning the present condition of the church.

28. (p. 113) *"Came Cephas, and the mighty Vessel"*: Respectively, these are references to Saints Peter and Paul. Cephas is the Aramaic name that is translated by the Latin Vulgate as Petrus (stone or Peter) in the Bible, John 1: 42: "Thou are Simon the son of Jona: thou shalt be called Cephas, which is by interpretation, A stone." In Acts 9: 15, Saint Paul is called "a chosen vessel," and Dante repeats this name for Paul in *Inferno* II: 28. This passage sets up the contrast between the early disciples of Christ, who are poor and accustomed to eating humble food, with the corrupt prelates of Damiano's and Dante's times.

29. (p. 113) *Now some one to support them on each side:* In ll. 130–135, the Poet's indignation becomes sarcasm. He says modern priests and prelates require an army of servants to attend them on each side, primarily because of their weight. These functionaries "hold their trains" (l. 132) and perform other tasks. Indeed, and historically, *braccieri* propped up the prelates on horseback; *portatini* called them or led them on their chairs; *caudatari* held their trains; and *staffieri* helped them on their mounts.

30. (p. 113) *"two beasts":* This would be the prelate and his mount covered by a single cloak.

31. (p. 114) *so loud a sound:* As the reader will discover in *Paradiso* XXII: 13–15, this tremendous noise derives from the cry the spirits around the Pilgrim and Peter Damiano raise for vengeance over the corruption of the clergy. Throughout the Sphere of Saturn, the Poet emphasized the lack of sound or music. Now, this sudden introduction of a deafening sound underscores the Poet's righteous indignation over the plight of the church.

CANTO XXII

1. (p. 115) *Oppressed with stupor:* Overcome by the tremendous sound he has just heard, the Pilgrim has not been able to make out the actual words spoken by the people who created the uproar. He turns to Beatrice, as a young child turns to his mother for protection.

2. (p. 115) *"After what wise . . . the cry has startled thee so much":* Beatrice now explains that the Pilgrim has been spared the full impact of the singing in heaven and her smile because they might harm him. Just imagine, she tells him, how much those would have terrified him if this cry of righteous indignation has had such an impact on him.

3. (p. 115) *"if thou hadst understood its prayers . . . before thou diest":* Realizing that the dim of the noise has obscured the content of the cries, Beatrice tells the Pilgrim the content and assures him that vengeance will be wreaked upon the corruption of the Church and evil prelates (the object of the cries). Some scholars have seen this vengeance in the humiliation of Pope Boniface VIII at Anagni or in the removal of the papacy from Rome to Avignon, but these events seemed to have increased, rather than to have destroyed, the corruption of the Church. This future punishment is best understood as a general desire and not any specific event of which Dante had any knowledge during his lifetime, even though Beatrice promises him satisfaction "before thou diest" (l. 15).

4. (p. 115) *"The sword... not in haste / Nor tardily"*: The sword of God's divine punishment always seems too quick for those who dread it but too late for those who desire it.

5. (p. 115) *spherules*: These are small spheres, small globes of light (the souls of the blessed in this sphere) that shine as they respond to one another's love.

6. (p. 115) *the largest and most luculent*: The largest and brightest of the spirits is that of Saint Benedict (c.480–c.547), founder of monasticism in the Catholic Church during the last days of the Roman Empire. The Rule of Saint Benedict (*Regula Monachorum*) established the kind of life the monks who followed his teachings should live. Benedict died at the Monastery of Monte Cassino, which he founded and which is perhaps the most famous of all such institutions in Europe. The Benedictine Order grew to become one of the most powerful and important in the Catholic Church.

7. (p. 116) *"the impious worship"*: Benedict's order was founded to combat pagan religions, which were still influential even at this late date, particularly in rural areas.

8. (p. 116) *"Here is Marcarius, here is Romualdus"*: Although there are several saints who bear the name Marcarius, Dante probably means either Marcarius the Elder, called the Egyptian (c.301–391), who spent most of his life praying in the Libyan desert, or Marcarius the Younger of Alexandria (d. 404), who directed the activities of thousands of monks and is generally identified as the founder of Eastern Christian monasticism, a contribution to Christianity that parallels that of Saint Benedict in the West. Saint Romuald (c.950–1027) founded the Camaldoli Order, also known as the Reformed Benedictines, and was born in Ravenna around 950. Dante must surely have known the famous monastery of Camaldoli, about 30 miles from Florence.

9. (p. 116) *"thee behold with countenance unveiled"*: The Pilgrim asks to see the human features of Saint Benedict in the flesh, so to speak, not distorted or concealed by the radiance that conceals him.

10. (p. 116) *"Brother"*: While the Pilgrim addresses Saint Benedict as "father" in l. 58, the soul replies in a less formal fashion, underscoring the idea that all souls in heaven are beyond such earthly titles.

11. (pp. 116–117) *"the remotest sphere . . . nor turns on poles"*: The remotest sphere is the Empyrean. As Saint Benedict notes, the Pilgrim will have his desire for vision, or total understanding, granted in the Empyrean, where he will see all the blessed in their human form. The saint then explains that only the Empyrean remains motionless and remains at rest, while the other parts of the heavens revolve and move about the universe.

12. (p. 117) *"our stairway"*: The ladder of contemplation recalls Jacob's ladder in Genesis 28: 12.

13. (p. 117) *"now my Rule . . . for mere waste of paper"*: Once again, one of the souls the Pilgrim meets denounces earthly corruption. Here Saint Benedict notes that the monks in his order claiming to adhere to his Rule are so uninterested in following the ladder of contemplation that they pay no attention to the Rule, reducing its parchment pages to waste paper.

14. (p. 117) *"as that fruit . . . or for something worse"*: Even the sin of usury does not displease God so much as the avarice of the priests and monks who keep the goods of the Church (intended to assist the poor) for the benefit of their own relatives or their concubines and bastards (the "something worse" of l. 84).

15. (p. 117) *"That good beginnings . . . to bearing acorns"*: Since human nature is so weak and corrupt, good beginnings or intentions do not last any longer than the time it takes the oak to form an acorn (see a similar idea expressed by Saint Benedict in *Paradiso* XXII: 136–138).

16. (p. 117) *"Peter began . . . the white changed into brown"*: Like a wilted flower that begins to turn brown with decay, the holy orders on earth have become corrupted from their uncorrupt origins in the poverty of Saint Peter, Saint Benedict, and Saint Francis.

17. (p. 117) *"In verity the Jordan . . . than succor here"*: Because of divine intervention, the Jordan River turned back and the Red Sea was parted, so it is possible that God may yet do something about monastic corruption.

18. (p. 117) *To his own band:* That is, to the group of the other contemplative souls.

19. (p. 118) *by a single sign . . . overcome my nature:* With a single gesture, Beatrice and the Pilgrim instantaneously rise up to the eighth sphere—the Sphere of the Fixed Stars. Her virtue overcomes his nature in the

sense that he seems to defy the force of gravity and also because he moves toward God even though his soul is not yet perfect.

20. (p. 118) *here below:* That is, on earth.

21. (p. 118) *my wing:* The Pilgrim is referring to his flight.

22. (p. 118) *Reader:* This is the last of the four addresses to the reader in *Paradiso* and the sixteenth in *The Divine Comedy*. The other three such addresses in this canticle are in V: 109 and X: 7 and 22. The Poet addresses his audience five times in *Inferno* (VIII: 94, XVI: 127, XX: 19, XXV: 46, and XXXIV: 23); he does so seven times in *Purgatorio* (VIII: 19, IX: 70, X: 106, XVII: 1, XXIX: 97, XXXI: 124, and XXXIII: 136).

23. (p. 118) *sign that follows Taurus:* This is Gemini.

24. (p. 118) *With you was born:* Dante was born under the sign of Gemini, between May 21 and June 21, 1265 (the exact day is uncertain). Note that here, it is the Poet Dante who is speaking, not the Pilgrim, as he looks back on his momentous journey to the afterlife.

25. (p. 118) *I with my sight returned . . . its ignoble semblance:* From the Pilgrim's heavenly vantage point, earth indeed seems an insignificant place when envisioned through the seven planetary heavens.

26. (p. 118) *And that opinion . . . doth account it least:* Those who hold the things of this world in high regard have mistaken their goals.

27. (p. 119) *the daughter of Latona shining / Without that shadow:* The daughter of Latona (Leto in Greek), a Titan, is Diana, or the moon. According to views of Dante's time, moon spots were only on the side of the moon facing earth; therefore the part of the moon that the Pilgrim sees is "without shadow." For an earlier discussion of moon spots, see *Paradiso* II: 52–148.

28. (p. 119) *Hyperion:* Another of the Titans, Hyperion was father of the sun, Helios, or Apollo. At this point in the poem, the Pilgrim can look into the sun, a testimony to his spiritual development.

29. (p. 119) *Maia and Dione:* Maia was the daughter of Atlas, and she was the mother of Mercury; Venus was the daughter of Dione. Hyperion, Maia, and Dione are all parents of gods whose names are also borne by heavenly bodies (the sun, Mercury, Venus).

30. (p. 119) *the temperateness of Jove / 'Twixt son and father:* The son of Jove (Jupiter) was Mars and his father was Saturn, and Dante considers Jupiter a temperate planet because it is between the hot Mars and the cold Saturn. During Dante's times, the movements of these heavenly bodies were observed and studied.

31. (p. 119) *all the seven:* From his position, the Pilgrim is able to see the position, movement, and size of the seven heavenly bodies: Saturn, Jupiter, Mars, the sun, Venus, Mercury, and the moon.

32. (p. 119) *The threshing-floor that maketh us so proud:* The inhabited part of earth is described contemptuously as a place where human beings fight over the grain that it produces (see the same metaphor in *Paradiso* XXVII: 85–87). Earth is an insignificant place when compared to the majesty of the universe.

33. (p. 119) *the eternal Twins:* The reference is to Gemini, the constellation through which the Pilgrim is turning.

34. (p. 119) *the beauteous eyes:* Compared with the physical and visible universe, Beatrice's eyes represent a spiritual universe that is far more beautiful and important.

CANTO XXIII

1. (p. 120) *Even as a bird:* The three opening tercets of this canto form the first part of an epic simile evoking an image of a mother bird protecting her offspring while she gazes toward the eastern sky, searching for the dawn of a new day so that she may provide food for them. This provides a beautiful term of comparison to Beatrice, who gazes upon the light of a new day that will allow her to provide spiritual sustenance for the Pilgrim. The rising sun is the image of the coming of Christ, who appears along with the Virgin Mary.

2. (p. 120) *the zone / Underneath which the sun displays less haste:* This is the meridian, where the sun seems to move less than it does near the horizon.

3. (p. 120) *from one When:* That is, from one moment.

4. (p. 120) *"Christ's triumphal march . . . Harvested by the rolling of these spheres!":* The vision of the Church Triumphant may be contrasted to the Pageant of the Church Militant in the earthly Paradise (*Purgatorio* XXIX–XXX). The "fruit / Harvested by the rolling of these spheres" may be interpreted as the most important souls of the blessed, such as the Virgin Mary, the Apostles, Adam, and even Christ Himself.

5. (p. 120) *Trivia among the nymphs eternal:* Trivia is another name for Diana, goddess of the moon. Stars accompany the moon as nymphs accompany Diana.

6. (p. 121) *A Sun that one and all of them enkindled:* Christ is the sun that provides light to the many stars of the blessed.

7. (p. 121) *lucent substance:* This is Christ's light.

8. (p. 121) *I sustained it not:* Dante's vision fails when confronted by the luminous nature of Christ.

9. (p. 121) *"the wisdom and the omnipotence":* In the Bible, 1 Corinthians 1: 24, Christ is defined as the power of God and the wisdom of God; this is the essence of the "lucent substance" mentioned in l. 32.

10. (p. 121) *"That oped the thoroughfares 'twixt heaven and earth":* Between the fall of Adam and the Advent of Christ, the road to heaven was closed to humanity. The virtuous could only wait in Limbo for the Advent of Christ to be rescued from sin. (In *Paradiso* XXVI: 118–120, we will learn that Adam spent 4,302 years in Limbo before Christ rescued him in the Harrowing of Hell.)

11. (p. 121) *As fire from out a cloud . . . against its nature, falls to earth:* Dante follows the science of his day (based upon Aristotle's views), believing that lightning occurs when air trapped in a cloud is compressed and escapes with an explosion, producing the noise of thunder and an ignition of lightning. Fire generally rises by its nature; however, in the case of lightning, it falls "against its nature," toward earth.

12. (p. 121) *cannot remember:* Back on earth, the Pilgrim can remember this mystical experience only with great difficulty, even though his mind had been expanded just as lightning expands a cloud.

13. (p. 121) *"look at what I am":* After experiencing the vision of the Church Triumphant and Christ as a sun, the Pilgrim is now prepared to gaze directly upon Beatrice's smile (her first smile since the two figures entered the heaven of Saturn).

14. (p. 121) *"the book that chronicles the past":* This is the book of memory.

15. (p. 121) *Polyhymnia . . . It would not reach:* She was the muse of sacred poetry. Beatrice's smile is so beautiful that human words cannot describe it even if Polyhymnia and the other eight muses had assisted the Poet. Once again, as is so frequent in the poem, the poetry underscores the unimaginable quality of the ineffable visions the Pilgrim enjoys.

16. (p. 122) *the sacred poem . . . his way cut off:* Now the Poet describes the ineffable nature of Beatrice's smile in much more humble terms, comparing it to a man who leaps over an obstacle when it stands in his path. Some aspects of Paradise are simply too miraculous to be described by human poetry.

17. (p. 122) *It is no passage for a little boat:* The opening lines of the second canticle (*Purgatorio* I: 2) had described the Poets' "little vessel of my genius" as it hoisted its sails to enter the second part of the afterlife. *Paradiso* II: 1 referred to the "pretty little boat" that followed behind the Poet's own vessel. Once again, the ship is used as a metaphor, here emphasizing the impossibility of expressing fully the Poet's vision.

18. (p. 122) *"the garden fair . . . under the rays of Christ is blossoming?":* Christ, shining like the sun, beams His rays upon the souls of the blessed, which appear as if they were a beautiful garden.

19. (p. 122) *"the Rose":* The Virgin Mary is known as the "Mystic Rose" in the liturgy.

20. (p. 122) *"the Word Divine":* This is a reference to Christ (see the Bible, John 1: 14: "And the Word was made flesh").

21. (p. 122) *"the lilies . . . whose perfume the good way was discovered":* These are the Apostles, whose fragrance (their acts) inspires mankind.

22. (p. 122) *the battle of the feeble brows:* Although the Pilgrim's eyesight is weak because of its mortal status, he fights to experience all of the vision of Paradise that he can comprehend.

23. (p. 122) *As in the sunshine . . . mine eyes, that were not strong enough:* The Poet compares the Ascension of Christ (no longer visible to the Pilgrim) to the sun rising above the clouds, yet still shining through them sufficiently to illuminate the flowerlike souls below. Christ has now arisen to the Empyrean. As the Poet declares in ll. 86–87, Christ does this in order that Dante may not be completely blinded by His brightness.

24. (p. 122) *"that fair flower":* The flower is the rose, symbol of the Virgin Mary.

25. (p. 122) *"the living star":* In the liturgy, the Virgin Mary is also referred to as the "Morning Star" and the "Star of the Sea."

26. (pp. 122–123) *a little torch . . . most sweetly soundeth / On earth:* The "torch" is usually taken to be the Angel Gabriel, since he creates a ring in the form of a crown around the Virgin, a reenactment of the Annunciation. As this angel sings, his song is described as more beautiful than any ordinary instrument. Some commentators refuse to identify this figure with Gabriel and prefer to see him as one of the Seraphim not specifically identified, primarily because Gabriel will eventually appear in *Paradiso* XXXII: 94–96, where in fact he will be singing the words of the Annunciation, "Ave Maria."

27. (p. 123) *the sapphire beautiful:* The Virgin Mary is always associated with the color blue, or lapis lazuli, in medieval paintings.

28. (p. 123) *"our Desire":* This is a reference to Christ.

29. (p. 123) *"The sphere supreme":* This is the ninth Sphere of the Primum Mobile, the realm that encircles the other eight revolving heavens—spheres made up of the seven planetary spheres plus the Sphere of the Fixed Stars (the location of the Pilgrim as this point).

30. (p. 123) *The regal mantle . . . With breath of God and with his works and ways:* Like a cloak or a mantle, the Primum Mobile encompasses and encircles all of the revolving spheres and is the nearest to God (and therefore most burns with desire for Him).

31. (p. 123) *Extended over us its inner border . . . where I was not yet appeared to me:* As the Pilgrim is on the "inner border"—the concave inner surface—of the Primum Mobile, it is still difficult for him to see it clearly.

32. (p. 123) *the incoronated flame . . . its own seed:* This is the Virgin Mary, who is about to rise up beyond the Sphere of the Fixed Stars near Christ (Mary's "own seed," or child) into the Empyrean, the tenth heaven.

33. (p. 123) *And as a little child . . . of whiteness upward reached:* The relationship between mother and suckling infant is now compared to the relationship between the Virgin and the souls of the blessed. Like a child holding its arms out to its mother after being breast-fed, the souls send their light toward the Virgin as she ascends. This maternal imagery recalls the tone of the opening of this canto.

34. (p. 123) *Regina caeli:* "Queen of Heaven" is the Latin hymn sung at Easter in praise of the Virgin.

35. (p. 123) *those richest coffers . . . for sowing here below!:* The souls of the blessed are now called rich coffers that have been filled with the harvest of the divine grace their good works have merited.

36. (pp. 123–124) *in the exile / Of Babylon, wherein the gold was left:* In the Babylonian exile (which came to be identified with earthly, as opposed to heavenly, life), the blessed on earth gave up earthly wealth, or gold, for spiritual wealth. In the Bible, Matthew 19: 21, Jesus instructs a man who asks how he must act if he is to be saved: "If thou wilt be perfect, go and sell that thou hast, and give to the poor, and thou shalt have treasure in heaven."

37. (p. 124) *There triumpheth, beneath the exalted Son / Of God and Mary:* The final sight that closes the canto is a vision of Saint Peter with the two keys mentioned in the Bible, Matthew 16: 19: "And I will give unto thee the keys of the kingdom of heaven." He stands in the Celestial Rose beneath Christ and to the right of the Virgin Mary (see *Paradiso* XXXII: 124–126). Following Church doctrine, Saint Peter stands at the entrance into heaven in Dante's poem.

38. (p. 124) *the ancient council and the new:* This is a reference to the most illustrious souls of the Old Testament and the New Testament, the prophets and the apostles.

CANTO XXIV

1. (p. 125) *"O company elect to the great supper / Of the Lamb benedight":* The Italian word Dante employs here is *sodalizio,* which early commentators on the poem construed as a reference to the apostles (figures who are about to appear in the ensuing cantos). A passage from Revelation 19: 9 is relevant here: "Blessed are they who are called unto the marriage supper of the Lamb." The "Lamb benedight," or the Blessed Lamb is, of course, Christ, as in John 1: 29: "Behold the Lamb of God, which taketh away the sin of the world." The marriage supper of the Lamb to which Dante alludes here represents the delight that the saints enjoy in their knowledge of God.

2. (p. 125) *"falleth from your table":* See the Bible, Matthew 15: 27: "Yet the dogs eat of the crumbs which fall from their masters' table." In *Il Convivio* I: x: 10, a work that alludes to this image in its very title, Dante writes that he has not yet attained a proper seat at the table of the philosophers or theologians, but that nevertheless he shares the crumbs of their wisdom: "Not that I sit at that blessed table; but, having myself fled the pasture of the common people, and taking my place at the feet of those who are seated, I gather some of what they let fall" (Ryan translation, p. 14).

3. (p. 125) *"his immense desire":* This is the Pilgrim's desire to know the truth or to participate in the banquet of the blessed.

4. (p. 125) *"bedew":* Dew is a traditional symbol of God's grace.

5. (p. 125) *"spheres on steadfast poles . . . the last one to fly"*: The souls remaining after the departure of Christ and the Virgin Mary are whirling around in different groups and at different velocities. Dante compares them to comets and to wheels in the works of "horologes," or clocks. Dante's image of the clockworks seems to reflect the cutting edge of this kind of technology in his day. In such a mechanism, a large wheel moves so slowly that it seems "motionless" (l. 15) to the naked eye, but its turning makes the smaller wheels turn so fast that they seem to fly.

6. (p. 125) *carols*: In Italian, *carole* are circular round dances that are similar to the movement of the spirits.

7. (p. 125) *of their affluence / Give me the gauge*: The degree of the beatitude, or joy, of each spirit can be measured by the velocity of its movements and radiance.

8. (p. 125) *From that one*: Later, in ll. 34–36, Beatrice identifies this spirit as Saint Peter. He is the brightest of the shining spirits.

9. (p. 125) *My fantasy repeats it not to me*: In this case, "fantasy" refers to the human faculty that retains images in the mind, but here the Poet wants his reader to understand that the human faculty of fantasy cannot recall such a powerful image.

10. (p. 125) *our imagination for such folds . . . a tint too glaring*: Here the Poet employs the metaphor of the artist, declaring that the "folds" of this image of light cannot be expressed with mere words. In Dante's time rendering the colors of the folds of garments required extremely subtle color, not merely dark shadows.

11. (p. 126) *"the great man . . . Lord delivered up the keys"*: The great man is Saint Peter, who received the keys from Christ to bind and unbind in heaven and on earth (see the Bible, Matthew 16: 19).

12. (p. 126) *"the Faith . . . on the sea didst walk"*: Before the Pilgrim can enter the Empyrean, he must be examined to prove his worthiness. In this canto, Saint Peter will examine him on Faith (appropriate since he tells Christ in the Bible, Matthew 14: 28–29, that if Christ orders him to walk on water, his faith will move him to do so). In canto XXV, Saint James will examine the Pilgrim on Hope. And in canto XXVI, Saint John will question him on Charity, or Love. These three theological or Christian virtues—faith, hope, and charity—are required for man to achieve salvation.

13. (p. 126) *As baccalaureate arms himself . . . the master doth propose the*

question: Saint Peter's examination of the Pilgrim on matters of faith follows more or less the pattern employed in the examinations (the *dis-putatio*) of the medieval university. The doctoral candidate (the bachelor) was required to give proofs, both for and against, a certain argument that the master proposed. The examiner would draw the final conclusion.

14. (p. 126) *turned I round to Beatrice . . . my internal fountain:* Note that during the Pilgrim's examination, he first turns toward Beatrice each time he answers a theological question. For the reference to the fountain, see the Bible, John 7: 38: "He that believeth on me, as the scripture hath said, out of his belly shall flow rivers of living water."

15. (p. 126) *"the great centurion":* In the Italian, Dante employs the word *primipilo,* addressing Saint Peter in his capacity as the first commander of the Church Militant as a Roman military officer, a centurion.

16. (p. 126) *"thy dear brother":* Saint Paul is called Peter's "beloved" or "dear brother" in the Bible, 2 Peter 3: 15. Dante's definition of faith in ll. 64–66 will follow that given by Saint Paul in the Bible, Hebrews 11: 1: "Now faith is the substance of things hoped for, the evidence of things not seen."

17. (p. 127) *"its quiddity":* That is, its essence, its substance (a Scholastic term). For more on this term, see endnote 22 to canto XX.

18. (p. 127) *"With substances and then with evidences":* As Saint Peter underlines, Saint Paul called faith a "substance" first and then an "evidence," or argument, only secondarily. The Pilgrim will correctly reply in ll. 70–78 that in matters relative to eternal life, Faith is the substance and is the equivalent in philosophical arguments of the evidence we demand in questions concerning earthly things. Arguments concerning religion are based upon belief, not facts.

19. (p. 127) *"Below by doctrine were thus understood . . . would there find place":* The Pilgrim's answer provides such a clear definition of Faith that no sophistic argument to the contrary on earth would be of any use.

20. (p. 127) *"this coin the alloy and weight":* These are two measures of a coin's worth. Thus the Pilgrim has passed two essential tests of a coin's true value, these tests standing for his theological correctness. It is probable that Dante meant the alloy or composition to stand for the substance and the weight to represent the evidences mentioned in l. 69.

21. (p. 127) *"tell me if thou hast it in thy purse?":* In contemporary vernacular, the Pilgrim has proved that he can talk the talk (define Faith correctly), but can he walk the walk (practice what he has preached)?

22. (p. 127) *"Yes, both so shining and so round":* The Pilgrim's resounding answer in the affirmative underscores the two tests of a coin: A coin shines if it contains the proper composition or alloy of metals, and its perfect round shape attests to the fact that it has not been shaved down around its edge to reduce its weight and therefore its value.

23. (p. 127) *"precious jewel":* This is a reference to Faith.

24. (p. 127) *"every virtue founded":* Hope and Charity, or Love, are based upon Faith.

25. (p. 127) *"The large outpouring / Of Holy Spirit . . . ancient parchments and the new":* God's grace, through the Old and New Testaments ("the ancient parchments and the new"), has inspired the Pilgrim's faith.

26. (p. 128) *"The proofs . . . nor anvil beat":* Asked in ll. 96–97 why he considers the books of the Holy Bible to be the word of God, the Pilgrim answers that the miracles described in the Old and New Testaments provide proof of the divine origin of these scriptures. Miracles are not natural occurrences, since Nature has no way to heat iron or to strike the metal on an anvil.

27. (p. 128) *"who assureth thee . . . naught else to thee affirms it":* Saint Peter now asks the Pilgrim what makes him think that the miracles actually happened: Offering the Bible as proof of the miracles involves a circular form of proof that would not normally be admitted in a logical argument.

28. (p. 128) *"Were the world to Christianity converted . . . the rest are not its hundredth part":* If the entire world was converted to Christianity without the miracles recounted in the Bible, this was the greatest miracle of all and certain proof of divine intervention. Other miracles would not be worth one hundredth of that single miraculous event. Obviously Dante exaggerates the percentage of the world that had been converted to Christianity. He repeats an argument found in Saint Augustine's *The City of God* XXII: 5 and in Saint Thomas Aquinas' *Summa contra gentiles* I: 6.

29. (p. 128) *"poor and fasting . . . Which was a vine and has become a thorn!":* The vineyard of the Lord has become corrupted (the "thorn") as a result of the degenerate clergy who have not followed Saint Peter's poverty and fasting.

30. (p. 128) *"One God we praise!"*: With his theologically correct responses, the Pilgrim has proven himself to be a true believer, and as a result the "Te Deum" ("We praise Thee, O God"), the famous Church song written by Saint Ambrose on the occasion of the conversion of Saint Augustine, is sung. This same hymn was heard in *Purgatorio* IX: 139–142 when the Pilgrim passed through the gate of Purgatory.

31. (p. 128) *that Baron:* The meaning is "that lord (Saint Peter)."

32. (p. 128) *"The Grace that dallying . . . And whence to thy belief it was presented"*: After successfully fielding questions on the definition of Faith, whether or not he possesses this Faith, from whence it is derived, and upon what theological foundations this Faith stands, the Pilgrim is now asked for his creed—the specific content of his faith and its sources. Note that in l. 118, Saint Peter attributes the correctness of the Pilgrim's answers to Divine Grace and not to any quality in the Pilgrim himself.

33. (p. 128) *"Towards the sepulchre, more youthful feet"*: According to the Bible, John 20: 3–8, Saint Peter's faith was so strong that it compelled him to enter Christ's Holy Sepulcher before John, who was the younger man.

34. (p. 128) *"In one God I believe . . . himself unmoved"*: The Pilgrim's credo follows the traditional Nicene Creed in most respects, although there are also some touches of Aristotelian ideas, such as defining God as the unmoved mover (l. 132). The idea that the entire universe is moved by God's love is, of course, Christian in origin.

35. (p. 129) *"Physical and metaphysical"*: The Pilgrim relies not only on Scripture but also on physical and philosophical or theological proofs of his faith. In *Summa theologica* I, q. 2, a. 3, Saint Thomas Aquinas offers five different arguments for God's existence based on God as first mover, first efficient cause, first necessity, first goodness, and first governing intellect.

36. (p. 129) *"Through Moses . . . the fiery Spirit sanctified you"*: In the Bible, Acts 2: 1–4 describes the time of Pentecost, when the Holy Spirit descended upon the Apostles as tongues of fire. These lines refer to other parts of the Bible that reflect writings after Pentecost: the Old Testament (Moses, Prophets, and Psalms of l. 136); the four Gospel books of the New Testament (l. 137); and the New Testament Epistles and the book of Revelation (l. 138).

37. (p. 129) *"so one and trine"*: The basis of the Pilgrim's credo is a belief in the Holy Trinity, which can be spoken of either in the singular ("one," using the Latin verb *est*, "is") or in the plural ("trine," or three, using the Latin verb *sunt*, "are").

38. (p. 129) *"this is the spark . . . dilates to vivid flame":* The belief in the Holy Trinity is the source of all faith. It is revealed through the Holy Scriptures and is an article of faith, but as a spark, it may blossom into a great flame, reflecting God's divine love.

39. (p. 129) *Three times encircled me:* Saint Peter now crowns the Pilgrim with three circular movements, just as he had crowned Beatrice in ll. 22–24. The three movements naturally reinforce the idea of the Holy Trinity as the center of Christian faith. The Pilgrim has passed his first examination with flying colors.

CANTO XXV

1. (p. 130) *If e'er it happen that the Poem Sacred:* The Pilgrim is about to be examined by Saint James on the second Christian virtue of Hope, and thus it is appropriate that in ll. 1–12, he expresses his lifelong wish to return to Florence and to receive the poet's laurel crown from his fellow citizens, who banished him to a life of exile.

2. (p. 130) *many a year:* Most scholars believe Dante took roughly a decade to complete *The Divine Comedy* while in exile.

3. (p. 130) *"the fair sheepfold . . . wolves":* Arguing his innocence of the charges brought against him that resulted in his exile, Dante asserts that the Blacks who drove him out of Florence are guilty of tearing apart his native city (l. 5, "the fair sheepfold").

4. (p. 130) *With other voice . . . Baptismal will I take the laurel crown:* Continuing the image of the innocent lamb and the sheepfold, Dante says he hopes to return to Florence in the future as the famous and respected author of this sacred poem. He underscores this wish in l. 7 ("with other voice"), suggesting that he would like to return not merely as the poet identified with other and lesser works of literature, such as his early love poetry. He would receive the poet's laurel crown at the Baptistery of San Giovanni in the center of the city outside its majestic Duomo (the Baptistery mentioned in *Inferno* XIX: 17–18).

5. (p. 130) *for her sake:* That is, for the sake of Faith.

6. (p. 130) *the firstfruits:* The reference is to Saint Peter, the first pope.

7. (p. 130) *"behold the Baron / For whom below Galicia is frequented"*: This is Saint James the Apostle, brother of Saint John the Evangelist and not to be confused with Saint James the Less, the brother of Jesus. This Saint James, according to tradition, preached in Spain, and his body was miraculously transferred to the capital of Galicia (Santiago de Compostela) after his death. During the Middle Ages, his tomb there was the most highly regarded pilgrimage site, after Rome and Jerusalem, in all of Christendom.

8. (p. 130) *one beheld I by the other:* The Pilgrim is referring, respectively, to Saint Peter and Saint James.

9. (p. 130) *the food:* See *Paradiso* XXIV: 1–6. The sight of God is food for the blessed souls.

10. (p. 130) *coram me:* The phrase is Latin for "before me."

11. (p. 131) *"the benefactions / Of our Basilica"*: The Basilica refers to the realm of heaven. Some commentators believe that this may be a reference to the Epistle of James 1: 5, 17, which speaks of liberality, or magnanimity. If this is the case, it would mean that Dante has confused Saint James the Apostle with Saint James the Less, traditionally considered to be the author of the Epistle of James.

12. (p. 131) *"As Jesus to the three gave greater clearness"*: In allegorical readings of the New Testament, the Apostles Peter, James, and John were identified, respectively, with faith, hope, and charity. They were also the three Apostles who witnessed three demonstrations of Christ's character: in the Transfiguration (the Bible, Matthew 17: 1–8), in the Garden of Gethsemane (Matthew 26: 36–38), and in the raising of the daughter of Jairus (Luke 8: 50–56).

13. (p. 131) *the second fire:* This is Saint James.

14. (p. 131) *mine eyes I lifted to the hills:* The two Apostles are described as if they were hills, in keeping with Psalms 121: 1: "I will lift up mine eyes unto the hills, from whence cometh my help."

15. (p. 131) *"our Emperor"*: This is a reference to God.

16. (p. 131) *"In the most secret chamber, with his Counts"*: Note how Dante has described heaven as if it were a feudal court inhabited by an emperor with his counts at his court, the "most secret chamber," or the Empyrean. The counts are His saints.

17. (p. 131) *"Say what it is . . . whence it came to thee"*: Recalling the questions posed by Saint Peter, the Pilgrim is ordered to define Hope, to say to what extent he possesses it, and to describe its source.

18. (p. 131) *the second light:* This is Saint James.

19. (p. 131) *the Compassionate:* This is Beatrice. Note that she prevents the Pilgrim's response to the second question in her subsequent remarks (l. 62), because it would presume arrogance on the Pilgrim's part to say to what degree he thought himself worthy of salvation. He will therefore answer only the first and third questions put to him by Saint James.

20. (p. 131) *"the Church Militant . . . into Jerusalem to see":* The part of the Church made up of all living Christians, as contrasted to the Church Triumphant of l. 54: "all our band" irradiated by "that Sun," (God); this group includes the blessed already in Paradise. The reference to Egypt (l. 55) and to Jerusalem (l. 56) refers, respectively, to the Church Militant and the Church Triumphant. Egypt stands for earthly life because of its role as the enslaver of the Hebrews in the Old Testament, while Jerusalem stands for the City of God that will be established after the Last Judgment.

21. (p. 131) *As a disciple:* Once again, the Pilgrim will go forward with his examination on Hope as if he were a student in a medieval university (see *Paradiso* XXIV: 46–48).

22. (p. 132) *"Hope":* Defining Hope as the expectation of future blessedness deriving from the race of God as well as one's previous merits follows a definition offered by Peter Lombard in *Libri sententiarum* III: xxvi, i. Saint Thomas Aquinas also discusses this definition in *Summa theologica* II, 2, q. 17, a. 1.

23. (p. 132) *"From many stars this light comes unto me":* The Pilgrim comes to this definition of Hope through the writings of many wise men.

24. (p. 132) *"chief singer unto the chief captain":* King David was author of the Psalms and therefore the chief singer for the chief captain, God.

25. (p. 132) *" 'Sperent in te,' in the high Theody":* In the Latin Vulgate, these are the opening words of Psalms 9: 10, "And they that know thy name will put their trust in thee." A theody is a sacred song.

26. (p. 132) *"the Epistle":* The Pilgrim addresses Saint James as if he were the author of the Epistle of James, a book in the New Testament

attributed to Saint James the Less, not to Saint James the Apostle. This brief book mentions man's hope in God's promise several times.

27. (p. 132) *in the guise of lightning:* Jesus calls James and John "Sons of Thunder" in the Bible, Mark 3: 17.

28. (p. 132) *"the palm and issue of the field":* As told in the Bible, Acts 12: 1–2, James was martyred by Herod Agrippa in the year A.D. 44, and palm branches traditionally symbolize martyrs; the "issue of the field" is a reference to the battlefield of life.

29. (p. 132) *"in her":* This is a reference to Hope.

30. (p. 132) *"Whatever things Hope promises to thee":* Just as Saint Peter asked the Pilgrim to describe the content of his faith, Saint James now asks him to describe what he hopes for in the life to come.

31. (p. 132) *"twofold garments":* In his reading of the Bible, Dante sees a reference to the unification of the body and soul in Paradise. The specific references are Isaiah 61: 7 ("therefore in their land they shall possess the double: everlasting joy shall be unto them"), and Isaiah 61: 10 ("he hath clothed me with the garments of salvation").

32. (p. 132) *Thy brother, too:* This is a reference to Saint John the Evangelist, who in the Bible, Revelation 7, describes the white robes of the blessed in Paradise.

33. (p. 132) "Sperent in te": Once again, as in l. 73 (see endnote 25 above), the blessed sing a Latin hymn to signify the Pilgrim's successful passing of yet another step in his "university" examination.

34. (p. 132) *all the carols:* Dante refers to the dancing circles of the blessed this way because their movements are similar to *carole,* circular round dances (see also endnote 6 to *Paradiso* XXIV).

35. (p. 132) *a light among them brightened . . . Winter would have a month of one sole day:* A third figure, Saint John, now appears. His brightness seems to equal the sun and would provide a month of continuous light from December 21 until January 21, when Cancer rules the night sky, if that constellation had such a powerful star within it.

36. (p. 133) *the two:* They are Saint Peter and Saint James.

37. (p. 133) *"the one who lay upon the breast / Of our own Pelican":* In the Middle Ages, the pelican was employed as a symbol for Jesus because it was thought that the bird nourished its offspring, or brought its dead offspring back to life, by feeding them its own blood. See the

Bible, John 13: 23, "Now there was leaning on Jesus' bosom one of his disciples, whom Jesus loved."

38. (p. 133) *"the great office":* After Jesus' death on the cross, John was entrusted with the care of the Virgin Mary (see the Bible, John 19: 26–27).

39. (p. 133) *the eclipsing of the sun . . . sightless doth become:* A number of solar eclipses could have been seen during Dante's lifetime, and it was a well-known fact that blindness would result if one looked directly at the sun for too long during an eclipse.

40. (p. 133) *"Why dost thou daze . . . the eternal proposition tallies":* The reason the Pilgrim is staring so intensely at the light that is Saint John is that, according to medieval legend, John ascended to heaven in both body and soul. Since the Pilgrim himself is traveling through the afterlife in his bodily form, it is natural for him to assume that the legend might be true. John's rebuke quickly destroys this myth. He shall remain in bodily form in his earthly grave until the Last Judgment, when the number of those selected by God as the blessed elect will undergo the resurrection of the flesh.

41. (p. 133) *"With the two garments . . . alone that have ascended":* Only the "two lights alone"—Christ and the Virgin Mary—entered heaven in both body and soul.

42. (p. 133) *Of sound that by the trinal breath:* When John begins to speak, the dancing of the three apostles and their singing cease.

43. (p. 133) *I could not see:* The Pilgrim is suddenly and temporarily struck blind, reminding the reader of the discussion of blindness caused by solar eclipses (see endnote 39 above). Since the Pilgrim was struck blind attempting to discern within the bright light of Saint John whether or not he retained his fleshly form, perhaps he is being punished for his temporary ignorance. If this is true, then his subsequent healing through the power of Love in the forthcoming canto represents an example of what all mankind can expect from God's love.

CANTO XXVI

1. (p. 135) *"Begin then . . . and not dead":* The Pilgrim will remain blinded during the entire examination on charity, or love (ll. 1–79), a subtle reference to the secular tradition that "love is blind." In a departure from his discussions of faith and hope, the Pilgrim never gives a definition of love or charity, and only expounds upon what he loves and why. After this third examination is completed, the Pilgrim is ready to enter the region of eternal blessedness through the Primum Mobile to the Empyrean. John also promises him that his sight is only temporarily blinded (l. 9) and will eventually be restored by Beatrice.

2. (p. 135) *"has in her look . . . Ananias":* In the Bible, Acts 9: 17–18, Ananias cured Saint Paul of blindness by laying his hands upon him. Dante thus suggests that Beatrice has this same miraculous power from God through her eyes.

3. (p. 135) *"Let the cure come to eyes . . . she with fire I ever burn with entered":* In Dante's youth, the sight of Beatrice kindled within him a burning desire and a secular love; now it will be appropriate for the Pilgrim to be cured of his blindness (and also his misguided love for the young girl) by her eyes, the portals through which this earlier love entered his heart.

4. (p. 135) *"The Good . . . that love reads me low or loud":* The good, God, is the beginning and end of all that is taught to the Pilgrim in the Holy Scriptures (the verb "reads" means "teaches," and the phrase "low or loud" refers to the fact that things may be taught with lesser or greater stress. Alpha (A) and omega (Ω) are the first and last letters in the Greek alphabet, the language of the New Testament, and therefore the Pilgrim is declaring that the beginning and end of his love rest in God. In Revelation 1: 8, Saint John wrote, "I am Alpha and Omega, the beginning and the ending, saith the Lord, which is, and which was, and which is to come, the Almighty."

5. (p. 135) *selfsame voice:* The voice is that of Saint John.

6. (p. 135) *"with finer sieve . . . aimed thy bow at such a target":* Just as a sieve is employed to separate the flour from the chaff, Saint John now tells the Pilgrim that he must more carefully define how he came to the love of God—who or what moved him to aim at making God the ultimate goal of his love.

7. (p. 135) *"By philosophic arguments, / And by authority":* That is, by human reason and by divine revelation from the Holy Scriptures.

8. (pp. 135–136) *"For Good . . . this evidence is founded":* The Pilgrim declares, following Aristotle, that goodness inspires love, and since all goodness resides in God, once this fact is perceived by the intellect,

man must love God. It is important to Dante to stress that an act of the intellect (understanding) precedes an act of will (love).

9. (p. 136) *"Such truth he . . . Of all the sempiternal substances"*: This is a reference to Aristotle, who taught that God was the unmoved mover for whose love the heavens are moved. The "sempiternal" or eternal substances are the angels and the blessed.

10. (p. 136) *"the truthful Author . . . 'I will make all my goodness pass before thee'"*: The author is God, and here Dante quotes from the Bible, Exodus 33: 19. God says this to Moses.

11. (p. 136) *"loud Evangel"*: The reference is to the biblical Gospel of Saint John. In the original Italian, Dante describes this gospel as *l'alto preconio*—employing the Latinism *preconio* ("proclamation"), and presumably a proclamation is loud. "Loud" should perhaps best be read as "great" or "sublime" or "strident." The Pilgrim is no doubt referring to the opening lines of this Gospel, which proclaim the Incarnation: "In the beginning was the Word, and the Word was with God, and the Word was God" (John 1: 1).

12. (p. 136) *"other cords"*: That is, other reasons.

13. (p. 136) *"how many teeth this love is biting thee"*: Most commentators construe this line as a somewhat incongruous reference to actual teeth biting, a metaphor for the strong attraction that Dante felt for the love of God. At least one commentator has suggested that the teeth in question are not human teeth but are, instead, the teeth of cogs and wheels of machinery, citing l. 56 as evidence that the teeth in question turn the heart toward God.

14. (p. 136) *the Eagle of Christ*: Saint John was identified with the Eagle, one of the four beasts cited in Revelation 4: 7 that symbolized the four Evangelists.

15. (p. 136) *my profession*: That is, my declaration.

16. (p. 136) *"All of those bites . . . placed me on the shore"*: The Pilgrim now begins to relate the "bites," or the secondary loves that have led him to direct his highest love to God. These include the existence of the world and his own existence, Christ's Redemption of mankind, and human hope. These things have led him away from "the sea of love perverse" (l. 62)—no doubt a reference to the carnal love that inspired Dante's love poetry and *La Vita Nuova*.

17. (pp. 136–137) *"The leaves . . . as he has granted them of good":* The Pilgrim declares he loves the creatures of God's creation ("the leaves . . . of the Eternal Gardener") in proportion to the goodness with which their divine maker has blessed them. God alone is loved for Himself.

18. (p. 137) *As soon as I had ceased, a song most sweet:* This song, "Holy, Holy, Holy," announces that the Pilgrim has successfully passed his theological examination on the three Christian virtues of faith, hope, and charity. Beatrice joins with the chorus of the blessed in singing this song, which appears first in Isaiah 6: 2–3, where the Seraphim chant it around God's throne, and later in Revelation 4: 8, where the Four Beasts sing it. That the word "Holy" is pronounced three times underlines once again the key to Christian doctrine: the Holy Trinity.

19. (p. 137) *And as at some keen light one wakes . . . passed from coat to coat:* The reader must remember that the Pilgrim has been temporarily blinded. His eyesight is now restored to him in a process compared to the way a waking man sees a bright light through his eyelids as a result of the stimulation of the "visual spirit" or the nerve that runs from membrane to membrane ("coat to coat") of the eye.

20. (p. 137) *did Beatrice / Chase every mote with radiance of her own:* It is Beatrice's radiance that reawakens the Pilgrim's eyesight.

21. (p. 137) *About a fourth light . . . "did create":* This will be revealed to be the light of Adam, who joins the three lights of Saint Peter, Saint James, and Saint John. Beatrice reveals Adam's identity when she describes him as "the first soul / That ever the first virtue [God] did create."

22. (p. 137) *Sometimes an animal . . . to give me pleasure:* Dante's simile has puzzled many commentators. Adam's soul reveals its joy to the Pilgrim by moving within its radiance much as an animal might reveal its motions by moving under a cover.

23. (p. 138) *"the truthful mirror":* This is the mind of God.

24. (p. 138) *"none makes Him parhelion of itself ":* All of creation is reflected perfectly in God, but no created thing can be a perfect reflection of God.

25. (p. 138) *"how long ago":* In the rest of the canto (ll. 109–142), Adam reads the Pilgrim's mind and enumerates the four questions the Pilgrim has for him: When was Adam created (ll. 109–110)? How long did he remain in the Garden of Eden (l. 112)? What was the nature of his sin ("the great disdain," l. 113)? And what language did he, the first human being, speak (l. 114)? The third question, the nature of Adam's sin, was obviously the most important, and Adam addresses this topic first.

26. (p. 138) *"the tasting of the tree . . . o'erstepping of the bounds"*: Adam's sin was not tasting the forbidden fruit but rather his disobedience, which resulted from the same kind of pride that brought about Lucifer's fall and constituted Original Sin.

27. (p. 138) *"thy Lady moved Virgilius . . . circuits"*: Adam spent 4,302 revolutions of the sun in Limbo, where Beatrice moved Virgil to assist the Pilgrim.

28. (p. 138) *"this Council"*: The reference is to the assembly of the blessed elect in Paradise.

29. (p. 138) *"all the lights / Of his highway"*: These are all the signs of the Zodiac.

30. (p. 138) *"nine hundred times and thirty"*: According to the Bible, Genesis 5: 5, Adam lived 930 years (he saw the revolution of the constellations of the Zodiac that many times). Adding the years of his life to the years Adam spent in Limbo (4,302) yields a total of 5,232 years that transpired between the creation of Adam and Christ's Crucifixion. (Christ freed Adam from Limbo in A.D. 34, during his Harrowing of Hell, immediately following the Crucifixion.)

31. (p. 138) *"quite extinct . . . under Nimrod were employed"*: Here Dante corrects an account of Adam's language from his earlier explanation in *De Vulgari Eloquentia* I: 6. In that earlier account, Dante had claimed all humanity spoke Adam's language until the confusion caused by the Tower of Babel (what he here calls the work done by the people under Nimrod) and then only by the Hebrews after the Tower of Babel was destroyed. Moreover, he held that this language was a divine creation and was unchangeable. Now he asserts that this language was the product of human reason and was susceptible to change or development. For the biblical account of the Tower of Babel, see Genesis 11: 4–9.

32. (p. 138) *"For nevermore result of reasoning . . . was durable"*: Dante declares that nothing human or the product of human reason lasts, for permanence depends upon the revolution of the heavenly bodies that affect the workings of Nature, while human affairs change according to human desire.

33. (p. 138) *"A natural action . . . To your own art":* The power of speech is natural for human beings, but precisely what language he does speak is left up to human devices and is not controlled by Nature.

34. (p. 138) *"Ere I descended":* That is, before Adam descended into Limbo.

35. (p. 138) *"El was on earth the name of the Chief Good":* In *De Vulgari Eloquentia* I: 4, Dante claims that the first name given to God ("the Chief Good") by the Hebrews was El, the first word Adam spoke. Longfellow's translation here differs from the original Italian text, which reads: I *s'appellava in terra il sommo bene* ("the Chief Good was called I on earth"). Dante may have changed his mind and taken *I* to stand for the first name of God after finding this idea in Saint Isadore's *Etymologiae* VII:i: 3. Moreover, the letter "I" can also be read as the number 1, which would underline God's unity. Finally, "I", or "J" (pronounced Jah), was the first letter of the sacred name the Hebrews used for their god Jah, or Jehovah. See Psalms 68: 4: "Sing unto God, sing praises to his name: extol him that rideth upon the heavens by his name Jah, and rejoice before him."

36. (p. 138) *"Eli he then was called":* Again, Longfellow's translation differs from the original Italian text, which reads: *e* El *si chiamò poi* ("and later He was called *El*"). Thus Longfellow's English version obscures the fact that Dante thought "El" was God's earliest name when he wrote *De Vulgari Eloquentia* but had, by the time he composed *The Divine Comedy,* changed his mind, using "I" instead of the name "El" in terms of antiquity. Jehovah and Elohim are the two most common names used in the Old Testament for the Hebrew God.

37. (p. 138) *"the use of men is like a leaf":* This simile is taken from Horace's *Art of Poetry* (60–63).

38. (p. 139) *"the mount that highest o'er the wave / Rises":* The earthly Paradise, or the Garden of Eden, is located atop Purgatory.

39. (p. 139) *"From the first hour . . . to the sixth":* Adam finally answers the Pilgrim's second question: How long did Adam remain in the Garden of Eden? He was there six hours, from the first hour to the seventh, when the sun completes a quarter or 90 degrees of its circle and begins moving into the second quadrant. At least one commentator has noted that Dante also spent six hours in the earthly Paradise as well as six hours in the eighth heaven.

CANTO XXVII

1. (p. 141) *"Glory be"... all Paradise began:* In *Paradiso* XXIV: 8, Beatrice had asked the blessed to "bedew" the Pilgrim; this is now accomplished as those who inhabit the eighth sphere of Paradise sing the liturgical "Gloria Patri" to celebrate the fact that the Pilgrim has passed his entrance examination and is now ready to travel through the Primum Mobile to the Empyrean, his final destination. In the original Italian, the lines are sung in Italian, not in Latin, and its full text would be "Glory be to the Father, and to the Son, and to the Holy Spirit, as it was in the beginning, is now and ever shall be, world without end. Amen."

2. (p. 141) *a smile / Of the universe:* The joy of the blessed at the Pilgrim's successful testing is communicated both by sound (the singing) and by sight—the universe seems to smile, transferring the act normally accomplished by Beatrice to all of creation.

3. (p. 141) *the four torches:* These are Saint Peter, Saint James, Saint John, and Adam.

4. (p. 141) *that first had come:* This is Saint Peter.

5. (p. 141) *As Jupiter would become... interchange their plumes:* Angered by the corruption of the Church in Dante's day, Saint Peter's light, white like that of Jupiter, becomes red like that of Mars but retains its size. The Poet compares this exchange to birds of different colors exchanging plumage when they molt.

6. (p. 141) *Providence... every side imposed:* Providence assigns not only the turns in singing in this eighth heaven but also the specific role each soul plays there. Here, Providence directs the souls to fall silent, awaiting Saint Peter's tirade on corruption.

7. (p. 141) *"If I my color change... usurps upon the earth my place / My place, my place":* Saint Peter's change of color from white to red results from his shame over the corruption of the present pope, Boniface VIII. Peter's repetition of the phrase "my place" three times underlines his anger and may be a reference to Jeremiah 7: 4, where the phrase "the temple of the Lord" is repeated three times Peter refers, of course, to Rome.

8. (p. 141) *"vacant has become":* The papal office is not actually vacant, since Boniface VIII reigned as pope in 1300, but Boniface's malfeasance has corrupted it.

9. (p. 141) *"the Perverse One":* This is Lucifer, or Satan.

10. (p. 141) *"below there is appeased!":* Satan takes comfort, or refuge, in Hell.

11. (p. 141) *With the same color:* The eighth heaven becomes tinted with the rose-colored hue of sunset or sunrise. Dante finds inspiration for this image in Ovid's *Metamorphoses* III: 183–184, where the Latin poet describes how the goddess Diana blushed with embarrassment when Actaeon saw her naked. She turned him into a stag, and his own hunting dog then killed him.

12. (p. 142) *From listening only . . . the supreme Omnipotence:* While Diana blushed when she displayed her naked body to Actaeon, Beatrice either blushes or turns pale in a similar fashion at the mere mention ("from listening only") of wrongdoing. Scholars have argued over whether Beatrice blushes or turns pale, but it seems more likely that her face turns red like those of the other inhabitants of this section of Paradise. At any rate, in ll. 35–36, the Poet compares the change in her complexion to the eclipse that occurred when Christ ("the supreme Omnipotence") died at the Crucifixion. While the biblical descriptions of this event in Matthew 27: 45, Mark 15: 33, and Luke 23: 44–46 treat the eclipse as darkness, Dante here interprets this event as a reddening of the sky's color.

13. (p. 142) *The very countenance was not more changed:* Saint Peter's voice was as changed as his appearance.

14. (p. 142) *"The spouse of Christ":* That is, the Church. From here through l. 66, Saint Peter denounces the evils of the medieval church.

15. (p. 142) *"of Linus and of Cletus":* Saint Linus became pope following the death of Saint Peter in A.D. 67 and was martyred around A.D. 76 or 79. Saint Cletus, or Anacletus, succeeded Saint Linus as pope until c.A.D. 90, when the Emperor Domitian martyred him.

16. (p. 142) *"in acquest of gold . . . Sixtus and Pius, Urban and Calixtus":* Unlike the present popes, the early popes after Saint Peter went in search not of gold but of eternal life ("this delightful life"). Sixtus I was pope from c.A.D. 115–125, during Emperor Hadrian's reign; Pius I was pope from c.142 to 155, during the reign of Emperor Antoninus Pius; Calixtus I reigned from c.217 to 222 and was succeeded by Urban I from 222 to 230. All four men were martyred.

17. (p. 142) *"Our purpose was not . . . and flash with fire":* Peter declares

that he and the other martyred popes of the early Christian church did not work toward dividing Christians into pro- and anti-papal factions (such as the Guelph and Ghibelline parties in medieval Italy). Nor were the keys of Saint Peter meant to be inscribed on banners used to lead troops against fellow believers (see *Inferno* XXVII: 85–90, a passage that describes how Pope Boniface warred against Christians almost exclusively). Nor did Saint Peter intend for his own image to be employed on the papal seal used to sell reinstatements after excommunication, indulgences, and other similar schemes to raise money ("privileges venal and mendacious," l. 53).

18. (p. 142) *"the Caorsines and Gascons":* In *Inferno* XI: 50, Dante identifies Cahors in southern France with usury; Pope John XXII, who reigned from 1316 to 1334, was from Cahors. His predecessor, Pope Clement V, who moved the papacy to Avignon, was from Gascony, a region reputed to be filled with avaricious men. Dante earlier mentioned John in *Paradiso* XVIII: 130–136 and Clement in *Inferno* XIX: 82–87, *Purgatorio* XXXII: 148–160, and *Paradiso* XVII: 82.

19. (p. 142) *"Scipio . . . Will speedily bring aid":* Saint Peter claims that the victory of the Roman general Scipio Africanus over the Carthaginian general Hannibal in the Second Punic War was the result of God's divine plan and that God's justice is assured in the future.

20. (p. 143) *"by thy mortal weight . . . open thy mouth":* The Pilgrim is commanded to return to the world of the living and to testify to what he has witnessed in the afterlife. In l. 64, Saint Peter mentions the Pilgrim's mortal condition, which is often underlined in the poetry of *Inferno*, implying that his time in Paradise is of limited duration.

21. (p. 143) *"As with its frozen vapors . . . with us had remained":* Dante describes the spirits floating away from the Pilgrim as similar to the activity of a snowstorm in the winter, when the sun is in Capricorn (the "celestial goat" of l. 69)—that is, in January. But the storm the Pilgrim sees is inverted, since the flakes return back toward the Empyrean. In effect, the perspective of the Poet is now that of God, to whom the returning souls or snowflakes would appear to be rising toward Him higher in the heavens.

22. (p. 143) *"Cast down / Thy sight" . . . the first climate makes from midst to end:* The Pilgrim looks toward earth for the first time since *Paradiso* XXII: 127–154. Medieval geographers divided earth and the heavens

into divisions of latitude called "climates," or zones. The first "climate" of l. 81 would correspond to the constellation of Gemini. As the Pilgrim glances down, he realizes he has traversed 90 degrees, or roughly a quarter of the circumference through the eighth heaven. Since 90 degrees in distance corresponds in time to one quarter of the revolution of the heavens around earth, six hours have passed in this part of Paradise.

23. (p. 143) *the mad track of Ulysses / Past Gades:* From his vantage point high above earth, the Pilgrim is able to see westward past the Strait of Gibraltar where, beyond the city of Gades, or modern Cadiz, Ulysses followed his "mad track" to his death, an event recounted in *Inferno* XXVI. While Ulysses' voyage ended in death and failure, the Pilgrim's even more heroic journey to Paradise will succeed.

24. (p. 143) *well nigh the shore . . . Europa a sweet burden:* According to Ovid's *Metamorphoses* II: 833–875, the shore where Jupiter (who had transformed himself into a bull) carried the nymph Europa was in Phoenicia.

25. (p. 143) *this threshing-floor:* As in *Paradiso* XXII: 151, the Poet employs this expression to underline the small importance earthly matters have to one heading toward Paradise.

26. (p. 143) *a sign and more removed:* While Dante is in Gemini, the sun is in Aries, and Taurus is between the two constellations.

27. (p. 143) *My mind enamored:* Even while gazing across the universe, the Pilgrim's mind is constantly "in love" with Beatrice, and when he sees her once more, she will have greatly increased in beauty.

28. (p. 143) *the fair nest of Leda:* This is a reference to the constellation of Gemini, since the twins Castor and Pollux were Leda's children from her relationship with Jupiter (who seduced her in the form of a swan). Jupiter placed the twins in the stars as Gemini after their deaths. See the source in Ovid's *Heroides* XVII: 55–56.

29. (p. 143) *the swiftest heaven:* This is the Primum Mobile, or the ninth heaven, the fastest of the revolving spheres in the universe.

30. (p. 144) *all so uniform . . . for my place:* In the first eight heavens, Beatrice had always chosen a specific place for the Pilgrim (a planet or a constellation). Since the Primum Mobile contains no heavenly bodies—the reason it is said to be "uniform"—the Poet is unable to state exactly in what spot Beatrice has placed him.

31. (p. 144) *"And in this heaven . . . the Mind Divine":* The Primum

Mobile is contained within the Empyrean, the tenth heaven. The Empyrean is inhabited only by God's mind ("the Mind Divine"), the source of the love by which the Seraphim, who are the Intelligence of the Primum Mobile, receive the power to move the Primum Mobile and to transmit this motion to the lower spheres.

32. (p. 144) *"light and love embrace it"*: The Empyrean contains the Primum Mobile and binds it with light and love.

33. (p. 144) *"As ten is by the half and by the fifth"*: The eight heavens beneath the Primum Mobile take the measure of their motion in the universe from the Primum Mobile's speed, just as the number 10 may be said to be "measured" by its half (5) and by its fifth (2), since the number 10 is a product of multiplying 5 by 2.

34. (p. 144) *"in such a pot... and in the rest its leaves"*: Dante metaphorically describes the Primum Mobile as the pot that contains the leaves of the lower eight heavens.

35. (p. 144) *"O covetousness... wildings the true plums"*: Beatrice launches into an attack upon humanity's weaknesses that will take up the rest of the canto. While man's will is essentially good (l. 124), it is the "uninterrupted rain" of corruption that diverts the will from its proper goal—that rots the plums by spoiling them on the tree.

36. (pp. 144–145) *"Even thus is swarthy... leaves the night"*: Lines 136–138 are difficult to interpret, but it seems clear that "him who brings the morn, and leaves the night" is the sun. Circe was the daughter of the sun and had the power to change men into beasts. Thus Beatrice is saying that the uncorrupted white skin of human nature turns black when it is corrupted at the first sight of worldly goods, in much the same way that Circe changed animals into beasts in Virgil's *Aeneid* VII.

37. (p. 145) *"Ere January be unwintered... centesimal on earth neglected"*: Until the Gregorian calendar in the sixteenth century corrected the errors in the Julian calendar, the year was considered to be 365 days and 6 hours long. Thus an error of about one hundredth of a day, or 13 minutes, was inherent in the system. As each century passed, the calendar would move the months a day forward into the next season. In other words, January would be "unwintered" and pushed into spring.

38. (p. 145) *"The tempest... fleet shall run its course direct"*: Lacking leadership, humanity has no hope, but with the proper temporal leadership—the "tempest" of l. 145—the "human family" of l. 141 will

become a fleet of ships that corrects its course, turning around toward the proper goal.

39. (p. 145) *"on the flower":* The Poet makes a sudden turn from one metaphor (humanity as a fleet changing direction in mid course) to the image of the rotten plums of l. 126, which now blossom as true or good fruit.

CANTO XXVIII

1. (p. 147) *imparadise my mind:* Dante invented this Italian verb (*imparadisare*) to describe the manner in which Beatrice dominates his mind.

2. (p. 147) *In similar wise... Love made the springs to ensnare me:* As Dante gazes into Beatrice's eyes—the eyes that once ensnared him with amorous love—he now sees reflected the light of God and of the angelic orders that shine through the transparent ninth sphere of the Primum Mobile from the Empyrean, the tenth heaven.

3. (p. 147) *in that volume:* That is, in that heaven (the Primum Mobile, the ninth heaven).

4. (p. 147) *A point... Light so acute:* God appears to the Pilgrim as a small point of exceedingly bright light.

5. (p. 147) *here:* The reference is to earth, where Dante the Poet is writing his poem.

6. (p. 147) *Thus distant round the point a circle of fire:* In ll. 25–36, the Poet notes the nine concentric circles turning around the point of light; these circles represent the nine angelic orders, the names of which will be given in ll. 98–126 of this canto.

7. (p. 148) *Juno's messenger:* This is the rainbow, or Iris. The seventh Sphere of Saturn is so great that a rainbow made into a circle would be too small to contain it.

8. (p. 148) *"From that point / Dependent is the heaven and nature all":* All heaven and Nature depend upon the First Mover (God) who is Himself the Unmoved Mover.

9. (p. 148) *"that circle most conjoined to it":* This is the Primum Mobile.

10. (p. 148) *"But in the world of sense... from the centre more remote":* Viewing the heavens from earth, the Pilgrim says, the parts of the heavens furthest from earth seem the most divine, but in fact from the heavenly perspective, the most divine parts of the universe are those farthest from earth.

11. (p. 149) *"According to the more or less of virtue"*: The wider the heavenly sphere is, the greater it reflects divine power in all its parts. As a consequence, the largest spheres have more influence upon earth.

12. (p. 149) *"this one which sweeps along with it / The universe sublime"*: The reference is to the Primum Mobile, the source of the entire universe's motion.

13. (p. 149) *The hemisphere of air, when Boreas . . . that cheek where he is mildest:* The reference is to the earth's atmosphere. In Greek mythology, the god Boreas is the north wind, often personified on maps of Dante's times as heads blowing three gusts of wind through the two corners of the god's mouth and through its center. The north wind could blow, therefore, in three directions (north, northwest, and northeast), and it is the latter of these three directions that represents the gentlest of the north winds and that is therefore "the cheek where he is mildest."

14. (p. 149) *those circles scintillated . . . all the sparks repeated:* The sparks represent the angels of the angelic orders.

15. (p. 149) *More millions than the doubling of the chess:* Dante employs a very elaborate story to say that the numbers of the angels is basically uncountable. In an Oriental legend, a king promises to give the inventor of the game of chess anything he asks. The inventor requests that the king place one grain of wheat on the first of the sixty-four squares on the chessboard, two grains of wheat on the second, four grains on the third, sixteen on the fourth, and so on until all the squares are covered. The king foolishly agrees, not realizing that the total number would reach about 18.5 million million million grains.

16. (p. 150) *the fixed point which holds them at the* Ubi: God holds each angel in its appointed place (*ubi* is Latin for "where").

17. (p. 150) *"Seraphim and Cherubim"*: The nine heavenly spheres are associated with nine angelic orders, listed here in ascending order of importance:

Moon: Angels
Mercury: Archangels
Venus: Principalities
Sun: Powers
Mars: Virtues

Jupiter: Dominions
Saturn: Thrones
Fixed Stars: Cherubim
Primum Mobile: Seraphim

18. (p. 150) *"Loves"*: These are angels.

19. (p. 150) *"the primal Triad"*: The triad is made up of the three most important angelic orders (Thrones, Cherubim, and Seraphim).

20. (p. 150) *"in the faculty which sees, / And not in that which loves, and follows next"*: Dante accepts the opinion (shared with Saint Thomas Aquinas, among others) that the intellect ("the faculty which sees") and not the will ("in that which loves, and follows next") is the key to blessedness.

21. (p. 150) *"And of this seeing merit is the measure"*: The power to see God is proportionate to the soul's merit, and this merit derives from grace and is assisted by the will. It is important to remember that in Paradise, the blessed attain the level of bliss that is in proportion to their power to see God.

22. (p. 150) *"The second Triad, which is germinating"*: Dante associates the second group of angelic orders—the Dominions, the Virtues, and the Powers—with blossoming flowers, an image that will reach its culmination in the figure of the Celestial Rose at the close of the poem.

23. (p. 150) *"sempiternal spring, / That no nocturnal Aries despoils"*: During Aries (March 21 to April 21), it is still possible that a sudden frost may destroy flower blossoms. This is not the case in heaven's eternal springtime (l. 116) where there is no danger of any changes in the environment.

24. (p. 150) *"Perpetually hosanna warbles forth . . . joy, with which it is intrined"*: Dante employs a verb (*sbernare*) that refers to the joyful song a bird makes upon the arrival of spring. He underlines the notion of the Holy Trinity with the invention of a verb *s'interna* ("is intrined").

25. (p. 150) *"three Divine"*: This is a reference to the three orders of angels. (Dante refers to angels as divinities in *Purgatorio* XXXII: 8.)

26. (p. 150) *"dances"*: The angels circle as if in a round dance.

27. (p. 150) *"The Principalities and Archangels wheel . . . angelic sports"*:

The final "triad" of angelic orders is made up of three groups: Principalities, Archangels, and Angels (not specifically named but implied). They are all joyful, suggesting a group at play.

28. (p. 150) *"upward all of them are gazing":* All the angels gaze upon God, but they do so in a sort of hierarchy, since the higher orders shed their power and influence upon those lower than themselves.

29. (p. 150) *"Dionysius":* According to Acts 17: 34, Dionysius the Areopagite of Athens was converted to Christianity by the preaching of Saint Paul and may have been martyred in or around A.D. 95. In the Middle Ages, a book entitled *De caelesti ierarchia* (*On Celestial Hierarchy*), incorrectly attributed to him, described the nine orders of angels in much the same manner as Dante does here. Dionysius, sometimes known as Pseudo Dionysius, is also mentioned in *Paradiso* X: 116–117.

30. (p. 151) *"Gregory afterwards dissented from him . . . he at himself did smile":* In a learned Latin work, Saint Gregory the Great (c.540–604) discussed the angelic orders, and in so doing proposed an order different from the one Dionysius and Dante set forth in *Paradiso* (see endnote 17, above). Gregory's order is as follows:

Moon: Angels
Mercury: Archangels
Venus: Thrones
Sun: Dominions
Mars: Virtues
Jupiter: Principalities
Saturn: Powers
Fixed Stars: Cherubim
Primum Mobile: Seraphim

It is worth noting that Dante accepted Gregory's order in his earlier *Il Convivio* II: vi; clearly, he revised his views between writing *Il Convivio* and *Paradiso*. Dante has Saint Gregory smile at his mistake when he enters Paradise.

31. (p. 151) *"For he who saw it here revealed it to him":* Dionysius correctly listed the order of angels, because Saint Paul ("he who saw it here") described the orders to him after ascending into the third heaven, as told in the Bible, 2 Corinthians 12: 2–4.

CANTO XXIX

1. (p. 152) *the children of Latona:* These are Apollo (the sun) and Diana (the moon).

2. (p. 152) *Surmounted by the Ram and by the Scales ... their hemisphere disturb the balance:* When the sun is in Aries (the Ram) and the moon is in Libra (the Scales), they are balanced for a moment on opposite sides of the horizon. This makes them appear to be a large pair of scales suspended by the zenith.

3. (p. 152) *So long ... at the point:* Beatrice gazes silently upon "the point" of God's light for as long as the sun and the moon remain in balance.

4. (p. 152) *"I have seen it / Where centres every When and every Ubi":* Beatrice reads the Pilgrim's mind and discerns his doubts about a number of questions (creation, the orders of angels, the rebellion of the fallen angels, the number of angels in heaven, etc.) because she gazes upon God, and sees his question reflected in God's mind. God is the point where every notion of time ("every When") and every notion of Space ("every Ubi") is centered.

5. (p. 152) *"Not to acquire some good unto himself ... 'Subsisto'":* God did not create the world to add to His goodness (since God is the essence of goodness), but He wanted other beings to share in His Goodness. In short, God's creation was an act of love. Other beings (God's "splendor / In its resplendency") were created so that they might declare, *"Subsisto"* ("I exist"), taking delight in the knowledge of their being.

6. (p. 152) *"new Loves":* These are the angels, who were the first created beings.

7. (p. 152) *"Nor as if torpid did he lie before":* One cannot speak of God's idleness before the creation, since God is beyond and outside of time. Time begins only with the creation.

8. (p. 152) *"Matter and Form":* Here Dante follows Aristotle in *De Anima* II: ii. The angels are spirit without matter, and are pure form, or pure mind. Pure matter is without spirit and includes the physical substances of earth and the lower orders of creation, such as the animals. Matter and form joined together would represent, according to some commentators, the heavens, and, according to others, mankind.

9. (p. 152) *"Came into being that had no defect":* When God's creation

issued forth in its three different manifestations, it was perfect and faultless.

10. (p. 152) *"three arrows from a three-stringed bow":* This is another reference to the Holy Trinity, the fundamental concept of Christianity, according to Dante's view. Here the idea of three refers to the three different manifestations of God's creations: matter, form, and angels.

11. (p. 153) *"substances, and summit . . . the pure act was produced":* These are the angels, created as God's highest beings ("the summit") and consisting of pure act.

12. (p. 153) *"Pure potentiality":* This is mere matter, the lowest part of creation.

13. (p. 153) *"Midway bound potentiality with act":* The heavens are subject to influences from on high and capable of exerting influence on things below them.

14. (p. 153) *"Jerome . . . a long lapse of centuries":* Saint Jerome (A.D. 340–420), best known for his translation of the Bible from Hebrew to produce the Latin Vulgate (from *editio vulgata*, or "common version"), believed that the angels existed for countless ages before the creation of the world. Dante rejects this view and agrees with the views Saint Thomas Aquinas sets forth in *Summa theologica* I, q. 61, a. 3.

15. (p. 153) *"this truth . . . By writers of the Holy Ghost":* Dante believes the correct view, that of Saint Thomas, has biblical support (see Genesis 1: 1 and Ecclesiastes 18: 1).

16. (p. 153) *"even reason seeth it somewhat":* Besides the revelations of writers of the Holy Ghost (the authors of such books as Genesis or Ecclesiastes who affirm the positions of Dante and Saint Thomas), human reason also stands against Saint Jerome's position. Angels were created for the purpose of moving the heavens, and if they had been created long before the rest of creation, they would have had no purpose or function.

17. (p. 153) *"three fires":* The Pilgrim's three fires are his three questions about angels—where, when, and how "these Loves" were created. Angels were created in the Empyrean; they were created contemporaneously with the universe (not before or afterward); and they were created perfectly good.

18. (p. 153) *"Nor could one reach, in counting, unto twenty . . . Disturbed the subject of your elements":* The time that passed between the creation and the fall of the rebel angels was extremely brief. Disturbing "the subject of your elements" may refer to earth, since in *Inferno* XXXIV: 122–126, Dante recounts that earth shrank back away from Satan when he was hurled from heaven toward earth.

19. (p. 153) *"The rest remained":* These are the rest of the angels who did not rebel. Note that Dante does not mention the neutral angels of *Inferno* III: 37–41, those who stood neither with God nor with Satan. Dante also does not discuss from which angelic orders the fallen angels came, although in *Il Convivio* II: iv he claims that some from each order fell.

20. (p. 153) *"this art":* The art is that of circling and contemplating the point of light that is God.

21. (p. 153) *"The occasion of the fall . . . Presumption of that One":* Satan's fall was caused by the archetypal sin of pride, or presumption.

22. (p. 153) *"modest . . . By the enlightening grace":* The angels who did not suffer from overweening pride are described as modest, for they waited for God's enlightening grace.

23. (p. 153) *"meritorious to receive this grace":* The degree of openness to grace depends upon love, something that is preordained.

24. (p. 154) *"They teach that such is the angelic nature . . . recollect, and will":* Beatrice now denounces the idea that angels have any memory, although they do have intelligence and will. This false doctrine was apparently taught in some schools of theology.

25. (p. 154) *"there below":* That is, on earth.

26. (p. 154) *"turned not away their sight":* Angels are so satisfied with the direct vision of God that they never turn away, and thus never have the need to recollect or to remember.

27. (p. 154) *"Believing they speak truth . . . greater sin and shame":* While some on earth are mistaken in their beliefs, it is far worse to maintain as truth what one does not even believe. Here Beatrice refers to ambitious and cynical theologians and preachers who substitute their own opinions for the word of God. What follows (ll. 85–126) is a digression by Beatrice away from her original subject (the orders of the angels) and a castigation of men who distort God's truths and who seek out their own personal glory.

28. (p. 154) *"One sayeth . . . whence to Spaniards and to Indians":* According to the biblical accounts in Matthew 27: 45 and Luke 23: 44, darkness fell over the land during the Crucifixion. However, the false preachers attacked by Beatrice maintain that a lunar eclipse caused the darkness and that it therefore darkened the entire half of the northern hemisphere from India to Spain. The orthodox account, however, describes the event as a miracle limited to Jerusalem.

29. (p. 155) *"not so many Lapi and Bindi / As fables such as these"*: These were extremely common nicknames for the names Jacopo and Ildebrando in Florence, and Beatrice declares that there were more fables preached by dishonest men on earth than people with this name in her native city.

30. (p. 155) *"the lambs"*: These are the unsuspecting members of the congregation who hear false ideas from sermons.

31. (p. 155) *"in the warfare to enkindle Faith . . . shields and lances"*: Sent by Christ to preach the true Gospel, the Apostles (unlike the arrogant priests of Dante's day) were armed with their faith, using it as a weapon to attack and as a shield for defense.

32. (p. 155) *"with jests and drolleries . . . The hood puffs out"*: Preachers who seek only the laughter or approval of their congregation puff up their cowls or hoods with arrogant pride and presumption when they succeed in making people laugh.

33. (p. 155) *"such a bird"*: This is a reference to the Devil, or Satan, who was often depicted in the Middle Ages as a winged demon.

34. (p. 155) *"what pardons"*: These are indulgences, which were bought in order to receive remission of sins. It is clear that Dante has no great faith in them, and views like his toward indulgences became crucial to the Protestant Reformation in the sixteenth century.

35. (p. 155) *"By this Saint Anthony his pig doth fatten"*: The symbol of Saint Anthony of Egypt (A.D. 251–356), regarded as the founder of monasticism, was the pig. The monks of the Order of Saint Anthony kept herds of pigs that were allowed to roam freely through the towns, and the credulous population, with their religious superstition, fed the pigs to fattening. Thus present-day preachers exploit the gullibility of the people for their profit, just as the pigs of Saint Anthony were fattened.

36. (p. 155) *"Paying in money without mark of coinage"*: That is, they used false coins. The meaning here is that the priests sold false indulgences.

37. (p. 155) *"digressed abundantly"*: Even Beatrice realizes that she has strayed far away from her topic—the orders of angels.

38. (p. 155) *"This nature . . . that can go so far"*: First Beatrice declares that neither human speech nor human fantasy could express the infinite number of angels—they are countless.

39. (p. 155) *"Daniel . . . Number determinate is kept concealed"*: In the Bible, Daniel 7: 10, the number of those who minister to God is countless.

40. (pp. 155–156) *"The primal light . . . diversely fervid is or tepid"*: Besides stating that the number of angels is infinite, Beatrice also contends that God's light is differently received by angels, so that the degree to which an angel may love is based upon its differing capacity to receive light.

41. (p. 156) *"The height behold now and the amplitude"*: The height refers to the entire angelic hierarchy, while the breadth or amplitude refers to the angels' infinite number.

42. (p. 156) *"so many mirrors"*: The angels reflecting the light of God are like mirrors, with God's light shining in each of them.

CANTO XXX

1. (p. 157) *six thousand miles remote from us*: In ll. 1–9, Dante describes the fading of the stars just before dawn begins to brighten the morning sky while noon (the "sixth hour" of l. 2) glows 6,000 miles away. Basically, Dante used the figure of 20,400 miles as the circumference of earth; from sunrise to noon, earth would revolve approximately one-quarter of its circumference, or about 5,100 miles. If the sun is 6,000 miles away from noon, and since noon and sunrise are six hours apart, there remains about one hour for dawn to break (one hour during which the sun will move about 900 miles). This sight is then compared (ll. 10–15) to the disappearance of the nine circles dancing around the central point of light that is God.

2. (p. 157) *The handmaid of the sun*: This is Aurora, the dawn.

3. (p. 157) *the most beautiful*: The most beautiful planet or star is probably Venus.

4. (p. 157) *the Triumph*: This is a reference to the dancing or whirling of the angelic orders.

5. (p. 157) *by what itself encloses:* Although the point of light that is God seems to be ringed by the angelic orders, it is actually God who contains them all.

6. (p. 157) *Scant . . . serve the present turn:* Nothing Dante has ever written about the beauty of Beatrice up to this point in *The Divine Comedy* could suffice to describe her beauty accurately here.

7. (p. 157) *the comic or the tragic poet:* Dante considered the style he employed in his epic poem to be "comic"—that is, written in a familiar style, as opposed to an elevated, serious, and tragic style. In addition, his poem has a happy ending, something Dante identified with comedy.

8. (p. 157) *From the first day:* In *La Vita Nuova* II, Dante claims that he was nine years old when he first encountered Beatrice.

9. (p. 158) *this sequence must desist . . . every artist at his uttermost:* As his poem draws to its conclusion, Dante announces that he no longer has the ability to describe accurately Beatrice's great beauty, as it becomes virtually synonymous with a beatific vision of Paradise. As he states, every artist must stop at his "uttermost."

10. (p. 158) *"from the greatest body . . . to the heaven that is pure light":* Beatrice announces that the two have passed beyond the Primum Mobile (the "greatest body" in terms of size when compared to the Empyrean) and into the Empyrean, the final part of heaven; it is composed to of pure light, which is the mind of God.

11. (p. 158) *"the one host and the other":* These are the angelic orders and the souls of the blessed.

12. (p. 158) *"Here shalt thou see . . . in the same aspects":* The Pilgrim is allowed to see the human souls of the blessed as they will be seen after the Last Judgment—their souls joined to their fleshly bodies. Earlier, in *Paradiso* XXII: 58–68, the Pilgrim had wished for such a vision, and now by a special privilege never afforded another living being, he has his wish granted.

13. (p. 158) *"at the final judgment thou shalt see":* Beatrice promises the Pilgrim that he will be saved and reside in Paradise with the blessed after his death.

14. (p. 158) *Even as a sudden lightning:* This is perhaps a reference to the experience of Saint Paul on the road to Damascus who, like the Pilgrim, experienced a blinding light (see the Bible, *Acts* 22: 6–11). Even

though in *Inferno* II: 28 the Pilgrim had protested that he was neither Aeneas nor Paul, he has actually managed to trump both of these famous figures in literature and religion by his own epic journey toward God.

15. (p. 158) *"Ever the Love . . . ready for its flame":* The Pilgrim is assured that every soul joining the blessed in the Empyrean experiences what he has just experienced: The new arrival is compared to the candle that must be made ready for the flame, or the vision of God it will soon receive.

16. (p. 158) *mine eyes were fortified against it:* The Pilgrim now begins to experience the rapture that all those who attain salvation will enjoy, a privilege that had to be prepared so that his sight could bear the power of his vision.

17. (pp. 158–159) *a river . . . rubies that are set in gold:* This river probably represents God's divine grace flowing freely. The souls of the elect are golden flowers on its banks and the ruby-red sparks (the angels) move as if they were bees in a flower garden. The ruby-red color suggests love.

18. (p. 159) *"The river and the topazes . . . foreshadowing prefaces":* The angels now change from ruby-red to topaz color (usually yellow), and these sights are identified as only mere "foreshadowing prefaces" of what the Pilgrim will later see.

19. (p. 159) *better mirrors:* These would be eyes that better reflect God. Note that up to this point, Beatrice's eyes reflected God's light, but now the Pilgrim's eyes become capable of doing so.

20. (p. 159) *Both of the Courts of Heaven:* These are the angels and the souls of the blessed.

21. (pp. 159–160) *There is a light above . . . too large a girdle for the sun:* The angels and the blessed see God through His light. God's light reflects upward from the convex outer surface of the Primum Mobile, giving that realm "vitality and power." The light "expands itself in circular form" (l. 103) and seems like a circle of light all around.

22. (p. 160) *in more ranks than a thousand . . . Rose in its extremest leaves!:* The souls of all those who "have from us returned," or who have earned a place in heaven and have returned there from their earthly life, are arranged in what is actually an amphitheater and what will also be called a Rose (l. 117). The Pilgrim sees the reflection of the blessed, all of whom gaze upward toward the vision of God.

23. (p. 160) *My vision . . . but comprehended all:* The Pilgrim now experiences the entire scene directly and without any limitations of distance. He has now passed beyond the point where space, time, and distance mean anything, where God reigns directly and not through secondary agents or natural events.

24. (p. 160) *the yellow of the Rose Eternal:* The center of the Eternal, or Celestial, Rose is yellow or gold in color, with the petals of the flowers being formed by the ranks of the blessed.

25. (p. 160) *"the white stoles":* The garments of the blessed are pure white, reflecting various verses in the biblical Book of Revelation, including 3: 4–5 and 7: 13–14.

26. (p. 160) *"so filled to overflowing . . . henceforward are few people wanting!":* The Celestial Rose, this heavenly amphitheater, is divided into two parts—one containing the souls of those who lived before Christ's time (souls rescued by Christ during the Harrowing of Hell) and those who lived afterward. The first part is already full, and the second part has only a few places remaining, underscoring Dante's belief that the end of the world was not far off.

27. (p. 160) *"Before thou suppest":* That is, before your death and your ascension to your place in this assembly of the blessed.

28. (p. 160) *"noble Henry, who shall come / To redress Italy":* The empty chair in Paradise awaits the soul of Emperor Henry VII (c.1275–1313), who is still alive back on earth at the time of the Pilgrim's journey in 1300. Henry was supported by Pope Clement V and elected Holy Roman Emperor in 1308. In 1309 he went to Italy to receive the imperial crown. Supporters of the empire, Dante among them, saw in him their hopes for a future free of the bickering that characterized medieval Italy. He was opposed by Guelph forces, especially those in Florence, and eventually lost the Pope's support as a result of French pressure. He died suddenly at Buonconvento, a small town near Siena and was buried in Pisa.

29. (p. 160) *"Blind covetousness":* Dante attributes the opposition to Henry VII to greed.

30. (p. 161) *"A Prefect . . . will not walk with him"*: The prefect is Pope Clement V, whom in *Inferno* XIX: 82–87, Dante has already assigned in the future to the circle of Hell punishing simonists. Initially supporting Henry, Clement withdrew real support after Henry's entrance into Italy because of the pressure exerted upon him by King Philip the Fair, who supported Charles of Valois' claims to sovereignty over portions of Italy.

31. (p. 161) *"he shall be thrust down . . . him of Alagna lower go!"*: These are the last words Beatrice utters in Paradise, and they express the same kind of righteous indignation that always characterizes Dante's treatment of the corruption of the medieval papacy. Beatrice's remarks here must be glossed with reference to Dante's treatment of the sin of simony in *Inferno* XIX. The term "simony," which signifies the buying and selling of church offices, pardons, or other favors, derives from Simon Magus, who in the Bible, Acts 8: 9–24, tries to purchase the power of the Holy Spirit from the Apostles John and Peter. In the eighth circle of Hell, simonists are stuck upside down, in vessels resembling baptismal fonts, with the soles of their feet burning. Dante places Pope Nicholas III in Hell for simony; when the Pilgrim approaches this sinner, Nicholas asks the Pilgrim if he is Pope Boniface VIII, since he knows that this pope will eventually come to replace him. As each new arrival reaches the spot in Hell where simony (a sin Dante particularly associates with the popes) is punished, the previous occupant is pushed farther down into the bowels of Hell. The fictional date of the Pilgrim's journey is 1300. Since Pope Boniface VIII died in 1303 (some years before Dante the Poet completed his poem), Dante the Poet can make a prediction that will prove to be true, at least with respect to Boniface's death. *Inferno* XIX also predicts the eminent arrival in Hell of yet another pontiff, Clement V (born 1264; ruled as pontiff 1304–1314), the man responsible for the "Babylonian captivity" of the Church, moving the papacy to Avignon, France. Beatrice confirms the earlier prediction of the damnation of both Boniface VIII and Clement V, indicating that Boniface ("him of Alagna"—a reference to Boniface's birthplace, Alagna or Anagni), designated as Nicholas III's replacement in the burning hole in *Inferno* XIX, will yield his place to Clement V and be thrust even deeper into the depths of Hell.

CANTO XXXI

1. (p. 163) *In fashion then . . . a snow-white rose:* While a red rose has been a traditional symbol of earthly love in European literature, Dante's white rose reflects heavenly love.

2. (p. 163) *the saintly host . . . the other host:* The "saintly host" refers to the souls of the blessed, as opposed to the angels, "the other host."

3. (p. 163) *Even as a swarm of bees:* The Poet compares the flight of the angels dipping into the flowers (the souls of the blessed) to swarming bees.

4. (p. 163) *To where its love abideth evermore:* That is, to God.

5. (p. 163) *They carried something of the peace and ardor:* Dante's simile is an inverted one, since the bees here carry something from God to the flowers, whereas in nature, bees carry pollen from the flower to their hive.

6. (p. 163) *Nor did the interposing . . . the sight and splendor:* Even though the beelike movement of the angels was before the Pilgrim's eyes, it did not obstruct the vision of God's light in the Rose by the blessed.

7. (p. 163) *with ancient people and with modern:* That is, with people from the Old Testament (the virtuous Hebrews) and with New Testament Christians.

8. (p. 163) *one mark had all its look and love:* All vision (a function of the intellect) and love (a function of the will) are directed in Paradise toward one goal, God.

9. (p. 163) *O Trinal Light, that in a single star:* Once again, Dante draws attention to the mystery of the Holy Trinity, three aspects of God joined in a unity.

10. (p. 164) *our tempest here below!:* The reference is to the confused affairs on earth.

11. (p. 164) *If the barbarians . . . the Lateran / Above all mortal things eminent:* Dante now compares the wondrous sights he witnessed to the amazement of the barbarians when they first encountered the splendors of ancient Rome. Helice (also known as Callisto), one of the nymphs, was exiled after being seduced by Jupiter, to whom she bore a son, Arcas. Jupiter transformed Helice into the constellation Ursa Major, the Great Bear or Big Dipper; and her son into Ursa Minor, the Little Bear or Little Dipper. For Dante's classical sources,

Ovid's *Metamorphoses* II: 496–530. A region every day covered by Helice would therefore be somewhere in the north of Europe, the origin (from the perspective of Dante and other Italians) of the barbarians. The Lateran refers to the Roman palace where popes in Dante's day resided. The building was destroyed by fire in 1308 and subsequently rebuilt in the sixteenth century. Dante probably means to use the Lateran as symbol for Rome in general, since the palace was supposedly donated by the Emperor Constantine to Pope Sylvester and was the seat of the Catholic Church before the Vatican Palace became its headquarters.

12. (p. 164) *And as a pilgrim . . . some day to retell how it was:* Dante compares the impossibility of describing what he sees to the experience of a pilgrim who vows to visit a shrine and then wonders how he will be able to describe his religious experience.

13. (p. 164) *And round I turned me . . . An Old Man habited like the glorious people:* Earlier on the Mountain of Purgatory, the Pilgrim turned to Virgil and discovered to his dismay that Virgil had disappeared (*Purgatorio* XXX: 40–54). Now, parallel to that experience, Beatrice disappears without a word, leaving the Pilgrim in the care of an "Old Man," dressed in white like the other "glorious people," the blessed. Line 102 will reveal this individual to be Saint Bernard, the abbot of Clairvaux (1090–1153) and the inspiration of the Second Crusade. Since Bernard was associated in his life and writings with mystical contemplation, he is appropriate to lead the Pilgrim to the final phase of his journey.

14. (p. 165) *"to the third round / Of the first rank":* Beatrice has resumed her customary position in the Celestial Rose. The Virgin Mary sits on the top of the tier, Eve sits under her, and Rachel (symbol of the Contemplative Life) below Eve. Beatrice earns an extremely choice seat from Dante, sitting to the right of Rachel. Thus symbols of contemplation and revelation are seated together.

15. (p. 165) *Reflecting from herself:* The Pilgrim is still unable to see God directly but instead sees Him through His rays reflected from the vision of Beatrice.

16. (p. 165) *"didst endure / In Hell":* In *Inferno* II: 52–108, the Poet describes how Beatrice descended into Limbo to ask Virgil to guide

the Pilgrim through Hell and most of Purgatory. In so doing, Beatrice imitated the actions of Christ in the Harrowing of Hell.

17. (p. 165) *"from a slave hast brought me unto freedom"*: The Pilgrim's journey toward knowledge and lack of sin is defined as giving slaves their freedom. Freedom from sin, the only true freedom, is the gist of the message of Dante's poem.

18. (p. 165) *"Smiled ... unto the eternal fountain turned"*: Beatrice's smile implies that Dante will attain his wish, eternal salvation.

19. (p. 165) *"will grant us every grace ... her faithful Bernard am"*: Saint Bernard finally identifies himself, guaranteeing the voyage to the vision of God because of his devotion to the Virgin Mary. In fact, Bernard's writings contain four homilies and nine sermons about the Virgin Mary.

20. (p. 166) *"As he who peradventure from Croatia ... By contemplation tasted of that peace"*: Dante now describes himself as a pilgrim from distant Croatia who comes to Rome to see the Veronica, the true image of Christ that was left on a cloth that a woman offered to Christ on his way to Calvary to wipe the sweat from his brow. On display at Saint Peter's Cathedral, the veil was an extremely popular pilgrimage destination. The pilgrims' amazement at seeing the true face of the savior is equal to the amazement the Pilgrim feels when he looks upon Bernard, a man who had already gazed upon the vision of God through contemplation.

21. (p. 166) *"Thine eyes ... But mark the circles to the most remote"*: Bernard directs the Pilgrim to look up toward God and the Virgin Mary and not down toward him.

22. (p. 166) *Surpass in splendor all the other front:* The Virgin Mary's radiance surpasses that of the other blessed.

23. (p. 166) *the pole / That Phaeton drove badly:* The myth of Phaëton has already been invoked in *Inferno* XVII: 106–108, *Purgatorio* XXIX: 118–120, and *Paradiso* XVII: 3. The pole refers to the axle, or shaft, of the chariot (the sun). When the axle broke because Phaëton lost control of the horses drawing the sun, the sun came so close to earth that it almost consumed the planet by fire.

24. (p. 166) *that pacific oriflamme:* The Angel Gabriel supposedly gave a standard to the ancient kings of France and they adopted it as their banner in wartime. The standard represented a flame on a background of gold. Here, the flame-shaped banner is used to describe the summit of the Celestial Rose, where the Queen of Heaven, the Virgin Mary, sits in glory. Naturally, this banner is peaceful, as opposed to the war-like associations of the French banner.

25. (p. 166) *Each differing in effulgence and in kind:* Dante shares the belief of his times that each angel was a different species, and so each differs in radiance and in its activities.

26. (p. 166) *A beauty smiling:* The Virgin Mary, like Beatrice, smiles to underline her joy.

27. (p. 166) *And if I had in speaking . . . I should not dare:* Out of reverence for the Virgin, the Poet refuses to describe her radiance and beauty in detail, and, indeed, would not be able to do so with all his literary skill.

CANTO XXXII

1. (p. 168) *Absorbed in his delight . . . office of a teacher:* Bernard seems to be completely absorbed in the contemplation of the Virgin Mary. I is possible that the Poet means to say that the mystic instructs the Pilgrim on the hosts of heaven without moving his eyes from the sight of the Queen of Heaven.

2. (p. 168) *"The wound . . . closed up and anointed":* By giving birth to Jesus, Mary provided humanity with the means to heal the wound of Original Sin.

3. (p. 168) *"She at her feet . . . who opened it and pierced it":* Eve sits below Mary; it was Eve who caused the original sin.

4. (p. 168) *"Rachel":* In *Inferno* IV: 60 Dante mentions Rachel, the second wife of Jacob and mother of Joseph and Benjamin (Genesis XXIX–XXX), as having been released from Limbo during the Harrowing of Hell by Christ, and again, in *Purgatorio* XXVII: 100–108, as being encountered in a dream. Rachel sits on the third horizontal row of the blessed, next to Beatrice, as we know from *Inferno* II: 100–102, where the reader has already learned that Beatrice was sitting by Rachel when the Virgin Mary sent Lucy to Beatrice to inform her of Dante's plight on earth.

5. (p. 168) *"in manner as thou seest":* To understand the arrangement being described by Saint Bernard, a diagram of the Celestial or Mystic Rose is useful:

The Celestial Rose

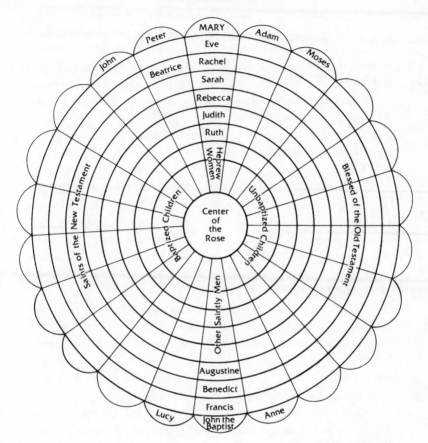

(adapted from Sayers, 1962)

6. (p. 168) *"Sarah, Rebecca, Judith"*: Sarah was the wife of Abraham and mother of Isaac; Rebecca married Isaac and became the mother of Esau and Jacob; Judith killed Holofernes, general of the Assyrians, and delivered the townspeople of Bethulia.

7. (p. 168) *"her who was / Ancestress of the Singer . . . 'Miserere mei'"*: Ruth was the great-grandmother of King David (encountered in *Paradiso* XX: 37), who committed adultery with Bathsheba, wife of Uriah. David wrote Psalm 51, a psalm of penitence: *Miserere mei* ("Have mercy on me").

8. (p. 168) *"through the Rose go down from leaf to leaf "*: Dante describes the seats occupied by the blessed as if they were rose petals.

9. (p. 168) *"And downward from the seventh row ... Hebrew women"*: Beginning with Mary at the top and followed by six other Hebrew women who are named specifically (Eve, Rachel, Sarah, Rebecca, Judith, and Ruth), the column is then occupied by other Hebrew women from the Old Testament. Dante does not name them for reasons of economy.

10. (p. 168) *"where perfect is the flower ... With vacant spaces"*: The principal division of the blessed in Paradise is between the saints of the Old Testament, who supposedly believed in Christ to come, and those of the New Testament, who believed in Christ already come. It is significant that while the partition of the Celestial Rose containing the Old Testament saints is completely filled ("where perfect is the flower"), the part of the Rose devoted to the other group still has a few vacancies ("with vacant spaces"). The assumption is that when these last seats are occupied, the world will come to an end, followed by the Last Judgment.

11. (p. 169) *"So opposite doth that of the great John"*: Directly opposite the column topped by the Virgin Mary and containing Hebrew women stands another column topped by John the Baptist, who was beheaded two years before the Crucifixion and who therefore had to wait in Limbo for that period until he was rescued during the Harrowing of Hell by Christ.

12. (p. 169) *"Francis, and Benedict, and Augustine"*: Under John the Baptist are seated Saint Francis of Assisi (*Paradiso* XI: 43–117), Saint Benedict (*Paradiso* XXII: 28–98), and Saint Augustine of Hippo. Dante mentions Augustine only briefly earlier (*Paradiso* X: 120). Born in A.D. 354, he was converted and baptized by Saint Ambrose in Milan in 387 and later became bishop of Hippo in Africa, dying there in A.D. 430 during the siege of the city by Vandals. He is best known for his *Confessions* and the *City of God*. The three men correspond respectively to Eve, Rachel, and Sarah on the other side of the Celestial Rose.

13. (p. 169) *"In equal measure shall this garden fill"*: According to Dante, Divine Providence had preordained that the same number of blessed would fill the Old Testament partition and the New Testament partition of paradise. Besides the poetic advantage of symmetry, this notion probably reflects Dante's view that the world would soon come to an end, for when all the places in Paradise have been filled, he apparently assumes, God will close up shop, as it were, and the Last Judgment will ensue.

14. (p. 169) *"And know that downward from that rank which cleaves . . . any true election had":* Saint Bernard explains that there is a horizontal division that divides the amphitheater-shaped Celestial Rose into lower and upper partitions. The lower section contains the souls of children who died before they reached the age of reason ("before they any true election had") and therefore before they could choose.

15. (p. 169) *"Now doubtest thou . . . fitted to the finger here":* Reading the Pilgrim's mind as occurs so frequently in the poem, Saint Bernard answers the Pilgrim's doubts about why some children have higher seats than others, since none won their place in heaven by their own merits or by the exercise of their free will based on reason. He will learn that their position in the Rose, and therefore their degree of beatitude, depends upon predestination, not on merit. "Eternal law" (l. 55) establishes this condition, and chance (causal point) plays no part, and the correspondence between a soul's merits and God's grace is precisely like the perfect fit of a ring on the finger. Dante's ideas here were not accepted by other theologians, such as Saint Thomas Aquinas, who denied that there could be different degrees of beatitude among the children in paradise.

16. (p. 169) *"sine causa":* This a Latin legal term meaning "without cause."

17. (pp. 169–170) *"The King . . . the effect suffice":* God ("the King") showers His grace upon humanity in ways that pass the human understanding. As Saint Bernard orders the Pilgrim, "Let here the effect suffice." Redemption is a matter of faith, not of reason, and the explanation for why some souls are predestined for salvation and others are not is simply beyond logic.

18. (p. 170) *"in those twins . . . to the color of the hair":* Saint Bernard argues that the mystery of predestination can be seen in the different treatment experienced by Jacob and Esau, the twin sons of Rebecca and Isaac, as told in the Bible, Genesis 25: 21–34. Apparently Dante believed that the favoritism shown to Jacob was caused by the fact that Esau had red hair, while Jacob did not.

19. (p. 170) *"their first acuteness":* God bestows the original capacity for grace when He creates the soul.

20. (p. 170) *"in the early centuries ... the faith of parents only":* During the period in the Bible from Adam to Abraham, the faith parents had in the coming Messiah was sufficient to ensure the salvation of their children.

21. (p. 170) *"After the earlier ages ... by circumcision":* After Abraham's time, circumcision was required for salvation of male children.

22. (p. 170) *"Without the baptism absolute of Christ":* After the Crucifixion, baptism was required for the salvation of children, and unbaptized children were destined for Limbo (see *Inferno* IV: 30–36).

23. (p. 170) *"Look now into the face that unto Christ":* Saint Bernard directs the Pilgrim to gaze upon the Virgin Mary to prepare him for the vision of Christ that is to follow.

24. (p. 170) *the holy minds:* These are the angels.

25. (p. 170) *And the same Love that first descended there, /* "Ave Maria, gratia plena": The Love is the Angel Gabriel, who descended to Mary to make the Annunciation *Ave maria, gratia plena,* or "Hail Mary, full of grace." See the Bible, Luke 1: 28, for the description of the event.

26. (p. 170) *Unto the canticle divine responded:* The entire host of the Celestial Rose responds in prayer.

27. (p. 171) *"Who is the Angel":* The Pilgrim asks this question, but the Poet has already told us that it is the Angel Gabriel. One of Dante's most interesting poetic inventions is that the Annunciation to the Virgin Mary by the Angel Gabriel will continue throughout eternity in Paradise.

28. (p. 171) *that one who delighted him in Mary:* This is Saint Bernard.

29. (p. 171) *the star of morning:* This is Venus.

30. (p. 171) *"who bore the palm":* In many representations of the Annunciation, the Angel Gabriel carries a palm branch.

31. (p. 171) *"the great patricians":* These are the patricians of the court over which Mary reigns.

32. (p. 171) *"Those two":* The two highest positions after Mary's belong to Saint Peter and Adam. They are called "the two roots of this Rose" (l. 120) because each represents the two groups of the blessed—those who believed in Christ to come, and those who believed in Christ who had already come. Adam sits on the Virgin's left (ll. 121–123), while

Saint Peter ("into whose keeping Christ / The keys committed") sits on her right side (ll. 124–126).

33. (p. 171) *"Augusta"*: This is a Latin term for Empress, referring to the Virgin Mary.

34. (p. 171) *"And he who all the evil days beheld"*: Sitting on Peter's right is Saint John the Evangelist, believed to be the author of *Revelation*, which foretold all the calamities of the Church in the future.

35. (p. 171) *"That leader"*: This is Moses, seated on Adam's left side.

36. (p. 171) *"Anna"*: Saint Anne, the mother of Mary, sits directly opposite Saint Peter, with John the Baptist seated on her left. Interestingly enough, Anne gazes constantly at her daughter Mary, not upon God, a human touch of maternal love.

37. (p. 172) *"Lucìa sits"*: Saint Lucy sits directly across from Adam, with John the Baptist on her right hand. She has already assisted the Pilgrim two times in the poem: first by sending Beatrice to his aid (*Inferno* II: 97–108), then by carrying the Pilgrim up the mountain to the gate of Purgatory (*Purgatorio* IX: 52–63).

38. (p. 172) *"as a good tailor . . . will turn our eyes"*: Saint Bernard now realizes that the Pilgrim's time is limited, and like a good tailor who makes the most of the cloth at his disposal, he urges the Pilgrim to gaze directly toward God.

39. (p. 172) *"As far as possible through his effulgence"*: The Pilgrim will now gaze upon God to the extent that grace and his preparation for this moment will allow.

40. (p. 172) *"Moving thy wings . . . that one who has the power to aid thee"*: The vision of God is not assured but must depend upon the Pilgrim's effort, assisted by prayer (l. 147)—symbolized by the image of the beating of wings—and by the assistance of the Virgin Mary, "who has the power to aid thee."

41. (p. 172) *And he began this holy orison:* The Pilgrim's prayer will be spoken for him by Saint Bernard.

CANTO XXXIII

1. (p. 173) *"Thou Virgin Mother"*: The last canto of *The Divine Comedy* opens with Saint Bernard's prayer to the Virgin to grant the Pilgrim the grace to see God (ll. 1–39).

2. (p. 173) *"the spiritual lives":* The reference is to the fate of mankind as spirit after death in Hell, Purgatory, or Paradise.

3. (p. 174) *"the Chief Pleasure":* This is God, the final goal of the Pilgrim's journey and of mankind in general.

4. (p. 174) *"sound thou mayst preserve / After so great a vision":* In addition to requesting assistance for the Pilgrim to experience the vision of God, Saint Bernard also asks the Virgin Mary to help the Pilgrim after he returns from "so great a vision" to earth again.

5. (p. 174) *"See Beatrice . . . clasp their hands to thee!":* This is the last mention of Beatrice in the poem, as the souls of the blessed join Bernard in his prayer and clasp their hands.

6. (p. 174) *The eyes . . . Eternal Light they turned:* Mary's eyes now turn toward Saint Bernard to indicate that she is pleased to entertain his entreaty. Unlike Beatrice, she does not smile before turning back toward the "Eternal Light" of God.

7. (p. 174) *but I already / Was of my own accord:* Now Saint Bernard disappears, leaving the Pilgrim alone with his contemplation of God.

8. (p. 174) *From that time forward what I saw was greater / Than our discourse:* Dante the Poet reminds the reader that he has returned from his journey and has recounted what he saw to the best of his limited, human ability.

9. (p. 174) *Ceases my vision:* Dante the Poet continues to speak, stating that after he has returned to earth, his vision of Paradise fades compared to the experience he lived through as Dante the Pilgrim.

10. (pp. 174–175) *Even thus the snow . . . soothsayings of the Sibyl lost:* The difficulty the Poet experiences in recalling his vision is now compared to the snow melting under the sun's heat or the leaves containing the Cumaean Sibyl's prophecies being scattered to the wind (see Virgil's *Aeneid* III: 441–451 and VI). In short, the experience of mystical vision is always ephemeral for mortal beings.

11. (p. 175) *O Light Supreme . . . sparkle of thy glory:* Dante the Poet (not Dante the Pilgrim) addresses God Himself and asks for enough inspiration to capture "a single sparkle" of His glory (l. 71). Note that here he no longer addresses the pagan muses or Apollo as he does in the first two canticles of the poem.

12. (p. 175) *I think the keenness . . . Which I endured:* the narrative voice of the poem shifts back to the perspective of Dante the Pilgrim, who now recounts his active participation in the final vision.

13. (p. 175) *the Glory Infinite:* God.

14. (p. 175) *I saw . . . one simple light:* Dante now attempts to describe what he saw when he gazed directly upon God. One explanation is that he saw the universe as if it were a single book, bound up by God's love (ll. 85–87). This beautiful literary image is then followed by a philosophical and theological one in ll. 88–90, as Dante explains how in God both substance and accident are joined together in a unity so that there is only "one simple light." Thus things existing in themselves (substances) and the qualities residing in substances (accidents) are fused together only in God.

15. (p. 175) *The universal fashion of this knot:* What the Pilgrim saw was basically the substantial form of the universe, what makes it what it essentially is and not the accidents that accompany its substantial form. This presumes that the Pilgrim saw into the mind of God, an experience impossible to reproduce in human terms or in poetry, but naturally Dante the Poet recounts this experience by describing its ineffability.

16. (p. 175) *more lethargy . . . the shade of Argo!:* Dante the Poet notes that in the present time on earth, one moment of this experience now recalled by his present memory involves more oblivion or loss of memory than is involved in recalling an event that took place more than twenty-five centuries ago, the voyage of the Argonauts in the ship named Argo on its way to seek the golden fleece. During that journey, the sea-god Neptune was amazed to see this first ship as its shadow passed over the water.

17. (p. 176) *Because the good, which object is of will:* The will's object is the good, and since all good is contained in God, the thought of turning away willingly from such an experience is impossible to consider.

18. (p. 176) *Shorter henceforward will my language fall . . . moisten at the breast:* Here is yet another image of the ineffability theme—in this case, the Poet's language has no more power than that of an infant.

19. (p. 176) *three circles . . . Iris is by Iris:* What the Pilgrim sees in the "High Light" are three circles of three different colors (another reference to the Holy Trinity), and each contains the other just as one rainbow (Iris) can produce a second rainbow (Iris).

20. (p. 176) *'tis not enough to call it little!:* In attempting a description of the Holy Trinity, the Poet once again emphasizes that he can recall almost nothing of what he has seen.

21. (p. 176) *O Light Eterne, sole in thyself . . . and smilest on thyself!:* This tercet, one of Dante's most famous, defines the self-contained quality of the Holy Trinity perfectly with its very structure.

22. (p. 176) *That circulation . . . painted with our effigy:* The Poet describes the final vision of the poem, that of Christ, the second person of the Holy Trinity. The vision is specifically Christ of the Incarnation, as within the light the Pilgrim discerns the human features, "our effigy," of Christ.

23. (pp. 176–177) *As the geometrician . . . A flash of lightning:* We now learn that just as mathematicians have been unable to square the circle (a problem posed by the ancient Greek philosophers), in like manner it is impossible to describe God in human terms. Nevertheless, again returning to the metaphor of wings ("my own wings," l. 139), Dante underscores that his own efforts to understand this vision were insufficient until "a flash of lightning"—a flash of understanding caused by God's grace—made him understand how the Incarnation might be possible, and how human nature can be united with divine nature in God.

24. (p. 177) *Here vigor failed the lofty fantasy:* At the very moment the Pilgrim understands the dual nature of God, he loses his ability to describe the event. Fantasy here means his power to receive images, not to make them. In short, the Pilgrim has reached the end of his capacity to receive the vision, a function of the intellect.

25. (p. 177) *But now was turning my desire and will:* The subject of this sentence is the last line of the poem: "The Love which moves the sun and the other stars" (l. 145). At the moment when the Pilgrim's fantasy falls short, he realizes that his will and his desire are in perfect agreement with God's love (his will and his desire turn like a perfectly balanced wheel because they are being controlled by Divine Love). God is, in effect, "the Love which moves the sun and the other stars," perhaps the most moving definition of God ever proposed. The poem ends on the word "stars" in the Italian original as well as in most good translations, just as the first two canticles, *Inferno* and *Purgatorio*, have done. Thus Dante reminds his readers that we are to look upward toward heaven if we are to attain happiness in this world and in the next.

Six Sonnets on Dante's
The Divine Comedy

BY

HENRY WADSWORTH LONGFELLOW

(1807–1882)

I

Oft have I seen at some cathedral door
　　A laborer, pausing in the dust and heat,
　　Lay down his burden, and with reverent feet
　　Enter, and cross himself, and on the floor
Kneel to repeat his paternoster o'er;
　　Far off the noises of the world retreat;
　　The loud vociferations of the street
　　Become an undistinguishable roar.
So, as I enter here from day to day,
　　And leave my burden at this minster gate,
　　Kneeling in prayer, and not ashamed to pray,
The tumult of the time disconsolate
　　To inarticulate murmurs dies away,
　　While the eternal ages watch and wait.

II

How strange the sculptures that adorn these towers!
　　This crowd of statues, in whose folded sleeves
　　Birds build their nests; while canopied with leaves
　　Parvis and portal bloom like trellised bowers,
And the vast minster seems a cross of flowers!
　　But fiends and dragons on the gargoyled eaves
　　Watch the dead Christ between the living thieves,
　　And, underneath, the traitor Judas lowers!

347

Ah! from what agonies of heart and brain,
   What exultations trampling on despair,
   Tenderness, what tears, what hate of wrong,
What passionate outcry of a soul in pain,
   Uprose this poem of the earth and air,
   This mediaeval miracle of song!

III

I enter, and I see thee in the gloom
   Of the long aisles, O poet saturnine!
   And strive to make my steps keep pace with thine.
   The air is filled with some unknown perfume;
The congregation of the dead make room
   For thee to pass; the votive tapers shine;
   Like rooks that haunt Ravenna's groves of pine
   The hovering echoes fly from tomb to tomb.
From the confessionals I hear arise
   Rehearsals of forgotten tragedies,
   And lamentations from the crypts below;
And then a voice celestial that begins
   With the pathetic words, "Although your sins
   As scarlet be," and ends with "as the snow."

IV

With snow-white veil and garments as of flame,
   She stands before thee, who so long ago
   Filled thy young heart with passion and the woe
   From which thy song in all its splendors came;
And while with stern rebuke she speaks thy name,
   The ice about thy heart melts as the snow
   On mountain heights, and in swift overflow
   Comes gushing from thy lips in sobs of shame.

Thou makest full confession; and a gleam,
  As of the dawn on some dark forest cast,
  Seems on thy lifted forehead to increase;
Lethe and Eunoe—the remembered dream
  And the forgotten sorrow—bring at last
  That perfect pardon which is perfect peace.

V

I lift mine eyes, and all the windows blaze
  With forms of Saints and holy men who died,
  Here martyred and hereafter glorified;
  And the great Rose upon its leaves displays
Christ's Triumph, and the angelic roundelays,
  With splendor upon splendor multiplied;
  And Beatrice again at Dante's side
  No more rebukes, but smiles her words of praise.
And then the organ sounds, and unseen choirs
  Sing the old Latin hymns of peace and love
  And benedictions of the Holy Ghost;
And the melodious bells among the spires
  O'er all the house-tops and through heaven above
  Proclaim the elevation of the Host!

VI

O star of morning and of liberty!
  O bringer of the light, whose splendor shines
  Above the darkness of the Apennines,
  Forerunner of the day that is to be!
The voices of the city and the sea,
  The voices of the mountains and the pines,
  Repeat thy song, till the familiar lines
  Are footpaths for the thought of Italy!

Thy fame is blown abroad from all the heights,
   Through all the nations; and a sound is heard,
   As of a mighty wind, and men devout,
Strangers of Rome, and the new proselytes,
   In their own language hear thy wondrous word,
   And many are amazed and many doubt.

Inspired by Dante and the *Paradiso*

Long is the way
And hard, that out of hell leads up to light.

—John Milton, from *Paradise Lost*

Poetry

Perhaps the greatest English-language legacy of Dante's *Paradiso* is John Milton's *Paradise Lost* (1667, second edition 1674), a twelve-book poem in blank verse. As a young student, Milton fantasized about bringing the poetic elocution of Homer and Virgil to the relatively young English tongue, just as Dante had done with his native Italian. Milton contemplated writing an epic for thirty years; as he thought about possible subject matter, he considered the King Arthur legends as seriously as the Christian figures Adam and Eve. His graceful, sonorous *Paradise Lost* is now often cited as the most influential epic poem in English.

A retelling of the biblical story of mankind's Fall from grace, *Paradise Lost* opens shortly after the dramatic expulsion of Satan and his army of angels from Heaven. A cosmic battle between good and evil quickly follows—one that ranges across vast, splendid tracts of time and space, from the wild abyss of Chaos and the fiery lake of Hell to God's newly created Garden of Eden. To tell this grand story, Milton invokes the Muse in the Homeric tradition:

What in me is dark,
Illumine; what is low, raise and support!
That to the height of this great argument
I may assert the eternal Providence,
And justify the ways of God to men.

351

Controversy still swirls around Milton's magnificent and sympathetic characterization of Satan. The portrait is so compelling that many critics and poets, including William Blake and Percy Bysshe Shelley, have maintained that Satan is the true hero of Milton's story. Blake wrote, "The reason Milton wrote in fetters when he wrote of Angels and God, and at liberty when of Devils and Hell, is because he was a true poet and of the Devil's party without knowing it." Indeed, in Milton's *Of Education* (1644) he promotes the study of poetry and the classics rather than of Christian thought. Milton most likely prized Dante's *Paradiso* as highly as he did the Bible, just as Dante gave equal weight to Christian doctrine and to classical figures such as Virgil and Ulysses throughout *The Divine Comedy*. Regarded together, *Paradise Lost* and *The Divine Comedy* form an epic cycle of man's descent and eventual apotheosis.

Throughout his life, Italian sculptor, painter, and architect Michelangelo Buonarroti revered Dante. Known primarily for his anatomically perfect statue of *David* (1504) and his masterly paintings in the Sistine Chapel, including the ceiling and *The Last Judgment* (1534–1541), Michelangelo is perhaps least remembered for his accomplished poetry. As was customary in his time among members of the elite, he started writing verse in letters to his friends and family. He quickly developed as a poet and began to compose sonnets, madrigals, and poems in terza rima—the metrical construction Dante used throughout *The Divine Comedy*. Like his better-known works in other media, Michelangelo's poetry reflects his humanism—a combination of Plato's philosophy, the stories of the Bible, and Dante's poetic legacy. It is almost as if Michelangelo set down in verse what he could not sculpt or paint.

Michelangelo spent much of his life in Dante's city of Florence under the tutelage of the Medici family, whose patronage essentially launched the Renaissance. During this time he wrote several sonnets in a style derivative of Dante's, as well as a number of explicit tributes to the author of the *Paradiso*. In his "Dialogue" on Dante, Michelangelo's contemporary Donato Giannotti uses Michelangelo as an interlocutor. Giannotti, a political theorist whose precepts overlapped with those of Niccolò Machiavelli (author of *The Prince*), has the painter recite an early version of "that sonnet you wrote a few days ago in praise of

[Dante]." In the finished draft of that poem—"Sonnet on Dante" (1546), here translated by Creighton Gilbert—Michelangelo laments that he cannot trade stations with the better poet:

> If I could have been he! Born to such fortune,
> To have his bitter exile and his virtue
> I would forego the world's most splendid portion.

In all of his poems about Dante, Michelangelo imagines the cycle of events described in *The Divine Comedy* as reflecting the poet's actual life and humbles himself before such an epic biography.

Statuary

In Dante's native city of Florence alone, statues of the poet turn up around several corners of the labyrinthine streets and cobbled mews. In the city's medieval Via Dante Alighieri, the Casa di Dante (House of Dante)—he is thought to have lived there before his exile—features a full cast of the poet standing gravely out front. The stern-faced Dante is depicted with laurels crowning his head and a lyre clutched in his left hand. In the Casa di Dante one can also see many documents relating to Dante, as well as a painting of the poet catching his first glimpse of Beatrice at the Ponte Vecchio.

In 1970 the Dante Society installed Italian sculptor Angelo Biancini's depiction of Dante in the main lobby of Canada's National Library. His sculptures are often panels that resemble architectural friezes and function much like paintings—that is, they exist mainly in two dimensions—with interesting and surprising textures coursing through them. His three-quarter-length bronze study of Dante pictures the poet in profile. The stiff folds of his robes emerge in hard angles from the wall at his back and in sharp relief in front. Dante's head emerges nobly from the top horizontal of Biancini's bronze. The moment evoked is one of Dante pausing to contemplate a stanza before committing it to his scroll, for the moment rolled up in his left hand.

Polish-born sculptor Bronislaw Krzysztof, known for his whimsical distortions of the human form, depicted the poet in 1984. Krzysztof's foot-and-a-half-tall sculpture portrays Dante from the lower torso, which is obscured by swooping robes, to his capped head. The piece is fashioned of bronze, nearly all of which is unpolished and black, though Dante's eyes and ears gleam with a golden luminosity. Krzysztof's major innovation with his *Dante* is the way in which the figure reclines at a thirty-degree angle, with the head lolling back unnaturally. The effect is of a figure who seems gifted—perhaps burdened—with insight and wisdom not afforded most mortals. Krzysztof received a Gold Medal for *Dante* at the VII Biennale Internationale del Bronzetto Dantesco in Ravenna in 1985.

One of the most impressive monuments to Dante's genius is a 13-foot-tall bronze and granite sculpture of the poet that can be seen in Cambridge, Massachusetts. The work was commissioned from Boston-born multimedia artist Richard Aliberti. Influenced by the Italian masters of the Renaissance, Aliberti's three-dimensional work focuses on the human figure, as well as on more unexpected and abstract forms. Aliberti's statue of Dante was donated to the Dante Alighieri Society of Massachusetts in 1997.

Comments & Questions

In this section, we aim to provide the reader with an array of perspectives on the text, as well as questions that challenge those perspectives. The commentary has been culled from sources as diverse as reviews contemporaneous with the work, letters written by the author, literary criticism of later generations, and appreciations written throughout the work's history. Following the commentary, a series of questions seeks to filter Dante's Paradiso *through a variety of points of view and bring about a richer understanding of this enduring work.*

Comments

James Russell Lowell

No one can read Dante without believing his story, for it is plain that he believed it himself. It is false aesthetics to confound the grandiose with the imaginative. Milton's angels are not to be compared with Dante's, at once real and supernatural; and the Deity of Milton is a Calvinistic Zeus, while nothing in all poetry approaches the imaginative grandeur of Dante's vision of God at the conclusion of the *Paradiso*. In all literary history there is no such figure as Dante, no such homogeneousness of life and works, such loyalty to ideas, such sublime irrecognition of the unessential.

—from *Among My Books: Second Series* (1876)

William Dean Howells

It is a great pity that criticism is not honest about the masterpieces of literature, and does not confess that they are not every moment masterly, that they are often dull and tough and dry, as is certainly the case with Dante's. Some day, perhaps, we shall have this way of treating literature, and then the lover of it will not feel obliged to browbeat himself into the belief that if he is not always enjoying himself it is his own fault. At any rate I will permit myself the luxury of frankly saying that while I had a deep sense of the majesty and grandeur of Dante's design, many points of its execution bored me, and that I found the intermixture of small local fact and neighborhood history in the fabric of his lofty creation no part of its noblest effect.

—from *My Literary Passions: Criticism and Fiction* (1895)

Charles Allen Dinsmore

Notwithstanding all that is scholastic and bizarre in the *Paradiso*, its most careful students are generally agreed that it is the fitting crown of the great trilogy. "Every line of the *Paradiso*," says Ruskin, "is full of the most exquisite and spiritual expressions of Christian truths, and the poem is only less read than the *Inferno* because it requires far greater attention, and, perhaps for its full enjoyment, a holier heart." In this wonderful book, which to Carlyle was full of "inarticulate music," poetry seems to reach quite its highest point. "It is a perpetual hymn of everlasting love," exclaims Shelley; "Dante's apotheosis of Beatrice and the gradations of his own love and her loveliness by which as by steps he feigns himself to have ascended to the throne of the Supreme Cause, is the most glorious imagination of modern poetry."

—from *The Teachings of Dante* (1901)

Charles Eliot Norton

Homer, Dante, Shakespeare stand alone in the closeness of their relation to nature.... Dante comes between the two, and differs more widely from each of them than they from one another. They are primarily poets. He is primarily a moralist who is also a poet. Of Homer the man, and of Shakespeare the man, we know, and need to know, nothing; it is only with them as poets that we are concerned. But it is needful to know Dante as man in order fully to appreciate him as poet. He gives us his world not as reflection from an unconscious and indifferent mirror, but as from a mirror that shapes and orders its reflections for a definite end beyond that of art, and extraneous to it. And in this lies the secret of Dante's hold upon so many and so various minds. He is the chief poet of man as a moral being.

—from *Aids to the Study of Dante* (1903)

T. S. Eliot

More can be learned about how to write poetry from Dante than from any English poet.... The language of each great English poet is his own language; the language of Dante is the perfection of a common language.

—from "Dante" (1929)

Questions

1. How literally do you think Dante wants us to take his geography in the *Paradiso*? Does he want us to believe that it actually looks like he describes?

2. Which of the following positions would you endorse? (1) Dante was mainly interested in telling a good story and demonstrating his poetic gift; (2) he was mainly concerned about distinguishing among and ranking the virtues as we experience them in life; (3) he literally and concretely wanted to depict the fates of the virtuous after death; (4) *The Divine Comedy* is essentially political—in the *Inferno* Dante settled scores with those who were against him; in the *Paradiso* he rewarded those who were with him; or (5) something else.

3. It doesn't seem fair, but the *Inferno* has always been more popular, has always inspired more art, commentary, and imitation than the *Paradiso*. It is more vivid to the imagination. It arouses more emotions. Why is that? Are we more interested in vice than in virtue? In these works, is there evidence that Dante himself was more engaged in writing the *Inferno* than in writing the *Paradiso*?

4. Was Dante's moral compass off, or do you feel that his allotting of punishments and rewards is essentially sound?

5. Has anything in the *Paradiso* convinced you that you ought to change your ways, that in something you do, you sin? Are what we call "sins" to be avoided because they lead to divine retribution or for other reasons?

For Further Reading

Bio-criticism

Anderson, William. *Dante the Maker.* London and Boston: Routledge and Kegan Paul, 1980. The most comprehensive biography of Dante, with extensive information about the poet's life and times.

Auerbach, Erich. *Dante, Poet of the Secular World.* 1929. Translated by Ralph Manheim. Chicago: University of Chicago Press, 1961. A classic by the greatest literary historian of the twentieth century; still required reading.

Bergin, Thomas G. *Dante.* New York: Orion Press, 1965. An older overview that is still rewarding.

Hollander, Robert. *Dante: A Life in Works.* New Haven, CT: Yale University Press, 2001. The best first book on Dante's life through his writings; includes important discussions about the critical problems that have occupied Dante's critics from the early commentators to the present.

Lewis, R. W. B. *Dante: A Penguin Life.* New York: Penguin Putnam, 2001. A brief discussion of Dante by one of America's foremost biographers.

Quinones, Ricardo J. *Dante Alighieri.* Second revised edition. New York: Twayne, 1998. An excellent and very readable examination of Dante's life and works with useful bibliography and information on translations of Dante's works.

General Criticism of Dante's Divine Comedy

Barolini, Teodolinda, and H. Wayne Storey, eds. *Dante for the New Millennium.* New York: Fordham University Press, 2003. A collection of academic essays on all aspects of Dante's literary career.

Bloom, Harold, ed. *Dante's "Divine Comedy": Modern Critical Interpretations.* New York: Chelsea House, 1987. Contains essays by different hands, including some of the most influential interpreters of Dante's poem, such as Ernst Robert Curtius, Erich Auerbach, and Charles Singleton.

Caesar, Michael, ed. *Dante: The Critical Heritage—1314 (?)—1870.* London: Routledge, 1989. This collection of historically important essays on Dante allows the reader to trace the changing views on the poet and his masterpiece from the first commentaries of the fourteenth century to the nineteenth century. Critics include important figures from Italy, England, France, Germany, and the United States.

Clements, Robert J., ed. *American Critical Essays on "The Divine Comedy."* New York: New York University, 1967. One of the best essay collections on Dante, reprinting classic essays by major Dante scholars working in America.

Freccero, John, ed. *Dante: A Collection of Critical Essays.* Englewood Cliffs, NJ: Prentice-Hall, 1965. Important essays by such diverse critics as Bruno Nardi, Gianfranco Contini, Luigi Pirandello, and Leo Spitzer.

Gallagher, Joseph. *A Modern Reader's Guide to "The Divine Comedy."* Liguori, MO: Liguori Publications, 1999. The original title was *To Hell and Back with Dante* (1996). A canto-by-canto discussion of the poem, useful for the student reader.

Giamatti, A. Bartlett, ed. *Dante in America: The First Two Centuries.* Binghamton, NY: Center for Medieval and Early Renaissance Studies, 1983. A fascinating anthology of essays linked to the birth of American interest in Dante created by the writings of Longfellow, Charles Eliot Norton, and James Russell Lowell, plus other more contemporary voices, such as T. S. Eliot, Ezra Pound, and other twentieth-century Dante scholars.

Hawkins, Peter S., and Rachel Jacoff, eds. *The Poets' Dante: Twentieth-Century Responses.* New York: Farrar, Straus and Giroux, 2001. An eloquent tribute to Dante's impact upon working contemporary poets, including essays by Eugenio Montale, Ezra Pound, T. S. Eliot, William Butler Yeats, W. H. Auden, and many others.

Iannucci, Amilcare A., ed. *Dante: Contemporary Perspectives.* Toronto: University of Toronto Press, 1997. A recent collection of fine scholarly essays on a variety of Dante topics written expressly for this volume.

Jacoff, Rachel, ed. *The Cambridge Companion to Dante.* Cambridge: Cambridge University Press, 1993. Useful introduction by a variety of experts to the major problems of Dante criticism arranged by topic (Dante and the Bible, Dante and the classical poets, Dante and Florence, and so forth). Essays are aimed at the student reader.

Lansing, Richard, ed. *The Dante Encyclopedia.* New York: Garland Publishing, 2000. Indispensable English-language reference to every imaginable topic, character, and problem in Dante's poem, containing nearly 1,000 entries by 144 contributors from twelve countries.

Lee, Joe. *Dante for Beginners.* New York: Writers and Readers Publishing, 2001. The amusing cartoon drawings and sense of humor in this student-oriented guide to the poem do not detract from its excellent canto-by-canto discussions of *The Divine Comedy.*

Mazzotta, Giuseppe, ed. *Critical Essays on Dante.* Boston: G. K. Hall, 1991. A collection of pieces by different authors, particularly useful for its reprinting of a number of the early medieval and Renaissance commentaries on the poem.

Criticism with Special Reference to the Paradiso

Botterill, Steven. *Dante and the Mystical Tradition.* Cambridge: Cambridge University Press, 1994.

Boyde, Patrick. *Dante, Philomythes and Philosopher: Man in the Cosmos.* Cambridge: Cambridge University Press, 1981.

Cornish, Alison. *Reading Dante's Stars.* New Haven, CT: Yale University Press, 2000.

Delumeau, Jean. *History of Paradise: The Garden of Eden in Myth and Tradition.* Translated by Matthew O'Connell. New York: Continuum, 1995.

Demaray, John G. *Dante and the Book of the Cosmos.* Philadelphia, PA: American Philosophical Society, 1987.

Foster, Kenelm. *The Two Dantes, and Other Studies.* Berkeley: University of California Press, 1977.

Gardner, Edmond. *Dante's Ten Heavens.* 1898. Freeport, NY: Books for Libraries Press, 1972.

Gilson, Étienne. *Dante and Philosophy*. Translated by David Moore. New York: Harper and Row, 1963.

Grant, Edward. *Planets, Stars, and Orbs: The Medieval Cosmos, 1200–1687*. Cambridge: Cambridge University Press, 1994.

Lewis, C. S. *The Discarded Image: An Introduction to Medieval and Renaissance Literature*. Cambridge: Cambridge University Press, 1964.

Mazzeo, Joseph. *Structure and Thought in the "Paradiso."* Ithaca, NY: Cornell University Press, 1958.

McDannell, Colleen, and Bernhard Lang. *Heaven: A History*. New Haven, CT: Yale University Press, 1988.

Moevs, Christian. *The Metaphysics of Dante's "Comedy."* New York: Oxford University Press, 2005.

Russell, Jeffrey Burton. *A History of Heaven: The Singing Silence*. Princeton, NJ: Princeton University Press, 1997.

Schnapp, Jeffrey T. *The Transfiguration of History at the Center of Dante's "Paradise."* Princeton, NJ: Princeton University Press, 1986.

Singleton, Charles S. *Journey to Beatrice*. 1958. Baltimore, MD: Johns Hopkins University Press, 1977. A very influential and learned discussion of Beatrice's role in *The Divine Comedy*.

Williams, Charles. *The Figure of Beatrice: A Study in Dante*. New York: Noonday Press, 1961. An intriguing consideration of the role of Beatrice in Dante's poem by another poet.

English Versions of Dante's Sources and Dante's Minor Works Mentioned in the Critical Notes to the Paradiso

Alighieri, Dante. *The Banquet*. Stanford French and Italian Studies, volume 61. Translated by Christopher Ryan. Saratoga, CA: ANMA Libri, 1989. An English version of *Il Convivio*.

———. *Dante's Lyric Poetry*. Edited and translated by Kenelm Foster and Patrick Boyde. Oxford: Clarendon Press, 1967. 2 vols. Dante's Italian lyric poetry with English translations and excellent commentary.

———. *The Inferno*. Translated by Henry Wadsworth Longfellow. Introduction and notes by Peter Bondanella. New York: Barnes & Noble Classics, 2003.

———. *Literary Criticism of Dante Alighieri*. Translated by Robert S.

Haller. Lincoln: University of Nebraska Press, 1973. Contains English selections from the various works by Dante (*De vulgari eloquentia, Il Convivio*, the *Letter to Can Grande, La Vita Nuova*, and the *Eclogues*) that discuss poetics, poetry, poets, and allegory.

————. *Monarchia.* Translated and edited by Prue Shaw. Cambridge: Cambridge University Press, 1995.

————. *The Purgatory.* Translated by Henry Wadsworth Longfellow. Introduction and notes by Julia Conaway Bondanella and Peter Bondanella. New York: Barnes & Noble Classics, 2005.

————. *Vita Nuova.* Translated by Mark Musa. Oxford: Oxford University Press, 2000.

The Bible: Authorized King James Version with Apocrypha. Edited by Robert Carroll and Stephen Prickett. Oxford: Oxford University Press, 1998.

Broken Columns: Two Roman Epic Fragments: The Achilleid *of Publish Papinius Statius and* The Rape of Proserpine *of Claudius Claudianus.* Translated by David R. Slavitt. Philadelphia: University of Pennsylvania Press, 1997.

Cicero. *On Duties.* Edited by M. T. Griffin and E. M. Atkins. Cambridge: Cambridge University Press, 1991.

Lucan. *Civil War.* Translated by Susan H. Braund. Oxford: Oxford University Press, 1999. A complete translation of the *Pharsalia*.

Ovid. *Metamorphoses.* Translated by A. D. Melville. Oxford: Oxford University Press, 1998.

Statius. *Thebaid.* Translated by A. D. Melville. Oxford: Oxford University Press, 1995.

Virgil. *Virgil, with an English Translation by H. Rushton Fairclough.* 2 vols. Revised by G. P. Goold. Cambridge, MA: Harvard University Press, 1999–2000.

Dante Websites Useful for a Reading of the Paradiso

Danteworlds: http://danteworlds.laits.utexas.edu. Perhaps the most useful website for the student and first reader of *The Divine Comedy* created by Professor Guy Raffa of the University of Texas. Extensive images of works of art indebted to Dante's poem.

Digital Dante: http://dante.ilt.columbia.edu/comedy. An interesting juxtaposition of two translations (Longfellow's classic version and the more recent version by Alan Mandelbaum) plus the Italian text. Created at Columbia University.

The Princeton Dante Project: http://etcweb.princeton.edu/dante. Created by Professor Robert Hollander at Princeton University, this website is probably best visited by the more advanced reader and requires registration (at no charge). It juxtaposes the recent Hollander translation with the original Italian text and includes much critical and interpretive information.

Look for the following titles, available now and forthcoming from
BARNES & NOBLE CLASSICS.

Visit your local bookstore for these and more fine titles.
Or to order online go to: WWW.BN.COM/CLASSICS

Title	Author	ISBN	Price
Aesop's Fables	Aesop	1-59308-062-X	$5.95
The Age of Innocence	Edith Wharton	1-59308-143-X	$5.95
Agnes Grey	Anne Brontë	1-59308-323-8	$5.95
Alice's Adventures in Wonderland and Through the Looking-Glass	Lewis Carroll	1-59308-015-8	$5.95
Anna Karenina	Leo Tolstoy	1-59308-027-1	$8.95
The Art of War	Sun Tzu	1-59308-017-4	$7.95
The Awakening and Selected Short Fiction	Kate Chopin	1-59308-113-8	$6.95
Babbitt	Sinclair Lewis	1-59308-267-3	$7.95
Barchester Towers	Anthony Trollope	1-59308-337-8	$7.95
The Beautiful and Damned	F. Scott Fitzgerald	1-59308-245-2	$7.95
Beowulf	Anonymous	1-59308-266-5	$4.95
Bleak House	Charles Dickens	1-59308-311-4	$9.95
The Bostonians	Henry James	1-59308-297-5	$7.95
The Brothers Karamazov	Fyodor Dostoevsky	1-59308-045-X	$9.95
The Call of the Wild and White Fang	Jack London	1-59308-200-2	$5.95
Candide	Voltaire	1-59308-028-X	$4.95
A Christmas Carol, The Chimes and The Cricket on the Hearth	Charles Dickens	1-59308-033-6	$5.95
The Collected Poems of Emily Dickinson	Emily Dickinson	1-59308-050-6	$5.95
Common Sense and Other Writings	Thomas Paine	1-59308-209-6	$6.95
The Communist Manifesto and Other Writings	Karl Marx and Friedrich Engels	1-59308-100-6	$5.95
The Complete Sherlock Holmes, Vol. I	Sir Arthur Conan Doyle	1-59308-034-4	$7.95
The Complete Sherlock Holmes, Vol. II	Sir Arthur Conan Doyle	1-59308-040-9	$7.95
A Connecticut Yankee in King Arthur's Court	Mark Twain	1-59308-210-X	$7.95
The Count of Monte Cristo	Alexandre Dumas	1-59308-151-0	$7.95
The Country of the Pointed Firs and Selected Short Fiction	Sarah Orne Jewett	1-59308-262-2	$6.95
Daisy Miller and Washington Square	Henry James	1-59308-105-7	$4.95
Daniel Deronda	George Eliot	1-59308-290-8	$8.95
David Copperfield	Charles Dickens	1-59308-063-8	$7.95
Dead Souls	Nikolai Gogol	1-59308-092-1	$7.95
The Death of Ivan Ilych and Other Stories	Leo Tolstoy	1-59308-069-7	$7.95
The Deerslayer	James Fenimore Cooper	1-59308-211-8	$7.95
Don Quixote	Miguel de Cervantes	1-59308-046-8	$9.95
Dracula	Bram Stoker	1-59308-114-6	$6.95
Emma	Jane Austen	1-59308-152-9	$6.95
The Enchanted Castle and Five Children and It	Edith Nesbit	1-59308-274-6	$6.95
Essays and Poems by Ralph Waldo Emerson		1-59308-076-X	$6.95
Essential Dialogues of Plato		1-59308-269-X	$9.95
The Essential Tales and Poems of Edgar Allan Poe		1-59308-064-6	$7.95
Ethan Frome and Selected Stories	Edith Wharton	1-59308-090-5	$5.95

(continued)

Far from the Madding Crowd	Thomas Hardy	1-59308-223-1	$7.95
The Federalist	Hamilton, Madison, Jay	1-59308-282-7	$7.95
The Four Feathers	A. E. W. Mason	1-59308-313-0	$6.95
Frankenstein	Mary Shelley	1-59308-115-4	$4.95
Germinal	Émile Zola	1-59308-291-6	$7.95
The Good Soldier	Ford Madox Ford	1-59308-268-1	$6.95
Great American Short Stories: from Hawthorne to Hemingway	Various	1-59308-086-7	$7.95
Great Expectations	Charles Dickens	1-59308-116-2	$6.95
Grimm's Fairy Tales	Jacob and Wilhelm Grimm	1-59308-056-5	$7.95
Gulliver's Travels	Jonathan Swift	1-59308-132-4	$5.95
Hard Times	Charles Dickens	1-59308-156-1	$5.95
The Histories	Herodotus	1-59308-102-2	$6.95
The House of Mirth	Edith Wharton	1-59308-153-7	$6.95
The House of the Dead and Poor Folk	Fyodor Dostoevsky	1-59308-194-4	$7.95
Howards End	E. M. Forster	1-59308-022-0	$6.95
The Idiot	Fyodor Dostoevsky	1-59308-058-1	$7.95
The Iliad	Homer	1-59308-232-0	$7.95
The Importance of Being Earnest and Four Other Plays	Oscar Wilde	1-59308-059-X	$6.95
Incidents in the Life of a Slave Girl	Harriet Jacobs	1-59308-283-5	$5.95
The Inferno	Dante Alighieri	1-59308-051-4	$6.95
The Interpretation of Dreams	Sigmund Freud	1-59308-298-3	$8.95
Ivanhoe	Sir Walter Scott	1-59308-246-0	$7.95
Jane Eyre	Charlotte Brontë	1-59308-117-0	$7.95
Journey to the Center of the Earth	Jules Verne	1-59308-252-5	$4.95
Jude the Obscure	Thomas Hardy	1-59308-035-2	$6.95
The Jungle	Upton Sinclair	1-59308-118-9	$6.95
The Jungle Books	Rudyard Kipling	1-59308-109-X	$5.95
Kim	Rudyard Kipling	1-59308-192-8	$4.95
King Solomon's Mines	H. Rider Haggard	1-59308-275-4	$4.95
Lady Chatterley's Lover	D. H. Lawrence	1-59308-239-8	$6.95
The Last of the Mohicans	James Fenimore Cooper	1-59308-137-5	$5.95
Leaves of Grass: First and "Death-bed" Editions	Walt Whitman	1-59308-083-2	$9.95
The Legend of Sleepy Hollow and Other Writings	Washington Irving	1-59308-225-8	$6.95
Les Liaisons Dangereuses	Pierre Choderlos de Laclos	1-59308-240-1	$7.95
Les Misérables	Victor Hugo	1-59308-066-2	$9.95
The Life of Charlotte Brontë	Elizabeth Gaskell	1-59308-314-9	$7.95
Little Women	Louisa May Alcott	1-59308-108-1	$6.95
Madame Bovary	Gustave Flaubert	1-59308-052-2	$6.95
Maggie: A Girl of the Streets and Other Writings about New York	Stephen Crane	1-59308-248-7	$6.95
The Magnificent Ambersons	Booth Tarkington	1-59308-263-0	$7.95
Man and Superman and Three Other Plays	George Bernard Shaw	1-59308-067-0	$7.95
The Man in the Iron Mask	Alexandre Dumas	1-59308-233-9	$8.95
Mansfield Park	Jane Austen	1-59308-154-5	$5.95
The Mayor of Casterbridge	Thomas Hardy	1-59308-309-2	$5.95
The Metamorphoses	Ovid	1-59308-276-2	$7.95
The Metamorphosis and Other Stories	Franz Kafka	1-59308-029-8	$6.95

Title	Author	ISBN	Price
Middlemarch	George Eliot	1-59308-023-9	$8.95
Moby-Dick	Herman Melville	1-59308-018-2	$9.95
Moll Flanders	Daniel Defoe	1-59308-216-9	$5.95
The Moonstone	Wilkie Collins	1-59308-322-X	$7.95
My Ántonia	Willa Cather	1-59308-202-9	$5.95
My Bondage and My Freedom	Frederick Douglass	1-59308-301-7	$6.95
Nana	Émile Zola	1-59308-292-4	$6.95
Narrative of Sojourner Truth		1-59308-293-2	$6.95
Narrative of the Life of Frederick Douglass, an American Slave		1-59308-041-7	$4.95
Nicholas Nickleby	Charles Dickens	1-59308-300-9	$8.95
Night and Day	Virginia Woolf	1-59308-212-6	$7.95
Northanger Abbey	Jane Austen	1-59308-264-9	$5.95
Nostromo	Joseph Conrad	1-59308-193-6	$7.95
O Pioneers!	Willa Cather	1-59308-205-3	$5.95
The Odyssey	Homer	1-59308-009-3	$5.95
Oliver Twist	Charles Dickens	1-59308-206-1	$6.95
The Origin of Species	Charles Darwin	1-59308-077-8	$7.95
Paradise Lost	John Milton	1-59308-095-6	$7.95
Père Goriot	Honoré de Balzac	1-59308-285-1	$7.95
Persuasion	Jane Austen	1-59308-130-8	$5.95
Peter Pan	J. M. Barrie	1-59308-213-4	$4.95
The Picture of Dorian Gray	Oscar Wilde	1-59308-025-5	$4.95
The Pilgrim's Progress	John Bunyan	1-59308-254-1	$7.95
Poetics and Rhetoric	Aristotle	1-59308-307-6	$9.95
The Portrait of a Lady	Henry James	1-59308-096-4	$7.95
A Portrait of the Artist as a Young Man and Dubliners	James Joyce	1-59308-031-X	$6.95
The Possessed	Fyodor Dostoevsky	1-59308-250-9	$9.95
Pride and Prejudice	Jane Austen	1-59308-201-0	$5.95
The Prince and Other Writings	Niccolò Machiavelli	1-59308-060-3	$5.95
The Prince and the Pauper	Mark Twain	1-59308-218-5	$4.95
Pudd'nhead Wilson and Those Extraordinary Twins	Mark Twain	1-59308-255-X	$5.95
The Purgatorio	Dante Alighieri	1-59308-219-3	$7.95
Pygmalion and Three Other Plays	George Bernard Shaw	1-59308-078-6	$7.95
The Red and the Black	Stendhal	1-59308-286-X	$7.95
The Red Badge of Courage and Selected Short Fiction	Stephen Crane	1-59308-119-7	$4.95
Republic	Plato	1-59308-097-2	$6.95
The Return of the Native	Thomas Hardy	1-59308-220-7	$7.95
Robinson Crusoe	Daniel Defoe	1-59308-360-2	$5.95
A Room with a View	E. M. Forster	1-59308-288-6	$5.95
Sailing Alone Around the World	Joshua Slocum	1-59308-303-3	$6.95
Scaramouche	Rafael Sabatini	1-59308-242-8	$6.95
The Scarlet Letter	Nathaniel Hawthorne	1-59308-207-X	$4.95
The Scarlet Pimpernel	Baroness Orczy	1-59308-234-7	$5.95
The Secret Garden	Frances Hodgson Burnett	1-59308-277-0	$5.95
Selected Stories of O. Henry		1-59308-042-5	$5.95
Sense and Sensibility	Jane Austen	1-59308-125-1	$5.95
Sentimental Education	Gustave Flaubert	1-59308-306-8	$6.95
Silas Marner and Two Short Stories	George Eliot	1-59308-251-7	$6.95

(continued)

Sister Carrie	Theodore Dreiser	1-59308-226-6	$7.95
Six Plays by Henrik Ibsen		1-59308-061-1	$8.95
Sons and Lovers	D. H. Lawrence	1-59308-013-1	$7.95
The Souls of Black Folk	W. E. B. Du Bois	1-59308-014-X	$5.95
The Strange Case of Dr. Jekyll and Mr. Hyde and Other Stories	Robert Louis Stevenson	1-59308-131-6	$4.95
Swann's Way	Marcel Proust	1-59308-295-9	$8.95
A Tale of Two Cities	Charles Dickens	1-59308-138-3	$5.95
Tao Te Ching	Lao Tzu	1-59308-256-8	$5.95
Tess of d'Urbervilles	Thomas Hardy	1-59308-228-2	$7.95
This Side of Paradise	F. Scott Fitzgerald	1-59308-243-6	$6.95
Three Lives	Gertrude Stein	1-59308-320-3	$6.95
The Three Musketeers	Alexandre Dumas	1-59308-148-0	$8.95
Thus Spoke Zarathustra	Friedrich Nietzsche	1-59308-278-9	$7.95
Tom Jones	Henry Fielding	1-59308-070-0	$8.95
Treasure Island	Robert Louis Stevenson	1-59308-247-9	$4.95
The Turn of the Screw, The Aspern Papers and Two Stories	Henry James	1-59308-043-3	$5.95
Twenty Thousand Leagues Under the Sea	Jules Verne	1-59308-302-5	$5.95
Uncle Tom's Cabin	Harriet Beecher Stowe	1-59308-121-9	$7.95
Utopia	Sir Thomas More	1-59308-244-4	$5.95
Vanity Fair	William Makepeace Thackeray	1-59308-071-9	$7.95
The Varieties of Religious Experience	William James	1-59308-072-7	$7.95
Villette	Charlotte Brontë	1-59308-316-5	$7.95
The Virginian	Owen Wister	1-59308-236-3	$7.95
The Voyage Out	Virginia Woolf	1-59308-229-0	$6.95
Walden and Civil Disobedience	Henry David Thoreau	1-59308-208-8	$5.95
War and Peace	Leo Tolstoy	1-59308-073-5	$12.95
Ward No. 6 and Other Stories	Anton Chekhov	1-59308-003-4	$7.95
The Waste Land and Other Poems	T. S. Eliot	1-59308-279-7	$4.95
The Way We Live Now	Anthony Trollope	1-59308-304-1	$9.95
The Wind in the Willows	Kenneth Grahame	1-59308-265-7	$4.95
The Wings of the Dove	Henry James	1-59308-296-7	$7.95
Wives and Daughters	Elizabeth Gaskell	1-59308-257-6	$7.95
The Woman in White	Wilkie Collins	1-59308-280-0	$7.95
Women in Love	D. H. Lawrence	1-59308-258-4	$8.95
The Wonderful Wizard of Oz	L. Frank Baum	1-59308-221-5	$6.95
Wuthering Heights	Emily Brontë	1-59308-128-6	$5.95

BARNES & NOBLE CLASSICS

If you are an educator and would like to receive an
Examination or Desk Copy of a Barnes & Noble Classic edition,
please refer to Academic Resources on our website at
WWW.BN.COM/CLASSICS
or contact us at
B&NCLASSICS@BN.COM.

All prices are subject to change.